D0318094

Twister

Jack Bickham, who lives in Oklahoma – the heart of tornado country – is the author of many books. The very successful Walt Disney Productions Film, The Apple Dumpling Gang, was based on one of his novels.

Jack M. Bickham
Twister

Pan Books in association with
Macmillan London

First published in Great Britain 1977 by Macmillan London Ltd
This edition published 1978 by Pan Books Ltd,
Cavaye Place, London SW10 9PG
in association with Macmillan London Ltd
© Jack M. Bickham 1976
ISBN 0 330 25380 8
Printed and bound in Great Britain by
Hazell Watson & Viney Ltd, Aylesbury, Bucks

for Janie, with such love

acknowledgments

Many persons contributed to the making of this novel.
Dr T. T. Fujita, noted tornado expert, provided early insights and inspiration with remarks made during his public lecture in my home city on May 29, 1974.

Fred Ostby, deputy director of the National Severe Storms Forecast Centre, patiently explained the workings of his organization, and provided invaluable background information.

Gene Lee and Joe Golden, scientists at the National Severe Storms Laboratory, answered many questions about tornado behaviour and weather satellite technology.

Dr John McCarthy, assistant professor of meteorology at the University of Oklahoma and formerly a staff member at the National Severe Storms Laboratory, not only answered hours of questions, but showed a continuing interest in technical aspects of the project, which was most encouraging.

Numerous – and anonymous – technical writers helped with their clear, concise pamphlets produced for the National Oceanic and Atmospheric Administration, which became part of the research materials.

The novel might never have been written if Harold Kuebler, my editor at Doubleday, had not come to Norman in June 1973, and, with his words, rekindled a fire. His encouragement and help continued throughout the writing and revision, and can never be adequately repaid.

J.B., Norman, Oklahoma, October, 1975

author's note

To avoid needless confusion, all time references in this novel are Central Daylight Time, even for areas which in reality would be in a different time zone, or operating on standard time. In addition, slight liberties have been taken with geography on two or three occasions. Most organizations named herein actually exist, but all the characters in this book are fictitious, and any resemblance to actual persons, living or dead, is purely coincidental.

Friday, April 4   2 p.m.–6:30 p.m.

NNNN
OOOXX23Z
CC X
WEATHER OUTLOOK
NATIONAL WEATHER SERVICE FORT WORTH TEXAS
REVISED FORECAST
ISSUED I P.M. CDT FRIDAY APRIL 4, 1975

... THUNDERSHOWERS MAY BE EXPECTED TO DEVELOP IN THE
WEST CENTRAL PORTIONS OF THE STATE OF TEXAS THIS
AFTERNOON AND MOVE EAST DURING THE LATE AFTERNOON AND
EARLY EVENING HOURS ...

THE OUTLOOK IS FOR LIGHT TO MODERATE RAINS FROM THESE
CLOUDS WHICH ARE EXPECTED TO BE OF MODERATE INTENSITY.
DEVELOPMENT WILL FOLLOW EASTWARD MOVEMENT OF A WEAK
LOW PRESSURE CENTRE IN THE UPPER ATMOSPHERE AND MAY
CONTINUE ACROSS THE STATE THROUGH AN AREA ROUGHLY
BOUNDED BY A LINE FROM SAN ANGELO TO ABILENE TO
TEXARKANA TO LONGVIEW AND BACK TO SAN ANGELO ...

EXCEPT FOR A POSSIBLE ISOLATED THUNDERSHOWER NEAR THE
AREA, THE REMAINDER OF THE STATE CAN EXPECT A
CONTINUATION OF UNSEASONABLY WARM WEATHER WITH GUSTY
WINDS. OVERNIGHT LOWS EXCEPT WHERE AFFECTED BY
THUNDERSHOWER ACTIVITY WILL RANGE FROM ABOUT 60 IN THE
NORTH TO 85 ALONG THE SOUTHERN TEXAS GULF COAST ...

SATURDAY'S OUTLOOK REMAINS FOR POSSIBLE SEVERE WEATHER
IN THE AFTERNOON HOURS ...

XXX

The weather was bright, hot and dusty across much of Texas, and
in the cities that had adequate water supplies, home gardeners
hosed their little plots while cowmen and oilfield workers, with
bigger problems, raked grit from their eyes and ritualistically
cursed. By 3 p.m., however, on a line a few miles east of Abilene,
and extending southward towards San Angelo, the endless blue
sky began to show vague silver forms, clouds beginning to build

higher and higher as the engine forces of heat and moisture combined.

The clouds did not amount to much at first.

At 4 p.m., the line of clouds had passed Abilene and San Angelo, giving neither city anything more than some lightning and thunder, and winds gusting to 40 knots at San Angelo's airport. A pilot on a flight plan into Mineral Wells, however, landed there at 4:25 to report severe turbulence in clear air ahead of the line of clouds, which he estimated topping out at 30,000 feet. There were telephone reports of very heavy rainfall at Breckenridge, Cisco, Brownwood and San Saba.

By 5 p.m., the line of clouds extended from near Mineral Wells to Temple, and was being watched by radar units at three offices of the National Weather Service. The clouds remained only moderate on the radars, but local reports included winds gusting to 60 miles per hour at isolated locations. A telephone call was made from the Forth Worth office to the National Severe Storms Forecast Centre in Kansas City, Missouri, and after some consultation, there was agreement to issue an immediate severe-thunderstorm watch for a large portion of an area north and east of a line from Austin to Beaumont.

Ed Stephens, director of the Kansas City severe storms office, which co-ordinated all national information on damaging weather warnings, studied the data briefly.

'I just don't think it's going to amount to much,' he told one of his forecasters, a man named Bright. 'There's just not enough temperature difference in there, and the winds aloft aren't going to create any wind-shear effect. If some solid thunderstorms do develop, they'll sit right where they are and just put themselves out.'

'We don't have the makings like we'll have them tomorrow,' Bright agreed.

'Right,' Stephens said with a twinge of worry about tomorrow. 'Keep a close eye on it, though.'

'Naturally.'

'You have a full crew?'

'Yes.'

'Well, you know the ropes. I don't see any reason why I can't go ahead and catch that handball game.'

Bright grinned at him. 'You've got in your seventy hours this week, boss. I think we can handle it.'

Still Stephens hesitated, reluctant to go – felt almost guilty about it. He tried to convince himself: 'With Congressman Tatinger coming in here the first of the week, I damned sure won't get on the court at all for a while if I don't make it today.'

'No problem,' Bright agreed. 'Go.'

Stephens glowered around the room. 'Get somebody to wash the ashtrays.'

'Clean-up for our congressman?'

'Tatinger is influential. Maybe you don't know how influential. Ways and Means listens to him. Everybody listens to him these days.'

Bright nodded. 'And what he's saying is, "I wanna be President." '

'He's too young for that, and that's not our problem anyway. But what *is* our problem is that he has clout. He went through some divisions of NASA like a Mack truck through tissue paper. Some of those divisions he visited – the ones that didn't impress him right – aren't even *there* any more.'

'He can't wipe us out.'

'He can hurt us.'

Bright looked glum at that. 'Okay. So we have a new crisis.'

'*I* do,' Stephens corrected him sourly. 'I'm the goddamn politician.'

'Well, you'd better get to the handball court, then, and try to unwind a little while you can.'

Stephens patted his flat midsection. 'Maybe I can lose two pounds.'

He had managed to convince himself. He left the great bronze-glass Federal Building in downtown Kansas City and headed for the gym.

It was 5:25 p.m.

At 5:48 p.m., in Killeen, Texas, Rick Mallory arrived home. Entering his small frame house, he caught the glad rush of his four-year-old son, Donny, and carried the boy into the kitchen. Mallory's wife, Cecilia, was just setting the table. She wore hip-hugger shorts and halter, and was barefooted.

Mallory kissed her. 'You look as good as that roast smells.'

'Hamburger Helper,' she told him solemnly.

'Ha!' But he went to the stove just to reassure himself.

'How did it go today?' she asked.

'Good. I'm getting the hang of it. Boy, it's *dark* outside!'

Frowning, she went to the window with him. Donny had retreated to the living-room television set again. 'It's looking *bad*,' she said.

'Well, we can use the rain, but if it gets any darker we won't be able to see that pot roast.' Mallory patted his wife's elegant posterior. 'We'll just have to go to bed for the night instead.'

'You're impossible,' Cecilia told him, pleased.

Thunder rolled. A sudden wind tossed the tiny trees they had planted only a few weeks earlier in the bare dirt of their tract house. The Bermuda grass sprigs, despite loving sprinkling, had not begun to spread yet because the weather had been cool, and the sudden wind hurled clouds of dust into the air.

The sky was very low. From horizon to horizon the clouds formed rounded, down-hanging pouches like the folds of an over-stuffed quilt. Through the window, Mallory and his wife could see grey wisps of cloud hurling along very fast, while the thick layers of parent cloud above seemed agitated, like an ocean of dirty divinity candy about to boil.

To the west it was even darker.

The wind increased. They could hear it singing overhead. Some metal weatherstripping in some of the windows began to vibrate, humming. Raindrops spattered down, increasing. Then the darkness deepened.

'I don't like this,' Cecilia murmured, frowning.

'Check the roast,' Mallory told her. He was concerned, too, but it was the man's place to hide this.

As he spoke, about six miles to the southwest, the densest and blackest centre of the huge rotating cloud put down an extension of itself. The extension was a pale grey. It rotated very, very swiftly. It came down and touched the ground, broke off a scrub-oak tree a foot in diameter, hurled hundred-pound chunks of sod and earth up into its own sucking maw, and began to move along the ground.

The tornado, not a very big one as tornadoes go, was some six hundred yards wide at its mouth. Its winds presently were about 165 miles per hour, but these, while quite sufficient to smash most man-made structures, were still building rapidly. The roar already was unearthly.

There was no way to predict whether the tornado, hidden in the murk and crashing rain of its parent cloud, would remain on the ground for many miles, would maintain its steady direction, or dissipate.

If it remained on its present course for another three minutes, however, it would hit the Mallorys' street.

'Rick,' Cecilia said, going to the window again, 'I'm scared.'

'They haven't blown the sirens,' Mallory said. 'If it were bad, they would have blown the tornado-warning sirens. Right?'

Cecilia went to the living-room doorway. 'Donny? Have they had any weather bulletins, honey?'

'They said thunderstorms a while ago,' Donny said brightly.

Wind blasted against the house, which had begun to seem very small and very frail. It was so dark, Mallory saw, that the street lights out front had come on automatically, as if it were night. The thunder boomed nearer, ominous, growling, and now the rain smashed down, driven by screaming winds that bent the little trees outside to the ground.

Downtown, at the police station, a radio message crackled in from one of the local patrol cars. Sent out as a spotter, the patrolman yelled that he had a tornado spotted, on the ground, moving directly towards the city.

The captain on duty unlocked an electrical-circuit box and mashed hard on a red button.

At the radio station, the disc jockey on duty heard the siren mounted atop a power pole only two blocks from the station. Knowing he would start getting calls within thirty seconds and having no information, he dialled the police number.

The girl on the city switchboard was named Rona Kentwhiler, and she was nineteen. 'Gosh!' she said excitedly. 'No one has told *me* there's a storm! It's raining and all, you know, but gee, if the sirens are going off, maybe it's just a mistake, because they're supposed to tell me right away!'

The disc jockey hung up and went on the air to try to avoid some of the inevitable hysterical calls.

At the Mallory house, Cecilia had just gotten the transistor radio out of the bedroom. She stood in the living-room doorway, her eyes wide with fright, as the little instrument rattled with the disc jockey's voice.

'Nothing to worry about, folks. I just called the city, and it looks like the sirens have gone off by mistake. We're experiencing some heavy rain, it looks like, but by gosh we can use it, huh? And—'

Downtown, the police captain went in to tell the girl on the switchboard about the tornado.

'Oh, my gosh!' she cried. 'The radio station just called and I told the man it must be a mistake!'

The captain stared at her for perhaps five seconds. 'For Christ's sake,' he said then, 'get him back and tell him it's for real!'

It was much too late for the Mallorys, who grinned at each other in relief and decided, independently and without words, to hide whatever worry they might still feel because of Donny.

The huge blackness swept across open fields and exploded a service station at the corner of the highway intersection. Sheets of metal weighing two hundred pounds were thrown hundreds of yards, crashing into plate-glass windows of the neighbourhood grocery. Power poles snapped, ripping heavy-gauge wires, and were hurled upward, becoming projectiles. The funnel smashed into the row of frame houses, filling the air with bits of wood and roofing. Walls crashed flat. Houses seemed to explode, and the air became a black soup of dirt and wreckage. The houses went down or seemed to blow up one after another, and a hellish roar, like a hundred jet airliners with all their engines screaming at full power, blanketed the earth.

Rick Mallory knew something very serious was wrong when he heard the wind suddenly become so strong and so evil that he could not wholly comprehend its force. He started toward his wife, intending to hurry her into the home's small central hallway, the best protection in the structure.

Cecilia turned toward him in the same instant, fear twisting her features.

An unbelievable force struck the house. Timbers screamed and shattered. The windows exploded in brilliant geysers of glass. There was a loud, splitting sound, and the walls began falling apart. Mallory just managed to touch his wife's hand when there was a hot, shocking impact, and he felt the whole weight of the roof coming down on his body. Over the stunning roar he heard Donny scream, but it was the last thing he heard, because three tons of wreckage came down on him and his wife and his son, and for them it was over.

```
ZCZC WBC 167
ACUS KMKC 051007
MKC AC 051007
MKC AC 051007
SEVERE WEATHER OUTLOOK NARRATIVE
VALID 051200 TO 052400Z
```

MODERATE TO HEAVY THUNDERSTORMS ARE EXPECTED AFTERNOON AND EVENING IN EASTERN TEXAS . . . SOUTHERN LOUISIANA . . .

LOCALLY HEAVY RAINS AND STRONG STRAIGHT WINDS GUSTING 50 K AND PSBLY HIGHER ALONG TEXAS AND LOUISIANA GULF COASTS AS ADVANCING SQUALL LINE AND WARM FRONT MOVE EASTWARD . . .
STRONG STRAIGHT WINDS WITH BLOWING DUST EXPECTED THROUGH MUCH OF OKLAHOMA AND SOUTHERN KANSAS . . .

THIS IS THE FIRST OF THREE LOW PRESSURE SYSTEMS OF PACIFIC ORIGIN EXPECTED TO MOVE ACROSS THE US IN THE NEXT 72 TO 96 HOURS. THE SECOND STORM SYSTEM IS MOVING INTO CALIFORNIA AT THIS TIME AND IS EXPECTED TO BRING SHARP DROPS IN TEMPERATURES AND PSBLY HEAVY SNOW TO PORTIONS OF UTAH AND COLORADO SUNDAY . . . SEVERE WEATHER MAY DEVELOP MONDAY FROM THIS SYSTEM . . .

THE THIRD LOW PRESSURE CENTRE NOW ORGANIZING IN PACIFIC IS EXPECTED TO MOVE INLAND MONDAY AND PSBLY CREATE MOST SEVERE CONDITIONS TUESDAY AND WEDNESDAY . . . CONDITIONS NOW APPEAR FAVOURABLE FOR WIDESPREAD THUNDERSTORM ACTIVITY FROM THIS THIRD SYSTEM ON WEDNESDAY . . .

XXX

Kansas City

Jake Kensington, the senior forecaster on duty in the National Severe Storms Forecast Centre, was startled.

Looking up from his slanted grey desk with its litter of tissue-thin weather charts and maps, Kensington had not expected to see Ed Stephens at this hour. Not that the pale, gaunt-eyed Stephens was a keeper of regular hours; everyone on the staff was accustomed to the fact that he sometimes seemed to live on the seventeenth floor of the Federal Building; but this was awfully early even for him.

'Insomnia?' Kensington asked with a slight smile.

Stephens, his dark tie slightly askew and his corduroy sports coat rumpled, did not smile back at him. 'Let's go over some of those charts on the Texas thing last night.'

So that was it. 'I was just looking at them myself,' Kensington admitted.

Frowning, Stephens grimly bent over the slanted workdesk. 'I want the five-hundred millibar chart first.'

Everything the men needed was in this room, the central nerve centre of NSSFC. A large room, somewhat longer than it was wide, it was brightly illuminated by fluorescent fixtures indented in the low, white acoustical-tile ceiling. At the far end, high tinted windows looked out on the darkness of near-dawn, the street lights of downtown Kansas City sprawled below. The walls were covered mainly by no-nonsense Masonite panelling, perforated to handle racks which held row after row of clipboard charts and reports.

Two rows of large, slant-topped grey workdesks dominated the centre of the room. Partly hidden by a partition nearby stood the local-area weather-information transmitter, a unit about the size of an upright freezer, with cassettes and glowing lights plugged into its front panel. Yellow ready lights glowed also on the panels of three tall facsimile machines nearer the central island. Two Sanders 720 cathode-ray-tube units, pale blue and grey, with Selectric keyboards, were positioned on work counters behind the desks, but neither TV-type display tube was lighted at present. There were three other men at work in the room, but it was a period of relative normality and only the continual chatter of teletypes from the nearby communications room punctuated the quiet.

For all the clutter of charts and records, it was a very orderly clutter, like the room of a packrat child with a very stern mother. The atmosphere was like that of a newspaper office: a touch grubby, utilitarian, with the faint odours of paper dust, stale tobacco and hot oil from the nearby teletypes. The men in the room were like newsmen, too: middle-aged, shirtsleeved, quietly businesslike. Pros.

Stephens said as he scowled over the charts. 'We didn't have a full-scale tornado warning out until three or four minutes prior to the time that damned thing hit Killeen.'

'We had a severe-thunderstorm watch,' Kensington pointed out.

'Yes. But everything in the data indicated that even that was going overboard in the direction of caution. Then this damned thing plows through there and kills seventeen people.'

'You know about the screw-up with the local radio station?'

Stephens's slightly puffy eyes tightened. 'Yes, I know about that screw-up. What I want to know is why we didn't give them more time to avoid such a screw-up.'

Kensington took a deep breath. He was beginning to understand clearly now. The one thing that everyone knew about Ed Stephens was his driving perfectionism. Things had gone wrong in Texas Friday night. As a result, Stephens probably hadn't slept very much, and today would drive himself even harder.

Kensington pointed out slowly, 'That tornado at Killeen was no normal twister. It was the only tornado we had anywhere in the country yesterday. Look at the daily activity report: a water-spout in Florida, a little hail in Pennsylvania, some rain here and there, and one fluke tornado.'

'We should have predicted it,' Stephens snapped, his eyes never leaving the charts. 'If we didn't forecast it in time, the Texas people should have picked it up on radar.'

'It was a fluke,' Kensington repeated.

'I know that everything we had indicated a far lower intensity of activity than what we got,' Stephens said. 'That's my *point*. Goddamn it, our predictors just aren't always sensitive enough!'

'Maybe so,' Kensington admitted. 'But if you stop to think about it, sir, we see ten thousand little squall lines like this every spring. How many of them, with this set of known factors, produce a tornado?'

Stephens raised his eyes from the data. There was a quiet, controlled havoc there. 'I don't care if this was a one-in-a-thousand or a one-in-a-million. Do you know where I was when that tornado hit Killeen? I was playing handball.'

Stephens pulled a cigarette from his shirt pocket and lit it with a quick, jerky, angry motion. He repeated, 'I was *playing hand-ball*.'

'What could you have done if you had been here?' Kensington

asked, knowing he was on dangerous ground, yet driven by see-ing an obvious truth.

'Maybe,' Stephens said bleakly, 'I couldn't have done a damned thing.'

'Right. We were staffed. We did everything.'

'I should have been here anyway.'

Kensington stared at his boss, absolutely at a loss for words.

Stephens turned and strode out of the weather room.

Going back to the weather maps, Kensington felt a deep, grudging admiration for Stephens, but it was an admiration mixed with something bordering on pity. No one could have pre-dicted the Killeen tornado with more than a few minutes' lead time. It had been the oddest and most isolated violent fluke that Kensington had ever heard of : one twister, developed out of a cloud of only moderate altitude, with most of the other classic tornado ingredients missing, on the ground only three miles and then in a skipping pattern, and then vanishing. Most tornadoes, as wildly unpredictable as they might seem, developed in known patterns, in response to generally predictable causes. This one had broken all the rules, and only the wildest and most impossibly perfectionistic dreamer would even think about the idea that any-one could have forecast its brief existence.

But no one had ever accused Ed Stephens of being less than a manic perfectionist, and that was among the reasons the forecast centre's record was as great as it was.

In a few minutes, Stephens came back into the weather room. He was in his shirtsleeves now, and had a plastic cup of coffee in hand.

'You're here for the day?' Kensington asked, newly surprised.

'I've got some telephone calls to make to Killeen and Norman,' Stephens said dourly. 'In the meantime, I want to see the new satellite pictures as soon as we get them. I may want to request some special shots a little later.'

'It does begin to shape up for a bad weather day in the South-west,' Kensington agreed.

'In the Southwest today,' Stephens said, 'and over a wider area Sunday, and worse on Monday, and even worse than that into the middle of the week – and we've got that goddamned Tatinger on our hands starting Monday, too.'

'You can't take every storm personally,' Kensington said sympathetically. 'I mean – I know you do. Hell. We all do. But it's crazy. We'll deal with Tatinger. And we'll deal with whatever else comes, too.'

'Yes,' Stephens retorted. 'And we're going to stay on top of things this time, too.'

Kensington stiffened. 'We stayed on top of Killeen.'

'I know,' Stephens said distantly.

'We always stay on top of them,' Kensington insisted.

Stephens looked up at him, and then his face softened. 'I know that, Jake. I know that.'

'You're not the only one who cares.'

'I'm sorry, Jake. I didn't mean it the way it sounded.'

But Kensington was angry too now, and tired. It had been a long night. 'Killeen was a fluke, a one-in-a-million. No one could have foreseen it. Something like that won't happen once every ten years.'

'Do you realize where I was when Killeen was hit?' Stephens asked as if for the first time. 'I was playing handball.'

Kensington exhaled loudly and turned away to his work.

Stephens watched for a while. He had to have reports from Killeen, and from the Severe Storms Lab at Norman, Oklahoma. He had to check his files to make sure he had all the handouts ready for Tatinger. He wanted to look over all the wires on Killeen, checking timing against verifiable facts. He knew it was stupid, feeling personally responsible, but that didn't change the fact that this was precisely how he did feel. The old driven feeling was in his gut again.

He went back to his office. He tried working. But the other thing on his mind kept nagging.

Finally he took the letter from his youngest sister out of his coat pocket and, scowling, read it carefully again.

Thursday

Dearest Ed,

Your letter was a lovely surprise. I hope it doesn't become the only one you write to us all year. I know this is the start of your 'busy season,' so hearing from you was all the more a nice surprise.

It's been busy here too. Mike has been completely engrossed in city business, and the next time we see each other, I can fill you in on why the last weeks have been especially trying for him. The kids are fine, I'm fine—

No, I won't lie to big old brother. My classes at the college are going right along and I suppose there are no obvious clouds on the horizon, but did you ever imagine dear, sweet, dependable little Mo would ever go just a little crazy? I sort of have, you know. I was into it a little last summer when you were here with us. The whole identity thing. Does that mean I'm starting to act menopausal already?

I'm functioning. Don't get worried. What has come through to me is that even as a child I tended to identify myself through the roles I was playing. I was 'a nice little girl,' or 'Mommy's helper,' or whatever. And then I was a good student, and then later I saw myself as Mrs Mike Coyle . . . as a good mother . . . as a housewife – never as *me!* Blame women's lib, huh? I think there's more to it than that. I've been reading a marvellous little book called 'Coming into Existence.' I wish I had come into existence as a little child. I wish I had done it even last year. But you can't cry over wasted years. I'm trying to make the grade now, as wrenching as that is. And I think, once I do make it, the struggle will have been worthwhile.

Now *don't* think I've gone crazy! I'm *fine.* I always did confide in you, and old habits are hard to break. I guess that's because I love you, big brother mine, and for just about the first time ever, I'm going to say that to you straight out, with no joke attached to hide behind.

You caught me in a thoughtful mood. That's why your letter was even more appreciated than normally. Please write again when you have time, and always remember I do love you.

Your nutty sister,
Mo

The letter had arrived at Stephens's house Friday afternoon, a remarkably fast delivery, which meant that his sister had written and mailed it very early the day before. The length of the letter and the speed of her reply to his brief note were almost as unusual as some of the content.

It troubled Ed Stephens. Was this his sunny little sister, beautiful Mo, the one to whom all the family pointed as the perfect child and the one with the ideal life? Wife of a mayor of a nice Ohio city, still quite young, with two children who were, as far as anyone knew, practically perfect kids?

Yes, she had had her moody moments as a child and young woman. But they had never somehow been as serious as others' moods. Mo had always been the one in charge of herself, sure of her identity, *happy*. And now this letter, which, to Stephens, reading between the lines, had an ominous, sombre tone.

Well, he was very damned busy. And you didn't meddle in others' business, right?

So he picked up the telephone, got an outside line, and direct-dialled the familiar number out there in Thatcher, Ohio.

A breathless female voice answered: 'Hello?'

'Jill? Hey. Sorry to disappoint you, but it isn't a boyfriend.'

'Uncle Ed?' She sounded delighted. 'My gosh! Are you in town?'

'No, I'm in Kansas City at work.'

'My gosh! You're calling us and it isn't even Christmas or something?'

He grinned. 'You really know how to hurt a guy, lady.'

'My gosh! I didn't mean it that way! Do you want to talk to Mom or Dad?'

'Is your mom there?'

'Sure! Just a sec.' She did not cover the mouthpiece when she hollered, and the noise practically broke Stephens's eardrum. 'Mom? It's Uncle Ed! Long distance!'

Stephens waited, the adult sound of Jill's voice taking him on a little memory trip. He had so often continued to think of Mo as almost a baby. But now her daughter sounded like a woman on the telephone, except for her exclamations, and she was almost a young woman herself. Now, if Mo was changing some way, was troubled—

'Hello?' And Mo, too, sounded breathless, so much like Jill.

'How's my baby sister?'

'Fine! I just wrote you a letter the other day.'

'I got it.'

Mo said nothing.

Stephens added, 'That's why I called.'

'I really am fine. Was that letter really dumb? After I mailed it, I got worried that it was awfully dumb.'

'It wasn't dumb. You sound out of breath, though.'

'We were in the back yard.'

'Is it warm enough for that?'

'You're the weather expert. Don't you know?'

'It may be a great shock to you, dear heart, but I do have a few things to do besides watch the forecast high for central Ohio.'

23

She paused. 'Ed, if my letter was dumb, I am sorry. I'm just fine, really. I'm making it through things all right. Really.'

'Mo, have you talked about this with anyone else?'

'You mean like Daddy? No. There are things you just don't – oh, you know what I mean. Why worry anybody else? I'm functioning. I'll make it.'

She said it cheerily, with confidence. The fact that she had to say it this way was even clearer indication to Stephens that she needed someone.

He asked, 'Have you and Mike talked it all out?'

'There's nothing to talk out, Ed. Not really. This is just a little personality reorganization, okay? Why worry Mike or anybody else? I didn't mean to worry you, either.'

'Maybe we'll get a slack period in a week or two. If we do, maybe I could come over that way.'

Mo said nothing, and the connection between them chirped and twittered with electronic murmurings.

'Okay?' he said finally.

'Yes, Ed,' she said in an entirely different and vulnerable tone. 'I think that would be very, very nice.'

'And hang in there in the meantime, right?'

'Right.' Her voice sounded like she smiled at that.

Stephens swallowed. 'Because listen, kiddo. I care about you, do you know that? Your letter wasn't dumb. Whatever's going on, you can hack it. You can do anything you want. Will you remember that?'

'Yes.' The single word was very bright, as if she might be laughing on the brink of tears.

'I mean,' he said slowly, feeling his way stupidly, 'we all go through stuff. So hang in there.'

'I will,' she said, and actually sounded better again.

'And thanks for cheering me up,' he added, to give her a change of pace. 'We had this damned stupid storm down in Texas that made me mad, and we've got a damned stupid congressman coming in here Monday to ask a lot of damned stupid questions, and there's a lot of damned stupid bad weather coming across the country in the next few days – and there's nothing like a snot-nosed kid sister to take a man's mind off his woes.'

She did laugh now. 'Even if she's damned stupid.'

'I'll call you again soon, Mo. And you call me if you feel like it. Right?'

'Yes, Ed. Thank you.'

He hung up and sat alone in his steel office, thinking.

70° West

The satellite plunged serenely through deep space. An internal stabilization system maintained its attitude perfectly so that its cameras, both visual and infra-red, could look unblinkingly back toward the earth, its home, 22,300 miles away. Its speed, 6,800 miles per hour, precisely matched the rotation speed of the planet so that its relative position was always the same, geosynchronous, poised over the Equator with its instruments focused unendingly on the North American Continent.

The satellite was called SMS-1. Launched on May 17, 1974, from Patrick Air Force Base, it was carried aloft by a Delta rocket.

SMS-1 was the most sophisticated weather satellite ever put into space. Weighing 535 pounds, screened from solar heat by ingenius thermal blanketing, power panels deployed in a golden geometry, capable of doing its work either automatically or on special radio command from the ground, and controlled by an elegant onboard computer, SMS-1 was the culmination of an intense weather satellite development programme dating all the way back to 1960, and TIROS-1.

Time did not exist for the satellite. It swept through light and dark, but its instruments could see in either condition. Far above the buffeting of the storms it helped men chart and predict, it knew no seasons, no punctuation to time except for the icy click of a relay or the whisper of a flywheel as it moved on across the fierce white light of the sun or the unbelievably vast panoply of the darkness, and the stars.

In the United States, daylight had crept about halfway across the continent.

From the East Coast came tiny radio signals which were picked up by the satellite's antennae and amplified by special, shielded receivers.

Tell us how you feel, the signals commanded. *Do you have sufficient power? Are you too hot or too cold?*

Obediently the satellite gave itself a quick physical, then radioed the results: *All is well*.

What do you remember?

The satellite dumped the picture data from its memory unit.

What do your cameras see now? What do your radiometers see now?

The satellite took a new scanning and sent it back.

Its view at the moment was a turbulent one. Cloud covered the Texas Gulf Coast where a storm was gnawing its way slowly eastward. Some blowing dust was just becoming visible in Oklahoma. A layer of high cloud covered much of California, signifying another storm. The radiometers detected more cloud about 300 miles out in the Pacific – great whorls of cloud which would appear light-coloured on the infra-red photo. The lighter the infra-red image, the cooler the cloud, and forecasters on the ground would interpret these cool clouds as being very tall ones, the kind that might produce the most violent weather.

The remainder of the nation was relatively clear, with traces of thin cirrus cloud extending in a circular path from Washington down into New Mexico, perhaps signifying jetstream activity. Snow showed clearly on the ground in Canada and some of the states in America's northernmost tier, while readings indicated both heat and high humidity in the South.

None of this was particularly unusual. Spring was the time of greatest contrasts in weather over the United States. As the movement of the earth around the sun changed the angles at which the sun's rays hit the planet, more heat radiated into the northern latitudes. But the struggle of the sun to overcome the winter's stored cold was a slow and laborious one. As they had done through the winter, enormous gobs of frigid arctic air continued to break off the polar regions, the global icebox, and drift toward the Equator. At the same time, air warmed by the sun's action near the Equator rose and pulsed northward toward the poles, being slowly chilled, slowly sinking, mixing with the polar chill. The earth's rotation and the engine forces of heat and cold created great global winds which mixed, collided, were shaped by surface features, flowed in wave motions west to east.

There were times, especially in the spring of the year, when the mixing and colliding of air masses coincided with seasonal changes in the great jetstream winds, and changes in the weather could be anything but tranquil. The meeting of air masses of drastically different temperatures and moisture contents can generate enormous energy.

Along the edge of an advancing cold mass of air, the warmer air being replaced is often forced upward. As it does so, it is cooled, and can no longer hold so much moisture. The excess moisture begin to condense out; clouds form rapidly, building. With the condensation, new heat energy is liberated. Electrical imbalances build. Lightning flashes, changing the very molecular structure of the air.

In a simple rainstorm, energy may be released that equals three Hiroshima-sized atomic bombs *every second*. In a big thunderstorm, or in that most violent of all weather phenomena, the tornado, this power may be multiplied many times.

The satellite SMS-1 existed in part to help man try to predict violent weather. The picture it was seeing today depicted conditions ripening for exactly this kind of weather.

For the moment, however, no new instructions came to the satellite. It continued to look down, working on its own schedule now until new orders came.

Norman, Oklahoma

Among the first to notice signs of the developing trouble was Bill Fredrick, a meteorologist at the University of Oklahoma. He did nothing about it because he knew that certainly others were noticing, too; signs like this did not escape notice along the network of thousands watching every weather development. But Fredrick took a wry pleasure in knowing he was spotting it very early on the charts.

A youthful, black-bearded giant, Fredrick had no particular business in the Meteorology Department on Saturday. He was primarily a classroom teacher and no classes met Saturday. But the visit was characteristic: weather was more than a business for him; it was a lifetime preoccupation. He had made his first rain gauge, a tin can with a ruler bolted to the side, when he was nine. A year later, his big Christmas gift had been a good aneroid barometer. By the time he was in his teens he had built, mostly out of junk parts, his own small but highly effective weather station with its own psychrometer, anemometer, and hygrometer, and was making up his own forecasts, poring over old synoptic charts at the local Weather Bureau office, and driving the forecasters there crazy with his questions.

There had never been much doubt about what Fredrick would do with his life if he was lucky. The last few years he had been known to draw up short with a little bark of pleasure, look down at his meteorological work, and say unbelievingly, 'They're *paying* me to do this!'

In addition to his teaching load, Fredrick held a part-time federal appointment with the National Severe Storms Lab, which had been established on the University's North Campus in Norman a few years earlier. Like the National Severe Storms Forecast Centre in Kansas City and numerous other offices, NSSL was a part of the National Oceanic and Atmospheric Administration. This parent organization was usually referred to as NOAA, pronounced by those in the trade like the name of the man who once built an ark. It had an incredible number of subdivisions, and was a jungle of acronyms. Even Fredrick didn't know all of them, although he knew a lot. He tried to concentrate on his own speciality, which happened to be severe weather in general and tornadoes in particular.

The Severe Storms Lab had been located in Norman because central Oklahoma was in 'tornado alley,' that broad band across the central and southern belt of the nation where tornadoes annually spawned the bulk of their death and destruction. Fredrick fit into the team of experts at the Lab very well.

Except incidentally, the Lab did not predict violent weather. Its job was to study the phenomena while in progress and to study data afterward. Fredrick had had some hair-raising adventures, chasing storms both by day and night, driving a specially instrumented van close under the fringes of enormous black clouds, chasing the snakelike tornadoes extending down out of them, visiting scenes of awesome devastation close behind the impact of the twister. He was not a poet, but he knew the poet's visceral thrill of discovery and awe in tornadoes. This most narrowly defined and destructive of nature's arsenal of weapons frightened him at a deep, elemental level even as he controlled the fear and worked as a scientist to try to understand it.

When Fredrick met someone who expressed an interest in tornadoes, he always asked the person early in the conversation if he was afraid of twisters.

If the person laughed and said he had no fear whatsoever, Fredrick knew he was a fool. People with intelligence respected these things.

Today Fredrick had come by his office casually, just to look at some of the many reports and charts that flowed into the building on teletypes and facsimile machines from arms of the far-flung National Weather Service, the 'umbrella under the umbrella' of NOAA. An upstairs hallway in the Meteorology Building on the campus was lined with these machines.

The reports, satellite photographs, facsimile maps and other synoptic data showed a somewhat typical spring day. The seasonal tilt of the earth on its axis had not yet brought the direct rays of the sun high enough into the north to dispel winter in much of Canada; two powerful high-pressure masses of very cold arctic air formed a dumbbell shape over the northern sectors of the continent, and patchy snow remained on the ground as far south as portions of Montana, North Dakota and Minnesota. Both coasts showed overcast conditions. The first of a trio of low-pressure centres was dragging a storm with it into Texas and Louisiana; a second was dissipating against the western slope of the Rockies, but would re-form tomorrow in New Mexico; a third low, extremely intense according to the chart symbols, was moving toward California from the ocean.

It would spawn some violent weather, that third low, just as the first was doing now and the second would do tomorrow and early in the week. The causes were many and complex, but when Fredrick was trapped into giving an after-dinner speech for a women's group or a civic club, he oversimplified things this way: 'Bring that cold, dry air south in a hurry; push that hot, moist, tropical maritime air up to meet it; where the two masses meet, you're going to have updrafts, downdrafts, sidedrafts, rain, hail, lightning, thunder, some cyclonic rotation, strong straight winds and possibly a tornado – and you'd better have your umbrella, friends, because it's likely to be a mess.'

It usually got a laugh.

Then Fredrick took pains to explain that he was not a hurricane expert. He told how a hurricane was a vast cyclonic circulation over a wide area, with driving rain, terrible visibility, and winds that sometimes topped 100 miles per hour, but frequently were less. Then he explained 'cyclone' and cyclonic,' which strictly speaking applied to any cloud mass in rotation, however slow, and he pointed out that many thunderclouds were cyclonic. And then he gave a simplified view of how the slow cyclonic motion of a cloud could become tightened, with a corresponding increase in rotational velocity, so that possibly a tornado could be born.

Then he talked about tornadoes, with their narrow track of a mile or less and their winds over 200 miles per hour, sometimes, and possibly even higher than that, and the associated straight winds that topped 100 miles per hour on occasion, and the huge hailstones that could kill, and the pressure differentials that could explode a strong building as the suction vortex of the twister moved nearby.

At this point the audience didn't smile any more.

Ah, well.

Turning now to another set of charts in the building hallway, Fredrick studied reports on the upper atmosphere. Each day, 185 ground stations used instrumented balloons to test the upper air. Most of these readings were taken at normal aircraft heights, but 25 stations were equipped to sample the air flow, temperature and other data at 10 millibars of pressure – 100,000 feet.

At this altitude flowed great invisible rivers of swiftly moving air, the jetstreams. Fuelled by the sun and affected by the earth's rotational forces, these winds sometimes travelled hundreds of miles in an hour. Ordinarily flowing in reasonably regular wave motions, the jetstreams carry new weather systems along with them as they flow west to east, sometimes moving high into the arctic cold and sometimes dipping well south into more temperate zones.

The 300-millibar chart today clearly showed the jetstream locations to the practiced eye. The lines of pressure and wind direction formed regular wavy patterns. But as Fredrick glanced along these patterns, he quickly noticed a small indention in the regularity in the Washington–Montana area.

The phenomenon was a short wave, an aberration in the usual steady pattern of the undulating jetstream. Cause: uncertain. Effect: possibly minimal.

Or possibly a great deal.

Sometimes the tiny indention became amplified into a deep wave, dipping the jetstream erratically deep into the south. If this happened, it was likely that stored cold air in the far north would break off and be carried southward at a high rate of speed.

If the deep wave developed now, Fredrick thought, in conjunction with the low-pressure activity, severe weather was almost a certainty.

That would mean extra work for him here or elsewhere. When the bad weather broke out he was likely to be asked to help follow it up, collecting data, whether it was in Oklahoma or New England. He didn't go as far away as New England very often, but he had a suitcase under the bed at home ready to be packed for fast travel at any time. His wife called it his 'tornado bag.'

Fredrick put the charts away and started home in his Volkswagen. It was not necessary for him to do anything about what he had noted right now; he was absolutely certain that others more skilled than he were noticing the same thing and doing whatever they could about it.

Around the world, he knew, tens of thousands of men and women devoted most of their waking hours to the weather, as their full-time job. Unlike most skilled people in other professions, very few of these people made any attempt to do more than observe and accept. Even the business of prediction and warning was the work of a comparative handful. And although weather control was popular in the Sunday supplements, and there had been some brave little experiments, mankind in the later days of the twentieth century did what it had always done with the weather: it watched and it took what came.

For centuries man had looked into the skies and had been afraid. He saw signs of a regularity in the sun, moon and stars, but did not fully comprehend. The weather and its vicissitudes were to him a part of the same deep mystery: rains came and his river flooded, ruining crops and killing livestock and people; then the river retreated, leaving miles of rich mud, so that the curse of flood was followed by the blessing of fertility; summer came and the earth dried out in intense heat, with more killing, and out of the north came frightening clouds with thunder and lightning, and later the chill of snow; man looked out of his cave or his hovel at the bleakness of winter and wondered if things would ever come back to life this time.

Modern man understands more than that, and yet his basic acceptance of the weather is no less instinctive or necessary. Like a frog at the bottom of his shallow pool, man sits at the bottom of his ocean of air and looks up and tries to understand. Because it is his nature, he tries to predict the future. Like the frog who knows that a patter of heavy rain on the surface of the pond means a flood of nutrients into his little world, modern man, too, can find causes and effects. In some areas his basic understanding is no better than that of his friend in the pond.

In the United States, the National Weather Service operates more than 400 weather stations. Every day of the year, its National Meteorological Centre processes 12,000 synoptic weather observations, 25,000 hourly aviation reports, 1,400 ship reports, 1,500 atmospheric soundings, a continuing automatic flow of data from buoys planted in the ocean, and countless satellite photographs. The flow of information is world-wide; even in the depths of the Cold War, weather information flowed freely from and to all countries.

For all this, however, man today may simply understand his weather. He does not control it.

Which, Fredrick liked to say, made it all the more interesting.

When he reached home, his wife said he had had a call.

'Who was it?'

'Mister Stephens.'

'In Kansas City?'

'Yes. He asked you to return the call.'

Fredrick direct-dialled the number in Kansas City. Stephens's voice sounded burry, as it sometimes did when he was tired or under pressure. 'Some of your people have gone to Killeen.'

'That's right,' Fredrick said. 'Paler and Hodges.'

'I've got a message for them that I didn't want to entrust to the switchboard out there at the Lab.'

Fredrick grinned. 'As if we were grand enough to have a switchboard anyway.'

'Right. Here's the message.' Obviously Stephens was in no mood for small talk. 'I want to get a preliminary report from Killeen as soon as I can.'

'You'll be on distribution, of course—'

'I don't want to wait for that. Ask them to dictate a cassette and mail it to me, tonight if at all possible. I'm very interested in this storm. It was highly unusual. Anything they can send back to me on track, damage, or anything else might be very helpful. I want anything they can tell me about this storm from people on the scene.'

'I'll get the message to them when they get back tonight,' Fredrick promised.

Stephens paused, then asked, 'Have you seen any of the data today?'

'Yes.'

'We're in for several damned interesting days,' Stephens said.

From another man, it might have been a casual comment. But when Fredrick hung up moments later, he went directly into the bedroom to his clothes closet.

His wife stuck her head in from the hall. 'What are you doing?'

'Getting my tornado bag ready,' Fredrick said.

'*Today*? You're going somewhere today?'

'Not today.'

'How do you know you're going to need it?'

'I'll need it,' Fredrick said grimly.

Sunday, April 6 1:20 p.m.–3 p.m.

NNNN//A
ZCZC WBC 337
TBXX6 KMKC 061300
SSFSS MKC SATELLITE NARRATIVE
BASED ON SMS-1 IR DATA THROUGH 1200Z

MKC FLOATING SECTOR IS B-3

CONFIGURATION OF CLOUD PATTERN OVER WEST TEXAS AND NEW
MEXICO INDICATES CYCLONIC CIRCULATION WITH APPARENT
UPPER LOW VICINITY 30 SOUTH ROW AT 12Z AND VORTICITY
MAX NEAR GDP . . . BOTH HAVE BEEN MOVING NORTHEAST 30 TO
35 KNOTS DURING THE PAST 6 HOURS.

CLOUD PATTERN OVER UPPER GULF . . . TEX-LA AREA WEAKENING
AND BECOMING DIFFUSE . . . SUGGESTING WEAKENING THIS SYSTEM.

JETSTREAM CIRRUS HAS BEEN NOTED DURING THE PAST 6 HOURS
NEAR A 26N 103W . . . DRT . . . MWL . . . OKC LINE WITH NO
APPARENT EASTWARD MOVEMENT. MIDDLE AND HIGH CLOUDS
ACROSS CENTRAL AND EAST MEXICO BEND NORTHWARD ALONG
THE TEXAS COAST AND LA AND SOUTHERN ARK. THE ANTICYCLONIC
BULGE IN THE CLOUD MASS NEAR 22N 99W . . . DRT . . . ACT . . .
SHV IMPLIES AMPLIFICATION OF THE UPPER RIDGE IN THE
SOUTHERN LATITUDES. THE LATTER BOUNDARY ALSO DEPICTS
POSITION OF THE SUBTROPICAL JET THAT REGION.

IMAGERY INDICATES CLOUDS FLOWING ACROSS CALIFORNIA INTO
IDAHO. WESTERN EDGE DRIFTING EASTWARD AT 15 KNOTS. HIGH
CLOUDS ALSO OBSERVED FLOWING EASTWARD ACROSS THE PACIFIC
WEST OF BAJA. WEAK PVA AREA OVER WASHINGTON INTO
MONTANA HINTS SHORT WAVE THAT AREA.

XXX

Kansas City

The most junior meteorologist on duty looked up sharply. He
turned to his co-worker. 'What in hell is the big man doing in
here on Sunday?'

'The same thing he does every other day,' the older man said
reasonably.

'Six days a week aren't enough for him?'

'You've seen the charts. You know we're in for another rough one in the Southwest today.'

'It was rough yesterday. Sixteen tornadoes. He was here from before dawn to well after dark, the way I hear it. Doesn't the man rest?'

'Well, he's on a tear right now. And things must look pretty bad to him, or he wouldn't be here.'

To Stephens, it did look bad. Saturday's storms had had the classic springtime pattern to them, and there had been no surprises. Only one of the day's severe storms had been near a city, and that one had only skirted a well-warned Dalhart, Texas. Today, however, appeared to promise worse, and the long-range forecast was all downhill toward a really major outbreak later. Stephens had conferred by telephone with his deputy, Harry Adams, after church, and that had decided him.

'You're going *where?*' his wife had protested.

'Work,' Stephens replied mildly.

'On a day like this?' The Missouri sky was clear and warm, streaked only by a few high cirrus clouds.

'You've been around me long enough,' Stephens told her, 'to know that nice weather here doesn't mean nice weather everywhere.'

She sighed. 'And nice weather today doesn't mean nice weather tomorrow. Yes, yes, yes.'

'I'll try to get home by eight.'

'Damn,' the lady murmured, more in resignation than anger.

Stephens, however, felt he had no real choice. He knew his staff could adequately handle any emergency without him. There were no one-man operations in the far-flung National Weather Service. And he also knew that any feeling of responsibility he might feel about Killeen was wholly irrational. But he had to discharge his tension in work. It was the way he was.

Driving downtown on Interstate 70, he exited at Thirteenth and pulled into the parking lot practically at the foot of the ramp. He rode an express elevator to seventeen, the floor shared by the Severe Storms unit and several related agencies. Walking past the River Forecast Centre, the next-door neighbour to NSSFC in the 1728 wing, he entered his own shop.

The front portion of the wing was like other offices, with white

35

tile ceilings, tan metal walls, contemporary furniture and gold carpet. Stephens's private office was in this area, but he didn't even pause there this time, going directly down the corridor into a small personal locker area which someone had dubbed the Ready Room. He poured a cup of thickish black coffee, then proceeded down the hall, past a wall of glass enclosing the big computer, past the communications room with its banks of hammering teletypes, and into the main weather room.

Glancing around, Stephens identified all seven persons on duty, a good crew. They were all male, all white, and most near the age of fifty. Meteorology took off as a science during World War II, and many men who learned their skills with the old Army Air Corps remain in the National Weather Service today. The present effort to recruit women and minorities is progressing slowly.

Harry Adams, a rotund man with a red face and hair to match, looked up from the chart talk that had been taking place at the workdesks. He walked over. As usual, his shirt-tail was half out and he looked totally disorganized. His appearance was not the reality.

'Howdy, howdy, Ed. We were just looking at some of this stuff.'

'How does it look?'

'Well, the first storm system, the one that busted things up in Texas yesterday, is playing out. The second one is going to give us some problems today, and the third one – the new one – is beginning to bug the hell out of me.'

'It's the third one that worries me, too,' Stephens admitted.

'If it gets going in a day or two, it's going to really raise hell through the middle of this country.'

'That's what I know.'

'We're just taking a look at the whole thing, if you want to join in with us.'

'Yes.'

They walked to the worktable area. The tables were strewn with the latest charts and maps, as well as numerous satellite photographs. Each man had some area of specialization, but they worked as a team without regard to specialization at times like these.

Stephens joined them casually, exchanging easy remarks, and began glancing over some of the materials. There was a tremendous amount of it, a mountain of data that Stephens, like his fellow workers, tended to take for granted. The large, flimsy charts depicted a broad range of weather information for many levels of the atmosphere, from ground level up well beyond the ranges of normal jet travel.

Two of the forecasters, Hedges and Bright, pointed out some obvious factors on the maps. Stephens did not push them into a formal discussion. It was his way to let the consensus develop as naturally as possible. He kept his own gnawing concern about that third storm system temporarily in the background.

'The first system,' he said, pointing to a collection of whorls in the eastern half of the nation, 'is still losing force.'

'I don't think it's much of a factor,' Harry Adams agreed. 'They're getting rain along the Gulf Coast, but there isn't a lot of support for it now.'

Stephens pointed to a second, more tightly packed whorl area in New Mexico. 'Isn't this one beginning to move out?'

'There's some movement,' Bridges said, 'but it isn't travelling as fast as we anticipated. Yet.'

'You think it will move out through this area?'

'Into the Texas Panhandle and then northeast. Yes. We've been saying snow for Colorado possibly today, but I think now it's going to come tomorrow.'

'Why won't the low move directly east and sock it to both Texas and Oklahoma?'

'Because of jetstream behaviour, among other things. We have a deep wave forming, and I think this low is going to catch the upswing side and go slamming up into the Great Lakes faster than hell.'

Stephens nodded. It was his own theory, but he had been testing as usual. 'A little weather through Colorado, Oklahoma, Kansas, Nebraska and Iowa, possibly, on Monday?'

Bridges grunted, 'More than a little in Colorado. They've got the moisture for heavy snow.'

'Nebraska?'

'Maybe. I'd guess no. I think the low will swing east faster than that.'

'We've already got gusty winds and some dust flying down through Texas and parts of western Oklahoma,' Bright chimed in. 'But they won't get anything worse than that because the air all through the central and southern part of the country is just too dry.'

'There's enough moisture off the Gulf Coast,' Stephens pointed out. 'Yesterday this time they were getting the hell beat out of them.'

'But the moisture is blocked by high pressure all through the South right now,' Adams argued. 'This second low-pressure centre will kick up the snow up here, and then possibly some light activity, but there just isn't enough humidity or heat in its way to provide a major storm outbreak, even if it sucks down some cold from Canada.'

'Okay, then,' Stephens said after a moment. 'It looks like some heavy snow in Colorado and possibly Nebraska, perhaps some activity we have to keep a careful watch over in the Oklahoma–Kansas–Iowa sector, and then not a whole lot farther east.'

'It's this third system we're all really concerned about,' Adams said.

Stephens studied the map. The third low was moving into California, with locally heavy rains and some high winds. 'What do you think this one is going to do?'

No one replied immediately, which was the signal for Bright, the most-junior man, to take a shot at it. He leaned over the table and traced a fingerline into Kansas–Oklahoma, then in a line roughly following the border between Kentucky and Tennessee, moving east. 'It will form again here in Kansas or Oklahoma and move east.'

'When will it get reorganized after crossing the mountains?' Stephens asked quietly, testing again.

'Tuesday.'

'Early Tuesday or—'

'Early Tuesday,' Bright replied. 'Then it will move across Kansas and part of Missouri on Tuesday, gathering punch and speed both, and we'll have some outbreaks because it's a hell of a big son of a bitch. But the worst will be Wednesday, because by that time it will have sucked a lot of cold air in behind it and all this Gulf moisture and heat up in front of it.'

Stephens studied the younger man's solemn face. 'How far do you think it will move Wednesday?'

'I think it will move faster than most. I think we'll have a real mess practically all the way to the Eastern Seaboard.'

Stephens was satisfied. 'We want to make sure we talk to Denver about this snow forecast,' he said. 'Just to be on the safe side. And I don't think it's too early to send out a message to make sure everyone in all RAWARC sectors knows what we're thinking right now in terms of Tuesday and Wednesday. We'll probably have a Skywarn Monday, for Tuesday. I feel virtually sure there will be a lot more interesting Skywarn Tuesday for Wednesday, although I wish something would make me a liar. It's still nice to-day, so let's run a routine test on all our local county communications, just in case we need them when the thing comes through here Tuesday, and let's send out a message advising all stations to complete any routine maintenance on their radars tomorrow – Monday – so everything will be ready if and when some of this starts hitting the fan.'

Communications would go out in a variety of ways. From the Centre's own communications room, messages would be prepared for practically instantaneous transmission directly and through the communications network computer in Maryland. Through the NOAA Weather Wire, information would go to more than 6,500 radio stations, 800 television stations, and 1,700 newspapers in some 3,000 communities. The news services would get extra information if desired.

In many major cities, the information would also go out over the weather radio system. These small, government-owned, automated FM transmitters would broadcast on 162.55 and 162.40 Hz to anyone with the special small receiver.

Telephone calls would be made. Locally, in the 38-county area which the Centre served as any other Weather Service office would serve a local area, all the special telephone lines and radio hookups would be checked to make sure warnings would come in and go out to the proper agencies at top efficiency if things later developed.

Although 'Skywarn' was the name of the entire programme designed to help communities and individuals spot and spread warnings about severe weather, a particular Skywarn message would be called to the attention of millions of people watching the NBC-TV 'Today' show.

'It looks,' Harry Adams said after a while, 'like we've got the show on the road.'

For Sunday, everything had been laid out. It was all routine and well oiled, and should have been comforting.

To Stephens, however, it was not.

Weather forecasting of all kinds had always had in it a dash of intuition. Stephens hoped he was wrong, but he had a very bad feeling about this third storm. It was a combination of factors, including the intensity and size of the low, its evident speed, the strange antics of the jetstream, all that extra cold air in Canada poised over all that potentially turbulent moist warm air in the Gulf – all the factors closing pincers on a nation largely basking under ideal spring weather when any tendency to pooh-pooh an adverse forecast would already be exaggerated.

Thinking of the known factors, and feeling the pressure of the ones that went to intuition. Stephens remembered other springs, other storm systems. He felt a sharp little pang in his gut. He was beginning to get worried. There just could not be any more Killeens.

ZCZC WBC4 071100
SPECIAL WEATHER STATEMENT
NATIONAL WEATHER SERVICE DENVER COLORADO
ISSUED 4 AM CDT MONDAY 4/7/75

. . . A HEAVY SNOW WARNING HAS BEEN ISSUED FOR THE
MOUNTAINS OF COLORADO AND THE NORTHWEST PORTION THIS
MORNING AND THIS AFTERNOON . . .

A FAST MOVING PACIFIC WEATHER SYSTEM HAS MOVED INTO
NORTHWESTERN COLORADO AND WILL TRAVERSE THE REMAINDER
OF THE STATE BY LATE AFTERNOON. THIS SYSTEM IS
ACCOMPANIED BY SNOW AND GUSTY NORTHWESTERLY WINDS OF
20 TO 35 MPH. HEAVY SNOW HAS BEGUN IN THE MOUNTAINS
AND IS EXPECTED TO CONTINUE THROUGH MOST OF THE DAY
WITH ACCUMULATIONS OF 4 INCHES OR MORE EXPECTED BY
MONDAY NIGHT. SNOW WILL DECREASE LATE MONDAY BUT
ANOTHER PACIFIC STORM SYSTEM WILL BE ARRIVING TUESDAY.

IN THE MOUNTAINS AND IN NORTHWESTERN COLORADO THE
HEAVY SNOW ALONG WITH BLOWING AND DRIFTING SNOW WILL
MAKE DRIVING HAZARDOUS. THE STORM WILL PRODUCE TRACES
TO 3 INCHES OF SNOW IN THE LOWER ELEVATIONS OF SOUTHERN
AND EASTERN COLORADO BEFORE ENDING MONDAY NIGHT.

ALL INTERESTS ARE ADVISED TO BE ALERT TO THE POTENTIAL
FOR HEAVY SNOW AND HAZARDOUS DRIVING CONDITIONS AND TAKE
WHATEVER PRECAUTIONS ARE DEEMED NECESSARY.

OTHER STATEMENTS WILL BE ISSUED BY THIS OFFICE AS
CONDITIONS WARRANT.

JOSEPHSON . . . WFSO . . . DENVER

Kansas City
At 6:50 Monday morning, Stephens was back at work again, in
his private office away from the bustle of the weather room. He
heard someone insistently hammering on the call bell at the re-
ceptionist's vacant desk out front. It was too early for secretaries
to be on duty.

Going out to find the source of the clamour, Stephens immediately recognized Congressman 'Buck' Tatinger.

Tatinger was tall, with rather long dark hair modishly teased around the ears. His long nose and wide-set eyes were the same as they had appeared on the televised hearings where he made a national image for himself by bullying witnesses. He was one of those men whose very stance betrayed that he considered himself irresistible to women, and the impression was heightened by his flared, foppish, western-style tan suit and pointed Gucci shoes.

Tatinger carried a slender briefcase, which he placed on the empty desk in the yawningly vacant secretarial area as Stephens approached.

'Who's in charge at this hour?' he asked brusquely.

Stephens immediately disliked him. 'Who do you want to see?'

'Stephens. But I suppose he gets here about ten, right?'

'I'm Stephens.'

Surprise lowered the sardonic eyebrow for an instant, but then came the cynical smile. 'Really up for me, eh? I'm Buck Tatinger.'

Stephens shook his hand. 'We have some weather developing. I've been here since five.'

'Right,' Tatinger grinned. 'You always work a ninety-hour week because you're so dedicated, and your office here is so under-staffed and in need of more money, eh? You bureaucrats never cease to amaze me. You're all alike.'

Despite simmering anger, Stephens held his smile. 'You're off to a good start, sir, maintaining your public image.'

'I expect to be here most of the week, Stephens. There is abso-lutely no sense in pretence on either side. My job is to protect the people's investments. Your job is to build up your office. I've never visited an office yet that wasn't fat – bloated with waste and inefficiency. Your budget request shows a nine per cent increase next year, and I'm here to find out why.'

'And slash it?' Stephens said. His heart was fluttering.

'And slash it, probably, yes.' Tatinger set his handsome chin. It was the expression that had become famous on TV and in count-less newspaper photographs as he confronted the secretary of state or a famous old admiral or those people whose major river-navigation project in the Midwest he had not merely trimmed, but scuttled.

'No need for either of us to pretend any great fondness for each other, Stephens,' he went on now. 'I'm here to ferret out your waste and inefficiency. You want to hide it. That's normal. Self-preservation: first law of the species. I don't hold that against you. But you're a bureaucrat and I'm a public servant. The relationship is an adversary relationship. No use pretending otherwise.'

'The job, in other words, requires you to attack whenever possible?'

Tatinger flashed a bright smile. 'Precisely. I may wind up liking you as a person, who knows? It wouldn't change a thing. My role here is to see you as a bureaucrat, and I hate bureaucrats.'

'Well,' Stephens grinned back at him, 'I hate politicians. So let's go to work.'

Thatcher, Ohio

It was 8.30 a.m. when Mike Coyle sat at the breakfast table on the glassed-in back porch of his home on Erie Street, alone with his second cup of coffee and his defeat.

It was not a day for this kind of pervasive depression. Robins flitted around the densely shrubbed back yard. The bright bloom of the forsythia contrasted with the dark green of pyracantha and nandinas coming out of winter dormancy. The bright-green lawn was mottled with sunlight out of a porcelain sky, and the maple trees, beginning to have some real size to them now, were in leaf.

Back inside the big Cape Cod house somewhere, Coyle's daughter Jill was playing her radio too loud again; the bass thumped, vibrating glassware. The noise mixed with the distant hum of Billy's hairdryer as he fluffed himself up into the proper state of chaos for the current high school fashion. Mo was in the kitchen, but she was quiet as she loaded the dishwasher. There was no room for adult noise these days.

Coyle heaved a long, uneven sigh, then loathed himself for it. He hated self-pity. People who felt sorry for themselves *were* sorry. People who believed in bad luck *had* bad luck. Now come on, Coyle, goddamn it. Shape up.

'Mo?' he called.

His wife appeared in the alcove doorway. Her face was soft from sleep and her blond hair was loose on the shoulders of a shapeless blue housecoat, but she looked pretty. 'More coffee?'

'Sit with me a minute,' he asked.

She smiled. 'Okay. I can manage that.' She sat facing him across the small table. 'Now what?'

43

'What do you really think about this whole business?' he asked.

'Oh, Mike. Don't ask me. It really is *your* decision.'

'It affects all of us.'

'I know. But it has to be basically your choice.'

Coyle rubbbed his face with his palms. 'It ain't easy, kiddo.'

Mo's smile faded and the more thoughtful side of her personality showed itself. 'Honey, another bond election failed last week. All right. That's not the end of the world. You can try it again . . . if we stay in Thatcher.'

'I'm getting a little tired of up-the-hill, down-the-hill.'

'I know. But you're still a popular mayor. It isn't as if you lost your own support by backing the bonds.'

'I'm popular,' Coyle agreed. 'As a caretaker.'

'Well, the people in Columbus say they're sure you can get the nomination for Congress. If that's what you want—'

'It's not that simple! What do *you* want?'

'Mike, we decided a long time ago on some things.'

'You've got your classes going now. A trip to Congress, assuming I could win—'

'You'd win.'

'—assuming I could win, would uproot us all. And I'd feel like I was running out on this job half-done, damn it.'

'Then stay,' Mo said with maddening calmness. 'You can run for Congress in two more years. It will still be there.' Her smile came back. 'I think.'

Coyle did not reply. It was, as it had been, an impasse. He had to decide alone, but could not begin to imagine all the possible side-effects. The people in Columbus were putting the pressure on, now that the bond election was settled, to get him to announce early, for a head start. But the bond defeats had savaged him worse than anyone, even Mo, suspected. He was being asked to make a crucial career decision at a time when he would have been hard-pressed to decide between baloney and spiced ham at the lunch-meat counter.

'As long as I stay,' he said, 'I'll keep bashing my head against the wall.'

'What do you really want to do, Mike?'

He looked at her. 'My God, if I knew that, I'd have it made, wouldn't I.'

She stood. 'I'd better get back to work in there. I hear loud radios being turned off. The children must be about due.'

He caught her hand. 'No easy answers for me?'

'Not for anyone.'

'You've changed, you know. You're strong.'

She looked at him with an expression he couldn't read. 'Wasn't I always strong?'

'Not like this.'

'Thanks. I think.' She went into the kitchen again.

Billy, a gangling sixteen-year-old, poked his head around the corner. 'Come on, Dad! I got to get down there!'

'We'll make it,' Coyle said. 'We always do.' He was aware of the hidden personal irony in this. He added, 'Cool it. Buzz off.'

Billy made a face. 'Now we have to listen to archaic slang on top of everything else?'

This kind of banter was superior, at least, to the kind of strained dialogue that often crept into their encounters these days. 'What's "everything else," Son?'

Billy rolled his eyes and racketed into the kitchen.

Coyle followed, finding Mo back at the dishwasher.

'I guess we're off,' he told her.

'Are you still planning to pick Jill up at the hospital on your way home this evening?'

'Sure.' He had forgotten it.

'If you get tied up, you can call me and I'll go get her.'

'The Council meeting shouldn't run us very late. All we have to do is sort over the wreckage a little and talk about cutting everything back another twenty per cent.'

Mo looked at him quickly, dried her hands on a towel, and came to him. 'Cheer up, darling. It isn't that bad.'

'Sure,' he said.

Seeing something in his eyes, she moved closer, watching his face intently and very seriously. 'Mike?'

For just an instant he had the horrible feeling he was going to cry. He patted her backside, forced a smile, and moved away. 'I'd better get going.'

Billy came in from the living room, no books as usual. 'Ready, Dad?'

Coyle forced brightness. 'Sure. Shag it.'

'The expression, Dad, is, "Let's shag." It's sort of an old-fashioned expression these days.'

'Then let's haul ass.'

'Mike!' Mo said ritualistically.

Backing the Chevy out of the driveway, Coyle tried to take note of superficial things in an attempt to shake the dark mood. Some of the new shrubs in front of the house were adding new leaf rapidly, beginning to fill in gaps along the basement wall where he had cleared out the ratty old shrubbery last year. Behind its trees, the house looked handsome, solid. Built in the late thirties, it had a solidity of line that newer homes just didn't approach, somehow.

The home's three thousand feet of floor space had been a real bargain when they bought it eight years ago, even though he had had to stretch to the limit for the down payment. Now its value had nearly doubled. It was a good house.

There had been, God knew, enough costly improvements: the new roof, furnace and air conditioning, floor refinishing throughout, new paint and wallpaper, a totally rebuilt kitchen, light fixtures, siding and shutter repairs, the storm doors and added insulation. There had been times when they had been near despair, wondering if they would ever get it into shape. But it was all done now except for small things here and there, and it had been worth the struggle.

Mike Coyle did not want to leave this place, with his workshop, with the formal living and dining rooms ideal for job-oriented entertaining that a public official had to endure now and then, with the big downstairs room with the fireplace and the TV, enough space for Billy or Jill to have friends in without everyone falling all over one another. He did not want to leave this street, with its huge old maples lining the curbs on both sides. It was a good place, right for all of them.

But was he willing – or able – to pay the price to keep it? Could he face more years of more defeats like the series he had already endured? He could *not* quit fighting for what he believed Thatcher needed. He was not the kind of man who could settle into comfortable mediocrity. If he stayed, and kept fighting, and kept getting smashed, he was afraid of what it would do to him.

He knew it was ironic that he should be so depressed about the possibility of moving up and out, into Congress. A man with any sense would view the post as mayor of a city like Thatcher as a springboard, and, after a defeat like last week's bond vote, would chortle at the opportunity to get the hell out.

But he was not that kind of a man, either.

Beside him, Billy sat silent now, increasingly withdrawn. The nearer they got to the school, the more he was a different person. Billy was changing very fast, and often Coyle was more than perplexed by some of the changes. Billy was moving away from him now, moving toward the judgment of his peers. He cared more about his friends than he did about his family now, Coyle thought bitterly.

But perhaps that was inevitable, too, like all change. Perhaps Coyle was fighting the only thing that could not be fought, change itself.

They drove the last few blocks to the school area. At the near corner, where a clutter of little shops existed to amuse students, a tall boy with very long hair was standing by the mailbox.

'Hey,' Billy said. 'You can drop me here, man.'

'This isn't school, *man*,' Coyle said.

'I've got time for a quick game of football first.'

'With the Ford kid?'

'He's a friend of mine.'

Coyle began to slow the car. He considered keeping quiet, but knew he wouldn't. 'Did it ever occur to you to go on to school five minutes early?' he asked, his voice tight.

'What for?'

'To study.'

'Dad, we don't have homework. That's old-fashioned.'

'What kind of a school is it if you never have homework?'

Billy grinned lazily. 'Progressive?'

But Coyle was angry for no identifiable reason, and driven. 'Maybe if you studied some, homework or not, you could get your grades up.'

'Crap, what's wrong with my grades?'

'C's?'

'That's good enough,' Billy said. 'That's average.'

Coyle approached his flash point. 'C's *aren't* good enough. Being "average" isn't good enough. Don't you want to excel? Don't you want to be the best?'

Billy honestly looked puzzled. 'Why?'

'Oh, God,' Coyle groaned. But he tried anyway. 'Listen. Vince Lombardi once told the Packers that the quality of a man's life is in direct proportion to how hard he strives for excellence.'

'Yeah. That was jock rhetoric.'

'That *wasn't* jock rhetoric! That was a fundamental truth that I happen to believe in . . . and try to live by.'

'Stop right here, Dad. This is fine.'

'Are you listening to me?'

'Sure, Dad.'

Coyle stopped the car. The gangly Ford boy waved and continued to slouch against the mailbox. Billy opened the car door, but Coyle caught his arm. 'Billy, okay. Maybe wanting to excel is Puritan Ethic. Right? I don't know. But look at it this way. You want to be free. That's the big thing with kids your age. Don't you see that your freedom is in direct proportion to your education?'

Billy smiled, and his eyes looked like those of a person dazzled by the sun. 'School? *Freedom?*'

'You're free in this country,' Coyle told him intently, 'if you have enough money. Without money, how much freedom do you have? To have money, you have to have a good job. To get a good job, you have to have a quality education. You have to excel.'

'Does that make it a just system?' Billy asked.

'Oh, Christ. I don't know if it makes it just or unjust or anything else. I'm talking about what's *out there*. I'm talking about reality – the world we have to live in. Do you think a guy making a hundred a week has the kind of freedom I do? Do you think I have the kind of freedom a Rockefeller takes for granted? If you don't fight to excel, to learn as much as you can and *be* as much of a man as you possibly can be, you're dooming yourself to the crummiest menial job, and you'll never have any freedom. Everybody will own you: the banker, the doctor, the grocer, everybody. That's why I'm hassling you. Don't you see that? I want you to have a good life.'

Billy stared at him thoughtfully. 'Dad,' he said finally, 'two things.'

'Yes?'

'First, we ought to talk about this sometime when I've got more time. Second, if I don't get out of this car, we're really going to have an argument.'

Coyle leaned back. 'You'd better get out, then.'

Billy got out, slammed the door, and walked toward the Ford youth.

Coyle drove away, stewing. There was probably no hope for

any real rapport now, he told himself. The die was cast and Billy would be what he would be, he told himself. *Let him go*, he told himself.

None of it worked very well.

Coyle knew he drove himself and others too hard. He had tried to be different, to ease off, but he had never found the formula. Here in Thatcher he had found an incredible problem to work on, and he worked on it every day of his life. He told himself that his ability to get results from employees and citizens meant that he wasn't totally inept or crazy. Why did he have so much trouble in his own home at times . . . with Billy, and with Jill to a lesser extent . . . and with his wife?

Driving, he convinced himself not to brood about it now. He had plenty of other things to brood about.

Cutting through the suburban neighbourhood, he reached the elevated interstate expressway that led downtown. He got on the super-road and drove fast. It was not far.

Begun as an early-day fort on the Olentangy River when west-central Ohio was still peopled by hostile Indians, Thatcher retained some of its character as a city built upon two bluffs overlooking the river. It had sprawled now, filling in between hills and growing well to the north, to Country Club Heights, and the college. Suburban shopping centres had diluted the sense of a central downtown. But as Coyle drove along the highway beside the bluffs, he could look down across the old houses perched precariously on hillsides, into the blocky geometry of the downtown business district, and across the curve of the river toward Southtown, the old, mostly squalid industrial area partially obscured by a haze of pollution. And it was not the worst place in the world, he told himself.

There were many things he could do for the place yet. He had been here long enough to know what was possible and what was not. He was not really whipped. Growth or no growth. Defeats or no defeats.

The city's population was now about seventy-five thousand. It had only two large employers, the glass works and the furniture factory, both in Southtown. Much of the old industrial area, deserted factories and dump-grounds, could have been cleared for new development if an Urban Renewal proposal had been passed two years ago. That, too, of course, had been defeated.

That was an old defeat.

Some new residential building was taking place on the city's east side. There were some new apartment complexes, stunningly ugly, to the southeast. There were trailer parks, too, and by way of contrast a rejuvenated local Preservation Society was working to refurbish the old Victorian homes along Canal Street. Much of the city was relatively comfortable, middle-class, settled, hanging on to the *status quo*.

And yet it was a good place to live. It needed a new police station and two outlying fire stations. It needed more hospital space and a new library. It needed new traffic-control systems, improved sanitation procedures, an expanded water-treatment plant. There was no youth centre worthy of the name, and the city parks were inadequate. The county bond proposal had failed, taking some of the needed improvements down, and last week the city's proposition had failed, too, putting the rest off into the indefinite – and unlikely – future. Thatcher couldn't even put up new traffic lights. It couldn't even scrape up the money to match federal funds to repair and extend its inadequate storm or other disaster-warning system. And yet it was *still* a good place to live, and Coyle loved it, and his sense of depression was so deep that it frightened him.

Knoxville, Tennessee

Les Korowiscz scrawled his signature at the bottom of the bill of lading, tore off a copy and handed it to the man on the shipping dock, walked around his hulking semi-trailer truck, tossed the clipboard inside, and climbed in after it. A glance at his watch showed it was past ten o'clock, late, but with such a beautiful day he could make up the time.

The man from the shipping dock walked around to the front and squinted up as Korowiscz fired up the engine and briefly wrestled the gears into position.

'Drive careful!' the little man called cheerfully.

Korowiscz saluted mockingly and tugged at the big steering wheel as he inched the truck away from the loading area. The rig was loaded heavily and his destination was a wholesaler in Dallas, Texas. A nice, short run, comparatively speaking. He would load for the return trip in Dallas late tomorrow and be out running in this direction again – heading home – very early Wednesday.

A burly man with a sense of humour, Korowiscz had no particular feeling about the trip one way or the other. He intended to drive hard, and he would get his usual backache. The signs on Interstate 40 said 55 *mph*, but he would highball at 70, the usual. The patrol was getting pretty nice about the speed limit these days. He seldom got a ticket any more. With his new CB radio, he could probably do 90 if he felt like it.

Within fifteen minutes, Korowiscz had the rig out on the interstate and was going up through the gears to his planned speed. It was a gorgeous spring day, clear, warm, little wind, with very clear air denoting low humidity. The tyres whanged their song on the pavement and the engine roared along smoothly. Korowiscz thought about his family back in Knoxville for a while, but then, as it always did, the passing of the miles began to insulate him from that reality and the truck became the reality.

Korowiscz got out a cigar and lighted up.

'Oh, my darlin',' he began to sing, 'oh, my darlin', oh, my *darlin*', ClemenTINE!'

The truck rolled west.

Monument Valley, Kentucky

'Land, it's warm!' Milly Tyler said to no one in particular.

Bustling around the small living room of her frame house, Milly continued wet-mopping the yellow linoleum floor. The farmhouse smelled of soapsuds and Clorox and room freshener, although every window stood open to the balmy spring breeze and the smells of springtime came in freely, wafting the chintz curtains.

The stem of her good Barling pipe clenched tightly in her teeth, Milly finished mopping the linoleum. It was one of the last things on her mental list. Squeezing out the mop in the galvanized bucket, she happened to look up and see her favourite cat, an old black tom named Spotnose, perched indignantly on the windowsill outside one of the living-room windows.

'I know you're plumb put out with me, Spotnose,' Milly told the cat. 'But you're just staying outside until this floor is good and dry. And you don't have to look at me like that, either!'

Spotnose continued to give her the same offended stare.

'My grandchildren are coming,' Milly explained to the cat as she dusted some tables that she had just dusted an hour before. 'You know how my son and his wife think I'm a crazy old lady, living out here in the country all by myself. They say, "Momma, you're eighty years old and you shouldn't live out there by yourself," They say, "Momma, you ought to come to the *city* and have *conveniences*, you can't take good *care* of yourself any more!"' Milly stressed the words with bustling sarcasm. 'Well, Mister Spotnose, when they get here with those tykes, they'll find this place spotless! Just like it always is when they show up! Then let them find *anything* to give them ammunition for saying this old granny ought to move into the city!'

She was a tall woman whom age had not succeeded in shrinking down. She had borne the last of her sons, the one who was coming with his two children Wednesday, at the age of fifty. It was not every woman of eighty who had grandchildren who were not even in school yet. That helped keep a body young. Thin now, with a heavily lined face, work-twisted hands and grey hair in a tight bun, she dusted with the busy determination she gave to every activity of her life.

Finishing the dusting, Milly carried the mop and bucket out through the kitchen to the latticed back porch. The apple and pear trees overhanging the back of the house were in riotous bloom. It had been so warm. Everything in this deepest east end of Monument Valley was early this year.

Milly went back through her little house to the front door. She needed cooling off a moment. She opened the screen. Spotnose tried to dart in.

'Shoo!' Milly caught him with her toe and twirled him back outside.

Standing on the wooden porch, she could look out at the sparse front yard, the fence, the dirt road winding past, the rolling weed field beyond, and the wooded hills and mountains stretching off to the south. It was a bright day and now almost hot. She could look the miles across the valley to the rising green bulk of Steptoe Mountain and see the ranger tower on its peak with exceptional clarity.

The cat walked around Milly's ankles, rubbing against her.

'You just fawn around all you want, Spotnose,' Milly said. 'You'll get in when the floor is good and dry, and not before. Land! Are you jealous just because the tykes are coming to stay with me for a few days? Don't worry. I won't forget to feed you.'

Spotnose would enjoy the tykes once they arrived on Wednesday, Milly thought. The other cats would, too. It would be a lovely visit all around. People might mutter about whether she was capable of taking care of a couple of feisty little boys, but she would show *them* a thing or two, as usual!

Thatcher, Ohio
It was past one o'clock when Mike Coyle plodded down Main Street from the City Hall to the corner drugstore. With him were Purvis Rawlingson, the city clerk, and two reporters.

They were an odd-looking group. Despite the long morning's tension and frustration, Mike Coyle remained immaculately neat in his grey suit and conservative tie and well-used but highly polished black shoes. Purvis Rawlingson, as usual, was a walking disaster area – a tall, heavy, shambling man with grey hair sticking out around soaring ears, a corduroy jacket that looked slept-in, cotton slacks that matched, and worn-out brown loafers which revealed flashes of bright-red socks. The young newspaper reporter had a notebook in his hand and two Leicas slung around his neck, and the radio man, even younger, looked like a juvenile thief with his Uher recorder and Sony cassette machine slung over his shoulders.

Traffic inched along the asphalt and brick street, going from one unsynchronized traffic light to the next. Overhead was a maze of power and telephone wires, signal-light wires, and the old double trolley wires for the electric buses that had stopped running ten years ago. The building fronts were mostly weather-stained brick, with some limestone thrown in. The rooflines formed an irregular border against the sunny sky, but none of the buildings along here topped three stories. Some of the fronts, as far up as the second-floor windows, had been covered with red-wood shingles or blue plastic or pink glass, to look modern.

The drugstore was grey and white plastic on the outside, but inside the old, narrow-plank floors creaked underfoot as Coyle and his companions entered and walked toward the back, where the soda fountain and lunch booths were located.

'Ho hum,' Purvis Rawlingson sighed, sidling into the booth. 'Another day, another dollar.'

John Meese, the young newspaper reporter, sat beside Rawlingson. 'After today's Council meeting, I'd say that dollar has been cut to forty cents.'

Rawlingson chuckled, and even his chuckle boomed. 'You have to take the bitter with the sweet.' He eyed the menu. 'Speaking of which, I think what I need today is a double cheeesburger, a piece of pie, and a shake.'

Mike Coyle made an effort to conceal the depression. 'What you need, Purvis, is some lettuce, no dressing, and some tea, no sugar.'

Rawlingson looked up sharply, his shaggy eyebrows twitching. 'You know my motto, friend. "Eat, drink and be merry, for tomorrow we diet." '

'Groan,' the radio man, Leroy Prendergast, said.

Rawlingson leered at him. 'Good, huh?' He chuckled again, and the chuckle grew with tidal action into a barking laugh. It boomed out, and Coyle saw people in the front of the store turn to identify the source of the sound.

'No sense being sour,' Rawlingson said. 'Happy day!'

'What's happy about it?' Meese asked dourly.

'Because that's my outlook!'

'You just got out of a City Council meeting,' Meese pointed out. 'It lasted almost four hours. The same old factions cut and snipped and bit at one another, and you ended up gutting your whole programme for the remainder of the year because your bond election failed. And you say "happy day"?'

Rawlingson refused to stop grinning. 'It's Monday.'

'So?'

'So it's close to the weekend.'

Meese looked puzzled. 'You can't *get* any farther from the weekend than Monday.'

'You're looking in the wrong direction!' Rawlingson said, and whooped again.

Coyle smiled despite himself. It was so typically Rawlingson. The man was a fine city clerk. He loved the work. He loved fussing with minor details. He loved talking with people from the Chamber of Commerce. He had been Thatcher's city clerk for almost thirty years and he knew everything – carried the most obscure records around in his head. He enjoyed working with details that would have driven anyone else crazy.

There was nothing you could actively dislike about Rawlingson.

Perhaps he had once known the existential agony. If so, Coyle thought, then he was the bravest man of all time. He was always the same: always cheerful, jovial, full of his mottoes that made absolutely no sense. Most men concealed themselves behind a veneer. Rawlingson was veneer all the way through.

'We'll make it through,' Rawlingson was cheerfully telling the reporters now. 'We always do.'

The waitress, a pretty girl who should have been in high school, came and took their orders: grilled cheese and black coffee for Mike Coyle; coffee only for the reporters; a cheeseburger, two cheese frenchies, an order of onion rings, and a chocolate malt for Rawlingson.

'Got to keep my strength up!'

Meese scowled over his notebook. 'Mister Mayor, as the result of this morning's retrenchment planning, where do we stand on hospital expansion?'

'There won't be any,' Coyle said.

'Did I understand that the proposal to name a regular Civil Defence co-ordinator was tabled right along with everything else?'

'That wasn't a bond item,' Coyle explained patiently. 'But we had to allocate operating funds to repair the old police communications gear, since the bond money for new stuff won't be forthcoming. The maintenance funds will be shifted from the account that we hoped to use to name some retired but active businessman as co-ordinator to work out Civil Defence matters.'

'Who needs Civil Defence anyway?' Rawlingson asked. 'Send us more Japs!'

'Just supposing,' Meese continued with his bulldog scowl, 'some disaster did hit Thatcher. Our wire, for example, has some stuff on it about severe thunderstorms through the Midwest Tuesday and Wednesday. How well is this city prepared to cope with a bad storm? A flood? An earthquake? Major fires? Even an enemy attack?'

Coyle hesitated. He could not let his own mood show through. He had to try to be positive. People did not want or need human leaders.

He said carefully, 'We have a weather wire in the police station, John. You know that. The sheriff's office can volunteer two or three cars for spotter duty. We have a siren system—'

'Parts of the city aren't covered. The last time you tested, some of the present sirens didn't work.'

'It's a matter of priorities,' Coyle said stiffly.

Rawlingson said, 'This area used to be a sacred ground for the Indians. Everybody knows that. The Indians camped here because they knew really bad weather never came. This county has never had a funnel or anything like that.'

'If you want a statement,' Coyle told the young man, 'I'll say that we plan to go back to the Committee for Civic Improvement. We'll ask them to look at all their priorities again.'

Meese bristled. 'Are you hinting at *another* bond election?'

'I didn't say that. I don't know. We'll ask them to look.'

'This city has rejected three bond proposals in the last twenty months. You guys walk up the hill and get your heads bashed in and then you start right up again. What chance would another vote have?'

'Are you looking for a fight, John, or a story?'

Meese groaned and put down his pencil. 'I know. Shit. But I get so tired of it. Are *all* towns like this – broken into factions, every bush-league businessman looking out for Number One, nothing ever getting done?'

'If I answer the question, I'm accepting the premise.'

'I don't know how you stand it,' Meese told him. 'I really don't.'

'Oh, it's not so bad.'

'You can't even get businessmen here to agree on how to paint new parking stripes on Main Street!'

Coyle gave him a painted-on smile.

Meese fumed, 'That's why the young people leave in floods as soon as they're old enough. Why stay here? Why fight it?'

Why indeed? Coyle thought.

The waitress came into view balancing two trays. One contained Rawlingson's lunch, the other everyone else's.

'One if by land,' Rawlingson chirped, 'two if by sea!'

Huntington, West Virginia

It was a pre-trial hearing, and the spectator portion of the huge old courtroom was vacant. Pale sunlight painted flyspecks and cobwebs on the high, greyish side windows.

The first attorneys for the oil companies began arriving at 2 : 15 p.m., well in advance of the scheduled start of the hearing, at 2 : 30. The Texon attorney, with two young assistants, brought in four briefcases jammed with legal papers, plus three heavy lawbooks. The Ampcor attorneys, three of them, carried in about a dozen books and a foot-thick stack of folders. Journeywell, a local firm, was represented by two men and one woman, all of whom carried in impressive stacks of documents and lawbooks if needed. Jarman Oil arrived at 2 : 22, two male lawyers and a slender secretary staggering under a new burden of manuals, ledgers, files and books.

The counsel table on the north side of the empty judge's bench filled up with heavy documents and briefs, lawbooks, file folders, notepads, attaché cases. Estron arrived – two attorneys – at 2 : 24. Books were moved to the floor, and began to pile up like trench-warfare sandbags between the oil company counsel table and the opposition table, which was silent, empty, gleaming.

Two more companies, four more lawyers, arrived simultaneously at 2 : 25. The last of the books were placed on the legal bunker between the tables. The lawyers, solemn, heavy-set men for the most part, wearing their power with gloomy ease, leaned toward one another and compared last-minute notes.

They glanced often at the opposition table, still barren, vacant. This was an important case locally, and could have landmark effects nationally. The majors were being sued by a small independent gasoline distributor who claimed they were in conspiracy to trade fuels between themselves, but refuse him sales in restraint of trade. Absurd, of course : how often did somebody take on the oil companies and win? But the case had required stern preparation, and all the lawyers had prepared hard and well, and were ready for the combat.

But where was the opposition?

At 2 : 29.30, by his gold Pulsar, George Abrams walked briskly into the room. He nodded coolly to his opponents – all seventeen of them – and lightly placed one very thin, fresh file folder on his empty table. He then sat down, crossed his legs, and looked out the dusty windows as if his mind were far away.

He was a tall man, greying, handsome, with a jutting chin well-known to the voters of West Virginia. Impeccably dressed in a dark-blue suit and gleaming black shoes, he looked like an ad for Hart, Schaffner & Marx.

He *looked* like the next governor, some voters said.

He was a son of a bitch, some of the oil company lawyers thought.

But this time he was going to get creamed. He had some grandstand play up his sleeve – Christ, what a cheap shot, bringing in one folder, typical of the kind of theatrics he always pulled – but it wouldn't help him. Not this time. All the law and precedent were on the oil companies' side.

The mobbed lawyers behind their bulwarks were secretly licking their lips.

2:30. The door behind the bench opened. Judge Orvis Powell swept in, cadaverous in his swirling black robes. Everyone rose. The bailiff announced court in session. The judge sat down. Everybody else sat down. George Abrams still appeared rather preoccupied and aloof.

'Queen Oil *versus* Journeywell *et al.*,' the judge said, reading from a folder. He looked up, noting the barricades of lawbooks. 'I assume defendants are prepared to proceed?'

The Texon attorney in charge rose to his feet. 'We are, Your Honour.'

'Plaintiff?'

George Abrams stood. 'Ready, if the Court please.' He had a very fine voice, very large and strong. He *sounded* ready.

The judge put on reading glasses and scanned pages from his own folder. 'All right. Do defendants wish to make any statement prior to discussion of the individual pleadings?'

The Texon man stood again. 'Your Honour, we believe this lawsuit is a form of harassment and we are eager to proceed.'

The judge turned to George Abrams. 'Mister Abrams?'

Abrams rose slowly to his feet. With very great care, he opened his file folder. There was one sheet of paper inside, neatly typed.

'If the Court please,' he said. He looked at his paper, obviously reading. 'November sixteen, last year. One hundred and twenty-two thousand gallons, no-lead gasoline, transferred from Texon to Journeywell Oil, tanker-truck delivery at the Journeywell facility southeast of Huntington. Delivery price forty-eight thousand, eight hundred dollars. Bill of lading number—'

Six opposition lawyers were on their feet at once, clamouring. Abrams stopped reading, pretending amazement.

The Texon man got the floor. His face blotched red. 'Your Honour, what is the meaning of this? What is counsel reading from? This is improper, irrelevant and immaterial!'

'If the Court please,' George Abrams replied, 'this case is about collusion. This sheet of paper is a record of collusive activities by defendant oil firms over a period of—'

'Where did you get that information!' the Journeywell lawyer yelled.

The Jarman Oil head attorney, looking shaky, was also on his feet. 'You can't read that information in open court! It's – it's prejudicial! It's confidential, and I don't know how you got it!'

Abrams did not look at any of them. His hawkish eyes remained on the judge as if no one had spoken. 'If the Court please, this information is accurate. Plaintiff prefers to read it into the record here, rather than release it to the press.'

The opposition lawyers behind their lawbooks were huddling in wild confusion, but the Texon man was quicker than the rest of them. His face was also the reddest because he had already grasped just how he and his colleagues had been screwed.

'Your Honour,' he said chokingly, 'defendants request a twenty-four-hour delay.'

The judge hardly paused because he understood, too. 'Granted.' The gavel whacked the bench.

George Abrams put his sheet of paper back into his folder and walked out of the room. It was 2 : 32.

In a way, Abrams knew and would have been the first to acknowledge, it had been pure theatrics. But it tickled him to death. He was still grinning to himself at the courthouse coffee bar five minutes later when one of the Ampcor lawyers came by, scowling.

Abrams could not resist twisting the knife just a little. 'You already have the law library back on the shelves, Tim?'

Tim's lips trembled a little, and he refused to look at Abrams. 'That was a cheap shot, George.'

Abrams grinned more broadly.

'You know,' Tim added, 'we'll have to offer a negotiated settlement. You have us over a barrel.'

'That's a very good pun,' Abrams observed.

'Goddamn it, how did you get that information? If that stuff gets out, it ruins us with the public! You could cause a federal probe!'

'I thought so myself,' Abrams agreed cheerfully.

'How did you get it, goddamn you? And what right—'

Abrams stilled his colleague with a steely hand on his forearm. 'I'm going to give you a free lesson, Tim. They tell it to you in law school. Legal practice is an adversary relationship. Adversary. That means *fight*. When you come into a courtroom against me, be ready to fight. I'm going to have your balls otherwise.'

'That's shoddy tactics!'

'No,' Abrams said, flaring just a little. 'I'll tell you why I beat your ass off today, and why I'll beat the ass off most people ninety per cent of the time. Number one. I work harder than you do. Number two. I'm smarter than you are. Number three. I fight, I don't play games.'

'You're a real bastard, George,' Tim said with real hatred in his voice.

Abrams touched the display button of his expensive gold watch. 'Excuse me. I have to appear in another court.'

'God help us if you get elected governor, George,' Tim said bitterly as Abrams started to move away.

Abrams swung back, genuine rage flashing through his bloodstream. 'I'm going to be governor, Tim. *Count* on it.'

He hurried to the elevators and upstairs to a courtroom where the criminal judge was sounding a docket for the month's felony trials. The district attorney, a young man with political aspirations, had announced a new policy under which he would try every case quickly, and would not seek delays, 'if my staff has to work twenty-four hours a day.'

The judge called thirteen cases in which Abrams was the defence attorney. He announced ready in all thirteen. This forced the district attorney to seek continuances in seven.

So much for district attorneys who got too involved in their own PR.

Abrams then went back to his office, dictated several memoranda, and took a telephone call from a distraught parent whose son had just been arrested on a heroin charge. Abrams said he would take the case through the first preliminary hearing for a retainer of five thousand dollars.

'That's more than I make in six months!' the parent said, shocked.

'We're not talking about six months of your life,' Abrams reminded him with brutal logic. 'We're talking about several years of your son's.'

The parent agreed. Abrams requested a cashier's check, by messenger.

At 3 : 55 p.m., the Texon attorney called to request formal talks on settlement of the lawsuit. Abrams agreed, but decided to let him stew until tomorrow.

At 4 p.m., he met with his campaign manager, approved plans for taping television spots to be used in later months of the campaign, made quick and extensive changes with a pencil on a brochure layout, called two supporters and raised twenty-five hundred dollars from each of them, and was alone in his office once more, not a hair ruffled, when the president of a large communications firm arrived at 4 : 50 to see if there was any way of legally collecting from a firm that had sold him more than one million dollars' worth of defective electronics gear.

The man didn't have a good case, but Abrams thought it sounded interesting. He took it. His preliminary fee was set at one hundred thousand dollars.

He was a man for whom everything in the world seemed to be going right. Up from a middle-class background, he had learned early, in the streets, that sportsmanship goes out of the window in a real fight. He had also learned that few succeed in this life, and they are likely to be the ones who are smartest, who work hardest, and who are willing to kick an opponent in the balls. He had been succeeding ever since.

Opposition lawyers hated him. Clients, despite his high fees, thought he walked on water. He had worked two sessions as a state legislator into his tight schedule, and the pundits said he would probably win his party's nomination to be the next governor.

No hint of scandal had ever touched George Abrams, although many opponents of many kinds had looked hard and long. He was married, he had a lovely wife and two lovely children, he went to church every Sunday – very visually – and he never took more than two drinks a day. Although his standard of living was very high, leaving him always only a few steps ahead of some bill collector or other, his income was enormous enough to compensate. He made tremendous amounts of money and spent it all. But that was not the stuff of genuine scandal.

George Abrams had only one weakness, and there were few who knew about that because ordinarily he was very careful. If he usually had another woman somewhere, it was always a woman he had checked out, to some degree, in order to make sure that she had as much to lose, proportionally, as he did in case of disclosure. The woman he was presently seeing, named Donna Fields, did not fit the usual pattern, because she was divorced, and a legal secretary. But he had hired an investigator who assured him, after diligent checking, that Donna Fields otherwise led a very quiet life, had had few lovers, had never been known to drink excessively, and had nothing in her background to suggest that she might take more from a relationship than present enjoyment.

It came as a distinct and unpleasant surprise to George Abrams, then, when his overfilled but satisfying day was jarred a few minutes before seven o'clock that night.

He was at home, hurrying through supper in order to attend a small neighbourhood political meeting at eight, when the maid informed him that a lady telephone caller was most insistent about speaking with him at once.

Abrams went out into the broad foyer of his huge home and picked up the telephone there, far from the nearest doorway where anyone might overhear. 'Yes?'

'George? I want to see you.'

His anger pulsed as he recognized Donna Fields's voice. 'I'm busy.' He lowered his tone. 'You're never to call me here. I call you. You don't call me. Understand?'

The young woman's voice was low, pleasure-filled. 'I think you're the one who doesn't understand, darling. Wednesday. Between two-thirty and three o'clock. At the Westside Lounge on Fillmore Street. Be there, because the fucking is all over, love, and I'm changing our relationship.'

Shock trickled down through Abrams's system. He managed to make his voice sound low, but normal. 'I don't know what you're talking about.'

'Be there,' Donna Fields told him, a harsh edge of spiteful glee coming into her voice. 'You're going to do what *I* tell you now, love, or you'll be very, very sorry.'

Then, before Abrams could react, she began whispering. The words were shocking, obscene, pronounced in a tone that viciously mocked all the times she had used similar expressions to goad him and pleasure him in bed. But the words were not out of love or pleasure now; they were explicit threats, reminding him how well she knew him and how much she could use against him if she wished.

The obscenities were still being whispered when he hung up the telephone.

Tuesday, April 8 3 p.m.–11:22 p.m.

ZCZC
WWUS9 RWRC 081500
MKC WW 081500
MKC 081500
ZZZZZ
BULLETIN

SEVERE THUNDERSTORM WATCH NUMBER 221
ISSUED 10 A.M. CDT APRIL 8, 1975

THE NATIONAL WEATHER SERVICE HAS ISSUED A SEVERE
THUNDERSTORM WATCH FOR PORTIONS OF . . .

SOUTHEASTERN KANSAS
CENTRAL AND EASTERN OKLAHOMA
SOUTHWESTERN MISSOURI

THE THREAT OF SEVERE THUNDERSTORMS WITH LARGE HAIL AND
DAMAGING WINDS WILL EXIST IN THESE AREAS FROM 10:30 A.M.
CDT UNTIL 5 P.M. THIS TUESDAY EVENING.

THE GREATEST THREAT OF SEVERE THUNDERSTORMS IS IN AN AREA
70 MILES . . . 60 NAUTICAL . . . EITHER SIDE OF A LINE FROM
OKLAHOMA CITY TO JOPLIN MISSOURI.

PERSONS IN OR CLOSE TO THE WATCH AREA ARE ADVISED TO BE
ON WATCH FOR LOCAL WEATHER DEVELOPMENTS AND FOR LATER
STATEMENTS AND WARNINGS.

THIS SEVERE THUNDERSTORM WATCH REPLACES WATCH NUMBER
218 ISSUED AT 6 A.M. CDT . . . WATCH NUMBER 218 WILL NOT BE
EFFECTIVE AFTER 10:30 A.M. CDT . . .

XXX

Kansas City
Ed Stephens lived his life pretty much as he played handball:
forthrightly, without pretenses, and with enthusiasm.

Congressman Buck Tatinger was a devotee of the indirect, the
opaque, and the verbal assault designed to get at truth by in-
flicting pain.

Which meant that Stephens, who detested frills and arrogance,
was having a very difficult time keeping his feelings about the
powerful young congressman from showing through.

Tatinger, today wearing a pale linen suit with his Gucci shoes, had been in the weather room most of Monday. He had been at Stephens's side through all of today, the slightly condescending look of amusement seldom leaving his face as Stephens alternated between fighting to keep up with fast-moving developments and explaining what was going on.

Standing in the weather room now, Tatinger beside him as usual, Stephens faced his aide, Harry Adams. 'Did you get out the thunderstorm watch updates while we were at coffee, Harry?'

Adams glowered around the busy room and clamped down harder on a dead cigar. 'Sure, but we're getting up to our armpits in alligators.'

Stephens knew exactly what Adams meant, but thought it might clarify his own thinking to get Adams to spell it out. 'Speak,' he said.

Adams pointed to the latest radar summary. 'We have this second system kicking up a few showers in Oklahoma and Kansas. Now it's moving into Missouri. We're going to get some thunderstorms, hail, and maybe worse along the front edge. But that isn't half what we're going to get when that third system gets itself together.'

Stephens turned to Tatinger. 'I explained that we're in the middle of three separate systems moving across the country—'

'Of course,' Tatinger said, cocking his right eyebrow. 'I understand perfectly. No need to elaborate. Just carry on.'

He managed to make it sound insulting, but Stephens gritted his teeth and turned back to Adams. 'What's with the third low now?'

'It's formed up out here in northern New Mexico and southern Colorado, it's already very intense, as you see on the chart, and it's moving like a bat out of hell.'

'But it hasn't kicked up any serious activity yet.'

'Amarillo just reported cumulonimbus building to the northwest. Tucumcari has winds gusting to fifty knots. The Oke City sequence reports show visibility down to eight miles with blowing dust. Dallas has southerly winds gusting to thirty knots and humidity up twenty per cent since their ten o'clock reading, just a little over five hours ago.'

Stephens bent over a table. 'Let me look at the charts a minute.' He shifted the two large sheets so they would be side by side, and became aware of Tatinger bending over his shoulder.

'Our computer, a CDC 3100, prints these,' Stephens explained. 'What it does is print information on to the map at the geographical point of origin of the information. If you want to know what's going on in Shreveport, for example, this charts prints the temperature and so forth at that location on the U.D. map.'

'What's this other chart mean?' Tatinger asked.

'Radar summary.'

Tatinger rubbed a finger through an eyebrow. 'Well, it may be clear to you. I fail to see the usefulness of spending all that money on such charts when you have the data in tabular form elsewhere.'

'Anytime we can put data together in a single chart, it helps show patterns of events,' Stephens explained testily.

'What do these charts show you, if anything?'

'In a nutshell, clear weather throughout the upper Midwest and South. Temperature range of fifty degrees at Detroit to seventy-seven at Birmingham. Winds light and variable. Humidity readings low. Our second low-pressure centre is creating some squall-line activity in Missouri, but it's beginning to lose the little punch it had.'

Stephens paused and traced a blunt finger across the northern sector of the map, and then again across the southern reaches. 'The clinker is in these areas. All through Manitoba, temperatures well below zero. In the Gulf, temperatures in the high eighties, and humidity in the same range. Get these two air masses together and the effects will be explosive.'

'What would get them together?' Tatinger asked, bored.

Stephens rapped a fingernail on the whorls depicting the deep low-pressure centre forming in New Mexico. 'This big bastard right here.'

'Say,' Tatinger said, and smiled, 'it would be really nice if you actually had some bad weather for me while I was here. I would enjoy that.'

'The victims wouldn't,' Stephens snapped.

As if sensing that he was preventing a possible sharp argument, Adams flipped a raggedly torn piece of teleprinter paper on to the top of the charts. 'This automatic buoy information shows an even steeper temperature and humidity rise in the Gulf than we had expected. I called New Orleans about it and they called a weather ship out there. The captain said it's like August down there. He said, "Take a deep breath and you could drown in this humidity." '

Before Stephens could reply, another meteorologist walked by and dropped another sheet of printer paper on the growing stack. 'Temperature is falling fast across the northern tier of states. Madison, Wisconsin, has dropped twenty degrees in three hours.'

Harry Adams lit his stubby cigar and glared. 'That makes the temperature differential between Madison and New Orleans at least sixty-six degrees.'

'Christ,' Stephens grunted.

Tatinger said, 'Does that mean storms are starting?'

'The cold air is sagging a little. No. This old stationary front has the heat and humidity temporarily blocked from moving northward, and developing flow out in front of the low will hold the cold air to the north for a while yet.'

Adams called to a man across the busy room: 'Dandridge? You got those new satellite pictures yet?'

Dandridge, a tall and lanky man with furrows in his forehead, came over with several limp photos in his hands. He arranged them on the table.

'No question about it,' he said. 'We have a deep wave in the jetstream now. You can see this cirrus across Arkansas and up into Pennsylvania.'

'Christ,' Stephens repeated. 'What about the high-altitude reports?'

'Bad.'

'Meaning what?'

Tatinger interrupted, 'Now, just a minute here. I'm a little bit lost. After all, I'm here on an important fact-finding mission. I don't want to interfere, but it's mandatory for me to understand what's happening.'

Harry Adams grunted, 'What's happening is that it's starting to hit the fan.'

Tatinger's cool, unfriendly eyes focused on the squatty man. 'Your name is Adams, isn't it? I fear, Mister Adams, that that kind of explanation just isn't very helpful.'

It was said with a subtle challenge underlying the words. Stephens wondered why young men in power had this quality of corrupt arrogance sometimes. Tatinger was looking for trouble, and there was no reason for it. It was his characteristic way of coming on: by being as abrasive as possible. Perhaps he thought he made people show their true colours this way. Perhaps this made him a cold manipulator.

Nevertheless, it was Stephens's turn this time to step in to avoid angry words. 'The reports mean the storm is developing faster and bigger than anticipated, and from the start we expected that it might be big and nasty.'

'Big and nasty how?' Tatinger insisted, goading him.

'Thunderstorms. Tornadoes. Hail. Flash floods. The works.'

'A few figures tell you that? Or are you guessing?'

Stephens took a deep breath. All right. Chalk talk. He told himself again to stay calm as he traced the New Mexico low-pressure centre with his fingers on the chart.

'A low-pressure centre creates a counterclockwise rotation of air around it. The drawing power of a low can affect air masses hundred of miles away. This low is becoming a very powerful one, with very strong rotational forces.'

Stephens moved his finger eastward across the chart, into America's heartland, and continued. 'As this low moves east, it will draw this intensely cold arctic air southward behind it in a circular pattern, and then push it out toward its southeast quadrant. At the same time, it will draw warm, moist air up in front of itself and curl it to the north.'

He paused again, making a quick pencil sketch. 'That's why the classic weather-map configuration shows a low-pressure centre with a cold front curling out of its lower-forward sector, and a warm front trying to go in the opposite direction above and ahead of it.'

Tatinger nodded, studying the diagram. 'The low mixes the dissimilar air masses, then, with potential for violence.'

'Yes, and in the case of this third low, we have immense quantities of cold air on one side and equally immense quantities of warm humid air on the other.'

'What was that about the jetstream? What was that all about?'

'A deep wave is a glitch in the jetstream that means high winds will plunge farther south than usual and then swing sharply north again. The jet is already beginning to blow cold air south. The low will also probably follow the jetstream, which means it will charge right across this line I'm drawing.'

Tatinger examined the new pencil line. 'From Oklahoma to West Virginia?'

'Precisely.'

'Does that mean the storms will follow that line too?'

'The frontal lines are likely to extend from Canada to the Gulf of Mexico, but the low's movement virtually assures serious problems all through Illinois, Indiana, Kentucky and Ohio – places where they aren't as well-equipped to deal with storm alerts as they are in the South and Southwest.'

Tatinger looked more sober. 'And I might as well try to understand the rest of it. High-altitude reports were mentioned.'

Stephens turned to Dandridge, who, with Adams, had endured the simplistic lecture. 'What about them?'

Dandridge frowned. 'Instability in the jet. It's blowing a hundred and twenty-five miles an hour at El Paso, but only eighty at Shreveport.'

Stephens digested this and turned again to Tatinger. 'That's more bad news. Instability in jetstream velocities is often associated with major outbreaks of severe weather.'

'Why?'

'There are theories, but it's complex.'

'Humour me,' Tatinger suggested, and then cocked an eyebrow. 'There were some people at NASA once, I recall, who didn't give me sufficient credit for understanding.'

Stephens very nearly lost his temper. 'Sorry. I'm too busy right now. I have some things to do in my office.'

'I'll come along,' Tatinger said.

'No you won't,' Stephens shot back. 'Stay here if you like. I'll be back in a little while.'

The youthful congressman's eyes registered a moment's surprise. Then the surprise faded, to be replaced by a softly venomous reappraisal. 'As you say, sir. It's your shop.'

Walking out of the weather room and down the hall to his office, Stephens wondered if the similarity had been intended: *It's your shop, it's your funeral.* Christ, maybe he was getting paranoid.

In his office, he made two calls to Norman, one to Denver, one to Chicago and one to New Orleans. He was doing everything he could personally to get all the gears oiled. Then, leaning back in his chair, his heart lurching around from the tension inside him, he opened his desk drawer and fought with himself about having one of his rationed cigarettes. While he was thinking about this, his eyes fell on the carefully folded letter from Mo.

It was absolutely absurd to worry about Mo and her family in terms of this severe-storm system. But she was still much on his mind. He knew the chances against a storm hitting Thatcher were astronomical. But astronomical odds fell true every day in this business.

Yielding to the impulse, he dialled the number again.

The distant telephone rang several times.

'Hello?' she said then.

'Mo. Ed again.'

'Ed? I can't believe this! My letter must have *really* been dumb!'

'Oh, I just felt like calling again. Are you okay?'

'Yes.' She sounded firmer today, like she meant it.

'I've got a congressman on my back here today, and a batch of bad weather developing. But I was thinking I might get over your way next week, or the week after. Would that be all right?'

'You know it would be.'

'I mean, I wouldn't be prying.'

'Would you believe I might really like to talk to you?'

'I'll try to get there, then.'

'Good.'

'Listen : how's your weather?'

'It's lovely,' she replied, sounding amused.

'It's not going to stay lovely much longer.'

'You mean you're actually concerned about flooding or something soon?'

'This storm is looking worse and worse. You might as well batten down the hatches. You're going to have it rough tomorrow this time.'

She responded seriously now. 'You must really be concerned to mention it.

'I am. Has Mike ever taken me seriously on any of this warning stuff?'

'Has he taken you seriously? Oh, yes. You've made a convert, big brother. But as to whether he's been able to get anyone else around here to do anything *about* it, that's another matter.'

'Maybe I ought to call him, gig him a little about making sure the system there is in as good shape as possible.'

'Well, Ed, I don't really think I'd do that today, if I were you.'

He sensed a problem. 'You said before that you've had a problem with the city there.'

'Another bond election failed last week.'

'Oh, boy. Poor Mike.'

'He took it hard this time.'

'How many does that make he's tried and lost? Two or three?'

'Three.'

'And knowing him, he won't give up.'

'No.'

Stephens thought about it. 'Well, okay. I won't call and bug the poor guy. But look, honey. Mention to him that I called again.'

'Ed, you know I will.'

'Not just that, but . . . well, hell. Listen, are you all right?'

'Just fine. Having classes and doing my housework like a good little girl.'

'And the kids? I didn't ask about Billy the other day.'

'The children are fine. Ed? Are you sure there's nothing wrong in the family somewhere?'

'Mo, has Mike ever gotten them to do *anything* about your sirens?'

'The sirens? Lord, no. The last time they tested, some didn't even go off.'

'Christ.'

'Is that what you called for, you big goof? To ask about our sirens? Aren't you finally letting that job of yours push you over the edge?'

'Mo, this is serious. We have some very bad weather coming up.'

'Well, thank goodness we don't live in Kansas or somewhere. I don't think we're up to any tornadoes.'

'Mo, you have had tornadoes in Ohio, too.'

'Weren't they flukes, Ed?' Then she seemed to reconsider. 'You mean you actually think *we* might get hit?'

'The chances are a million to one against,' he admitted. 'But this outbreak looks *so* serious right now, I got to thinking about you, and I – just – well, I'm taking every *other* precaution I can think of.'

'Ed, when is all this supposed to come?'

'Over there, tomorrow. We're going to have some rough stuff farther west today on a continuing basis. But your area . . . tomorrow. Late.'

She was silent a moment. 'I'll tell Mike you called, Ed. I'm sure he has everything in as good a working order as he possibly can already, though.'

Stephens had a sinking feeling. He was acting stupid. He was still reacting somehow to Killeen. Was he Thatcher's caretaker? Or anyone's? They were adult people. And the chances of trouble in Thatcher were astronomical, against.

He said, 'Just call it big brother's whim.'

'Well, it was nice of you to call, anyway. Even if it took a fright about the weather to make you do it.'

She was amused, and she probably had every right to be, Stephens thought. Hell. 'You say hello to Mike and the kids for me.'

'I will, Bunny.'

No one ever called him that besides Mo. Only a handful of people even knew of the crazy nickname. 'So long, Sis,' he said.

After hanging up, he sat at his desk awhile, lost in thought. He would go home soon, he decided, and try to get to bed early so he could be on the job *very* early tomorrow.

He was not worried about falling to sleep. He had a pill.

Birmingham, Alabama

The air was as soft as a julep.

A dozen friends had come to the Kristofsen house for this particular garden party. They were pretty people, youthful in fact or thanks to lives which allowed indolent attention to cosmetic expertise. Few of them had ever had to worry much.

The patio and large swimming pool behind the mansion tinkled with the pleasant sounds of laughter, conversation, and swimming.

Two female friends stood off the edge of the pool patio, near the matching twin cabanas. One was blond, the other brunette, and both were lovely. Their sleek, bikini'd bodies had been slammed into shape at the same expensive winter spa.

'Susan looks lovely today,' the blonde said, covertly eyeing the pretty young woman poised on the diving board.

'She knows how to give a nice little party,' the brunette agreed.

'She learned fast, didn't she?'

'Yes. And she learned well, too.'

'She's charming, don't you think?'

'For *nouveau riche*.'

'Shame on you,' said the blonde, amused.

'A party over the weekend, this one today, and I understand she has another scheduled for tomorrow,' the brunette said. 'Now, honestly, my dear, wouldn't you say that's just a bit much?'

'She might need parties to take her mind off . . . things?'

The brunette glanced up at a second-floor window. 'Do you suppose he's up there as usual, locked in with his typewriter?'

It was idle speculation. The truth was that David Kristofsen *was* upstairs, *was* locked in with his typewriter.

His typewriter, the dusty pages, the liquor, and a growing sense that he was through.

Wearing a tee shirt and baggy cotton slacks, he stood in the centre of his book-lined study. Only the faintest sounds of the pool party came to him. The highball glass in his hand was almost empty and he was just a little swacked. For a while there, after the trouble began for him, a few drinks had helped a little. Now they didn't. Nothing did.

For Kristofsen it had been a long trip to the top. He had been hailed as a meteor on the literary scene just three years ago, when, at thirty-nine, he had watched one of his novels go to the top of the bestseller lists. 'Effortless . . . the work of a born storyteller,' according to *The New York Times*, showing its predilection for errors stated in tones of infallibility. There was no mention of the nineteen years it had taken him to learn how to make it appear this effortless: no talk of the agony.

No. It had been assumed everywhere that the first big book, *Southern*, had been dashed off easily, with no prelude of the years. The second one had probably looked just as easy to them, as had the third, now atop the list. Some people had it made, the critics implied. Some people were just natural-born writers.

Only Kristofsen and a few others really knew the price he had paid. The newspaper days, the years of teaching college kids how to write literate sentences . . . the salaries that ranged from $3,900 at the paper to the munificent $11,000 per year he had been making at the college just before *Southern* took off. That sort of thing did not make good flap copy.

Neither did the millions of cigarettes, the all-night writing, the dozen novels that had preceded *Southern*, with his hopes and his guts in them . . . the twelve books that were published and then sank out of sight without so much as a ripple.

No. He was an instant success, a new star without past, without anguish. That was the way Americans wanted their heroes, even those in such dying professions as literature.

He had paid the price, Kristofsen thought ironically now, re-filling his tumbler with whisky, and he had, as a result, Every-thing. With a large *E*, please. He had worked hard and been lucky and he and Susan were now among the Elite. Capital *E* again, please, Mister Editor. They had their $400,000 estate, their cars – a Corvette for him and a Mercedes for her and a Mazda just for the slumming hell of it – and the swimming pool, the private plane, the trips, the clothes that hadn't even been worn yet, all of it. They had it made, and they had it all.

They even had – *he* had, rather – something he could never have afforded back in those days when he was making $3,000 a book: a six-month case of writer's block.

Symptoms: characters who walked through the motions like living dead; plot developments that went nowhere; pages that piled up but said nothing; a feeling inside the brain that he had written it all out, that he was suffering a terminal fatigue.

Prognosis: uncertain.

For a man like Kristofsen, every aspect of living had always been bound up in some way with the creative process. If he felt happy, he wanted to write about it; if he felt bad, or sad, that too became grist. And when he was working well, every imagined turn of phrase or act by a story person immediately suggested a hundred – a thousand – new possibilities in plot development, theme, interaction of characters, meaning – and it was all a great, glorious, maddening, compulsive puzzle, and there was nothing like it . . . when it was going well.

Now it was nothing like that maddening joy. He had *succeeded* – made it big – so of course he had to do it again, to prove it was no fluke. Every word he wrote, he subconsciously compared with *Southern*. Every character, he tested against those characters who had been so praised. He was no longer a creator, he was a man making comparisons.

And Christ, he was tired . . . so bone-achingly *tired*.

The prospect of filling all those pages, making his mind create all those syntheses, was a numbing one. And yet the slump, or block, affected how he saw everything else in life. He was drink-ing too much. He had moved away from his wife, from everyone and everything, tunnelling deeper into himself in search of emo-tions yet to be mined. So that the quest took him ever farther from the goal, and he was dying.

Kristofsen clinked the ice cubes together in his empty glass. Well, he told himself bitterly, not to worry, right? Only rich writers could afford slumps like this one. He was now in the same class with Scott Fitzgerald . . . wasn't he?

Kristofsen went to mix another drink, filled with the ache of self-hatred.

Below, of course, at poolside, the two women could not know any of this.

'At the rate she's spending his money,' the brunette was saying, 'I suppose he *needs* another bestseller.'

'But from what I hear, his real affair these days isn't with the typewriter; it's with the bottle.'

'No!'

'That's what I hear. Far be it from me to spread idle gossip, but I have it on good authority. He's been positively swoozled the few times he has appeared at any of the poor dear's parties lately. And today he hasn't appeared at all.'

'Susan does look a little tense, doesn't she?'

'Wouldn't you, if your sugar daddy were running short on ideas?'

'Oh, dear. I hate to think that's true. It *is* such fun to have a literary lion as a next-door neighbour.'

Across the broad expanse of patio, Susan Kristofsen climbed from the pool. Towelling herself, she spied the two women watching her. She waved gaily.

'Well,' the blonde sighed, 'I suppose we might as well go over and be nice to the poor dear. It's the least we can do, isn't it? I mean, these parties must be costing her a fortune!'

Thatcher, Ohio

It was past eight o'clock when Mike Coyle pulled into his driveway, manoeuvring around a dark-blue Oldsmobile. The dinner meeting had left him savagely tired, and the blue Olds irritated him.

It belonged to Martin and Lisa Hegstrom, whom he pigeonholed as Mo's friends . . . some of her college friends . . . rather than his. He had always been pleasant enough with them, and vice versa. But tonight he was in no mood for unexpected visitors.

He started towards his front porch, fumbling a bit in the growing darkness. He would be nice if it killed him, he decided .

75

'Careful there, neighbour!' a friendly voice called.

Coyle turned to peer into the yard next door. He spotted the two figures. 'Hello.'

The figures moved across the next-door yard and toward the driveway. As they did so, they became clearer. Walt and Helen Shyer, the neighbours, evidently had taken advantage of the day's beautiful weather to do some yard work. The grey-haired Shyer wore dungarees and a paper hat, and Mrs Shyer had some sort of bulky grey work apron over her dress.

Shyer pointed a thumb toward the wheelbarrow and a bag of peat moss in his front yard. 'I'm glad you came home. If the hard-working mayor is ready to call it a day, I guess I can too.'

'We'll finish the mulching,' Mrs Shyer told him. 'We have a little light left, and we'd better use it. They say rain tomorrow.'

'Oh, it won't rain.'

Coyle smiled. 'When I talked with Mo a while ago, she said her brother called from Kansas City. That's twice he's called in the last couple of days.'

'Is that the one who chases tornadoes?' Shyer asked with interest.

'No, he doesn't chase them. His office tries to predict them. It gets out those warnings.'

'And was he calling to say we'll have storms?'

'He seems to think so.'

'Good argument against the possibility, then,' Shyer grunted. 'I'm not criticizing your brother-in-law, or anything like that. But, by golly, the way those boys get out forecasts for bad weather all the time, then nothing ever happens.'

'Maybe they'd rather be safe than sorry,' Mrs Shyer observed.

'If they say bad weather,' Shyer countered, 'I'll lay my money on clear and warmer. They're alarmists.' Then the older man seemed to think of his manners. 'I like your brother-in-law,' he assured Coyle. 'Nice fellow. Next time he comes back, we're going to go fishing up at Coon Hollow. But I'll bet my boots that if his office says bad weather, we can delay the mulching for a week.'

'He's concerned,' Coyle said.

'Then maybe we'd better *not* mulch,' Shyer said hopefully.

'We finish mulching,' Mrs Shyer said firmly, 'tonight.'

'Yes, but if it's going to rain, maybe we could just wait?'

'Tonight,' she said.

'Slave driver,' Shyer sighed.

'You love it,' Mrs Shyer assured him.

'Does your wife ever treat you this badly?' Shyer asked.

Coyle summoned a smile. They were really very nice people. 'Not often, but I'm late right now. No telling *what* kind of trouble I'm in.'

'You'd better get in there, then,' Shyer assured him. 'My trouble is enough for the entire block.'

Coyle chuckled and headed for his own front door.

The Shyers had lived in the same house for almost forty years. They had conceived children here, brought them home from the hospital, raised them, and seen them come back again with children of their own. The two biggest trees on the block, a pair of magnificent maples, had been planted as seedlings by Walt Shyer in the late 1930s. Now a man could not touch his hands when he encircled the trunk with his arms, and it hurt your neck to stare up to their tops, and it made you dizzy to stare up at them against the sky that way for very long.

More things he would miss, Coyle thought, if he left this place.

He went into his home.

In the living room, Mo was seated on the white leather couch. Lisa Hegstrom, a slender brunette, sat beside her. Martin Hegstrom sat in one facing chair, and Coyle had the added unpleasant surprise of seeing a tall, unkempt, leggy woman in the other chair. Her name was Thelma Pruitt, and she taught in the English Department of the college, as Hegstrom did.

'So there really is a Mike Coyle,' Thelma Pruitt said in her usual ironic, masculine way.

'There is,' Coyle grunted, working hard at being civil despite his fatigue. 'How are you, Thelma? Hello, Lisa.' He shook hands with Hegstrom, a man taller than he, somewhat younger, with full hair and a square jaw.

'We've been talking about the latest bond election,' Hegstrom told him.

'Have you?' Coyle sat between Lisa Hegstrom and Mo. He was very angry; when he was this tired, didn't Mo realize that he didn't welcome company?

'It's a shame, Mike,' Lisa Hegstrom said.

'Yes,' Thelma Pruitt smiled. 'I believe it was Pepys who said

77

he was pleased mightily to see what a deal of business goes off of a man's hands when he stays by it. But in your situation, alas, the business came to a bad end, Mike.'

Coyle tried. 'The questions got confused. I keep telling myself that the truth will carry most of these proposals if we can once show how false the arguments against really are.'

'Yes,' Hegstrom said as if uncovering a precious gem. 'But wasn't it Aquinas who pointed out that truth and falsity are not really opposites. The truth deals with what really is.'

'But,' Mo countered, amused, 'it was Horace Greeley who said that government deals with the given, not the abstract ideal.'

Hegstrom pretended good-natured horror. 'Ah, Mo, Mo. If we could just save you from that Journalism Department!'

There was a moment of silence which began to become awkward. There were finished drinks on the coffee table, and Lisa Hegstrom raised her glass and dawdled her pink tongue at the ice cubes. She was an attractive woman, and for a split-second Coyle translated her actions in his imagination, seeing her in bed with him. Had it become that bad with Mo in bed?

But he did not linger on the question. The silence was still there, and as Lisa put down her glass, Coyle knew it was his place to offer fresh drinks, and now. They were waiting for that.

He lit a cigarette and leaned his head back.

'You're tired,' Thelma Pruitt said, not unkindly.

'Yes, and I've got a batch of reports to go over yet tonight.'

'And miles to go before you sleep?'

Christ, would they never stop their games? He did not reply.

'Well,' Hegstrom said, slapping his knee.

'We really do need to get on,' Lisa said.

'No need to run off,' Mo said.

But they were on their feet. Hegstrom smiled down at Coyle. 'I hope those reports don't keep you up too late, my friend.'

'Well' – Coyle smiled back – 'tomorrow is another day. Margaret Mitchell.'

Hegstrom's face froze slightly, but then he dutifully chuckled. Coyle stayed where he was, and let Mo show them out. He waited, listening to his headache as a background for their final chatter at the door. When Mo came back into the room, she was decidedly cool.

'What was that all about?' Coyle demanded.

'Just a friendly visit.'

He got to his feet. 'I better go do those reports.'

'Yes, I suppose now that you've run my friends off, you can do that.'

'Did I say something not sufficiently intellectual?'

'Mike,' she told him grimly, 'I'm not going to fight with you.'

'Why not?'

'You're tired and depressed. I suppose I shouldn't have invited them in when they appeared at the door. But I didn't realize you'd come home in quite such a bad mood.'

'I get the feeling I'm an outsider when those people are here. They take over my house.'

'It's *my* house too.'

'They're phoney intellectuals. I don't like them.'

'*I* do.'

'I approve of your school,' he said slowly. 'I think it's great, and we agreed a long time ago that every woman has to find a way to try to be her own person. But goddamn, those people bug me!'

A smile lurked at the corners of her mouth. 'You made that clear with the Tara quote.'

'I'm surprised I had it in me after the day I've had. Every day is the same. I want a change in billing, and I have to argue with six people because it was "always" done the old way. I ask somebody to make four copies of a letter, and they make three because that's "always" been the norm. You can't get anybody to do anything without a quiet little struggle.'

'Inertia.'

Coyle put out his cigarette and reached for the pack again. 'Is that what you call it?'

Mo uncoiled from the couch and walked to the portable bar. 'I think you want a drink before supper.'

'I had supper, remember? Cold cuts and tapioca. The great mayor's staple diet.'

Mo put down her drink, walked around behind his chair, and put cool fingers to his neck. She began rubbing the tense muscles there. 'Calm down, now. Try to calm down.'

And so she was mothering him.

And there was nothing else he could say.

Again, and even more startlingly so than earlier, he realized that he was on the verge of tears. It frightened him a little. He was even more tired than he knew. He had no idea how much of the feelings about Mo and her friends were real and how much over-reaction. He was suddenly confused and scared.

He had this decision to make at a time when he was in the worst possible shape to make it.

The stationery he could use in a campaign was already printed, the first nudging gift from the power brokers in Columbus. The boxes of neatly imprinted paper and envelopes, with just his name on them, were already stacked in his office at City Hall. So the first step had already been taken toward the campaign he was not sure he really wanted.

But he could not go on this way, either. He knew this.

Out of the dilemma came a sudden, brief, very clear picture. He saw the Smith & Wesson revolver in the upstairs chest of drawers. He saw himself driving out into the country someplace and get-ting out of the car . . . no sense spoiling the inside of the car . . . and putting the barrel of the revolver in his mouth.

The instant's picture was more vivid than any imagining he had ever had. It stunned him. He had never truly thought of sui-cide before.

It would be such a mess for Mo and the kids.

My God you've got to get yourself together.

He wondered, however, if he could keep it from happening now that he had once visualized it so clearly.

This thought frightened him. He told himself to relax. He con-centrated on Mo's cool fingers massaging his neck. They felt very good. Strong fingers . . . loving fingers . . . and suddenly he some-how made a connection between her hands and the brief fantasy he had experienced with Lisa Hegstrom. There was a small, elec-tric quickening in him.

He reached up and put his hand over his wife's. 'Hey.'

She bent low to his ear. 'Hey what?'

He slid his hand down the length of her arm to her waist, then let it steal upward to curve the heavy firmness of her breast. He found and massaged the ripe nipple. It began to harden under-neath the material that covered it.

'Are you serious about this?' Mo asked huskily, 'or is this fatigue tension talking?'

In the exhausting last weeks of the bond campaign there had never been time or energy. He could not actually remember the last time they had made love. The tensions of the job, the unspoken angers over some of her friends, over things the kids did or didn't do, and over his mounting uncertainty about their whole future, had made their existence together sexless for what now, suddenly, seemed clearly a very long time.

He took her hand and guided it across his chest, and lower. 'Does that feel like fatigue to you?' he asked huskily.

Feeling the bent thickness of his hardened penis under her fingers, Mo was surprised yet not surprised. He had been so preoccupied, so meteoric and emotionally unpredictable these last months, that their sex life had dwindled to nothing. This had worried her, but in a way it all fit together . . . made other things much easier for her.

She felt a soft burst of pleasure in knowing that he wanted her now. One ear attuned to the sound that would warn her of Billy or Jill approaching the closed living-room door, she gently massaged his hardness through his trousers. She bent closer to his ear and licked inside.

Mike caught her wrist and squeezed it. 'Let's be old folks and go on to bed early.'

'The children,' she protested automatically.

'They won't even notice.'

She nodded, pleased, and went with her husband into the hallway and upstairs. Competing stereos echoed from opposite ends of the hallway, but the sounds were faint in their own corner bedroom, off its own short corridor.

She locked the door carefully. A night light glowed softly in a corner, providing sufficient illumination. It was a large, faintly old-fashioned bedroom with one of their prized antiques, a great canopy bed, in the centre.

Mike was already undressing. He caught her watching, and grinned. 'I hope we haven't forgotten how.'

She began unsnapping buttons, her breath uneven. 'I think it's like riding a bicycle, darling.'

She had not known there would be an affair with Martin Hegstrom. Prior to meeting Martin, she had been faithful throughout her married life. There had been only two other men before Mike, and both had been very brief encounters; she had gone to bed with her husband a virgin in mind if not in fact.

Of course she had briefly, guiltily, fantasized lovers. But she had never imagined it would really happen until that afternoon when she attended the reception given by the English Department in Martin's honour, marking publication of his textbook. She had had a class with him, and admired him . . . had even fantasized once, or perhaps twice . . . but was genuinely startled when he managed to get her aside late in the party.

'I'm glad you came to my party,' he told her, smiling.

'I didn't know if I should. There aren't many students here.'

'I asked you because it was important to me.'

'To have *me* here?'

He did not blink. 'We could slip out in another few minutes. Will you come with me? I think we both need a drink that's superior to old Mrs Caulfield's punch.'

Try as she might, Mo had never been able to recreate the steps that had followed; her memory blurred because of the mounting excitement and sense of recklessness she had experienced. She left the reception and waited outside, and in a few minutes he joined her, his eyes alight with pleasure and mischief. Without explanation, he took her to a cocktail lounge on the far side of the city, and they each had martinis. Paranoid about being seen, she protested that she had to get home soon, and that his wife must be expecting him. Nonsense, he told her. His wife was out of the city, and it was only four o'clock in the afternoon.

And then he had very simply told her that he wanted her.

She did not remember what she had said. She knew what she had always imagined she would say in such a situation, but he was a strong, attractive man. Her loneliness sprang out at her, catching her by surprise. The martinis, perhaps, made it possible to respond in a way she could never have responded otherwise.

Thinking she was dreaming an insane dream, she seemed to watch herself leave with him. She was incredibly frightened and shocked. Her emotional state bordered on panic. But the desire was boiling through her, having lain in hiding, denied from recognition, perhaps longer than she knew.

He took a motel room. She waited in the car in an agony of fear . . . of discovery, of recognition, of failure or guilt. But on watery legs she walked with him into the room and he locked the door and he took her into his arms for the first time.

Now, in bed with Mike, Mo gently stroked his back as he sucked at her nipples. His erection was hard against her thigh and she knew he would mount her soon. She ached for this.

A part of her cried *whore!*, and hated her; another part of herself sang with a dual fulfilment that was unbelievable in its intensity.

Darkness crept across the nation. Knowledgeable forecasters looked at the data with a feeling of watching a bomb tick.

Humidity readings across the South began to inch upward as the low drew nearer, bringing warm, moist air northward; readings doubled at Shreveport and Mobile within a few hours.

The latest reports from eighty-six stations sampling the upper atmosphere with radio balloons showed more disturbing evidence at 500 millibars, an altitude between 18,000 and 20,000 feet. Cooler air had begun to override warmer air across a vast expanse of the central plains. Thunderstorms could only maintain their buoyancy and continue to grow as long as they were warmer than their environment; the high-altitude cool temperatures guaranteed an upper-air environment in which great cumulonimbus, once begun, could burgeon.

The winds aloft were also disturbing. They were strong and gusty. These would carry uprising currents ahead of forming clouds, hurling rain away from the centre of the cloud so it could not cool itself out by having its rain fall down into its own centre.

Given windless conditions at high altitudes, thunderstorms often did extinguish themselves. As the clouds grew, precipitation was formed in the upper levels. Without shearing winds aloft, the forming precipitation would fall right back down into the updraft which had caused it, decreasing the intensity of the updraft itself.

Storms along the Gulf Coast often suppressed themselves within thirty minutes by this self-damping machinery.

Given high-speed winds aloft, however, the story was different. As the precipitation was formed, it was carried out ahead of the cloud by the wind-shearing effect; the cloud's updraft was actually intensified by the process of wind carrying the precipitation ahead, and a self-fueling process of convergence on one side and precipitation on another was set in motion.

It was a combination of temperature differentials aloft and vertical wind shear which the latest data showed, and these factors, in conjunction with others also showing on this and earlier reports, made conditions ripe for the most violent weather.

Just at dark, a line of moderate thunderstorms marched across Oklahoma, with intense lightning and small hail reported at El Reno, Oklahoma City, Moore, Norman, Noble, and many other communities in the middle of the state. The line in Oklahoma seemed to scatter and lose punch as it moved on eastward, but it provided distant fireworks in the sky for residents of the Tulsa area, who were on severe-weather watch at the time.

There were confirmed reports of three tornadoes in Kansas, at Pratt, Great Bend, and Salina. The twisters moved through rural areas and unroofed a few farm buildings. A farmer named Echenrode was treated for a broken arm in Salina.

Emporia had pea-sized hail.

A special severe-weather statement dispatched from Kansas City outlined the situation carefully. Virtually everything from Kansas City eastward could expect possible severe weather on Wednesday.

At 11 p.m., Louisville reported humidity had doubled in five hours. North Platte, Nebraska, reported blinding snow. The temperature difference across Kansas, west to east, was thirty degrees. The wind-chill index at Liberal was minus ten, and in St Louis a few hardy souls were playing in heated motel swimming pools.

The satellite's pictures in the infra-red spectrum showed a patchy band of cloud from near Rapid City, South Dakota, to San Antonio, Texas. The line was thickening and building as the storm gathered itself in the night.

The storm now would come, bringing its entire panoply of ill effects. All indications were that the effects would include the worst possible : tornadoes.

The time, location, path, duration and general behaviour of a tornado cannot be predicted. Forecasters can only say where they might appear – and then issue warnings after they are spotted. Unlike the hurricane, the tornado does not form slowly, following a pattern.

This much is known : when conditions in and around a towering cumulonimbus cloud are just 'right,' it will form one or more tornadoes. As the cloud itself rotates, so does the tornado, but with infinitely greater speed and over a much more restricted radius. People think of tornadoes as sucking things upward in their path, and this does take place; but there is evidence of enormous downward wind forces too, at least as some tornadoes first touch the ground.

Sometimes the tornado's funnel shape is very apparent. Others look like pale or dark-coloured snakes. Others are great black areas beneath clouds with no discernible shape, due to the obscuration of flying dust or debris or rain. The tornado may not be seen at all before it hits; it may be too dark, or the victim may be unfortunate enough to have the funnel touch down very, very close to where he happens to be.

There was a popular motion picture once in which the principals were notified that a tornado 'was on the way,' and then prepared for several hours until the twister finally obligingly showed itself miles away on the horizon. People who know tornadoes know this is nonsense. Tornadoes are seldom so predictable or obliging.

The tornado will usually travel generally southwest to northeast, but does not necessarily do so. The famous tri-state tornado of March 18, 1925, which wrecked parts of Missouri, Illinois and Indiana, killing about 700 people, moved in this way. But the worst tornado ever to strike New England, the one that hit Worcester, Massachusetts, on June 9, 1953, travelled generally northwest to southeast, and others have been reported moving in other directions. Some have been tracked through colossal U-turns, and research by Theodore Fujita of the University of Chicago indicates that some, at least, may start tracking sharply northward during the declining phase of their lives.

Direction is not the only unpredictable aspect. Some tornadoes have been tracked on the ground for hundreds of miles. Others touch down so briefly that only a house or two out of an entire city will be severely damaged. Some move slowly while others travel 60 miles per hour or faster. There is no foolproof way to predict the force of a tornado from its forward speed, although the factors may be related. The tornado's rotational forces, too, may vary from only 50 miles per hour or so – enough to knock down an occasional sign or do light tree damage – to speeds that may exceed 250 miles per hour – enough to sweep house foundations clean and turn automobiles into flying projectiles.

The width of the tornado's path may also vary from a few hundred feet to several miles.

Although late afternoon and evening are 'prime time' for tornadoes, they have struck at every hour of the day or night. Although most people think they know the tornado-prone areas of the country, they do not know that in 1973, for example, every state in the Union reported tornadoes except Alaska, Utah, Washington and Rhode Island. And although the United States has more tornadoes than any other country in the world, few realize that many other nations do have them, including England.

Tornadoes have struck before the rain, during the rain, and after the rain. They have been seen moving across snow-covered ground, lakes, rivers, rolling terrain and even mountains. They have been seen in the open countryside and in cities like Dallas, Louisville and Huntsville, Alabama.

The ordinary American home cannot stand up to a tornado. Neither will the average school building. Light-metal structures such as many motels and shopping centres are even more vulnerable. Although a few states like Arkansas have now begun enforcing a law to require mobile home manufacturers to build retaining straps and cables into the walls of these units, mobile homes remain notorious as the most unsafe places of all.

Nothing can stop a tornado. A good warning system and enlightened public response can minimize the resulting death and injuries.

That was why the wires were so busy this night of April 8. The messages were of various kinds, but they all said the same basic thing. Their translation was:

'It's coming. Watch for it.'

Wednesday, April 9
7:30 a.m.–10:50 a.m.

ZCZC WBC 114
ACUS 9 RWRC
MKC WW 091000
MKC 091000
ZZZZZ

BULLETIN

SPECIAL WEATHER STATEMENT
ISSUED 4 A.M. CDT WEDNESDAY APRIL 9, 1975

THE NATIONAL WEATHER SERVICE HAS ISSUED A SKYWARN FOR A
LARGE SECTION OF THE UNITED STATES EFFECTIVE FROM 5 A.M.
CDT UNTIL MIDNIGHT.

THE AREA INCLUDES ALL OR PORTIONS OF NEBRASKA, KANSAS,
OKLAHOMA, ARKANSAS, MISSOURI, IOWA, WISCONSIN, ILLINOIS,
INDIANA, KENTUCKY, TENNESSEE, MISSISSIPPI, ALABAMA,
GEORGIA, OHIO, WEST VIRGINIA, VIRGINIA, NORTH CAROLINA
AND SOUTH CAROLINA.

EXTREME SOUTHERN PORTIONS OF MICHIGAN MAY BE ADDED
LATER.

THE NATIONAL WEATHER SERVICE SAID AN EXTREMELY FAST
MOVING LOW PRESSURE SYSTEM NOW LOCATED IN KANSAS AND
OKLAHOMA WILL MOVE INTO THE OHIO VALLEY AREA OR BEYOND
BY NIGHTFALL WITH THE THREAT OF SCATTERED SEVERE
THUNDERSTORMS AND SCATTERED TORNADOES OVER THE BROAD
AREA OUTLINED.

LOCAL NWS OFFICES ARE INSTRUCTED TO TAKE ANY FURTHER
STEPS DEEMED NECESSARY TO ASSURE OPTIMUM OPERATION OF
RADAR AND COMMUNICATIONS SYSTEMS. EXTRA PERSONNEL
SHOULD BE PLACED ON ALERT AS NECESSARY.

A SERIES OF SEVERE THUNDERSTORM WATCH AREA ALERTS WILL
BE ISSUED STARTING AT 4:20 A.M. CDT.

XXX

Kansas City
Ed Stephens was puzzled.
He had gotten to the Severe Storms Forecast Centre before 7 a.m.

in order to try to stay on top of developments. But now, after thirty minutes, he was finding the data confusing.

In the communications room, airport-terminal sequence reports, flooding in on a vertical stacked array of high-speed teletypes covering part of an inside wall, showed cool, blustery conditions in much of the west-central region of the country, with everything from blowing dust to snow showers and fog. In Wyoming, Colorado and the Dakotas, the data indicated IFR conditions – instrument flight rules only due to sharply reduced visibilities. Much of Oklahoma and Texas reported southerly winds gusting to 40 knots, and more dust and haze. Through Kansas, portions of Nebraska, Iowa and Missouri, and parts of Louisiana and Arkansas, gathering clouds at high altitudes were being reported, with a few symbols indicating developing cumulonimbus – thunderstorm clouds – at lower levels.

Much of this was normal. But as Stephens scanned the reports across the country, he seemed to find developing clouds at random intervals. Cleveland reported lowering visibility, but Chattanooga was clear. Cincinnati reported a few thunderheads, beginning to build, and yet Indianapolis reported nothing. The Memphis radar summary showed no activity, while Nashville showed numerous small echoes building up. The storm's effects were popping up in what seemed to be a crazy-quilt pattern.

Frowning, Stephens left the communications area and went into the main weather room. The extra personnel he had ordered were on duty. On organizational charts, men who worked most directly with severe-weather watches and warnings were designated a separate unit, SELS, for Severe Local Storms unit. In practice, although each man had his own job and did it without immediate supervision, there were no cubbyhole divisions of labour. It was a single big team with a single big job.

Stephens conferred with the forecasters. Bright went over the surface and 500-millibar charts with him, and they compared conclusions. With both charts showing high winds, chilled air aloft and humidity on the upswing, there was little argument about the gloomy prognosis.

A man named King went over the latest satellite pictures with Stephens. They showed broad smudges of cloud all the way to the East Coast, in no discernible pattern and with many wide breaks. The low-pressure centre itself had gathered enormous shelves of clouds around it, and resembled a great hairy octopus.

'The whole thing is moving like a bat out of hell,' King pointed out, 'and it seems to be accelerating.'

Stephens pointed to a line of thin cirrus pointing away from the low and toward the northeast. 'It's going to follow the jet.'

'We'll have activity popping up farther east faster than we thought.'

'The watch areas will contain everything.'

'Oh, right, sure. But some of this stuff trying to get started clear over in Ohio is *really* early.'

Sephens grunted and turned to cross the room. He wanted to verify the Cincinnati cloud data.

In an alcove off the main room, behind a wall of file cabinets, a technician was perched on a high stool, his body bent over a glass-topped worktable. A yellow light shone up through the tabletop and a large, semi-transparent map on which he was working.

The map was an outline of the United States, with many principal cities marked in. Working from data flowing in over the wires, the technician was sketching in a national pictorial summary of what the radars in various areas were seeing. Taking the report from a given city, he could centre that city on a compass-rose diagram on the illuminated glass; then, by referring to magnetic azimuths and mile markings on the compass rose, which the light super-imposed on the thin map, he could draw in radar echoes precisely where they were reported.

This national radar plotting chart was prepared every hour. It was almost finished. It showed the same puzzling patchwork of cloud reports that Stephens had visualized from the data.

Stephens walked back to where Bright waited. 'I almost tend to think a few places like Cincinnati have made mistakes.'

Bright grinned crookedly. 'You know we're all perfect.'

'I think I'll just see for myself.'

So saying, Stephens turned to the row of narrow, olive-drab facsimile machines that stood just inside the weather-room entrance. Each machine had rollers on top with a slanted printout surface. The lower portions were characterized by telephone dials, switches, some rows of steadily glowing yellow lights, and a telephone receiver on a side hook.

Stephens flicked briefly through a small card file on the left-hand machine and took out a white plastic card about the size of an oil-company credit card. It was filled with small, rectangular slot-holes. On the top edge was printed its designation: CINCINNATI.

Lifting the telephone receiver, Stephens inserted the plastic card in the slot behind the cradle. He pushed a *start* button on the telephone base. The card fed itself upward out of the slot, being 'read.' On the receiver came a high-pitched warbling tone which showed that the connection had been made.

The facsimile machine itself began to make a swishing sound. The paper rollers began to turn very slowly and the paper began to feed up out of the machine. The machine began painting, dark grey on white, a picture of the Cincinnati radarscope.

Cincinnati was on a 250-mile scan. The precipitation portrayed was scattered, but a line appeared to be developing in central Kentucky, with other clouds scattered widely through Ohio and Indiana. The radar operator had scrawled intensity notations on his scope with a grease pencil; an arrow indicated the most severe echo currently on the scope.

The machine took ninety seconds to complete the picture.

'They didn't lie,' Stephens said, rubbing a slight ache in his lower chest. Was the ache worse than usual today?

'Let's look at Nashville,' Bright suggested.

They repeated the operation.

'This damned storm isn't playing by the rules,' Stephens complained. 'The pattern is all mixed up.'

'Don't let Congressman Tatinger hear you talk like that.'

'Hell, don't mention him. Maybe he'll oversleep all day.'

Machine bells began whanging in the communications centre. Both men rushed in. The message was already being printed.

The day's first tornado had already popped up, near a town named Trafalgar, in Kansas.

Trafalgar, Kansas

Near Trafalgar, a farmer named J. M. Stine was at that pleasant time of morning when he dawdled over a second mug of coffee. The kitchen light was on and there was unusual darkness at the windows. Stine was not enjoying his coffee as much as usual because he was sweating. It was too hot for so early in the morning. Stine thought, *It's going to come up a cloud, and then it's going to come a humdinger of a rain.*

Maybe that would cool it off. Cooling was needed. A light, hot, moist breeze ruffled the faded cotton curtains at the open windows. Outside, bits of dust and debris flew around the barnyard and the trees rustled nervously.

Stine's wife was in the bedroom, and his two sons, fifteen and twelve, were out at the barn. A pink Arvin radio was playing on the sinkboard.

In a moment the music stopped on the radio and the announcer came on. 'That was the man you know so well, the late Jim Croce, and this is Billy Lewis at WKY radio in Oklahoma City. And now a look at the news at thirty minutes past the hour.

'The National Weather Service here in Oklahoma City has issued a severe-weather watch covering a large portion of Oklahoma and Kansas. The people at the Weather Bureau warn of the possibility of scattered severe thunderstorms and scattered tornadoes, with possible heavy rain, some hail and damaging straight winds—'

'Dad!' It was the voice of Stine's older boy, Mark.

'Just a minute!' Stine called, concentrating on the radio.

'—a line extending from Tulsa through Trafalgar, Kansas, and south to Atwood, and a second area sixty miles either side of a line from—'

'Dad! Quick!'

This time Stine recognized the shrill quality of the yell. The dregs of his coffee sloshed on to the tablecloth as he jumped to his feet. As he moved toward the back door, he realized that the wind had suddenly stilled. Everything was darker and the still was unearthly.

Stine chilled. Like a man watching a film, he watched himself open the screen door, step on to the little enclosed back porch with its crates and sacks and stored empty jars and the sweet smell of decaying fruit. He flipped the light switch and the overhead bulb glowed yellow.

'Dad! Hurry!'

'Coming!'

He stepped out into the yard.

There was an eerie greenish light now. Mark and Tony stood near the doors of the barn and their faces were bathed in the strange light. They were looking to the south and west, a direction Stine could not see from the porch because the house blocked his view.

Mark pointed.

Stine ran into the yard, turned, and looked.

He could look across the yard and the road, across the fence line and out over miles of slightly rolling open field. The sky was covered with towering grey clouds, and those nearby had a pearly quality, with greyish strands hanging down from their bellies. The illumination was like that of a half-moon.

But there was enough light to see the darker cloud, a huge black cylinder extending out of the clouds about two miles away. The blackness extended downward from the cloud to the ground, and at its base was a kind of haze, and the entire cylinder, of enormous proportions, was twisting sinuously, like a snake.

Then Stine heard the distant roar, like express trains. Beneath the roar was a rattling sound of some kind, a crackling.

Lightning veined the clouds overhead and thunder clapped. A hot wind gusted, shaking the trees. The barn door flew open.

'In the cellar!' Stine shouted. 'Right now!'

The boys turned. They ran to the cellar, an earthen cave dug halfway between the house and the barn. Fill-dirt made the top of the cellar a grass-covered hump about two feet high, and into the fill were set timbers on which the heavy oak door was hung.

Mark swung the door up and open.

Stine saw no more. He was already in the house. '*Mary!*'

She appeared in the door that led from the living room to the kitchen. 'Is it—?'

'*Come on!*'

She moved, but instead of coming toward him, she vanished back into the living room.

Stine ran after her. It was blacker outside now, and the roaring had already built to a thunderous level. Wind lashed at the house, and in the flash of lightning he could see trees whipping wildly.

Stine's wife was at the end table, struggling to get a large object – the family Bible and family record – out of the lower shelf.

Stine grabbed the Bible for her and propelled her out through the kitchen. He almost knocked her down, pushing her out the back door and across the yard. Wind buffeted them and dirt stung bare skin. A few spatters of rain hit and they were shockingly cold. The air had the smell of electricity.

Mark and Tony stood by the opened door of the cellar. Tony had a lantern.

'Get inside! Get inside!' Stine yelled.

They plunged down the rickety steps into the dark, and Stine pushed his wife in after them. He saw their dog running around the yard, panicked.

'*Skippy!*'

The hound somehow heard, and bolted over to him. Stine shoved him down below, too, stepped down three steps himself, and, his waist still above ground level, reached for the handle of the door.

The wind slammed him sideways into the supporting timbers, sending skyrockets of pain through his ribcage. Lightning and thunder crashed simultaneously. Grabbing for the door handle again despite his pain, Stine was turned so he could look directly at the storm.

It was upon them. He saw an inferno of whirling debris and dirt just across the road, and objects – *fenceposts* – flying in all directions. Then the blackness moved across the road and the bottom of the spinning mass became narrow and clearly defined, perhaps only fifty yards wide, and Stine clearly saw it whip viciously and lift up off the ground. A tremendous bolt of crimson lightning smashed into the ground nearby, sending up clouds of smoke and steam.

The roar was like nothing Stine had ever heard. All around him was whirling motion, a briny green all around, a blackness at the centre. Shingles began flying off the roof of the house. A great pressure sucked at Stine's ears and he cried out – the sound of the cry was lost – with the sharp pain. He threw his head back in reflex action, and gasped.

The funnel had lifted up and was passing directly over him. He could not tell how high it was but it was not very high, perhaps a few hundred feet. It whipped and writhed, a great pale whorl of cloud rotating at incredible speed. The mouth of it seemed alive. From the rotating mouth hung three or four mini-twisters, ugly little black snakes whipping and twisting as they spun around the mouth and spun on their own axes as well.

He could look far up into the tornado. The cloudy walls spun, tubular rolls of cloud, and slender veins of lightning flickered constantly up and down on the insides, lighting the central cavity which seemed clear. Farther up – Stine had no way of guessing how high – there was constant lightning flashing in a greenish murk.

Transfixed, Stine stared up into the funnel. The sound had deafened him. Someone was pulling on his legs and he looked down and saw Mark yelling at him, but no sound came. He looked up again.

The mouth was larger. It was swooping down again.

The barn exploded.

Stine dived for the bottom of the cellar.

Columbus, Ohio

Holding the helicopter on a steady, slow, east-west course as he made another pass over downtown Columbus, Rudy Murphy studied the flowing traffic below. In his headset he listened to the announcer give him his cue.

'All right,' he said into the microphone briskly. 'This is Rudy Murphy in the Earlybird traffic chopper, and traffic is moving right along in good shape this morning. The interstates are moving nicely, we have just a little congestion along High Street near Broad Street, as motorists move into the underground parking, but traffic is in good shape both east and west . . . and north and south. They're still working that accident there near Fifth Avenue, but traffic is moving around quite nicely. Looking north, it appears there's a small delay on the River Road near Lane Avenue, but nothing at all serious. It looks good this morning, folks, and this is Rudy Murphy in the Earlybird Whirlybird, returning you to the studio.'

He flicked off the transmit button and listened to the disc jockey start introducing the next record. Turning the chopper to the west, he swung out across the river and began a long, slow pass that would carry him out to the west side for his next report on the traffic around the General Motors and Westinghouse plants.

It was warm over Columbus this morning. There was a dense heat-haze. But the morning was perfectly normal.

Rudy Murphy sighed. It was a hell of a way to make a living.

Monument Valley, Kentucky

High clouds haloed the sun. A mist of humidity cloaked the valley in a gold-tinged grey. From the old rocker on her porch, Milly Tyler could not quite make out the forest-ranger station atop Steptoe Mountain, although she knew its precise location. It would rain today.

Moving her pipe from one side of her jaw to the other, Milly lightly inhaled a little Sir Walter Raleigh. Smoothing her big hands over the freshly ironed pleats of her grey dress, she looked up and down the dirt road, paying special attention to the area to the right, where the road twisted into woods and vanished from sight. It was time for the children to be here.

'They'll be late,' she said aloud. 'I've been ready for two days, and they can't get themselves here on time. Land!'

Spotnose the cat, draped over the porch railing, opened one eye to look at her.

'Probably,' Milly went on, 'they'll be put out about it, too, and fussing between themselves. A million modern time-saving gadgets, a fancy new car, colour TV, even a fancy new watch that lights up and shows you numbers so you don't have to be able to tell time; and they're *still* late.'

Spotnose yawned.

Milly lapsed into silence; there was no use talking to a sleepy cat.

Milly's son Thomas lived and worked in the city of Henderson, fifty miles away. His business trip would be taking him to Miami, Florida, for two days. Milly thoroughly approved Thomas's taking his wife Nina along. Husbands ought to take their wives to conventions; more wives, less foolishness and trouble. And Milly would obviously enjoy watching after the tykes – Kent, eleven, and Adrian, ten.

Naturally there had been a small fuss over whether Milly would leave the farm and go to the city to babysit. Thomas had wanted it that way, of course. Bringing the boys to the farm forced them to miss two days of school, he had argued, and you'll enjoy having all the conveniences, momma.

To which Milly had momma'd right back that she knew all about big cities in this day and time, and she went there once a month to pick up the welfare check, and that was plenty, thank you. And the boys would learn more in two days in the country than they would in a week at that fancy school, and that was an end to the discussion.

So now Thomas was getting back at her by being late.

Milly had two apple pies cooling on the drainboard by the pump, and a rabbit stew cooking. She had shot the rabbit yesterday afternoon, stalking out into the pine wood behind the house, climbing a couple of old fences and going through some gullies and a briar patch, seeing the cottontail sitting, kicking him out and yelling 'shoo!' because it just was not sporting to shoot a creature sitting that way, food or not, and then knocking him over with one shot from her old 12-gauge. She had taken him home, skinned him, gutted him, meticulously picked out the shot, and put him in cold brine overnight to ease off the wild taste a little. The stew had been cooking since early morning.

And later this morning, before the stew, she had planned to take the tykes down the dirt road and into the brush to show them the baby squirrels she had found. Boys needed to see things like that, learn about nature. But if Thomas didn't get them here pretty soon, it would be too late to go before lunch. You couldn't turn the thermostat down on a wood cooking stove; you timed things out as best you could, and you accepted the inevitable.

Not that Thomas would understand any of that. He was now twenty minutes late at least.

'Land!' Milly complained.

The road remained empty. It came out of the deep woods on the right, having snaked down the hill that blocked most of the view to the west, and then came through this flat meadow within fifty yards of the house, going along parallel with the smooth wire fence out in front, past the mailbox that still had J. G. TYLER painted on it, although he had been dead almost ten years now, and then down over the plank bridge spanning the creek where the willows were, and then over a rise and on east, toward the county road a mile away, where the nearest neighbours, the Lovetts, lived.

Milly had no car, but the telephone nearly always worked and she could call for a taxi, which usually arrived within an hour.

In the decades that Milly Tyler had lived in the far eastern end of Monument Valley, many things in the world had changed drastically. She had kept them at a distance. From day to day, her life now was much as it had been in the 1940s and even earlier, although the Depression had been on earlier, and things had been *really* hard then. But the earth and the sky were the same, year after year, and the hill to her right gave a solid frame to her outlook, the landscape flattening a bit across the road, humping out toward the horizon in a series of increasingly choppier little hills, finally rising by degrees to the distant crest of Steptoe Mountain, the lumpy, green-shrouded shape she had known all of her life.

There was more open ground to the east, but the willows along the creek hid that from Milly's view, and she liked it that way because she was a hill woman: open spaces made her uneasy; there was a nakedness to them that did not set well, did not close in a person's eyesight with borders that could be catalogued and memorized and made a part of perspective.

Milly still could not make out the ranger tower on the mountain. It was very wet in the air today. And very warm. She felt the perspiration in the deep wrinkles of her neck. Well, a little rain would be all right, and the haze at least kept that forest ranger from using his binoculars to spy on her.

She knew the forest ranger spied on her. She had definitely *seen* him in his tower, looking right at her house with his big field glasses, big as life there in the bluish field of her spyglass as she watched him from behind the curtains of the parlour. Some people had no sense of decency at all.

Milly's pipe had gone out. She cracked a wood match on the arm of the rocker and fired up again. She just had the pipe smoking well again when she heard the car engine. Striking the pipe sharply on the porch railing, she showered hot ashes into the petunias and put the hot bowl into her apron pocket.

A red station wagon tooled down the dirt road and turned into the yard. Thomas was at the wheel and Nina was in the front with him. The boys were in the back – all over the back, actually, as they clamoured to be let out.

'All right! All right!' Thomas yelled, his voice penetrating the closed windows because, naturally, they were running the air conditioning. He shut off the motor. The back window slid down and the boys climbed out.

'Hi, Grammaw!' Kent and Adrian charged for the porch. Kent was a year older, but Adrian had grown faster; they looked like towheaded twins.

'Hello, dickenses,' Milly laughed as they piled into her lap.

'What are we gonna do, Grammaw?' Adrian asked excitedly.

'Are we gonna go fishin'?' Kent demanded.

Getting out of the car, Nina called sharply, 'Be careful with Grandmother now!' She was a pretty girl, slender, wearing a summer suit that Milly thought was too severe. The poor girl lacked flair. 'You're too big to go jumping on Grandmother like that!' Nina scolded, coming onto the porch.

'Leave 'em be, child!' Milly told her.

Thomas came to the porch, too, the step boards groaning under his weight. He was getting much too heavy and his red sport coat and cream-coloured trousers emphasized this fact. His hair was too long, too: on to his collar.

He bent to brush his lips across Milly's cheek. He did it very quickly, as if he were afraid he might catch old age. ' 'Lo, Mom. Sorry we're late. We'll have to just drop the boys and get headed back.'

'All right, dear,' Milly said. She returned her gaze to Nina. 'You look very pretty, dear.'

Nina smiled. 'Tommy bought this new outfit.'

'It's real pretty. Would you like me to shorten it for you? It will just take a minute.'

Nina glanced down at her skirt, which caught her trim legs well below the knee. 'This is the style this year, Momma.'

'Foof,' Milly said. 'Thomas wants *you* to *think* it's the style. You've got lovely legs, dear. You ought to show them off.'

'Mom!' Thomas said, genuinely – poor thing – shocked.

'And the bodice, here,' Milly went on, reaching out to pinch the material under her daughter-in-law's breasts. 'This should be taken in a mite, see?'

Thomas said grimly, 'The suit fits perfectly.'

'Thomas, let Nina speak for herself. The way you run over this girl is a disgrace. Nina, you have the legs and you have the figure. My goodness! Do you think the good Lord gave you a nice body to hide under a sack? If Thomas gets nervous about other men watching you, maybe that would be good for him.'

Nina blushed deeply. 'We have to be hurrying along, Momma.'

'I could take it up for you in five minutes.'

'No,' Thomas said definitely. Then, to ease the tone, he asked brightly, 'What do you think of *my* new outfit, while you're commenting on our clothes?'

Milly sniffed. 'Makes you look like a drum major.'

Kent and Adrian had giggling fits.

'Ouch!' Adrian yelped after a moment. He hopped off Milly's lap and jumped around. Then he plunged his hand into Milly's apron pocket before she could stop him. 'I burned myself and it was this!' he cried, holding her pipe aloft.

Thomas put on his stern face, the way he always did when imitating his late father. 'You've been smoking again!'

'I've been blowing bubbles, dear.'

'Mother.' He always got formal when he was being righteous. 'You know what the doctor said about your heart.'

'Foof.'

'And cancer—'

'A little smoke kills germs, Thomas. It probably makes a body last longer.'

'That's ridiculous!'

'Haven't you ever heard of smoking a ham or a turkey to make it last?'

'Mother, this is no joking matter.'

'Smoking also keeps your weight down, Thomas. Maybe you should try it.'

Her son sighed and gave up. 'We have to get back. The boys' clothes are all in the suitcase.'

Milly nodded, then nodded several more times as poor Thomas went through his entire planned itinerary for her again, presumably so she would know where he was going to be at any instant of the day or night. Thomas had it all memorized, with contingency plans and everything else. He planned more than anyone Milly had ever known. It was depressing.

Finally they moved to the car.

Nina said, 'The radio said we're having some bad weather west of here. I hope you don't get stuck with these two boys in your house because of rain for the whole two days.'

'If they give me trouble,' Milly said, 'I'll fill them so full of pie they won't be able to budge off the floor.'

'Oh, boy!' Kent grinned.

'Yow!' Adrian whooped.

'Brush your teeth after every meal or snack,' Thomas told them.

Nina said, 'I think they have a weather watch out for the valley, Momma. I know I worry too much—'

'You certainly do,' Milly replied crisply. 'We could always go to the root cellar if something did happen, but nothing will. This entire valley used to be a campground for Indians. Indians would never camp where there might be a cyclone or anything like that.'

'How did the Indians know?' Thomas asked.

'I wouldn't expect you to understand that,' Milly told him.

'You'll be all right, though?' Nina insisted.

'Snug as bugs in a rug.'

Adrian giggled. 'What kinda bugs?'

'Rug bugs,' Milly told him.

'What do rug bugs look like?'

'Can't miss 'em,' Milly replied. 'They take naps.'

Both boys stared. Then they got it. Kent groaned. Adrian fell to the ground and rolled.

As the car pulled away, the two boys grew serious. Milly could see in their eyes that they were already thinking about getting homesick.

'What're we gonna do, Grammaw?' Kent asked.

'Well, young gentlemen, I have to go to the kitchen to check on our dinner. It won't be ready for a while, yet.'

'I'm hungry now, Grammaw,' Kent said.

'Me too!'

Milly nodded. 'Go out to the cellar, then. You remember where it is. You'll find jelly on the shelves. The bright red is strawberry. Bring up a jar. I baked some bread this morning. You can have some jellybread to hold you over.'

'Oh boy!' Kent said.

'Oh boy!' Adrian said.

They jumped off the porch, cut through the petunias, routing Spotnose, and tore around the side of the house.

Smiling, Milly gave the sky a last glance before she went in. Off to that part of the western sky she could see, there were many tall clouds, their tops golden in the high sunlight. That part of the sky looked like piles of meringue, and the clouds marched off to the south as far as anyone could see. They were growing, becoming real giants.

They were far away yet, though, Milly decided. There would be plenty of time for a walk down the road to the woods before it rained.

Thatcher, Ohio

Horace Greeley, Charles Dana, *et al.*, had been fascinating men.

Maureen Coyle was working hard to convince herself of this.

Back from her morning classes at the community college, she postponed household chores and immediately went to the living-room desk where she spread out her notebooks and texts, intent on catching up with the course that had been giving her the most trouble this semester: history of journalism.

Not that Mo had any real intention of becoming a journalist. But in the three and a half years she had been taking classes as she could fit them in, it had become apparent to her that it was fine to say you were in 'pre-law,' but the practical person should be careful to make the *pre*-portion of her studies fit into some occupation, just in case.

After years of being a wife and mother, and telling herself that this was enough, Mo had gone back to college with nothing but fears and self-doubt. She *knew* she was being silly . . . a middle-aged housewife filling in spare time, now that the children were older, just another vaguely discontented, restless female seeking she knew not what, playing at self-fulfillment – whatever that was – when she had enough. When she started, she also *knew* she probably wouldn't make it, couldn't compete with these bright young students . . . couldn't study any more after the years away. She had never been that good a student in the few courses she had taken before she left school to get married, she told herself. And now she was middle-aged, rusty, a very competent housewife, thank you, and not ashamed of that . . . but nothing more.

She had been surprised at her progress.

Not that any of it had been easy. God knew she had worked. Mike did not know how hard she had tried. No one knew. It was a casual joke around the house, the nights she stayed up until 2 a.m. or later, poring over the freshman compositions, over the philosophy that just *wouldn't* make sense, over the biology that had come so close to really wiping her out. There had been many times when she knew she had been right in the first place, and that probably she ought to quit kidding herself, and go to the church group where she could make finger-paintings and talk about getting into oils, or write magazine fillers, and talk about a novel, and never do either.

She had always so detested those strange, outwardly confident, inwardly mushy older women who talked so much about asserting themselves, and were clearly never going to accomplish anything. So her fear of becoming like them had driven her even harder.

And then the professor in the English course had told her she obviously had talent in writing, and the professor of Law Survey – a woman – told her she had a mind that might do well in law.

And her grades started coming back at the top of the course list with such regularity that she wondered if there wasn't some mistake.

So now Mo was committed, of sorts, and as she moved ahead, her thinking had changed. She would study law, there was no question about that. She might be fifty before she finally finished the exams, if she continued to study only a part-time load. But better to reach her goal at fifty than not at all. She was hedging her bets, too, *just in case* she couldn't quite hack it: in another two years she could get her BA in journalism, and if things happened, she could find work on a newspaper somewhere.

Much of this was unspoken between her and her husband. She knew he did not really see the way she was thinking. It was not a source of conflict. He was a good man. He truly wanted her to fulfill herself, be her own person. He did not, because he could not, understand where her own destiny-seeking might one day lead her.

Now he was preoccupied about the latest bond-election failure, was agonizing over his own decision about the future. She was supporting him in every way she could. Although it did not enter his mind that she might even consider doing so, she had already thought deeply about her own future, and what his move away from Thatcher – if it came – might imply for her. She had thought about it a long time, and carefully, and had decided that she would go with him if he chose to run for Congress, and won.

Mike would have been stunned to suspect that she had ever seriously entertained the opposite option. But she had done so *most* seriously. The children were almost grown. Accommodations could be worked out where they were concerned. She might stay here, finish her first degree, plan to go on in law.

But she had decided against this. If he chose to move, she would go with him this one more time. She could study in Washington. She had contracted to be a wife and mother, and she would complete the job with the children. There was so much pain with both children now, as they began to try to grow up, reject their parents for reasons even they did not understand, build the courage to move away ... they needed a mother for this, and Mike needed a wife.

Mo hoped that the day would never come when her and Mike's goals became so in conflict that they were forced to make ultimate decisions. She loved him. She loved the children. But just as she could face the possibility now of leaving this home, which she also loved, if she had to do so, she knew that the larger decision might also come.

The years had changed her. There was no hostility in self-assertion. She *would* complete her degree. She *would* practice law. She thought it could all be worked out with Mike. If it could not be worked out, somehow, then she *would* have the strength to be her own person.

Studying her journalism history notes now, she knew that Mike suspected so very little of this ... just as other things in her life were not known to him any more. There were times when she felt deep stabs of guilt. But she was discharging her obligations, and she knew what love was ... and how it could differ from one man to another, now ... and she loved her husband. But in the long run she could only love from her own stance of completion. Nothing would stand in the way of her own completion as a person, an integrated personality, a woman with real freedom and choice.

It was not the time to talk about any of this with Mike. Especially not now. The sea tides of change that had been moving through her would continue, and even she did not know where they would take her.

She was not afraid.

Only her compassion made her worry that Mike ... and others ... might one day not really be able to understand.

In the meantime, she would help him all she could.

Frowning, she tried to force herself to concentrate on Mr Greeley. The wind sighed outside the house.

She was concentrating hard enough that the telephone actually startled her.

She hurried to answer it, preoccupied.

'Hello again,' the voice said quietly.

Mo quickened inside. 'Hi.'

'Are you alone?'

'Yes.' Already she thought she knew why he had called ... as he sometimes called during the day. She felt the old rent in her personality strain. But her heart was beating faster already.

'I have a couple of hours,' Martin told her, his voice thick with feeling. 'Would you like to meet me?'

He did not have to specify more. There was a room now, a rear unit in a small apartment complex that catered primarily to retired people ... or others with a need for a secure, clandestine hideaway. You could drive the car directly into the unit's garage, with its electronic door. No one could see.

Remembering her lovemaking with Mike, Mo felt a stab of guilt. 'I don't know,' she said softly.

'An hour,' he said.

God, it was not love or anything like it.

That was why she could not resist.

'All right,' she said.

'Can you leave now?'

'Yes.'

Wednesday, April 9
11:10 a.m.–12:40 p.m.

VV

ZCZC

SDXXI RWRD 091530

GRAND ISLAND RADAR SUMMARY . . . APRIL 9, 1975

AT 10 A.M. CDT MIXED RAIN AND SNOW WERE INDICATED BETWEEN
OMAHA . . . YORK . . . AND COLUMBUS . . .

AN AREA OF INTENSE ACTIVITY WITH SOME CLOUD TOPS
EXCEEDING 40000 FEET EXTENDED IN A LINE SIXTY MILES WIDE
FROM HASTINGS SOUTHWARD TO RILEY KAN . . .

MOVEMENT OF THIS LINE OF HEAVY THUNDERSTORM ACTIVITY
WAS EAST AT 50 MPH . . . MANY INTENSE ECHOES OBSERVED
FORMING IN AND AROUND THIS LINE WITH APPARENT EASTWARD
DEVELOPMENT . . .

XXX

Kansas City

Unstable air had swept into the Kansas City area itself, and for
the NSSFC personnel on the seventeenth floor of the Federal
Building downtown, the situation had complicated itself a hun-
dredfold.

The Centre, in addition to its national duties, was the local
weather station for a thirty-eight-county area. While work on the
national scale continued at a hectic pace, Ed Stephens had moved
into the radar room and was wholly engrossed in the worsening
local situation.

Although the radar room was about fourteen feet square, it
seemed much smaller because it held so much equipment. Tile-
floored, with a low acoustical ceiling studded with light fixtures
and ventilation louvres, it was very dimly lighted to facilitate
operation of its main component, the hulking radar console.
About eight feet long and five feet tall, the thickness of a colour
television set, the console was shaped like an old-fashioned theatre
organ, its side panels canted inward toward the operator, who sat
facing the centre. In this central section was the largest of three
scopes, a round one more than a foot in diameter. A swiftly rota-

ting white sweep painted greyish blotches on the dark screen as outgoing radar signals encountered precipitation and bounced back.

Pushing some papers and extra equipment back off a side table, Ed Stephens glanced at Buck Tatinger, standing like his faithful – and irritating – shadow in the doorway.

Tatinger gave him the cocked eyebrow. 'Have time to explain?'

'Come take a quick look,' Stephens snapped. 'Then I'll just have to run you out of here.'

Tatinger came around the far end of the console. He peered at the centre screen. 'Lots of clouds.'

'Precipitation,' Stephens corrected him. 'This kind of radar can look out two hundred and fifty miles. It sees precipitation, not clouds that have little water in them.'

'Is this on two-fifty scan?'

'No. It's too close for that, the storms are right on top of us. We're on one-twenty-five scan now. That strongest line of echoes – that string of very bright splotches – is to our southwest and coming at us.'

The radar technician twiddled knobs under the right-hand smaller screen, making tall zigzag pictures dance.

'That gives us a vertical picture of the clouds, how high they go,' Stephens explained. 'Since cloud height and severity are often closely related, that's important.'

'How about this one on the left?'

'Those zigzag greenish peaks represent readings on intensity of the echoes. Again, it helps us tell how heavy activity is in a given cloud.'

Tatinger nodded knowingly. 'So that's how you people can detect a tornado far away. Can you show me a hook echo?'

'Radar isn't infallible,' Stephens said, conscious of the need to hurry. 'People make a lot of the hook echo on the radar screen, and often it's there. But sometimes there can be a hook and no tornado, and there can damned surely be tornadoes and no hook. Hail can fool a radar, too.'

'Then,' Tatinger said, his eyes narrowing, 'radar is just so much weather-service PR.'

'Christ, no! It's valuable.'

'How do you know when to trust it?'

'You trust your operator.'

Tatinger smiled thinly. 'Ah, yes. The human element. Would that explain why budget figures show such a ghastly rise in projected salaries for some of these people?'

'You're going to have to get the hell out of here right now,' Stephens rasped. 'I'm going to be just too busy to talk for a while.'

Tatinger stepped back. 'I'll be outside.'

Stephens ignored him and moved behind the far end of the radar console to a narrow table jammed between the console and the wall. There was just room for him to stand facing a repeater scope. It glowed brightly and changed to a pie-shaped configuration as the operator beyond stacked cabinets scanned only the southwest quadrant. He was looking at the worst portion of the advancing cloud mass, and had programmed the radar to see only echoes of intensity 4 or above. The scope still showed five brilliant, irregular blips.

Stephens hurriedly checked out his communications gear.

A gadgeteer would have been impressed. A science-fiction *afficionado* might have been disappointed. There were plenty of gadgets crammed into the four-foot working space, but the proliferation of unmatched telephones, speaker boxes with makeshift plastic tape affixed to them, battered hand microphones and little card-file boxes, stacked on other equipment in no apparent order, was a far cry from the antiseptic order of *Star Trek*.

'Look at Olathe,' the radar operator said suddenly.

Stephens snapped his attention to the repeater scope.

A large, irregular echo a few miles southward of Olathe had suddenly changed its configuration and brightness. Shrouds of cloud seemed to form a pattern like that of astronomical pictures of distant nebulae. Stephen's eye immediately picked up a bright curling tip in the southwest quadrant of the echo – the characteristic 'hook.'

Olathe had been warned fifteen minutes earlier that heavy activity was moving in. This message had been on top of the earlier watch information. Olathe had an excellent spotter system, mostly policemen and civilian volunteers who moved to good lookout positions at times like these in order to watch for possible tornadoes.

Still, Stephens did not hesitate. He grabbed a telephone and pushed the send button. 'Olathe sheriff, this is Kansas City Weather.'

One of several small loudspeakers tacked to the wall near the ceiling scratched back: 'This is Olathe, go ahead.'

'We have a radar indication of a possible tornado—'

The spotter telephone jangled loudly.

'Hold on,' Stephens snapped, and grabbed the phone.

'This is Herndon down at Ottawa,' a nasal voice said excitedly. 'There's a tornado just came down out of the cloud here and it's on the ground about five miles north of town. It's moving northeast about thirty, forty miles an hour.'

Stephens slammed the receiver down and said into the other, 'Olathe, we have radar indication of a possible tornado about twelve miles southwest of you. Take appropriate action.'

'Okay,' the officer's voice came back. 'We don't have anything on it from our spotters yet, but we'll let you know.'

Stephens broke that connection, reached around with his left hand, and pulled a long loop of perforated teletype tape off a hook in the Masonite partition. At the tape's top was printed in Magic Marker: *Urgent TEWN Message. TORNADO! Local loop only!*

'Mike!' Stephens yelled.

Mike Collins, his first assistant in times like this, was already inside the doorway.

Stephens tossed the loop to him over the cabinets. 'Ottawa and northeast.'

Collins fled.

Stephens grabbed up a microphone and pushed a transmit stud. This cut him directly into the weather-information transmitter standing just beyond the door. People listening to their own weather radios would hear an interruption of the casette information that had been playing, and what he now had to tell them directly. Perhaps more vital, as he pressed the transmit stud, the transmitter sent out a special tone signal at 1050 Hz. This would activate special receivers in those schools, hospitals and public buildings which had them; the receivers would go off 'standby' and broadcast the warning at high volume.

'This is the National Weather Service in Kansas City,' Stephens said. 'We have a report by the public of a tornado on the ground about five miles north of Ottawa, in Franklin County. This tornado' – he glanced at the repeater scope and saw, on sector scan, a single brilliant blip in the correct location – 'is confirmed by radar at this time. This tornado is on the ground about five miles north of Ottawa. It is moving toward the northeast at about forty miles per hour.

'This is a tornado warning for persons in Franklin County, southern Douglas County, and Johnson County.' As he spoke, he was turning to his wall map. 'This storm appears to be moving toward Olathe and the Overland Park area.'

Outside, Mike Collins was back from the communications room. The prepunched tape was already sending the tornado warning out on the local wire circuits. Collins was at the transmitter now, jamming a cassette in the panel. Stephens knew that it contained the standard precautionary information broadcast after a warning: take cover, go to a storm cellar or basement or a central hallway, etc. Stephens released the microphone key.

The spotter phone jangled.

Someone else – Harry Adams – somehow squeezed into the tiny space and picked that one up. Stephens got through to Ottawa. Adams asked the radar operator for some help and was given azimuths and a range reading to the southwest. Using the plastic-covered map, he swung a mileage ruler centred on Kansas City out to the proper azimuth, chalked off the mileage, and put an X on the plastic with a grease pencil.

Adams was saying into the radio transmitter microphone: 'a funnel cloud aloft just north of the John Redmond Dam and Reservoir in Coffey County. Persons in Coffey County should be on the alert.'

Stephens took the microphone out of Adams's hand. 'This is a tornado warning for Olathe, Kansas. There is a tornado on the ground less than ten miles southwest of Olathe, moving directly toward Olathe, at this time.'

One of the small loudspeakers on the equipment cabinet came to life: 'This is Troop A, Lees Summit. We have a rotating funnel cloud directly over—'

The spotter phone rang again and Stephens got it as Adams took action on the Lees Summit report.

'This is Bonner Springs,' the voice said on the telephone. 'It's raining really hard here. Did you mean to include us in that tornado warning?'

'No, not right now, sir,' Stephens said calmly, glancing at the radar. 'Keep watching, though.'

For the next few minutes, every facility was swamped. A third tornado was reported outside Lawrence, in the countryside. Topeka was also threatened. Heavy hail and high winds were pounding communities on the Missouri side, too, as the activity seemed to leapfrog Kansas City in its haste to develop eastward. Going across a bank of black wall telephones, Stephens touched base with several state police offices, keeping them up-to-date. The loudspeakers said the Olathe tornado was in that city and carving a path of destruction.

The coffee in the white plastic cup tasted rancid. Stephens knew the taste was that of his own tension. *How badly was Olathe getting socked?* The tornado was still grinding northeast, following a path that roughly paralleled Interstate 35.

Stephens got a cigarette and paused for an instant as he inhaled. His eyes fell on the compact blue Nova computer directly behind the radar operator. This was part of a digitalized radar-information experiment. No one was paying much attention to it right at the moment. When lives were at stake, equipment could not always get the job done. When the chips were down, it always became a question of the people.

And not just the people here, or in the other NWS offices.

The citizens had to do their part – had to help themselves. They had to listen and be alert and know what to do.

The spotter phone sounded. Stephens picked it up.

'This is Jenkins near Olathe. I've got the tornado in view and it's back up in the cloud at this time.'

A loudspeaker grated, 'Tornado north of Olathe is in the cloud.'

Another telephone rang. 'This is Lees Summit and we have winds gusting to seventy and hail the size of golf balls.'

As he swung into new action, Stephens distantly thought of the way it was going to be someday – instantaneous communications with *every* fire department, sheriff and police chief in the area being served. This ideal had not yet been realized here, and it would be years before it could become a reality on a national scale. But one day, local weathermen would be able to push a single button and talk instantly to all officials in their areas of responsibility.

The radar repeater screen showed a burgeoning, furry clutter in all directions. The operator had switched out the Video Integrator and Processor, the selective unit on top, and had contoured the scope to look at everything in the 125-mile circle. And there was a lot to look at.

Rain hammered the glass windows of the office beyond the radar-room door. Lightning displayed brilliantly, and the sound of thunder rumbled over all the other commotion.

Chicago, Illinois
In the Chicago office of the Associated Press, the machine fed by scattered circuits around the state banged its bell several times and began to chatter. Brad Dillingham, the assistant bureau chief, went over to read the story coming in.

XXCV
Helena bjt
BULLETIN
Helena bjt
by THOMAS PIKE
HELENA, Ill. (AP) – A tornado smashed through this community of 2,700 early Wednesday afternoon, killing at least fourteen and leaving scores injured.
Property damage was estimated at more than $1 million.
The tornado, described by Helena residents as 'a great silvery snake in the sky,' roared directly through the downtown section, demolishing a large percentage of the buildings in that area.
It smashed through the Rockley Memorial High School, where at least five students were reported killed.
MORE   MORE   MORE

The machine spat the rolled paper higher, and was silent for a moment. Then the bells clanged again and the teletype-printer began slamming away once more.

BULLETIN
BULLETIN
Kirkerstown hit
by LAYMOND CRIM
KIRKERSTOWN, Ill. (AP) – A huge, roaring black tornado brought death and destruction to this small western Illinois community today. Civil defence officials said five persons are known dead.
MORE   MORE

Dillingham rolled the paper up as the machine fell silent for another few seconds, and carried the scraps of news into the other room where a dozen reporters and editors were frantically busy.

'More storms?' Dillingham's superior, a man named Gilbert, asked.

Dillingham tossed the paper down. 'Just a start. Helena and Kirkerstown.'

Gilbert scowled at the paper. He was an old-timer, and looked it. 'When will they ever learn?' he asked bitterly. 'Everybody out there thinks his tornado is the best tornado. Every clown out there types his by-line at the top like he's got the story of the century. Don't *any* of those dummies know how many tornadoes we've *got* today?'

Gilbert turned and flung the sheet of paper at a senior reporter nearby. 'Here's some more stuff for the tornado roundup. Hang loose. I've got an idea there's a lot more coming.'

Thatcher, Ohio

'Don't fire,' the voice said behind Mike Coyle, 'until you see the whites of their eyes.'

Coyle slowed his pace and let Purvis Rawlingson fall in step. Rawlingson, wearing a rumpled scarlet blazer and grey slacks, waggled his bushy eyebrows in a leer. 'Want to hear something else inspirational?'

'I guess I'll pass,' Coyle said, forcing a smile.

Rawlingson looked ahead of them down the City Hall corridor. 'Meeting Mr Glass Factory now?'

Coyle nodded. 'Meeting Mr Glass Factory.'

Rawlingson veered off to enter his own office. 'I'll just leave. Good luck, friend.'

Coyle walked on by himself. He didn't blame Rawlingson for ducking out. Bert Andrews, the president of Thatcher Glass, was not going to be in a friendly mood.

Harrigan at the Chamber of Commerce had called almost two hours ago, about eleven, to warn them that Andrews might be putting in an appearance. This was not so much a gesture of good will on Harrigan's part, although superficially the Chamber did always co-operate, as it was part of the ongoing feud between Harrigan and Andrews personally and between the glass-factory management and downtown merchants in general.

There had been a time – a very long time – when Thatcher

Glass ran the city just about as it pleased. With a payroll of almost two thousand in those days, it had had the clout to do so. In later years the plant's payroll was half what it once had been, still very large but not an overwhelming single force as it once had been. And other forces had risen : the downtown businessmen, banded together in the Chamber of Commerce, promoting different interests, seeking different priorities. Now Thatcher Glass was the city's only significant large industrial employer in Southtown. It was a vital industry. Bert Andrews wanted to use this fact as a lever to have things his own way, as his father had. It wasn't working out for him very well, but his clout guaranteed that no one else could get much done, either.

Andrews was the leading opponent of all bond questions that did not emphasize Southtown development above all else. This put him squarely at odds with the Chamber, and especially with Cecil Upshaw, whose father had been the biggest business force *north* of the river. If businesses had armies, Coyle thought, then the Thatcher Glass Knights and the Upshaw Department Store Warriors would be having it out at the middle of the Southtown Bridge right this minute.

Instead of that, Coyle thought as he entered his office, they were playing capture the flag. He was the flag.

Andrews, a heavy-set man with a sunburned bald head, was fidgeting in a waiting-room corner.

'Come in, Mr Andrews. Sorry I was held up briefly.'

'Bert,' Andrews grunted. 'You're to call me Bert. I've told you that.'

Coyle put an arm lightly over the older man's shoulders and guided him into the working office.

'I'll get right to the point,' Andrews glowered across the desk. 'People are sick and tired of these bond issues. Now it looks like you're in cahoots with Upshaw and the rest of them to start laying out propaganda for another one already.'

'The committee will probably recommend another bond election in the early fall,' Coyle agreed.

Andrews thumped a stubby fingertip on the desktop. 'There isn't going to be any more taxation in Thatcher.'

'Isn't that for the people to decide?'

'They've decided! How many times are you going to try?'

Coyle knew it was going to take awhile, this one-sided argument. Andrews and Upshaw, two of the most important individuals in the city, had never gotten along. If one backed something, the other was almost certain to be against it. Andrews had graduated from Ohio State, while Upshaw was a Notre Dame man; so it even went to football.

But right now the bond question was the football, and so was Coyle.

As Andrews went on thumping on the desktop to make his point, Coyle thought of the fine printed stationery nestling in the closet. It was a first step, so he would run for Congress, get away from this, start again. He would make *progress*.

But he had talked about progress so much that he hated the word. How often did progress mean tearing down a tradition, and erecting a quonset hut? What was wrong with staying in a job like this for the rest of your life, if you could?

But he couldn't. He was too tired. Even Andrews' cliché arguments on the bond questions right now seemed to pound into him, shrivelling him inside. He thought again of the city's problems, its splits, its intransigence . . . and then he thought about his family and everything else.

People did kill themselves, he thought. It was not so unreasonable. If you couldn't work things out, it was far better to put a clean end to it than to face years and years of being unhappy, trapped.

The session with Andrews took forty minutes. When it was finally over, Coyle left the City Hall and walked down the street to the drugstore for a cup of coffee alone, so he could think. A brisk, gusty wind drove dirt and bits of trash along the street with him. The humidity was fierce, and a halo was around the milky sun.

Norman, Oklahoma

The National Severe Storms Laboratory on the north campus of the University of Oklahoma is a long, low, contemporary structure of pink brick and horizontal slabs of concrete. The entrance is of slabbed blue glass. Beyond a small parking lot and flagpole on the south side there is a grassy knoll studded with stilt cabinets and poles containing weather-sampling devices. There is a plastic-domed radar antenna nearby. The building is numbered 1313. The federal government eschews superstition.

It was almost lunchtime at the Lab, and on the second floor Bill Fredrick had just arrived from the main campus meteorology department as part of his usual split-schedule commuting. He was at a table studying satellite photographs which showed the amazing development of the storm when the telephone-paging loudspeaker overhead came to life.

'Bill Fredrick, line two. Bill Fredrick, line two.'

Fredrick walked to a nearby office suite and picked up the telephone.

'Bill?' the voice said over a long-distance connection. 'Do you want to go chase storms?'

Fredrick recognized the voice of Van Davidson, one of America's leading research experts on violent weather. Leader of a group of scientists at the University of Michigan, Davidson worked closely with the better-known Fujita team in trying to solve the ancient riddle of precisely what triggered tornadoes, and what went on inside them.

'Are you talking about going today?' Fredrick asked.

'Today, tomorrow and maybe several days after that.'

Fredrick thought of ways he could rearrange his schedule. He was not surprised, because he had been watching the reports. 'I can get ready. What's the programme?'

'Bill, it's unbelievable. This thing is really cutting loose now. We have an enormous area we have to cover as soon as possible.'

'I know it's bad. I've been watching the wires.'

'The wires are running far behind. There just aren't enough circuits. I just talked with Ed Stephens and he's having trouble just keeping the log up-to-date.'

'What have we had? A dozen tornadoes already?'

'More like thirty, I'd guess.'

Fredrick breathed sharply. '*Thirty!*'

'Yes, and it's just getting started real good.'

'I can be ready anytime,' Fredrick decided. He boggled a little mentally at the thought of thirty tornadoes already confirmed in Davidson's mind. Characteristically, a storm outbreak brought many reports of twisters that later were not borne out. If Davidson said thirty, he had already done some probability math, and the number of reports was far higher.

And thirty tornadoes was an incredible number.

Davidson was saying, 'I've got Johnson on the other line and he has the Learjet. He can be down there for you in about an hour. You'll fly to St Louis and meet your pilot there. You'll fly in a Cessna 172. Brooks and Holding are going to be up, too, and Ted Fujita has his people getting ready. We'll co-ordinate out of Chicago.'

It was going to be a long, hard project, Fredrick thought. The usual procedure was for teams, working in light aircraft, to make aerial surveys of storm damage, taking thousands of photographs. Individual tornadoes had to be located, measured and codified by their ground track. Later, members of the Davidson team, along with people from NOAA, would move into the devastated areas and conduct interviews along with more ground-level picture-taking.

Work that hurt, because of the suffering one encountered. Work that fascinated, too – and had to be done if violent storms were ever to be better understood.

'Bill?' Davidson's voice came over the receiver now.

'Yes.'

'I thought we got cut off.'

'No.'

'Shall I send the Learjet, boy? This is the granddaddy of them all. Incredible data.'

If there had been any question in Fredrick's mind, that would have dispelled it. *Incredible data.*

'I'll be ready here at the airport,' Fredrick said.

'Great.' The connection broke.

Fredrick was left standing there for a moment, listening to the dial tone. From his desk he could look out to the west through the broad tinted windows. The sky was rapidly clearing, and a brisk north wind whipped the greening, tufted prairie grass along the adjacent airport's runways. The temperature outside was forty-six.

It would not be like this in Alabama, Fredrick thought, or in the Ohio Valley. He knew what to expect in those places. He *knew* . . . and a deep shudder of anticipation went through him.

Birmingham, Alabama
Standing behind the curtains of his upstairs study, David Kristof-sen watched the couples emerge from the cover of the mansion's front porch and make their way to the cars parked along the broad curve of the driveway.

Dark cloud overhung the estate now, and the sycamores stood deathly still in the humid heat. But the couples now departing looked happy. The swimming party evidently had been a success despite the threatening weather.

From where he stood, Kristofsen could not see his wife, Susan. But he could tell by the final smiles and waves of the departing pretty people that she was in the elegant front doorway which the porch roof screened from his view. Evidently she was being the perfect hostess right to the last.

Of course, he thought with bitterness.

Sipping his ice-cold Henry McKenna, Kristofsen watched the Busseys' Lincoln pull away from the curved curbing, move grandly past the portico, and turn out along the driveway that curled through the trees toward the street seventy yards away, beyong the ivied stone wall. The Busseys were in real estate. They were also the last to leave.

Kristofsen walked the length of his book-lined study, giving the dusty chaos of his so-called worktable a wide berth. He had worked very well at a kitchen table in a duplex, at a card table in the corner of an eight-by-ten bedroom, in a converted garage. Now he had the kind of place to work that he had always fantasized. So now, of course . . .

He left the study. He was slightly sloshed, a feeling he had begun to learn to like. He went down the curving staircase, through the empty gilt foyer, past the downstairs study and living room, and through the terrazzo-floored back-porch area to the pool patio.

The large, pear-shaped pool extended out from the patio. An irregular collar of pale-grey concrete decking around the edge made the water seem bluer and more sparkling. All around the well-kept lawn were signs of the party: little tables and chairs scattered about, still bearing the litter of paper plates, cups, utensils and scraps of food; the trestle table with the wreckage of *hors d'oeuvres* and cunning little fruit-punch bowls with scraps of decaying lemon and orange floating in their dregs; gleaming wet footprints everywhere in front of the two shake-shingle cabanas where the pretty people had changed clothes for their dip, and cigarette and cigar stubs crushed wetly here and there on the pavement.

As Kristofsen had expected, Susan was back in the pool. She was doing languid laps, her pale hair streaming free in the water, golden body and emerald bikini creating multi-coloured spangles in the foam stirred up by her strokes.

As she turned at the far end, she saw him. He held up his glass in recognition. She showed nothing, kept swimming.

Susan had come through, Kristofsen thought dully. Somehow none of it had touched Susan very much, not deeply, not where she really lived. She looked at least ten years younger than he, a stunning blond goddess. She had kept herself whole through all the bad years, and when the times had suddenly become very, very good, she had moved into the new life with an ease and grace that astounded him.

He wondered how she had made the transition so beautifully, so easily, while for him it had been a maiming. He did not think he hated her for it.

Seeing that she would not stop swimming just yet, Kristofsen walked aimlessly around the pool area. He picked up a few of the cigar butts and put them in the ashtrays that were everywhere. Some willow leaves on the lawn here, too; had to mention that to the gardener. And the vinca definitely looked shabby, needed fertilizer or something.

The door of the women's cabana stood ajar. By some impulse of curiosity, Kristofsen glanced inside before he shut it. There was a bloody tampon on the wet concrete floor along with several shredded cigarette butts and some tissues.

He stepped inside, crouched, and picked up the bloody thing. He tossed it into the wastebasket. Then, shaking inside, he raked the wet floor with his fingertips, collecting as much shredded tobacco and tissue as he possibly could. The goddamned whores, he thought. Just like it was a goddamn public restroom, and not *his house*.

Sweat dripped off his face as he went back outside. Susan was just emerging languidly from the shallow end of the pool near the patio. As she began to towel herself, water streamed down her golden body, crossing her belly and slipping into the folds of the bikini bottoms and along the sleek strength of her thighs.

'Nice party?' he asked, walking over to her.

'Yes,' she said, not looking at him.

He reached out to brush water from her shoulder with his fingertips.

She pulled back. 'Don't.'

His anger boiled. 'Why?'

'I've got suntan lotion on.'

'Are you afraid I'll get you dirty, or what?'

She looked sharply at him. 'You'll make marks.'

'If you marked that easily, Susan, you'd be covered with marks.'

'You've been drinking.'

'If you marked that easily, you'd have Paul Clinger's finger-prints all over you.'

She stopped towelling. 'What is that supposed to mean?'

'I saw the two of you in the pool a while ago.'

'So did everyone else. We were playing Marco Polo.'

'Is that what you call it?'

'You weren't even here.'

'I was in the upstairs window.'

'If you were so interested, why didn't you come down to meet people?'

'I was trying to work. Remember, work? W-O-R-K? It's something the middle-class folk do.'

'God, David, you're really drunk.'

'To hell with that. To hell with your friends, too.'

'You made that clear to them, snubbing them.'

'I gave them just what they want: the picture of the big, hard-working author so busy on his next million that he can't even come to his own party.'

'It was rude of you.'

'What was I supposed to do? Sit here for a couple of hours and watch Clinger leech all over you in the pool?'

Susan's tan became pale around her eyes, which became a most amazing and angry green. 'I told you we were playing a game.'

'He was doing everything but fucking you.'

'You wouldn't expect us to do that in public, would you?'

He went cold. 'What does *that* mean?'

'Nothing.' Coldly she stared past him.

He grabbed her arm and dragged her back.

'Let go of me, David!'

'What did you mean by that?'

'Nothing!'

'I let you have these stupid parties. I don't talk to you about what they cost.'

'I know. You talk very little to me.'

'I'm talking to you now, goddamn you! Maybe I'm just a little old-fashioned, but if you think the money lets you be some kind of a swinger with any son of a bitch that—'

She pulled loose from him. 'Let me go!'

'He was trying to make you.'

'What if he was?'

'What?'

'What if he *was*? I fended him off, didn't I?'

'*Did* you?'

'Yes, you bastard!' she spat. '*This* time I did!'

'*This* time? *Now* what the hell are you—?'

'Don't you think every woman likes to feel desirable?'

'He was practically shoving it in you right there in front of all those people!'

'Why should *you* care? You hate those people. And somebody could be fucking me seven nights a week and *you* wouldn't know it! When was the last time *you* were able to—'

He hit her.

He, who had not hit anyone since about the third grade, and then in a fight he had very quickly lost.

It was not a very effective blow. It slid off her cheek. He came nearer falling than she did. But her head shot back. She was a big girl, but the blow rocked her.

Tears bolted from her eyes as she stared at him in disbelief.

He could not believe it. He had *hit* her. He could not believe it, and an enormous self-loathing rose up to engulf him.

'Oh, hell, Susan,' he said thickly. 'I'm so sorry—'

She turned and ran into the house.

Kristofsen rubbed his eyes in continuing disbelief. Then he became aware that someone was watching. He turned and saw that the black maid had come out of the house, evidently to start cleaning up. She was an old woman in a neat dark uniform, and she was staring in horror.

'What are you staring at, you black bitch?' Kristofsen screamed. 'Get busy, goddamn you! Can't you see it's going to rain after a while?'

The maid turned to her work.

Kristofsen rushed into the house after his wife.

ZZZZZ
091800
BR 22

BULLETIN

SEVERE THUNDERSTORM WARNING
EANS REQUESTED
NATIONAL WEATHER SERVICE INDIANAPOLIS INDIANA
ISSUED 1 P.M. CDT APRIL 9, 1975

A SEVERE THUNDERSTORM WARNING IS IN EFFECT UNTIL 2 P.M.
FOR PERSONS IN THE INDIANA COUNTIES OF HENDRICKS . . .
MARION . . . HAMILTON . . . HANCOCK . . . AND MADISON.

A SEVERE THUNDERSTORM WITH DAMAGING WINDS TO 80 MPH
AND 2 INCH HAIL WAS REPORTED BY THE STATE HIGHWAY PATROL
1 MILE NORTH OF NEW WINCHESTER AT 12:45 P.M. THIS
THUNDERSTORM IS MOVING EASTWARD AND SLIGHTLY NORTHWARD
AT 30 MPH. THIS THUNDERSTORM HAS BEEN REPORTED DOING
DAMAGE TO FARM BUILDINGS IN THE NEW WINCHESTER AREA AND
HAS THE POTENTIAL FOR DEVELOPMENT OF A TORNADO.

A TORNADO WATCH REMAINS IN EFFECT FOR THE ENTIRE STATE
OF INDIANA UNTIL 6 P.M. TONIGHT.

IF THREATENING CONDITIONS ARE SIGHTED, BE PREPARED TO
MOVE TO A PLACE OF SAFETY. TO REPORT LARGE HAIL OR
DAMAGING WINDS . . . PLACE AN EMERGENCY CALL COLLECT TO
THE INDIANAPOLIS NATIONAL WEATHER SERVICE OR ASK THE
NEAREST LAW ENFORCEMENT AGENCY TO RELAY YOUR REPORT
TO THE NEAREST NATIONAL WEATHER SERVICE OFFICE.

XXX

Indianapolis, Indiana

In a hospital on the west side of Indianapolis, Frank Reynolds
stood in the emergency-room corridor with his wife, Dora, and
his older brother, Ches. Reynolds' midsection was a sour ball of
shock as he tried to read the doctor's face.

'She'll have to go directly to surgery,' the doctor said.

'What is it?' Reynolds asked huskily. 'What happened to her

when she fell?' He had this childish faith that it would be all right if he knew precisely what was damaged inside his mother's body. 'Tell me *exactly* what's wrong.'

'It was a bad fall. Her spleen is damaged. There's considerable internal bleeding. We have no alternative but immediate surgery to learn the exact extent of her injuries, and to take corrective action.'

Reynolds glanced at Dora and Ches, then back to the doctor. He swallowed hard. 'She's seventy-five years old, Doctor.'

'Mr Reynolds, we have no choice.'

Ches stirred. 'What are her chances?'

'There's no way of knowing. I would say it's fifty-fifty. Don't be pessimistic, but don't be optimistic, either. We'll just have to go in there and see.'

The family stood there, staring at him.

The doctor, whose name was Courtney, knew there was nothing more to be said. The crew in emergency had finished pumping the old woman's stomach by now and she was headed for surgery. Courtney murmured a few more words and hurried to the elevator, which carried him up to the surgical suite.

He dressed quickly and scrubbed up, and by the time he walked into the operating room, his patient was on the table. Anaesthesia was already being administered. The clock stood at 1 : 30 p.m.

Courtney gave the old woman's face only a glance, noting the poor colour and shallow breathing. It was going to be difficult.

The other doctors and nurses stood waiting. Around the table, the banks of complex life-sustaining equipment puttered softly and hummed. She was on a respirator and intravenous pacemaker.

'Well,' Courtney said cheerfully. 'Let's begin, shall we?'

Taking the scalpel, he bent over the patient's abdomen and made a long, quick, deep incision.

Thatcher, Ohio

The tiny apartment was spartan. Maid service kept it immaculate.

'They act like high-school kids on days like this,' Martin Hegstrom said as he stripped. 'Somebody says rain coming, and half of them cut class like they had to go play before their mommies make them go indoors for the rest of the day.'

Mo sinuously slipped her hardened breasts out of the filmy bra, aware of the effect her body always had on him. 'Well, Professor, sir, isn't that what you're doing, too? Playing before it rains?'

Martin grinned, and, already naked, came over to push her back on to the bed with a pleasurable roughness. 'There's probably a literary reference there somewhere, but I'm too hot to think about it.'

Mo threw her head back in pleasure as he slid her panties off and buried his face between her legs.

'And how,' he whispered in a moment, moving up on the bed beside her, 'do you propose to achieve your shocking, indecent, and absolutely marvellous multiple orgasms today?'

She could be direct with him in a way that she had never achieved with her husband. She did not know why this was so. But now, with the usual but always new feeling of complete freedom, she shoved him on to his back and deftly slipped one thigh over his hips, straddling him.

'Oh, that,' he said, trying to make it light but not quite succeeding.

Reaching down, she grasped his penis. It was huge and hard. He had never failed her. He had only half-jokingly explained to her once that this was what an affair was all about: the partner having only the best of the other person.

He was so big and engorged that, as she often did, she felt a tiny qualm as she tucked him up and inside her body. She held her breath in an agony of longing and caution, and slowly began letting herself down on his great length. He stretched her, filled her, and she settled her weight very carefully.

'Stopping there?' he taunted, watching her.

Through slitted eyes, she adored him. He was fully inside her now. His tip pressed firmly into her very deeps, nudging almost painfully against the mouth of her cervix. But her buttocks were not all the way down to his hips yet, she still held much of her weight on straining thighs.

She wriggled, tried somehow to relax herself, and sank slightly lower. There was almost real pain now, but she had almost accommodated him fully. She waited, gasping for air, her legs stabbing fatigue pains into her belly and back. She would have him all. She knew it was always possible. She rotated her hips from side to side, teasing him, stretching herself. Her nipples tingled with pleasure. Head thrown back, she closed her eyes and concentrated only on the pleasure rioting through her body.

He nudged upward at her.

With a sob, she lowered herself fully down so that her weight rested on his hips.

'Oh my God,' she breathed. 'The way you fill me *up!*'

'Shut up, lady,' he whispered, and, grasping her hips, he began to thrust.

Gasping, she began to ride.

Even at this moment there was a guilt. Across her mind flew a picture of her home, empty . . . of Billy . . . of Jill . . . of Mike. It was not right. *Why was she like this? Why was she doing this?*

She knew that she was not the same person who had begun the affair. She did not know how much longer it could endure. There would have to come a time . . . perhaps soon.

But for now there was the sensation, and she rode.

Kansas City

Fatigue had begun to send the familiar and always-frightening flutters through Ed Stephens's heart when a secretary came into the weather room to tell him about the personal telephone call. He left Buck Tatinger in Harry Adams' hands and went to his private office.

'Hello?' He got into the desk and lit a cigarette.

'Ed?' It was his wife.

'Yes.'

'You sound so hoarse, like you're extra-tense, dear.'

'I am, babe,' Stephens sighed, deeply inhaling the blessed smoke.

'They just had a little news special on TV. They showed tornadoes in several cities. Then the weatherman showed a Skywarn over practically the entire eastern half of the country.'

'Great. I'm glad they had a special. The more word we can get out, the more people are warned.'

'I thought you might want to know.'

'I'm glad you let me know.' The fluttering got very bad for a moment, catching his breath. He heaved another sigh, trying to ease the uncomfortable sensations in his chest.

'Is it so bad, Ed, that you won't be home for supper?'

'I'll tell you what, honey. Don't look for me at all tonight. I'll call later and let you know how we're doing, but whatever rest I do get tonight, it better be right here on the couch in the office.'

'Oh, Ed,' and her voice sounded worried, 'is that really wise?'

'I don't know if it's wise,' he grunted. 'It's necessary.'

'I know you haven't been feeling well some days. *When* are you going to go have a new physical?'

When, indeed? Ed Stephens had known for more than a year that it was not only time for a physical, but that a physical was clearly indicated. There were the nerves, the insomnia, the fluttering in his chest, on rare occasions even a twinge of pain. He was secretly a little scared. But if he went to the doctor and the doctor told him to take it easy – find some job with less strain – what then? *Could* he quit this job? Would he have any life without it?

'I'll see the doctor real soon,' he promised, lying.

'Have you had lunch?'

'No time.'

'Did you take your Valium to the office?'

'No, I didn't bring the goddamn Valium, babe.'

'Oh, Ed! Do you want me to bring it to you? I can drive down—'

'No. How could I take a damned tranquilizer? Don't you know I have to be just as alert as possible? This is a hell of a mess we're in on this storm system, and I'm supposed to be the boss-man!'

'But you need a tranquilizer, Ed! You've got all that responsibility, and that awful little congressman there, hanging over your shoulder—'

'I'm fine,' Stephens lied, putting a hand on his chest where he could feel the sickening lurching. 'You just sit tight, okay? We didn't lose any shingles in that wind or anything, did we?'

'No, everything is fine here. But ... I worry about you, do you know that? I *wish* you would try to take it just a little easy!'

'I am,' he told her. 'Right now, for example, I'm just talking to my girlfriend.'

'Oh, you're just impossible.'

'And I love you, old lady.'

'I love you too.'

Hanging up, Stephens finished his cigarette in the beautiful peace of the quiet office. His heart thudded and gyrated. His stomach hurt. *Take it easy*, he told himself. *Relax. It's just tension.*

He wished briefly that he could be home. It would have been nice to go home early today, and take his wife out to supper somewhere, and maybe even go somewhere different afterward, and listen to music.

God, how long had it been since they had listened to music?

He got to his feet. The storms were on the move. He had to get back to the weather room. He started down the corridor.

Halfway there, just as he passed the 'ready room,' a sharp stroke of pain rocketed through his chest. He felt dizzy and nauseated. He caught his breath and went into the washroom.

He leaned over a toilet and was thoroughly sick to his stomach.

Flushing it away, wiping his face with a wet paper towel, he found himself bathed in a cold sweat. The face that looked back at him from the mirror was the face of a stranger – chalky, bloated, with deep circles under the eyes. *My God, I'm really getting old.*

But he had to get through this. Sure, there were a dozen men out there who could handle it, but none as well as he. The responsibility was his, the job was his. He had to do it.

He leaned over the lavatory as another spasm of nausea passed through him.

'Well,' a voice boomed behind him. 'There you are.'

Stephens straightened up and turned, fighting for composure as he faced Tatinger. The congressman, pink-faced and immaculate in today's mod suit of pale green, was watching him closely, although the usual sardonic expression was on his face.

'Just taking a little breather,' Stephens said.

'I plan to do that myself,' Tatinger said, leaning toward the mirror as he brushed at his flowing hair. 'Thought I might take a little walk to clear the cobwebs.'

It would be a relief. 'You plan to come back later today?'

'Oh, I won't be gone very long. It looks to me like the fun is just starting in the Midwest. I wouldn't miss it.'

'If you consider people getting killed "fun,"' Stephens said, 'you may well be right.'

'Is that another slam?' Tatinger asked, his face blotchy. 'I'm getting a little tired of being slammed, you know.'

'Sorry, I'm tired.'

'When I get back,' Tatinger retorted, clearly angry, 'there are a number of questions I want to discuss with you. But that doesn't mean there's anything personal in it. I'm just doing my job, the same as you are. My job happens to be protecting the interests of the common taxpayer against boondoggles and featherbedding.'

'You've said that many times before, Congressman, and if I seem snippy now and then, possibly it's because you continue to insist that there *is* boondoggling and featherbedding when I know that idea is stupid.'

'We'll see, Mister Stephens. We'll see.'

Hating the man's arrogance, Stephens started for the door.

'Just remember it's not personal,' Tatinger repeated.

Stephens turned back. 'It's not personal if you imply that you intend to try to cut our appropriation? It's not personal if somebody in there loses a job, or we fail to get a new piece of needed equipment, or we lose a facility somewhere that helps me do my job?'

Tatinger's eyebrow cocked again. 'You know, you bureaucrats are all alike.'

Stephens was almost felled by the lurch in his chest. He turned, sucking wind, and rushed out of the restroom.

He went back into the confusion and noise of the weather room, with the men bumping into one another as they rushed about. He caught Bright's eye. 'What do we have on the Topeka damage and casualties?'

Bright shrugged. 'Not in yet.'

'Damn it! Call them again.' He had to get Tatinger out of his mind . . . had to get his own physical discomfort out of his mind. 'Where are the new satellite shots?'

'Five minutes, they said.'

The latest SMS-1 photos were being processed into a continuous 16mm loop. The loop, when projected, would show hours of cloud movement in moments, helping make patterns clearer.

Stephens badly wanted this new set of pictures. Reports flooding in from a dozen states continued to puzzle him: severe weather in one place, clear weather nearby, in no apparent pattern. The storm system had become an evil giant, but its precise pattern was not yet completely clear.

Another five minutes of waiting for the loop, Stephens told himself now, probably meant nothing. He was only feeling his own anxiety. The chances were strong that the pictures would only confirm what all of them already knew: they had a hell of a storm on their hands, and it was bursting out all over the place.

Like every other weatherman in the world, Stephens was not one hundred per cent sure how valuable satellite photography might become. Use of the pictures was in its infancy. It was a case of technology providing something before anyone knew exactly how to use it. Pictures from space helped locate and track hurricanes, and had other valuable uses. But much of the data from pictures was only visual confirmation of what was already known in other ways.

On Stephens's request, the satellite was not going through its usual cycle of a complete national picture every thirty minutes. The satellite had been instructed to scan only the eastern half of the United States, producing a new picture about every quarter hour. The loop that they were awaiting now would compress a number of these shots into seconds, giving a much clearer view of what was going on.

The latest individual photos had begun to indicate a cloud pattern that Stephens believed might hold the key to the mystery of conflicting reports from proximate stations, and he was all the more anxious for the five minutes to pass.

Fidgeting, he reflected briefly on how quickly new miracles were accepted. He should have been marvelling, he told himself, that the pictures were collected at all.

From the satellite twenty-two thousand miles out in space, the feeble radio signals, compressed onboard by a minicomputer, were beamed to a thirty-foot, dish-type antenna at Suitland, Maryland. There the signals were 'massaged' – partially unscrambled – and then sent to the World Weather Building nearby where another team of computers further refined them and put them in picture format. The entire process, from camera to print, took only about seven minutes, and much of that time was in the picture printing, the simplest procedure involved.

No one could look at a satellite picture and tell which clouds might be developing tornadoes. But the height of clouds was one correlative to intensity, and their pattern sometimes gave valuable tips, too.

Harry Adams hurried across the room. 'First report on Topeka.'

'What is it?'

Everyone in the room paused to listen.

'Looks like eight or nine dead, about twenty injured.'

Someone whistled grimly.

'They got off real, real light,' Adams pointed out.

'All the warnings worked.'

Bright called from the door of the communications centre, 'Another tornado at Paducah.'

'In the city?'

'In the city.'

'I'm trying to keep a total,' Adams said. 'That has to make thirty-five we can be sure about.'

'I want more information ón Topeka. Where were the people killed? Why didn't they get the warning? What's the first estimate on total property damage? Are we sure there was just one funnel?'

Adams nodded as he studied wire reports. 'Large hail in Detroit. We didn't expand the watch into Michigan any too soon.'

'It's clear into Canada now.'

'I know, and this line down here by Peoria is really very bad. Tops over fifty thousand. Then it weakens a little bit, but it's bad through this part of Kentucky.'

'The biggest clouds of all are down in Alabama,' Stephens pointed out needlessly.

'Well, we've had four tornadoes for sure down there. Huntsville has this unbelievable line of echoes solidly to their west. Tuscaloosa is getting the hell pounded out of it right now.'

'Huntsville?'

'Not yet. They had some patches of sunshine a few minutes ago.'

'This squall line is acting very peculiarly.'

Both men knew that the actual passage of a frontal system did not always carry the worst severe weather. Often, for reasons not fully understood, a squall line will form fifty to one hundred miles ahead of the actual front. Sometimes the squall line passes, dumping the worst weather, then leaving a gap of amazingly gentle conditions between it and the parent frontal system.

Deviations from normal expectations all over the country, and especially in Alabama, led Stephens to believe that there might not be just one squall line in front of the system. There might be parts of two. The satellite pictures might confirm or disprove the theory, and he hoped he was wrong because two squall lines meant double trouble.

'Where's that satellite loop?' Stephens muttered again.

'More names on the report, here,' Adams grunted as another man hurriedly wrote the locations of more reported tornadoes on the clipboard.

Stephens glanced down the lengthening list : Lincoln, Decatur and Anchor in Illinois; Paducah and two other small Kentucky communities; towns in Missouri, Arkansas, Alabama. Scanning the list, he had a sinking sensation because he knew the worst was probably all ahead. If this system followed the norm, the time period between about 4 p.m. and midnight would see the most tornado reports.

Bright came out of the communications centre. 'Bloomington, Indiana.'

'In the city?'

'On the edge.'

'Christ.'

'Here's the satellite loop.'

Four of them went into the enclosed room, shutting the door behind them. Stephens quickly threaded the loop of film into the projector. He started the motor. 'Okay. Lights.'

As Adams punched the overhead light buttons, Stephens started the projector bulb and drive mechanism. On the portable screen across the room, a swirl of grey and white appeared in a rectangle of brilliance. It took only moments for the loop to complete itself and start over, so that the cloud movements seemed almost to pulse and fall back again.

'My *God*, that thing is moving!' someone said.

'Look at the pattern,' Stephens snapped. 'Look at the pattern.'

A great swath of dense cloud angled across the centre of America, denoting the low-pressure system and its fronts. Far out in front of it, into Pennsylvania, West Virginia, North Carolina and Georgia, another clearlý defined line of cloud could be seen building.

In the haze across Ohio, Kentucky, Tennessee and Alabama, a second line was clearly formed and on the move.

A third line extended through Illinois and part of Indiana.

'*Three* squall lines?' Harry Adams said incredulously.

There was no doubt about it, and all the questions were answered ... the reports of clear skies between stations reporting bad weather, the strange pattern of the clear reports, the violence popping up in so many separated places at once.

Each squall line was developing its own severe thunderstorms. The loop showed how swiftly they were building, and moving eastward.

Many areas were going to be hit not just one time by killer storms, but two or three times.

'Speak,' Stephens commanded no one in particular as the loop ran yet another time.

No one replied, and the silence, marked only by the ratcheting of the projector, attested to the gravity of the situation far more adequately than any words.

Monument Valley, Kentucky
'And who would like just a little more pie?' Milly Tyler asked.

Her grandsons, Kent and Adrian, groaned in unison. Under the yellow glow of the electric light, turned on against the gathering afternoon darkness, both boys looked puffy and flushed.

'No?' Milly asked, pretending surprise. 'Land! Do you city boys fill up that easily?'

'I had three pieces already!' Adrian gasped.

'I had *four!*' Kent topped him.

'Foof. They don't make boys the way they used to. I remember when your father would eat an entire berry pie by himself, and then ask for jellybread.'

'Yeah, but he's fat!' Adrian explained.

'Well, he's gotten a little plump. I agree with you about that.'

'I'd eat a lot more,' Kent said, 'but it's just too hot.'

'It *is* sultry,' Milly agreed. 'Why don't you two go outside and cool off while I wash the dishes, all right? Then we'll talk about what to do next.'

Turgidly, the boys obeyed, practically waddling out of the kitchen. Pleased with herself, Milly began putting dishes in the sink. When she had them all in, she pumped up about three inches of well water, enough to cover everything. Then she carried the big iron pot from the stove, careful with the heavy potholders, and poured in sizzling hot water until she judged the dishwater would be just right. After putting the pot back on the wood stove, she began doing the dishes rapidly, sloshing them in and out of the Ivory Flakes and then dipping them in the pan of rinse water before putting them in the yellow plastic rack on the drainboard behind the pump handle.

The visit so far was going nicely. Milly knew Thomas and Nina worried that the tykes would be too much for her. Actually, the reverse tended to be nearer the truth: the hike into the woods had left her fresh, but the boys worn out. They were good boys, but city boys. All the good food on top of a little exercise would likely put them flat on their backs for a nap pretty soon. Then she would enjoy the quiet, having artfully arranged it for herself, and smoke a pipe.

The pipe always seemed to taste better on rainy days, and it was going to rain soon now.

'Grammaw!' Kent called from the front door.

'What is it?'

'There's a guy here to see you.'

Adrian yelled, 'He's got a red truck!'

That would be Jason, the Lovetts' hired boy, Milly thought. She went through the parlour to the front porch and found the gawky Jason standing beside his ancient Ford pickup. The tykes were staring up at him as if he were a king or something. Jason was skinny and pimply, homely as could be, but he was a good boy, too. The Lovetts were lucky to have him.

'Hello there, Jason. What brings you by this time of day?'

'Hello, Miz Tyler. I wondered if you have any old canvas or other kind of tarp material around?'

'Canvas? Well, no, Jason. But I do have some heavy plastic sheeting back in the shed. You're welcome to use that if you like. Do you mind if I ask what you need it for?'

'The cow is fixing to have her calf. That's why I got out of school early, to come check on her. And she's fixing to calve real soon. I've got her in the Lovetts' little shed, but you know how beat up it is, and it's going to come a rain. I thought I could rig some extra shelter for her.'

'Well, the plastic is in my shed, Jason.'

'A calf!' Kent gasped. 'A cow is gonna have a calf?'

'It's not a very earth-shaking event,' Milly said.

'*I* never saw a cow have no calf!'

'Me neither!' Adrian added.

'How does a cow have a calf, anyway?'

Jason said, 'I'll go get the plastic.'

'I'll help!' Kent yelled, and loped after him.

'Me too!' Adrian yelled, and followed.

Milly sighed at the thought of boys practically into their teens who had never seen a birthing. That was the way life was in the city. You never got close to anything. My land, you got your vegetables in plastic bags instead of covered with honest dirt; you never noticed when it got too hot or too cold; you didn't have to work for anything like your water. In a modern city you never got very close to what life was really all about.

Milly had a great many theories that explained problems of the modern world for her, and one of them went to why the younger generation spent so much time standing around on street corners and defying parental authority: the children had no idea what life was really about. When the most you had ever had to worry about was whether the thermostat was set at 72 or 73, you had lots of time for mischief. And when you had known no more adversity in your entire life than a wet diaper – and then only for the length of time it took Momma or Daddy to sprint to change you the first time you bellowed – it was easy to imagine you were immune from anything bad happening, and could risk assaulting the whole civilized world. If children knew the facts of life and a little deprivation and consequently some honest fear, Milly reasoned, they would be a lot better off. And a lot more cautious about the games they played with other people's lives.

Kent and Adrian, never even seeing a birthing, were a good example of the sort of thing Milly was thinking about. What kind of view of reality did you have, for heaven's sake, when you didn't even know how life began, with pain and blood? No *wonder* the younger generation was such a mess; they didn't even know how it started. If you didn't know even that, it followed that you could get all kinds of related crazy misconceptions in your head, like no one ever had to suffer in this world, and nothing could happen to you no matter what you did, and the world was a benevolent place that owed you a living.

Milly was not, under these circumstances, disturbed when Kent and Adrian legged it back around the house ahead of Jason, their loginess forgotten.

'Jason says we can go!' Kent yelled.

'Can we, Grammaw?' Adrian pleaded. 'Can we? Huh? Please?'

'Go where?' Milly asked, playing dumb.

'With Jason! To see the cow!'

'Yeah!' Adrian said. 'And we won't get dirty, Grammaw, we *promise!*'

'And we won't talk to strangers,' Kent added.

'And we won't talk dirty,' Adrian added to the litany, 'and we won't throw rocks, and we won't—'

'Land!' Milly sighed as Jason tossed the big roll of blue plastic into the back of the pickup. 'Did you tell these boys they could come with you, Jason?'

Jason grinned. 'Sure, if they want.'

'They won't get in your road?'

'They won't get in my road at all. I might even let 'em help.'

'See?' Kent jumped up and down. 'So, can we go? Can we?'

'*Please?*' Adrian added.

'I don't see why not,' Milly said, 'provided—'

'Yippee!'

'Yow!'

'—provided,' Mill repeated sternly, 'you do exactly what Jason tells you—'

'We will!'

'Yeah! We promise!'

'—and provided you can have them back by six, Jason.'

'No problem,' Jason said. 'Mr and Mrs Lovett ought to be back from work about five-thirty, and I have to get back into town this evening for my evening class.'

'You go to school *at night?*' Kent asked.

'Part of my classes, yes.'

'Ugh! Why?'

'Because I have to,' Jason replied soberly. 'I have to work for a living part of the daytime schedule. But I have to get my education, too. Nobody ever got anywhere in this world without his education.'

Right on, Jason.

'Don't your mom and dad take care of you?' Adrian asked.

'They're dead,' Jason said. 'I take care of myself.'

The two small boys looked up solemnly at the seventeen-year-old. Yes, Milly thought, this visit might be good for the tykes in more ways than one.

'You'd better get along,' she said. 'That old cow might not wait.'

'Can we ride in the back?' Kent asked, climbing up on to the tailgate.

'No,' Jason said. 'Road's bumpy. Ride up here with me.'

The two boys obeyed instantly. Jason started the truck, backed out, and drove down the road, with the two boys waving excitedly as if they were going to the North Pole rather than one mile up the road to the east. Milly waved back, and, when they had gone out of sight beyond the willows, fished her pipe out of her apron.

Spotnose emerged from hiding under the porch.

Distant thunder rolled, like great iron dominoes falling in line. The sound echoed a long time from mountain to mountain. Overhead, the clouds were low and in constant agitated motion. The sense of oppressive humidity was stronger than before.

'I believe I might just turn on the radio,' Milly told Spotnose. 'Do you see all that black out beyond Steptoe Mountain, kitty? I'm not sure I like the looks of that.'

She went into her house.

Indianapolis, Indiana

A particularly large and energy-charged cumulonimbus cloud discharged one of its many lightning bolts just west of Indianapolis. The charge of 175,000 amperes crashed blue-white into a power substation. Chunks of metal flew under the impact and sparks showered in all directions. Wires, kicking flame from their severed ends, lashed like whips along the ground. Instantly the grass on the hillside around the lonely transformer site was licked by hundreds of little tongues of flame.

The main lines carrying power out of the site and into the high-power lines above were broken. They twisted in the smoky air and then hung listless.

The outage at the substation created a peak drain along more than three hundred miles of lines in the immediate area. Safety switches slammed, and about a hundred and forty square miles suddenly had no electricity at all.

In the hospital operating room, the lights went off without warning. The life-sustaining equipment around Dr Courtney's patient stopped too, and for a shocked instant there was nothing but total blackness and an incredibly complete silence.

Courtney stopped exactly where he was, with his hands inside the old woman. 'Lights!'

'Emergency unit will come on in ten seconds, Doctor.'

'Is the goddamned equipment all shut down too?'

'Some of them, but the—'

The lights flickered and came on. All around the table, life-sustaining equipment filled the silence with whispers of re-assurance: little motors hummed, a valve wheezed, air moved, blood was pumped.

Courtney breathed again.

'Doctor.' The nurse spoke just as Courtney realized what had happened.

To hell with why. To bloody hell with precisely how.

The patient was fibrillating.

Courtney barked orders as he went to external heart massage. Each time his fist smacked on to the back of his hand on the old woman's chest, her lungs grunted air. The monitor showed wildly ineffective heart activity.

'Pressure is sixty,' someone said. 'Fifty ... forty ... pressure is—'

'Shoot that directly into the heart muscle!' Courtney told a doctor rushing over with a syringe of digitalis. 'Nurse, hurry with that goddamned machine!' He grabbed the leads from the equip-ment, ready to apply electric shock in an attempt to galvanize the heart into activity.

Fifteen minutes later, he walked slowly from the operating area. He was drained and stunned out of all proportion to the loss of one elderly patient. It had been going so well. And then the power failure ... only a few seconds ... but enough. *Enough.*

Courtney wondered bitterly how he was going to explain it to those people waiting downstairs. *'I'm sorry, your mother was killed by a power failure. I'm sorry, your mother was killed by lightning, probably. These things happen. Tough.'*

He knew he would not try to explain it all. How did you ex-plain blind, insane bad luck?

The old woman would not be counted as among casualties of the storm, which at this hour stood at 118 known dead, about 450 injured.

Birmingham, Alabama

Standing in front of the typewriter with the drink he didn't want, David Kristofsen tried foggily to think about what to do with this life that he no longer wanted, either. Susan was locked in the bedroom, and outside, the storm had broken: rain pounded the casement windows of the study, and for the first time since they had lived in the old house, the howl of wind penetrated sharply, making bits of cut glass in the chandelier vibrate and turn in the stillness.

The force of the wind was actually making the old house tremble.

Kristofsen walked across the study to the windows that looked out of the front of the house. Rain, driven parallel to the ground by the shrieking wind, obscured even the nearest trees, which whipped in agony. The driveway was flooded. The rain pounded on the glass like soft hammers.

He remembered that he had stood here only a little while ago, watching the guests leave. He should not have gone downstairs then. He should not have had the stupid fight with Susan, all of it tied somehow to the wretched stimulus of that bloody tampon tossed onto the floor of the cabana . . . tied to the vivid visualization he had had, of some sleek, supposed friend, pulling it out and tossing it down, not caring because they would never know which one had done it, and so it was all right.

Somehow that unseen act symbolized so much of what sickened him about their lives now. He thought of the line from Fitzgerald about careless people, going along without thought, wrecking lives.

He had fought about that with Susan upstairs just a few minutes ago, after he had struck her and she had rushed away. He had followed and tried to apologize, and then they were screaming at each other again.

'Do you know what one of your fine, upstanding friends did in the cabana?' He knew he was practically hysterical, that it wouldn't make sense to her. But he told her.

'What difference does *that* make?' Susan had cried.

'It makes all the difference. Oh, Christ, don't you see? It makes *all* the difference! That's what they are. That's what they think of us. Throw your goddamned *rag* on the floor, let us pick it up! It's the – the—' He boggled, fighting for the word – 'the *brutality* of it, don't you see that?'

She started to turn away.

'Don't turn your back on me! I'm trying to talk to you!'

'Is that what you came in here for?' She had stripped off the bikini, and stood there before him stark naked, every muscle magnificently tense with anger. 'I thought maybe you wanted to hit me again.'

'I'm sorry. I told you that. I'm *sorry!*'

Again she started to turn away.

He took her arm. 'Talk to me. Please!'

'Is there anything to say, David?'

'Oh, Christ,' he groaned. 'Now are we going to get the ice-maiden act?'

'There's nothing to say!'

He tried. He tried bleakly as she put on a white terry-cloth robe and began brushing her hair, her back to him. He tried to explain about the book and how nothing in life went right for a man when the book was going so badly. He tried to explain how frightened he was. His voice began shaking as he went on because she did not respond, remained with her back to him as if she didn't hear, and he was torn by the urge to grab her, hit her again.

He was amazed.

The first blow had been a kind of accident. It had sprung from unsuspected depths. But now he wanted to hit her again, and more carefully. He wanted to feel his knuckles mash facial bone, break cartilage, cave in teeth. He wanted her down, on the floor, on her knees, and he wanted to pound her, make her pay—

—for *what?*

Outside, then, the rain had begun suddenly, and hard. It silenced him for a moment and gave Susan the chance to walk to the window and look out.

Her face was glacial. So very calm and under control.

'It's storming,' she said.

That was how she had beaten him.

She was so strong . . . too strong for him. With a woman's strength, she could reject him at will. The one strength that woman had learned over the centuries was this one, the one no man could overcome: the power to freeze, go inside herself, become a waxen statue whose remoteness could kill something in a man without a word being spoken.

Kristofsen knew he had strengths . . . had had strengths, once. But these did not equip him to deal with this kind of ultimate rejection any more than a big-game hunter was qualified, or a caveman might have been qualified, or a president. Women talked so much of love, and yet this was their final use of love. And Susan would never yield from this stance now unless he wooed her again, slowly fawned over her and tried to win her back again, showed his abjectness, pretended good humour when there was no good humour, feigned happiness out of agony, cut off his own balls and wagged around her like a snivelling urchin puppy, coming on himself if she so much as petted his head.

The self-loathing Kristofsen felt as he realized this was so intense that he had bolted from the bedroom to the study. Then he stood at the typewriter ... sterile typewriter ... and thought of how he should have explained himself, what he should have said, the speeches and replies marching through his head like dialogue in a book.

You always come back to this typewriter, he thought. You have a failure, and you come back to work it out. You have a success, and you come back to prove that it wasn't a fluke and you can do it again. This machine is at the centre of your existence, and now it has failed you too. But if you give it up, you have nothing left.

Standing at the window, Kristofsen felt that the storm in some way mirrored his own inner conflict. It was big enough, fierce enough, with destruction enough within it. Ah, God, to be a Shakespeare and to be able to work it out truly in all the words that were *really* the right words to carry this weight!

He sipped his whisky. *Kill your brain*, he thought in a new spasm of self-hate.

The storm increased its intensity, raging with a wild fury. Rain screamed through the wind, battering at the glass. Trees were bent double. He could not see the wall gate or the street beyond. Everything was darkening. There was a sharp peppering sound on the stone walls and the roof, and Kristofsen saw that small hail had begun plunging down with astonishing volume and force. Each tiny fragment of ice hit the flooded driveway hard, bouncing six feet into the air and falling again. Everything was covered with it in seconds.

Lightning veined the black clouds. Thunder slammed, making the floor vibrate. Bits of tree limbs and shrubs flew through the air. More lightning crashed, very close, red in his peripheral vision, and the thunder rocked him.

The rain was even harder. The driveway had become a lake out into the trees. Over the wind's roar came a sharp breaking sound, and he saw an old oak split, teeter, and fall. The rain was suddenly cold because his breath fogged the window glass. He rubbed a spot in the fog with his fingers. The glass was cold. The glass was trembling.

A new sound came over all the others, a continuous insane hammering. Bigger hail, the size of grapefruits, hurtled down.

It was darker. Much darker. Very fast.

There was another new sound, a great banshee roar.

Panic struck cold fingers into Kristofsen's gut. He dropped his drink and ran for the door. As he grabbed the doorknob, something crashed behind him and cold wind swept in. The window had imploded, glass flying like diamonds, wind and rain and hail filling the room. White things flew everywhere: manuscript pages.

Kristofsen got the door open and was propelled by the wind into the hall. Susan had run from the bedroom. Her face was slack with terror.

He grabbed her hand and pulled her toward the stairs.

There was a very loud *cracking* sound. The house staggered. The hallway chandelier swung spastically and came down, and part of the ceiling came down, too, and *there was no roof there*, just open sky and the rain lashing in.

Kristofsen dragged Susan down the stairs, which bucked like they were made of rubber. He had a crazy instant's recollection of a fun house. *Next we slide through the barrel.* A piece of plastered ceiling fell past them and smashed to bits on the downstairs foyer floor.

He got to the downstairs. A huge mirror on the inside wall fell, crushing a table. The front door blew open, torn from its hinges. The lights went out. Lightning pulsed vividly into the foyer through the rain. From somewhere far away came the distant sound of a siren, but then it was lost again in the screaming of the storm.

There was a closet beneath the staircase. Kristofsen pulled the door open. The wind tearing through the house almost knocked him off his feet, but he held on to Susan and pushed her into the closet ahead of him where she sprawled against something – Christ, his stupid golfclubs.

There was no thought in Kristofsen now of the property. Even the manuscript made no difference. He was terrified, and everything had been stripped away except for one overwhelming certainty.

He wanted to *live*.

He threw himself into the closet on top of his wife, trying to shield her with his body, and around them was the hellish sound of the house being torn to pieces.

Thatcher, Ohio

Earlier, it had been possible to see that Thatcher lay under an immense shelf of cloud extending from horizon to horizon, north and south. Now, as Mike Coyle walked to the police station, he noticed that the clouds had moved farther over the area and extended in all directions solidly. The deck seemed to have lowered, too, and here and there lighter grey puffs scudded along rapidly, swirling as they travelled generally northeast. It was warm and a little windy. Without the breeze, the humidity would have been stifling; Coyle could not ever recall the air being any closer or more oppressive.

In the back room of the station, window air conditioners chugged away, dripping puddles of moisture on to the cheap carpet of the squad room. One policeman, a man named Hendrix, was having coffee.

'Hope you have your umbrella, Mr Mayor,' Hendrix said.

'We need umbrellas under those window units, Sam.'

'Never saw 'em sweat that bad.'

'Is the chief around?'

'Yes sir, in his office.'

Chief Merrill had a window air conditioner, too, but he was working in his shirtsleeves and there were large dark stains of sweat under his arms. He looked up from his paperwork with an expression almost like relief as Coyle entered.

'Busy?' Coyle asked.

'Nothing that can't wait, sir.'

'What's new on the weather wire?'

'I just looked at it. They're having some rough stuff to the west.'

'Moving this way?'

'Yes sir, it looks like it. Of course we don't have anything to worry about. The river would turn any tornado or anything like that. You know the Indian legend.'

Coyle hesitated. He felt a little silly, yielding to his slight concern. He recognized that he was partly idling away some time, doing something that he had some control over after the frustration of trying to deal with Bert Andrews. But it was part of his job, too.

'If things do get hairy,' he said finally, 'will we have some spotters out?'

'Well, you know the emergency plan, sir. We'll send a car over to the west side, and one south of the river. And I was talking to the sheriff's office a few minutes ago, and old crazy Barney is already out there somewhere.'

'Barney Reilly?'

Merrill grinned. 'Who else?'

'Barney is a good deputy.'

'Yeah, but you know how he is. He's a nut on bad weather. He must cost the county a thousand bucks a year, just chasing around after clouds.'

'Well, he's from tornado country, right?'

'Yeah, Bluejacket, Oklahoma. But, good lord, he's lived up here ten years now. He ought to know we don't have storms like Oklahoma does.'

Coyle did not comment on this. He had heard Barney Reilly on the Civil Defence radio during a thunderstorm passage. Reilly was considered eccentric, or worse, by just about everybody. A thoroughly likeable man, and completely dependable, he went ape when storms threatened. The sheriff had long since given up, and let the man drive out wherever he wished at times like this. It didn't do any harm, the sheriff said, and when you had a good man, you humoured him a little.

'We haven't sounded the sirens or anything, have we?' Coyle asked now.

Merrill frowned. 'No, sir. This is just a watch. You don't blow the sirens unless you have a warning – you know, a storm coming right at you. We've never had that.'

'When you tested the sirens last month, some of them didn't work.'

'Two. That's right. The one in Liberty Heights, and one of them south of the river.'

'Have they been fixed?'

Merrill's forehead wrinkled. 'By golly, now that you mention it,

I don't remember.' He turned to a pile of papers. 'That report ought to be in here somewhere.'

'It's not that important, probably.'

Merrill shuffled around. 'Well, now, just a minute. I'm sure that information ought to be right here . . .'

Coyle waited and controlled his impatience. He knew which areas of the city were covered by sirens, and which were probably too far from the nearest unit to hear. Except for a partisan debate on the Council a year ago, Thatcher could have had new sirens and complete coverage. But the same old split had wrecked everything. Each of the 128-decibel sirens cost about $7,000, after all, the opposition said, and even with matching funds from Washington meeting half the cost, that was a lot. When the city was so strapped for operating funds, and running new bond elections up the flagpole every thirty minutes, how the hell could a responsible councilman vote to buy a bunch of new gadgets that were never used anyway?

Some of the sirens dated back to Korean War days, when installation had been part of the military buildup. These were so old that it was a miracle if they worked at all. Others, installed hit-and-miss fashion in later years, did not provide overlapping coverage in all areas. In the last test, the Liberty Heights siren hadn't worked at all, and one of only two units south of the river had wailed for a few seconds, then issued a wisp of smoke before falling silent.

The police, with city maintenance-crew help, had been ordered to check them out.

'Here we go,' Merrill said now, pulling some papers out of the pile. 'Hum. Looks like Liberty Heights was fixed. We haven't tested it yet. I guess we should have remembered to do that. Now on the one south of the river, let's see . . . Here we are . . . Nope . . . It's burned up. We sent the guts to Columbus, but we haven't heard yet whether they can fix it or not.'

Coyle returned to his own office. The sky was darker. He thought about what might happen if severe weather ever did move into the city. Back at his desk, he made some notes for a presentation to Council next week. They would vote it down, six to four, but he would at least try.

He called his home and talked to Mo. She said Jill was working at the hospital again this afternoon and might miss supper. Billy had called from school and said he wouldn't be home until later, either. He and some friends are going to do some cruising, he said.

'Cruising,' Coyle repeated. 'Great.'

'Mike.'

'Okay, okay. I'll try to get home early. Maybe we can go out to eat or something.'

'If the weather comes along as bad as Ed said it might, I imagine we'll be happy to settle for sandwiches at home.'

'Well, think about supper out. Unless you're too tired from your shopping.'

'Shopping?'

'I tried to reach you a while ago and you weren't home.'

There was a slight pause. 'I had to go get just a few things.'

'Well, think about supper out, then, okay? Meantime, we'll see how much of an alarmist old Ed really is these days.'

Wednesday, April 9   2:45 p.m.–3 p.m.

XC56YYO
081
ZZZZZ

BULLETIN
TORNADO WARNING
EANS REQUESTED
NATIONAL WEATHER SERVICE NASHVILLE TENNESSEE
ISSUED 3 P.M. CDT APRIL 9, 1975

A TORNADO WARNING IS IN EFFECT UNTIL 4 P.M. FOR PERSONS IN
THE TENNESSEE COUNTIES OF TROUSDALE ... MACAN ... AND CLAY.

A TORNADO WAS REPORTED BY THE PUBLIC 4 MILES NORTHEAST
OF HARTSVILLE AT 2:50 P.M. THIS TORNADO IS CONFIRMED BY
RADAR AND IS MOVING TO THE NORTHEAST AT 35 MPH.

THE TORNADO WARNING ISSUED AT 2:25 P.M. IS STILL IN EFFECT
FOR PERSONS IN OVERTON AND FENTRESS COUNTIES. THIS TORNADO
IS STILL ON THE GROUND AND IS BEING TRACKED BY SPOTTERS
AND RADAR. IT IS PRESENTLY AT OR NEAR THE COMMUNITY OF
TWINTON AND IS MOVING TO THE NORTHEAST AT ABOUT 40 MPH.

IF THREATENING CONDITIONS ARE SIGHTED ... BE PREPARED TO
MOVE TO A PLACE OF SAFETY. TO REPORT A TORNADO ... PLACE
AN EMERGENCY CALL COLLECT TO THE NASHVILLE TENNESSEE
NATIONAL WEATHER SERVICE OR ASK THE NEAREST LAW
ENFORCEMENT AGENCY TO RELAY YOUR REPORT TO THE NEAREST
NATIONAL WEATHER SERVICE OFFICE.

XXX

The storm system lay across the heartland of America, moving
eastward at speeds sometimes approaching seventy miles per
hour. It continued to draw cold polar air down its west side and
tropical maritime air up from the Gulf in its path, mixing the ingredients to create new cloud colossi along each of its three squall
lines.

There were by now five clouds in the system that towered over
sixty-five thousand feet. Warm air rushed up through these
clouds so rapidly that it burst into the stratosphere, an invisible

fountain of new turbulence in the strong winds aloft.

Blizzard conditions extended into central Nebraska now. Where creeks still raced out of control beyond their banks, snowflakes mixed into the slippery mud. Red dust rode into Oklahoma on winds gusting to fifty knots. In Clear Creek, West Virginia, the temperature hit eighty-four degrees, and an amateur meteorologist rechecked his instruments when his wet-bulb reading showed a relative humidity of 80 per cent.

Near South Bend, Indiana, a bank of blue-black cloud dropped a white funnel approximately one-quarter mile in diameter. Moving in excellent light under the cloud, the tornado cut across a large riverbed, which tornadoes were really not supposed to do, destroyed a farmhouse and some outbuildings, changed direction slightly to the north, and moved into the community of North Liberty. Within two minutes, the town was a tangled wreckage, its streets covered with broken trees and power poles, houses smashed beyond recognition. The same cloud was seen just south of Elkhart a few minutes later, but the funnel was aloft.

Near Bowling Green, Kentucky, a farmer named Hoffbreener was alone in his home, reading a newspaper. He noticed that the light was failing and got up to turn on a floor lamp. He happened to glance outside and saw a big maple tree sail by like a low-flying aeroplane. He ran to his back door and dived into his storm cellar just as the house started flying to pieces behind him. Hoffbreener had earlier filled out a coupon for insurance information in the newspaper he left behind. A woman in Columbia, more than sixty miles east, would find the newspaper in her back yard the next morning and mail it back to Hoffbreener.

In Dickson, Tennessee, a high-school boy named Cameron was out in his 1956 Chevrolet sedan, joy riding with his girlfriend after they had both cut afternoon classes. They were astonished to see a tornado dip out of a cloud and into a field only a few hundred yards to the left of their position on the highway. The girl began crying. The boy didn't know what to do, so he kept driving. The funnel moved to the road, picked up the car and tossed it four hundred yards down an embankment, and crushed it, killing both occupants.

Nearby, after the same twister or a related one, a farmer named Coverton drove through a driving rainstorm to his neighbour's farm because he had seen the tornado pass very close to the neighbour's house. The house was smashed and the neighbour couple were wandering around in a daze. Trying to get them under some kind of shelter from the rain, Coverton led them to the chicken house, which appeared miraculously unscathed. Opening the rickety door, Coverton found the floor covered with feathers. Fourteen fine hens sat on their roosts, stone-dead and as naked as if they had been plucked by a careful hand. A local science teacher was later quoted as saying this phenomenon had been reported before. It had something to do, possibly, with the intense low pressure of the passing tornado drastically changing the air pressure inside the feather quills so that they exploded out of the skin.

In northern Alabama, a vicious hailstorm swept across a prize beef ranch. The owner went out minutes later to find seven head of cattle battered to death by hailstones measuring five inches in diameter. Four more head were destroyed later when they could not be salvaged from similar injuries.

Flash flooding ravaged more than fifty towns in Missouri, northeastern Oklahoma, northern Arkansas, Indiana, Illinois, Kentucky, Tennessee and Alabama. Messages crackled across the wire network reserved for river information. Flash-flood warnings were sent out by centres in Smithville, Missouri; Joliet and Willow Spring, Illinois; Barbourville, Cumberland and Williamsburg, Kentucky; Baton Rouge, Louisiana; Bartlesville, Oklahoma, and others. Near Brookport, Illinois, an old man, living alone in a house on the edge of the stream, stood on the roof of his front porch and watched the rescue boat putter up to save him. As he prepared to step into the boat, he heard his dog yapping in the house. Telling his rescuers to wait just a minute, the old man went back inside the house through a bedroom window. Seconds later, the entire house tipped and slid down the muddy bank into the full current of the river, turning on its side and being swept downstream. It would be six hours before the old man's body would be fished out of the house where it wedged under a bridge. The dog would still be yapping, and would be saved.

In a town called Duncan, in Tennessee, a small tornado struck without any advance warning from local spotters. Two hundred and twenty-eight houses were smashed and many others badly damaged. Survivors wandered around in a daze, in a town that looked like a huge pile of kindling. The Red Cross would count eighty-seven dead. Duncan, being in a valley between high mountains, had always assumed a tornado could not strike there. Also, being in a valley made local TV reception poor, and every home that had a set was on the cable. While television stations in Nashville were breaking into programming to warn of radar echoes that indicated Duncan was threatened, the local Duncan TV sets were turned to a rerun of 'I Love Lucy,' broadcast from New Orleans, where the weather was only blustery.

Even those television viewers receiving accurate local bulletins from live TV were likely to be getting it from less-than-expert hands. Of the two hundred and fifty major market cities in the United States, only about seventy had a professional meteorologist on their staff. All the others doing weather were only announcers, commercial readers or 'weather girls' who simply read the wire with no real understanding of what it was all about.

In Louisville, two couples met as prearranged at a suburban motel, rented a room, had group sex, and took turns taking pictures of various couplings by each other. Some drinking was done, and a cassette player was maintained playing prerecorded tapes at a fairly high sound level to mask the sounds of the bed activity. When one of the women finally happened to part the closed draperies an inch or so to glance outside, she nearly fainted. The street and parking lot were full of emergency vehicles. Power poles were down, and the shopping centre across the highway was a disaster. A tornado had passed within a hundred yards of the motel while they were playing. The two couples dressed hurriedly and departed, legal partners together. One couple went from the motel directly to a church and prayed a long time.

Straight winds gusting over one hundred miles per hour smashed windows in Chicago. A plate-glass store front collapsed, decapitating a customer.

And still the storm grew, feeding upon itself.

Huntington, West Virginia

Smoothing her skirt over a snug hip, Donna Fields walked into the lounge. It was a long, narrow room, very dark and intimate, with black leather booths and only the dull glow of soft lights off bottles and glasses behind the bar for illumination. Donna immediately saw him in a booth toward the rear. She walked back toward him, savouring her power. She walked slowly, hips undulating, proud of her body and what it had won for her.

She slid into the booth facing him. 'Hello, darling.'

George Abrams looked older today, perhaps as a result of her telephone call and the explicit language she had used to get him here. Even in the dimness the haggard quality around his eyes was apparent. His business suit, of course, was very expensive and perfectly right; so were his blunt, manicured hands, the freshly trimmed neatness of his iron-grey hair, the cut of his silver-blue tie. But he seemed somehow shrunken inside the expensive clothing, the everyday armour of his political wars.

When he spoke, however, Abrams's voice was under steel control. 'All right, Donna. Let's make this fast, shall we?'

'You're not going to buy me a drink?' Donna turned and signalled the bartender. 'Oh, but I want a drink.'

'Goddamn you, Donna.'

The bartender came over. She ordered a whisky sour. Abrams waved the man away. Donna said nothing until the bartender had come back with her drink, and then she continued to be silent while Abrams stared at his folded hands on the tabletop. She would force him to lead the conversation at first. She was enjoying this.

Finally he looked up. 'You said it was urgent.'

'Yes.'

'What do you want?'

'Money, love.'

'You bitch.'

'Is that any way to talk to your mistress, darling?'

His hands became impotent fists. 'You were never that. A few casual meetings—'

She laughed softly. 'Is that what you call them now? My God! I'd like to see what you call a *serious* night! When I think of some of the things you did to me ... and had me do to you. Yum. Casual? I—'

'I don't have much time, damn you! Tell me what you want!'

'Just a little money right now, love.'

'I don't have any money.'

'Of course you have money. Or you can find money. You have a family and further political ambitions. I think you'll find the money to keep me happy. When I'm unhappy, you know, I tend to want to pour my sorrows out to other people – sometimes total strangers. If I were to be very sad, and tell certain people about some of our fun and games together—'

'No one would believe you,' Abrams said, although he had paled. 'You can't trick me into blackmail.'

'Did you know,' Donna asked sweetly, 'that I had a tape recorder in my bag a couple of those times? Like the night in the Poconos.'

Abrams visibly flinched. His eyes burned into her. 'Tapes?'

She sighed. 'After Watergate, I know that's dreadfully unoriginal. *Another* politician biting the dust behind a tape recorder? It almost strains one's credulity, yes? But they are nice little tapes. Some of the sounds and instructions are really shocking. I'm sure your wife, for example, would be terribly shocked.'

'It won't work,' Abrams grated. 'I won't pay.'

'Your famous voice comes through several times with remarkable fidelity, sweet. Isn't that a funny word to use under the circumstances? Fidelity? I made a pun.'

'Listen, you little whore, if you think—'

'Name-calling? Naughty, naughty. Can't we be calm and rational about this? I have a service – silence – and you have the ability to purchase that silence. It's a simple enough transaction.'

Abrams's face was well known. But no television camera had ever seen the hardness that was in his face now.

'How much?'

'This time, ten thousand.'

'I don't have that kind of money!'

'Oh, of course you do, love. I read yesterday that your campaign treasure chest is already past the hundred-thousand-dollar figure.'

'I can't dip into that!'

'I don't care what you dip into, George. I just have this need for my ten thousand.'

'Suppose I just tell you to go to hell?'

'Then, to be sordid about it, your wife will receive a nice letter and a copy of the tapes. So will the opposition and two television stations.'

Abrams's expression was so shocked and anguished that Donna reached across to pat his hand patronizingly.

She said, 'Don't take it so badly, darling. I won't be too harsh in my demands. Ever.'

'This is just the first instalment, is that it?'

She examined, without feeling, the face that had become havoc. 'Let's just say that you played, and now you begin to pay. I certainly don't anticipate being too greedy. I have a standard of living to uphold, and that does cost money. But it's certainly far better for me if you remain happily married and happily in public office. I won't ruin you. I'll just ask for my small share.'

Abrams stared at his hands, which balled and opened spasmodically on the tabletop. 'You want cash, I assume.'

'Yes, please.'

'Where and when?'

'You can have it deposited in my account, dear. And anytime tomorrow will be just fine.'

'How do I get that much cash by tomorrow? How do I get it into your account without being recognized? I can't run that risk—!'

Donna patted his hand again and quickly slipped out of the booth. 'You'll manage, George. Good-bye for now.'

She walked out of the lounge. She was very, very pleased with herself. She knew he would meet the demands . . . this time and the time after that, and on and on. He could not afford to do otherwise.

It felt so good, not just the prospect of all that lovely money, but knowing that now he would dance to *her* song, do as *she* demanded. Through him, she would have her revenge on all men.

The feeling of power surged within her so strongly that she shuddered with the pleasure of it. As she walked, she realized that she was quite wet between the thighs.

As she got into her Ghia, the first raindrops pattered down.

Near Kingfisher, Missouri

At the end of a brief, sizzling flight north in the Learjet, Bill Fredrick was met by a research-team co-ordinator, Phil Gates, and a trim, youthful woman wearing a lemon-coloured sweater and matching miniskirt. Her name was Barbara James, and she was to be the pilot of his Cessna for the low-altitude tracking of tornadoes that had passed only hours earlier.

Gates filled Fredrick in on radio frequencies and co-ordination matters, handed him some charts with hasty numbers X'd in, and hurried off somewhere else. Fredrick took this and his camera and recording gear to the Cessna 172 parked nearby and climbed aboard.

Barbara James started the aircraft, and within moments they were climbing away from the airport. Fredrick glanced at the sweet line of leg revealed by the tiny skirt as she manipulated a rudder pedal.

She glanced at him. 'Anything wrong?'

'I've never had a woman pilot on one of these jobs before,' Fredrick admitted.

'I can fly,' she said rather grimly, setting her pert chin.

'It's the legs that are distracting.'

She instantly cooled. 'Enjoy. But I think I should tell you that my boy friend is a leftside cornerback for the Denver Broncos. He's already uptight about some of my flying jobs. Just last month a man on a charter got a little fresh. I told Danny. The guy gets out of the hospital next month.'

'Okay,' Fredrick grinned. 'That wasn't what I had in mind anyway, but we understand each other.'

'It's just that Danny gets so violent sometimes. It scares me. He's six-three, two-thirty-five.'

'Lady,' Fredrick told her, 'relax. My wife, whom I love, frightens *me*. She's five feet, ninety-nine.'

Barbara James looked quickly at him and grinned. 'Okay!'

That had been an hour earlier, and now the sky was fast clearing over north-central Missouri. A strong north wind buffeted the Cessna as it descended through four thousand feet toward rolling hills ahead. Fredrick, in the right-hand seat, slammed a film cartridge into another of his Leicas, then bent over between the seats to get a cassette tape recorder ready. A jounce in the air almost made him drop the recorder.

'Sorry,' Barbara James murmured.

Fredrick recovered. 'Not as bumpy as it was for a while there, anyway.'

She nodded as she trimmed the controls. 'Bumpier at lower altitudes. That north wind has plenty of oomph. I must have a thirty-degree course correction set in, and we're still drifting a little.'

'How cold is it?'

She flipped the sunshade up momentarily to peer through the top of the windshield at a thermometer set outside. 'Right at zero centigrade.'

They were flying in an area now well behind the front. Although high cloud formed a scud over portions of the sky above them, and to the south, the sky was clear to the west and north. Off on the eastern horizon, the tops of gigantic cumulonimbus stood golden in the sunlight.

Fredrick consulted the area chart. 'Is that Kingfisher Mountain off to the right, there?'

'If it ain't, we're durn sure lost.'

Fredrick sat up in the seat to see better over the nose. 'That ought to be Frederickville up there, then.' He could see breaks in the rolling green countryside and a tin roof glinting in the sun.

'Named after you, I guess,' Barbara James said.

'Spelled different.'

'Shame.'

Fredrick turned on the cassette machine and spoke into the microphone. 'Two-fifty the afternoon of Wednesday, April ninth. Near Kingfisher Mountain, Missouri. First report, the Farmington tornado, identified on the preliminary Davidson-Fujita list as number thirty-seven. Track not yet sighted.'

Barbara James banked the plane slightly. 'Think I've got it over here.'

Fredrick peered out of his window as the plane came around, still descending. Below, the ground rolled along under a blanket of timber. As Barbara James manoeuvred and pointed, Fredrick quickly spotted the break in the green – a yellow streak across the woods like a fresh firebreak.

'That's it,' Fredrick said.

She brought the Cessna around along a descending path that would intersect, then parallel, the path of destruction. They had now slipped below the altitude from which Farmington was in view behind a series of hills, but the view of the tornado path was very good.

Fredrick clipped the microphone to his lapel and dictated as he began shooting pictures. 'The point of origin is an estimated twenty-five statute miles southwest of Farmington, near Dean Mountain. The beginning point of the tornado track is very clearly defined by a broad circular splotch of fallen timber, and the track heads northeast on a line toward the town.

'At the point where the track begins, large trees can be seen thrown outward to all points of the compass as if a single explosive downdraft marked onset of rotation. After this initial downdraft, marked by severe throwing and splintering of trees up to at least two feet in diameter, trees along the path suggest that rotation began almost instantaneously in the usual counterclockwise way. Trees along the path after initial impact are strewn in circular fall patterns both left and right.

'The path is approximately one-eighth-mile wide along the entire length presently being photographed. The bright object in the photos on the first magazine, first camera, appears to be a felled windmill of some kind, but there is no sign of habitation in this area.'

Fredrick kept snapping pictures. As Barbara James levelled the plane and swept along the path of felled timber, Fredrick tried to keep his voice from showing the excitement he always felt at times like these. 'This was a powerful tornado. Some trees show evidence of being thrown all the way down the hillside. At an altitude of—' He glanced at Barbara James. He knew they were five hundred feet above ground level, but wanted altimeter figures.

'Thirty-one hundred,' she said.

'—thirty-one hundred feet, some of these trees can be seen to be old and well-developed. Ahead I have a deep ravine in view, and the tornado went right down the side of the hill into the ravine, crossed a brook, and went up the far side, angling across that hill as if it did not exist. The track continues through rough country, and there are some frames in here toward the end of the roll that show the earth torn up alongside a county road. The single-lane concrete bridge appears to have been broken in half, and some of the pieces aren't there any more.'

As the Cessna continued to drift along the path, big flaps extended as Barbara James used slow-flight technique, Fredrick kept talking as he worked and reloaded the cameras. This was only one of many tornadoes he had tracked, and, as far as he could tell, not a very special one. But it had had power and it had continued for miles, and the straightness of its path was remarkably true. Many tornadoes that chose to run along for miles did show a fairly straight course for at least a part of their lives, but this one seemed to have moved as if it had some fiendish navigation system of its own.

The tornado also further served to continue the mounting pile of evidence against the old theory that terrain could seriously affect a twister. There had been cases where a hillside or river evidently turned a tornado from its original path because of friction or something similar, but since the studies of the April 3, 1974, storms, the theory was in considerable disarray. The Fujita team at that time had found a tornado which touched down in a valley in northwest Georgia, climbed a 3,500-foot mountain, and went down the other side with sustained power. In southern Kentucky, tornadoes had run along adjacent valleys. In the Brandenburg area, a funnel had crossed a wide section of the Ohio River, doing serious damage on both sides. It was a myth, presumably, that terrain could save any location from a tornado, although many still believed it. Fredrick was pleased to have more evidence to help bury the old idea.

'The track seems to narrow somewhat as we approach the hills blocking our view of Farmington,' he dictated now. 'The track appears straight toward Farmington. We are now moving over the hills and getting our first view of Farmington.'

Ahead, the broad yellow path of destruction went straight and true, and there in the path was a broad area of barrenness. It looked like a great open sore. The pattern of a highway was faintly discernible. The area was strewn with toothpicks and tin cans, only the toothpicks were lumber, the tin cans cars and trucks.

A water tower lay on its side. Wisps of pale smoke moved up from mounds of blackened wreckage, and the wind carried them off in long, inky stains. Fredrick could see felled power poles, shattered roofs, here and there a broken wall or part of a chimney. Foundations glowed grey in the sunlight, and lots that had been vacant before noon today were green and less littered.

Fredrick saw some people standing in one of these clearings, and nearby was the flashing red of ambulances or police cars. Some of the people looked up as the Cessna passed over. Their faces glinted pale for a split second, then were gone. No one waved.

'We have the town in view,' Fredrick said huskily as Barbara James swung the plane around for a second pass. Then Fredrick got busy with the cameras, but he did not speak again right away, or for some time.

*

Kansas City

Ed Stephens knew that his job needed the press. It was the news media that carried the warning message, very often, when a storm was threatening a community. Every year, men from NSSFC and other agencies travelled the country, fulfilling speaking engagements, trying to increase public awareness of what severe-weather warnings were all about. Therefore, even though he considered many reporters ill-informed pests who got as many things wrong as they got right, Stephens had a personal vow to handle the press gently whenever possible.

The reporter from the Kansas City *Times* was testing that resolve at the moment.

His name was Patterson, and he had been in the weather room for some time. Several people had given him some answers, but he was waiting for Stephens. He wanted an interview for the next paper. Although he was sorely tempted to point out that he simply could not spare even a few minutes right now, Stephens finally relented and tried to be cheerful about it as he took Patterson back down the corridor to the administrative offices, and then into his own corner room.

Sunlight was bright beyond the tinted windows.

Patterson was a tall man, young, with a scant dark beard. A cigarette dangled from his lips and he squinted through the smoke. 'I'll try not to keep you too long, Mr Stephens.'

'I want to be helpful if I can,' Stephens said politely.

'What do you think characterizes the situation at this hour, in layman's terms?'

In layman's terms. That was the trouble. You could not avoid oversimplifying some of these things if you used layman's terms.

Stephens, however, tried. His chest hurt a little.

'We have three bands of storm activity extending from Canada almost to the Gulf Coast. There are three exceptional hot spots right now. One is just west of Brandenburg, Kentucky. One is not far away, in a place called Monument Valley. The third is here northeast of Birmingham. Birmingham was just hit, hard.'

'Wasn't Brandenburg hit hard just a year or two ago?'

'Unfortunately, that's right.'

'Does your radar show a lot of tornadoes right now?'

'Our own radar looks out only two hundred and fifty miles. We can get facsimile pictures of other radar sites spotted around the country, and we have teletype information. But that isn't the way it works. Once we know that a broad area is a possible target for severe weather, we issue a watch. These are studied and updated, changed if necessary. After that, it's essentially your local National Weather Service office that gets information and issues the local alerts.'

Patterson looked irritated, and his tone betrayed it. 'I'm not interested in technicalities, and neither are my readers. Do you have some bad storms other than the three places you mentioned, or don't you?'

Stephens swallowed his harsh reply. You ran into reporters, especially some young ones, who thought you did business that way, by conducting a mini-Inquisition instead of an interview. Patterson was not being irritating by accident; it was his technique. Mike Wallace and Dan Rather had not done journalism education a service with some of their performances on the tube.

Again, however, Stephens tried.

'We have several cells – clouds – that extend up to an altitude of sixty-five thousand feet. That's a fantastic height for a cloud of this nature. The energy is unbelievable. I'd bet those clouds are producing tornadoes.'

'You'd bet? Don't you know?'

'I could check the wires. That isn't my job at the moment. Others out there are keeping tabs.'

'Keeping tabs?' Patterson's jawline hardened as he tried to look menacing. 'Isn't there something more you ought to be doing?'

'Like what?' Stephens asked.

'I don't know. I'm asking you. People are getting killed out there. I'm asking what you're doing about it.'

'Everything you saw out there in the other room. The local offices are working their heads off.'

'Don't local news media get out most of the information?'

'Yes, to the public. They get it from us.'

'What about people out in the country, where there isn't a local TV station?'

'There's always a radio station fairly nearby. Hopefully, they might be in range of a NOAA weather station. Those are very important.' Stephens wanted to talk about these.

Patterson waved it aside. 'What if they don't have a radio?'

Stephens sighed. 'Then we hope they're watching the clouds.'

'If a person has a sturdy house, won't he be all right, nine times out of ten? Aren't most of these houses that get wrecked really kind of flimsy houses?'

'No. That's not true.'

'Houses I see in tornado pictures always look like trash.'

'You're seeing them after the tornado has thrashed them, friend.'

Patterson's eyes glinted. 'Will a well-built house survive?'

'Directly in the path of a tornado?'

'Yes.'

'No,' Stephens said firmly. 'No way. The ordinary well-built home simply can't hope to stand up to the kind of forces we're talking about here. Straight winds themselves may cause structural damage at these velocities. With a tornado, you also have twisting forces, wind speeds that exceed two hundred miles per hour, tremendous pressure differentials. We've seen pressure drops of twenty millibars on a barometer when a tornado passed close by. The instrument simply goes down all the way to the bottom peg. Most modern structures leak a lot of air, and there are different opinions on this, but I personally believe that the pressure drop outside a structure can be so sharp – so fast and so severe – that parts of the building simply explode. That's the theory behind the old idea of opening a few windows when a tornado is coming close. I still don't think it's a bad idea.'

Patterson was scribbling notes swiftly. 'Anything else a tornado may do to you?'

'Sure. At those wind speeds, you have all sorts of projectiles flying around: boards, signs, planks, rods, power poles, steel I-beams—'

'I find it hard to believe that you very often see a damned steel I-beam flying around.'

'They fly,' Stephens said, maintaining his cool, 'and they hit things. It's not uncommon to find pieces of poles or trees driven right through the walls of houses. I've seen a steel I-beam weighing six hundred pounds carried several hundred yards and driven four feet into the ground.'

'But newer houses, made of brick, sitting on a good basement, will stand up to a lot, right?'

'Not to a tornado.'

'No?'

'A brick-veneer house is one of the worst kinds. The bricks fly off like confetti. And people at Texas Tech, where they're doing a lot of work on structural damage caused by severe weather, suggest that older houses, seated on raised foundations with a crawl space, may actually sustain less damage than the kind you're talking about. Houses like that will slide off their foundations, and absorb a hell of a lot of energy in the process. The fixed structure will just start coming unglued.'

'Wait a minute, wait a minute,' Patterson grunted, his pencil flying.

Stephens obeyed. Although he had been rationing out his cigarettes to himself all day, and wasn't supposed to have another for twenty minutes, he lighted up. He wondered what was going on in the weather room. Well, they knew where he was.

Patterson caught up. 'What does a person do if he sees a tornado coming?'

'Depends on where you are. If you're in a car, for example, and can clearly see that the thing isn't bearing right down on you, you might figure out which way it is going, and then drive in the other direction. But often that isn't possible, and you're safer in a ditch, even, than in a car, which usually gets tumbled and smashed.'

'In a house what do you do?'

'If you have a cellar, get in it.'

'Aren't cellars a little old-fashioned?'

'Not in parts of the country where they have a lot of these things. You can buy a prefabricated concrete shelter for about a thousand dollars, and it takes only a couple of days to install it.'

'Well, fine. But what if you don't have a shelter like that?'

'If there are public shelters, and there's time—'

'No public shelter,' Patterson snapped irritably, 'and no basement. *Now* what?'

'Say a prayer, for one thing.'

'I'm trying to be serious, Mr Stephens.'

'So am I, friend. So am I. If you've never been in one of these things, there is no way you can imagine what it's like. All the laws of physics seem repealed. You face forces that nothing in your previous experience has equipped you to deal with. Shock and stark terror are common reactions.'

'Because you see everything getting ruined, yeah,' Patterson said impatiently.

'Because you're afraid you're going to *die*.'

'So where do you go if you're stuck in your house?'

'Away from windows. A central hallway is often best. A bathroom may be good. The plumbing in a bathroom gives the walls extra reinforcing, the pipes. The southwest corner, contrary to popular opinion, may be the worst place to hide.'

'Should you get under a bed or something like that?'

Stephens wondered where Patterson had come from. 'No, because the thing you get under might fall on you. It might not hurt to wrap in a blanket or mattress—'

'Could houses be made tornado-proof?'

'I seriously doubt it. Not at a cost anybody could afford, and not in a style anyone would want to live in. Concrete pillboxes aren't that fashionable. But I have,' Stephens added, sensing Patterson's hostility rising again, 'seen studies that indicate most American homes could be provided a small, storm-proof closet that would cost only a few hundred dollars.'

'How would they work?'

'An existing hallway or closet would be braced up with extra timber in the walls and overhead.'

'Why aren't homes already built with a place like that in them?'

'Why aren't homes built with automatic sprinkler systems for fires, or complete burglar-alarm systems as standard equipment? Money. People generally won't pay the extra cost just for a somewhat safer place that they think they'll never need.'

Patterson grinned. 'Sounds to me, sir, like you guys haven't been doing a very good job selling the public.'

The stab of rage almost made Stephens say something regrettable. He caught it just in time.

'Well,' he said quietly, 'we've tried. Maybe you're right.'

'You said something about pillboxes. Would that be a good building for heavy weather?'

'Steel-reinforced concrete buildings hold up fairly well, although they do sustain some damage.'

'How about schools? Are they pretty good generally?'

'The old ones are stouter, but they're a horror because of all the windows, the threat of broken glass flying all over the place.

Many newer schools are constructed out of modular steel panels, with open-girder roofing and the like. They're not that strong. Gymnasiums and cafeterias are usually the worst-hit part of a modern school, because the roof spans are so long in those areas. Modern schools are often just like most of your newer grocery stores, motels, other prefab metal structures. I wouldn't want to be in any of them if a bad storm was coming.'

'If you were a school administrator, what would you do? Run?'

'No. I'd have copies of an excellent NOAA booklet on school safety in storms – and I'd follow what the booklet says.'

'I noticed reports of damage to trailer homes all over the place. Is that what they do? Roll along and collapse? Are they okay if you tie them down?'

'Some are better than others, but if you don't tie them down, they will roll over and over and be crushed.'

'And if you do tie them down?'

'It helps, sometimes, but sometimes the trailer squashes *inside* the tie-down. Paradoxically, trailers are too well sealed for their own good; they don't leak, and a tornado pressure change can explode them.'

'Why do so many people live in the things, then?'

'Probably because they like them, or can't afford anything more substantial. Or maybe they figure they won't get hit. I don't have the precise figures at my fingertips, but the chances of a given point being hit by a tornado are really pretty slim, you know.'

'Tell that to the people getting hit today.'

Stephens smiled grimly. 'That's why we're here.' He rubbed his aching chest.

'And yet you're so calm about it,' Patterson snapped.

The word surprised Stephens. 'Calm?'

'All this wreckage! All this suffering! And you sit here, puffing cigarettes, like you were talking about laboratory animals!'

Stephens stared at the unpleasant young man, struggling with a flash-point temper. 'I'm not calm.'

'You certainly look it to me.'

'I'm not calm. I've missed a couple of meals, and I'll miss some more. I've missed some sleep and I'll miss some more of that, too. I'm doing everything I can to get warnings out, just like everybody else here is – like everyone is across the country. What are we supposed to do? Get hysterical? Scream and shout? What goddamned good would any of that do?'

Surprisingly, Patterson grinned as he jotted a note. Then he looked up as he put his pen in his pocket. 'So you *do* care. Good. I was just testing.'

'Get out,' Stephens barked. 'I've got work to do.'

XXXXXXXXC
284
ZZZZZ

BULLETIN
TORNADO WARNING
EANS REQUESTED
NATIONAL WEATHER SERVICE LOUISVILLE KENTUCKY

ISSUED 2:50 P.M. CDT APRIL 9, 1975

A TORNADO WARNING IS IN EFFECT UNTIL 5 P.M. FOR PERSONS IN
THE KENTUCKY COUNTIES OF LATIMER, JENKINS, FLOYD,
FRANKLIN AND JONES.

A TORNADO WAS REPORTED BY THE PUBLIC 7 MILES NORTH OF
CLINE AT 2:38 P.M. THIS TORNADO IS MOVING TO THE NORTH
AT 35 MPH.

A FUNNEL CLOUD ALOFT WAS REPORTED BY THE POLICE AT
BAXTER SPRINGS AT 2:39 P.M. THIS FUNNEL CLOUD IS MOVING
NORTHEAST AT 40 MPH. HIGH WINDS AND HAIL UP TO 1 INCH
IN DIAMETER HAVE BEEN REPORTED NEAR THIS CLOUD.

A TORNADO WATCH REMAINS IN EFFECT FOR THE ENTIRE STATE OF
KENTUCKY. THIS WATCH IS VALID UNTIL 8 P.M. THIS WEDNESDAY
NIGHT.

IF THREATENING CONDITIONS ARE SIGHTED . . . BE PREPARED TO
MOVE TO A PLACE OF SAFETY. TO REPORT A TORNADO . . . PLACE
AN EMERGENCY COLLECT CALL TO THE LOUISVILLE NATIONAL
WEATHER SERVICE OR ASK THE NEAREST LAW ENFORCEMENT
AGENCY TO RELAY YOUR REPORT TO THE NEAREST NATIONAL
WEATHER SERVICE OFFICE.

XXX

Monument Valley, Kentucky
The old radio in Milly Tyler's kitchen had scarcely warmed up
when it abruptly went dead in the middle of whatever irritating
song it was playing at the moment. At the same time, the kitchen
seemed unusually quiet against the backdrop of wind humming
outside, and Milly realized that her electric refrigerator and clock
had also stopped.

She went into the living room and flicked light switches there, getting no results. The room was grey, as if it were evening.

'Foof,' Milly said to herself.

Not that power failures were so uncommon in this isolated rural portion of Monument Valley. Once every month or two, the lights flickered or went out for a few minutes. Once, the power had been off for seven hours. This failure, however, was especially irritating because Milly wanted to hear what the weatherman had to say. She was beginning to be just a little uneasy about the clouds. She did not want Kent and Adrian soaked to the skin if she could avoid it.

Relighting her pipe, Milly walked to the front porch. A freshening hot wind buffeted her, carrying sparks out of the Barling's bowl. The clouds overhead had lowered and darkened, and the underlayer now had a shape and texture that reminded Milly of marshmallows, the way they looked when they were melting into the hot chocolate. Each big marshmallow was ivory-coloured in the centre, and in the interstices was a blue-green brightness as if the clear sky was trying to shine through.

The clouds seemed to be rushing in all directions.

Milly looked out southwest, toward Steptoe Mountain.

It was much darker in that direction. She saw one particular cloud that appeared very dark and very tall, moving fast over the mountain from the south. She saw another dark cloud to her left, moving toward Steptoe Mountain from this opposite direction, which seemed very odd.

High wind sang overhead.

As Milly watched, the two darker clouds, trailing others in the general marshmallow texture of the sky, continued to sweep rapidly toward one another. They were still miles apart but definitely on a collision course. A bolt of lightning forked down from the near cloud, and this was answered immediately by bright explosions of light inside the far one. It was as if the two were speaking to one another.

Wind gusted, first hot and then cool. Dust flew. Thunder rolled, rattling windows of the house. The trees in the yard bent and lashed under a new gust. Then it was hot and still again, and out toward Steptoe, across the miles, the two clouds had moved with amazing swiftness and were starting to move together.

Milly's uneasiness grew. She *knew* there could not be a tornado in Monument Valley. But she had never seen clouds act exactly like this before, and the smell of the air itself was odd, too: muggy, dank, with a funny electric odour. She suddenly wished she had not let the two boys leave her side.

It might not be a bad idea to call the Lovett house, she thought. The Lovetts had an extension bell on their telephone outside so they could hear it when they were gardening. If she let it ring a long time, the sound might reach Jason and the boys in the shed and they might answer it.

She went inside and lifted the telephone receiver. It was dead.

'No lights,' Milly fumed, 'no radio, no telephone. Land! Doesn't *anything* work around here any more?'

Distant thunder called her back to the porch.

Dust blew thickly in the air. The electric odour was stronger. Thunder growled continuously. Bracing herself against the porch post, Milly looked again toward the mountain.

The two clouds had come together and increased sharply in size. Their blue-black base enveloped Steptoe Mountain. Off to one side there was an area of pale-greenish clarity, and even at that great distance Milly could clearly see that the cloud above this greenish space was moving rapidly, in rotation.

As she stared, a long grey-blue tendril extended down from the cloud base. It danced for a moment, and then went back up.

Milly held her breath.

Two more tendrils came down, danced around each other, moved back up. Then another. But this one came down farther, was thicker at its base, changed colour as it extended itself, glowed with internal green lighning.

The tendril began to go back up as two others appeared. But the main one did not go all the way back up. It maintained its position, extending halfway downward toward the placid side of Steptoe itself. Then it moved on down, lengthening, and reached the side of the mountain. It instantly changed colour to a blacker hue, and began to twist.

'No,' Milly said aloud.

It was impossible.

The clouds overhead rushed along now, flying toward the funnel. The wind howled.

Jason would be busy with the cow. The boys would be watching *him*, not the sky. The plastic, stretched above them for extra shelter, would block off most of the view unless someone purposefully walked out from under it to look, which was not very likely. Milly could not call them and they would not have a radio; the houses along here shared a power line.

They had to be warned, and Milly was the only one who could do it.

Dropping her beloved pipe, she ran off the porch, across the yard, into the roadway. She started east, running clumsily, the wind a heavy pressure at her back.

Birmingham, Alabama

The insane racket outside the closet had begun to subside. The roar had diminished, and the sounds now were different – wind and thunder and the sounds of water.

It took a long time for David Kristofsen's shocked senses to register these facts.

Finally he opened his eyes. Light was leaking through cracks in the walls. He was wet; water was dripping onto him from above.

Rain.

How could it be raining inside the house?

Susan was crying softly beneath him.

Kristofsen sat up. 'Susan. Are you okay?'

'Yes,' she said hoarsely. 'I – think so.'

'It's all right. Everything is fine now. We're safe. The closet held together. '

'What *happened?*'

'I don't know. It had to be a tornado, I guess.'

They sat huddled together. There was not very much light. Kristofsen was so shaky he was not sure he could stand, but they were getting wetter by the minute and he had to know now what was outside. He feared this knowing.

'Susan, I'm going to open this door.'

'No!'

'It's all right now. It's all right.'

She said nothing, trembling violently.

He said, 'I'm afraid it might be bad out there. Our house might be all torn up.' He had a strange impulse to shield her from seeing it, if the house was severely damaged. It was as if he were responsible.

He got shakily to his feet, grasped the doorknob, mentally braced himself, and pushed. The door swung back a few feet, grating, and then hit something and stuck.

Rain was pounding down in the foyer. A bright-greyish light bathed walls and carpet streaming rainwater. There were chunks of plaster and pieces of panelling everywhere.

Kristofsen emerged from the closet.

The front wall of the house was not there any more. He stood in the foyer with the rain beating down on him and could look out through a crazy geometry of fallen timbers and broken rock, past a V-slashed framework of wreckage formed by the caved-in front porch, into the flooded driveway and lawn beyond. The driveway looked like dump trucks of trash had been unloaded. The trees – those still standing – were draped with things that looked like bedsheets and clothing.

Turning, Kristofsen saw that the front portion of the east wing of the house had vanished. Looking up the staircase, he could see into what resembled a crude cutaway drawing of a construction project: walls sheared off, with protruding studding; the upstairs floor, sagging disastrously in the middle, broken cleanly so that joists and subflooring stuck out like the edges of a thatched roof; then more ruined walls higher up, the partially collapsed roof-line high above, open to the sky, rain pouring down from solid grey clouds. The storm had cut a huge pie-slice out of the house from top to bottom, and there was rubble everywhere: boards, planks, broken stone, pieces of roofing and tile, strips of sheet metal, broken furniture, shredded insulation, shattered doors, Sheetrock, Masonite, ripped carpeting, ruined paintings in ruptured frames, smashed tables, chairs, lamps, dressers, cabinets.

Fire sirens sang in the distance.

Kristofsen saw that the west side of the foyer tilted crazily, signifying that the entire west wing had been twisted, wrenched off plumb. There was not a right angle anywhere. He could not get a familiar line for reference, and for an instant was dizzied by the feeling that he was utterly lost, in some new dimension.

Behind him, Susan cried out brokenly. He turned in time to see the shocked expression on her face as she emerged from hiding.

'We're okay,' he told her quickly. 'We're okay. We made it.'

'The house,' she said. 'The *house*.'

'The staircase held, see? It saved us.' He pointed to the intact staircase. Rain was running down the carpeted steps in a little waterfall.

Susan turned all the way around, her eyes holding a look that Kristofsen knew he would never forget.

'It's . . . ruined,' she said dazedly.

'It doesn't matter, Susan. We're alive.'

Her eyes changed. 'Mrs Jackson!'

The maid. Kristofsen had forgotten her. He boggled for a moment, trying to think where first to look. Of course she was all right, he told himself. In the west wing. In the kitchen?

Clambering over a pile of wet plaster and other rubble, he made it to the west-wing corridor. The door was stuck, but he wrenched it open. The hallway beyond the door seemed intact, but it was not square any more. Kristofsen moved through the hall, aware of his wife close behind him. Ahead he could see into the large kitchen. There was a counter with dirty dishes on it, still intact. He took new hope.

'Mrs Jackson?' he called.

There was no reply.

He entered the kitchen, aware as he did so that the light was not normal: it was grey, but much too bright.

The back wall of the kitchen had been mostly windows. This wall was not there any more. It had been knocked in, filling the kitchen with jewel-like shards of broken glass which coated every surface. The big copper exhaust hood over the range had come down, bringing part of the ceiling with it. A great tree limb, bigger around than Kristofsen's thigh, and with dozens of smaller branches and countless rain-shiny green leaves still attached, had been hurled into the room and now lay across the middle of the floor, straddling a smashed worktable.

Susan pressed past Kristofsen and skirted the mounded debris. She looked down and then she screamed.

Kristofsen climbed through the mess to get to her side.

Mrs Jackson had been working at the sink area fronting the glass wall when it was crushed or blown inward. The maid had taken the full impact of flying glass and perhaps the tree limb itself. She lay sprawled on the floor, face up horribly, arms and legs akimbo, and there was absolutely no doubt that she had died instantly.

Susan put her hands over her face and began to sob. Kristofsen clumsily tried to put his arm around her.

She pulled away. 'No. Don't touch me.'

He looked at her, shocked.

'I can't stand it,' she choked, 'and if you touch me—'

She left it unsaid, but he suddenly understood. Touch now would break the last shreds of her control.

A memory he hadn't known was still in his head came back instantly. It went back to high school, his first year. One of the dreams, then, had been about sports. He had gone out for the football team quite confident that it was the beginning of a glorious career. On the fifth day of practice, before he had so much as gotten into a scrimmage, the coach had gently told him to turn it in.

The practices had been a continuing little hell, a series of demonstrations that he was neither big enough nor fast enough to be much of a player, and the coach's speech had left him only numbed. He was ashamed, but he told himself he could live with it; he went home and announced at the supper table that at least he had been honoured in the very first group to be cut.

Which might have ended it.

But that night, late, just as he was about to go to sleep, he had been startled to see his door open, his father come into the room. His father sat on the bed in the dark and awkwardly spoke for what seemed a very long time about life and its disappointments. And when his father finally went away, Kristofsen had lain there in the dark and felt the tendrils of his father's kindness and love move around in his consciousness, and the kindness broke his control, and he cried, fighting to stifle the sounds, for a long time.

Kristofsen knelt beside Mrs Jackson's body now. He carefully pulled her skirt down to cover her knees. Taking off his rain-soaked sweater, he covered her face. He could not think of anything more to do. He felt as if something within him had withdrawn to a very great distance. He was shivering. He was not cold.

Taking Susan's hand, he led her through the broken wall to the rear patio, littered with debris. By some fluke, the fragile roof over the patio was intact, and sheltered them from the rain. He headed along the back of the house, intending to re-enter through the living room.

'My God, look!' Susan said.

She pointed into the yard.

The big trees had been shattered, broken off to jagged stumps. One old elm had been uprooted and lay on its side, its great root ball filling the area where the twin cabanas had been. There was no sign of the two little buildings except the slab foundations. The yard looked like a scene from a war movie, total devastation.

Then Kristofsen realized that Susan was not looking at any of this, but at the pool itself.

The pool, a long, curved, concrete shell, was empty. The funnel had sucked out forty thousands gallons of water and taken it off somewhere else.

Lightning sizzled overhead. The enormous thunderclap drove them into the house again.

Thatcher, Ohio

'I suppose I can't make you change your mind,' Thelma Pruitt said with ironic finality.

'Not this time,' Mo smiled.

'You would enjoy it, and it would be good for you.'

'A conference on how the media cover legal questions? Of course. It hits both my areas of interest. And they have some wonderful speakers.' Mo took a deep breath. 'But right now, no.'

'Two days in St Louis,' Thelma Pruitt added thoughtfully. 'When you feel you *can't* get away is when you probably *should* get away.'

'Possibly. But I really think I'm needed here these next few weeks.'

'Trapped by your wifely duties?'

Mo met the slightly older woman's eyes. 'You know me better than that.'

Thelma Pruitt was an impressive woman, perhaps in part because she no longer tried to be. Tall, almost gaunt, she wore no makeup, and her greying hair seemed so bushy and unkempt that it was likely to fly right off her head. Her skirt-suit was simple, almost plain, and her white blouse in a style that once would have been pronounced 'mannish.' She wore sturdy shoes and no hose. Despite what seemed a conscious attempt to be everything a man might ordinarily consider unattractive, she was, Mo knew, very attractive to most men strong enough not to be frightened by her. She was very strong and very alive.

'I understand your feelings, Mo,' Thelma Pruitt said now. 'I was just indulging my usual tendency to test you a bit.'

'I'm fine,' Mo told her.

'Are you really?'

'Yes.'

'And Mike?'

'He's very low right now. I'm worried about him.'

'Because of the election?'

'That and other things.'

'It's none of my business, but—'

'No,' Mo cut in calmly. 'Martin has nothing to do with it.'

'Have you been seeing Martin again?'

'No. That really is finished.'

'I understand.'

'We're friends now,' Mo explained. 'That's the way it's going to be.'

Thelma Pruitt stretched her long, athletic legs. 'Yes, but I think poor Martin will never quite accept that. Some men are like that, poor things. Ownership becomes a part of their whole outlook.'

'With Martin, that's an oversimplification,' Mo said.

'I know it is. Testing again. I talk too much. Martin sincerely cares for you.'

'I know that,' Mo replied. 'I care for him. But our lives are committed to others, and we knew that from the start, and maybe that's the only reason we could ever get together, even for a little while.'

Thelma Pruitt frowned. 'I don't understand.'

'We were both messed up intellectually and emotionally, trying to find ourselves, scared, unsure of our identity, *far* too accustomed to hiding our true feelings from our marital partner to be able to admit the confusions we were going through. So we found each other, and we could be safe with one another because we could be honest and not scared of disillusioning one another ... or losing one another, because, you see, we never really had any *claim* on one another.'

'And you were trying to declare your independence as a person,' Thelma Pruitt added.

'And a lover is always part of that pattern?' Mo asked sharply. 'Oh, God, Thelma, please don't make it sound that cheap!'

'I didn't mean it that way, Mo.'

Mo knew this was so, and said nothing. She had not had a really close friend since childhood, until Thelma Pruitt came along. Professional in her work, outspoken, vividly independent, and perhaps, Mo suspected, even a lesbian, although there had never been any hint of an overt suggestion in that regard toward Mo. Thelma Pruitt had often seemed to Mo many of the things she so yearned to become, a self-realized woman. And so their friendship had grown and deepened.

But today Mo had lied about her relationship with Martin, had calmly said it was over, when Martin's semen was still sticky and warm inside her body. Why? Were the subtle changes she was undergoing also altering her relationship with Thelma? Had Mo now come to the point where she no longer could be the wholly open, pathetically candid and confused disciple of the older, seemingly wiser and tougher woman?

Mo did not know the answer. But when Thelma Pruitt left a little later, walking hurriedly to her car because the sky was darkening and a stiff, moist breeze whipped the trees, Mo let her go without calling her back, as she felt an impulse to do, and telling her that it was a lie . . . that part about being finished with Martin.

Alone in the houuse, she wished she had not lied – not to Thelma Pruitt, not to Mike, not to herself. She had, she felt, begun to drag herself free of all the constraints that had bound her tightly for so long. She was liberated sexually now, and knew her own capacities of intellect, and was beginning to face feelings in herself that her life of acting the lady would have forced her to deny. She could stand on her own feet now . . . almost.

And she needed no props, but the affair, which had been a desperate learning experience and an escape and a prop, continued.

She longed to be finished with it. She wanted to enjoy all the pleasures with Mike, now, as a sharing woman, unafraid and uninhibited. She could proceed very slowly with him, as if making glad discoveries, and in sharing totally with her husband she could become free as she had been with Martin.

This was what she now wanted: to be her own woman, and to be truly free, yet free with her own husband, lovingly, as she wanted it to be.

She wondered if she would ever reach this state.

Muncie, Indiana

The sky over Muncie's outlying residential neighbourhood changed rapidly from mildly threatening to a lightning-filled ebony. Then the wind began, and rain blasted the sides of the metal prefab classroom building like bullets. The lights inside had already been on, but now they became vital because it was like night. School buses were lined up a few hundred feet away, yellow lights flashing, headlights obscured by the driving rain. But no one was boarding.

The twenty-three first-graders watched their teacher with eyes that were round and frightened.

Jennifer Fogel gave them her brightest smile. 'Isn't this fun, children? We're getting a lot of nice rain!'

It didn't fool a single child. They stared at her. Thunder rolled and the rain came down even harder. Jennifer Fogel kept her silly smile pasted on her face. She had to keep them from being more scared.

'We won't try to run through this rain for the buses,' she said brightly. 'No need to get soaked. We'll just wait a few minutes.'

A little blond boy held up his hand.

'Yes, Teddy?'

'Is the roof going to blow away, Miss Fogel?'

'Of course not, Teddy! This is just a nice, hard rain.' Jennifer cast about mentally for something more to say, and then she had an inspiration. 'Tell me, now. Can anyone tell me? What does a good spring rain like this do? Does it help us?'

Several hands went up. This was more like it.

'Darla?'

'Makes flowers grow.'

'That's right. Very good, Darla. The rain makes flowers grow. Now can anyone—' Thunder obliterated her voice for an instant— 'Can anyone tell me anything else the rain helps?'

Hands went up again.

'Jimmy?'

'Puts water in the river and we drink it up.'

'Good! Very good, Jimmy. That's right. The rain puts water in the river, and we have dams on the river to hold the water back, to save it, remember? Very good. How many of you remember the story we read about rivers and big dams?'

Several children shot up their hands. Jennifer asked about details of the story, and incidents about the girl and boy in the story were repeated. Jennifer prattled on awhile about the rain helping farmers, too, and how farmers grow crops to feed hungry people, et cetera.

Beneath the prattle, Jennifer Fogel was getting more and more worried. She was twenty-three years old and in her second year of teaching. Nothing like this had ever happened to her before. She knew this was no ordinary storm. She and other teachers had chatted about the violent weather to the west earlier in the day, speculating hopefully that school would be dismissed, and the children home, before anything developed around Muncie. But now the storm was upon them, and the school buses might be in the parking lot, but she was not going to risk sending these kids out into this shrieking wind and rain, and she knew no one else would, either.

Running to the buses was just as out of the question as was running the thirty yards to the main school building. The children simply could not make it safely.

Jennifer wished desperately that they were in the main building. It had stood for seventy years, and no mere storm could do anything to it, she thought. She had no faith in this prefab with its thin metals walls and tin roof. But she had no choice. She was stuck and the children were stuck and she had to keep them occupied.

'That was very good, Johnny. Now let's play a game. Let's pretend we own a big farm. Let's make a list of all the things we have on our farm, tractors, and cows, and everything. All right? Good. We have pictues of all these things on the blackboard railing, see? Underneath the picture, we have the word. You can copy the words down on your tablet. All right. Let's do that now.'

There was a general shuffle as lunch pails and book bags, poised atop desks for the run to the buses, were put on the floor and tablets and pencils gotten out. Many of the children already had their rain slickers and hats on, but they accepted the inevitable with good grace.

The rain continued to pound the prefab. Jennifer saw that it was leaking around the windows and running down the inside of the walls in several places, puddling on the floor. Thunder boomed, and she felt the floor tremble. *My God, we could get blown away in this thing.*

What was even more terrible to her was that each prefab unit stood alone. She knew there were other teachers and children isolated in others along this row. There was no intercom, no way of knowing anything.

The children had begun laboriously block-printing in their tablets.

Jennifer walked down the rows of desks and went to the rear door. Looking out, she saw the bus lights through the rain and wind. She could barely make out the lights in the main-building windows. Lightning briefly illuminated a nightlike sky.

She was helpless.

Something very elemental stirred in Jennifer Fogel. She had never before actually known any fear for her life. Now her skin crawled. She suddenly knew how fragile these walls were . . . how fragile she was, and the children.

Incredibly, the wind increased its ferocity. Rain puttered through cracks in the window frames. Some of the children looked around, more clearly frightened now. Jennifer could see the west wall of the prefab *moving* – pulsing in and out as if it were breathing.

One of the children began to cry. Another, a boy, stood and lowered his head. Jennifer saw his lips moving.

Getting together the shreds of her composure, she walked up the aisle. 'Sammy, what are you doing?'

'Prayers,' Sammy grunted, and squinted his eyes tight again.

'That's a nice idea, class!' Jennifer beamed. 'Did you hear what Sammy said? He's saying his prayers. Isn't that nice? I'll tell you what. Let's stop playing the farm game for a minute. If you want to, you can take a minute out of your busy day and say something to God.'

Some of the children appeared startled, some bowed their heads, three or four made quick signs of the cross and got right with it. A hand went up for a question.

'Yes, Ginnie?'

'What if we don't know about God?'

Jennifer took a deep breath. She was probably already in trouble with the Supreme Court. 'Well, Ginnie, then you just close your eyes and sort of *hope* for whatever you want to come true.'

'Do you know any prayers?'

'Why, yes, Ginnie. I think so.'

'Will you say a prayer?'

Jennifer hesitated. The School Board would have cats if they heard about it. And Jennifer agreed that it really *wasn't* right for public schools to teach religion.

Thunder made the walls vibrate.

'Our Father,' Jennifer said in a trembling voice, 'who art in heaven—'

The children began to join in.

No one, either inside or outside the scientific community, would ever suggest a cause-effect relationship, but no tornado struck near Muncie. There were strong straight winds and some hail, but the school suffered no major damage and no children were hurt.

Wednesday, April 9
3:45 p.m.–4:15 p.m.

NNNN
ZCZC
WWUS7 RWRB 092030

SEVERE WEATHER STATEMENT AND RADAR WEATHER
NATIONAL WEATHER SERVICE TALLAHASSEE FLORIDA
ISSUED 3:30 P.M. CDT WEDNESDAY APRIL 9, 1975

LOCALLY HEAVY RAINS WITH SHOWERS AND THUNDERSTORMS ARE
MOVING ACROSS THE TALLAHASSEE AREA AND APALACHEE BAY . . .

AT 3:25 P.M. SHOWERS AND THUNDERSHOWERS EXTENDED FROM
NEAR ST. TERESA THROUGH TALLAHASSEE AND TOWARD MOULTRIE
GEORGIA. LOCALLY HEAVY RAINS ACCOMPANIED THE STORMS . . .
WINDS IN DOWNTOWN TALLAHASSEE WERE GUSTING TO 60 MPH
AS THE STORMS MOVED EASTWARD 15 TO 20 MPH. OTHER SHOWERS
AND THUNDERSHOWERS WERE WIDESPREAD OVER THE COAST AND
MUCH OF NORTHWESTERN FLORIDA FROM PENSACOLA TO DEAD
MANS BAY AND INLAND NORTH.

NNNN

Near the Indiana-Ohio line, two great cumulonimbus clouds began to emerge as the giants in their squall line. Clouds through much of the line in this section towered more than forty-five thousand feet tall, but these two, side-by-side, each several miles broad at the base and only four miles apart, began, for unaccountable reasons, to build further.

Driven northeasterly by high- and middle-altitude winds of great velocity, cool air moved in on one side of the clouds. Warmer air nearby was pocketed, and struggled to rise, creating turbulence. Under the clouds, and within them, warmer air was shoved rapidly upward, cooling as it rose. The moisture in this air, as it cooled, was condensed out, droplets of rain forming around microscopic particles of dust and salts, and this condensation released new heat energy. Complex electrical imbalances developed, with positive charges building toward the cloud tops, now rushing upward to form ice-crystal anvils above forty thousand feet, and negative charges collected nearer the earth. The earth itself was positively charged, with the seething air acting as insulator between cloud base and ground, but as the charges built, a process of ionization suddenly formed a channel, creating a momentary path of conduction from cloud to ground, and a bolt of lightning flashed, equalizing charges to some degree. This electrical discharge possibly contributed to formation of millions of new rain droplets high in the cloud, and these were carried still higher, hurled out ahead of the cloud line. Other raindrops whirled around in the freezing temperatures near the top, became solid globs of ice, and only then plunged earthward as hail.

Some of the colder air on the forward side of each monster cloud formed downdrafts; this air mixed with warmer currents being driven northward; the cooler and warmer air currents met and mixed, swirling north, while drafts on the far side of the cloud swirled south; the result was the beginning of a slow, counterclockwise rotation, the entire cloud beginning to turn on its own axis.

The two burgeoning giants near the Indiana-Ohio line began rotating about their centres almost simultaneously, becoming cyclonic. At the same time, they began rotating very, very slowly around one another. Their tops broke through fifty thousand feet and continued to build. Rain and hail thundered from their ebony bases, lightning blasted, hail as well as freezing rain plunged down. Conflicting temperatures, conflicting electrical charges, conflicting wind currents and conflicting moisture contents warred within the mini-system, rotation speeded up, the ice-crystal anvils burst through sixty-thousand feet, and violent equalizations of pressures near the surface became so intense that first one, then two, then several black funnel-like appendages dipped down from the green-black base that the two clouds now shared as one.

Within the funnels, the rotation of the parent system was presented in violent miniature. Over diameters ranging from a few feet to four hundred yards, identifiable tornadoes extended their black bodies like evil snakes, lengthened, reached ground, touched, began to move. Their rotational winds smashed objects flat in their path; the lifting forces of the partial vacuum created in the centre of the vortex sucked off roofs, uprooted trees, tossed large objects about.

Within the mouth of each of the large tornadoes were two to five smaller suction vortices, like tornadoes within tornadoes.

These had been the subject of speculation until 1974, when scientists photographed them, confirming the theoretical.

These vortices, spinning at fantastic speeds, also rotated around the centre of the parent funnel. Although the entire tornado could do grave damage, the vortices were the points of maximum destructiveness. Their factual confirmation in 1974 had explained many previously puzzling tornado-damage reports.

To understand the path that a multiple-vortex tornado will describe on the ground, cup your hand as if you were holding a baseball or an orange. Now turn your hand over in that position and place it so that the curled fingertips rest lightly upon a flat surface. Move your hand along the flat surface in a straight line, rotating your hand slightly so that your fingertips trace individual patterns. The resulting patterns, if drawn out, would resemble the coils of a child's toy, the Slinky. In places, the fingertip tracings – the suction vortices – will coincide and cross one another; in another area, no vortex path at all will be drawn. This is one reason why a tornado may seem to 'select' only certain houses on a block for maximum devastation, why some may seem to be skipped.

After the terrible storms of April, 1974, scientists found 'the Slinky pattern' clearly drawn in wheatfields of the South. In another place, aerial photography showed clearly how suction vortices had happened to strike two houses, while missing a third. People in the third house said they assumed the tornado had lifted for an instant, or skipped.

Science does not yet know why one tornado will form and run on the ground for hundreds of miles, while another may start to form, touch down only briefly if at all, and then retreat into the parent cloud. They do not know, either, why one funnel will form as many as five suction vortices, while another seems to have only one. In this area, like others, science sometimes resembles the blind man exploring the elephant.

In both Dayton and Cincinnatti a little before 4 p.m., however, radar operators observed hook echoes in the rotating monster clouds crossing the line into Ohio. It was not difficult to chart the general direction of the storm system, and to extrapolate a line onto a road map indicating where the two superclouds were likely to move.

The line extended directly through Thatcher, Ohio.

Kansas City

The tornado-warning message out of Dayton in one hand, Ed Stephens stood at the radar facsimile machine with Harry Adams and watched the picture of the Cincinnati radarscope being drawn. Stephens's chest was lurching and galloping, and he was trying consciously to breathe very slowly and deeply. The slight pain he felt now, he told himself, was only tension.

Behind him and Adams, Buck Tatinger, fresh in a pale-yellow leisure suit after being gone from the Centre for some time, pointed at the screen imperiously. 'All those blobs are clouds?'

'Precipitation,' Stephens corrected automatically.

'What's your interpretation?'

'They're bad echoes, very intense.'

'You and Adams, here, were talking a few minutes ago about the storm losing some of its punch.'

'That was wishful thinking,' Adams grunted around the stub of his cigar.

'Not very scientific,' Tatinger observed.

'Maybe,' Harry Adams said bitterly, 'we just didn't want to face the fact that Ohio is going to get plastered just the way Illinois and Indiana and Kentucky have been getting plastered.'

'Is your communications system better in Ohio?' Tatinger demanded.

'It's the same kind of system,' Stephens said. 'Why?'

'You had that terrific lag in Indiana. Your wire was sending out warnings after tornadoes had already hit.'

'The circuits jammed because you simply can't put four messages on a wire simultaneously,' Stephens replied testily.

'On one occasion, didn't a message have to wait almost three minutes?'

'Yes, goddamn it, and what are you implying now?'

Tatinger's eyebrow came up in sardonic amusement. 'My conclusions will be incorporated into a formal report to the Congress, and to the people of the United States.'

Bastard!, Stephens thought, and turned to Adams. 'I'm going to call Dayton about this situation. There are a lot of small towns along that way with no warning systems of any kind. Possibly we can get a national TV network break-in again and reach some people with the alert that way. Possibly we can get people in Cincinnati and Columbus to make some calls to the smaller communities to help, too.'

Adams nodded. 'Did you see this Huntsville report?'

'Yes. Also the way it's building into Florida.'

'That one area in Kentucky is a real hot spot now, too.'

'Is that,' Tatinger interrupted again, 'Monument Valley?'

'Yes,' Stephens said. 'Do you know the area?'

'No. Do you?'

Somehow it sounded insulting. Stephens straightened up, ignoring the flipflop of his heart. 'We can't know every place. We can't do everything.'

'Oh, come now. Isn't that a little melodramatic?'

'This is hardly a normal day, Congressman.'

Tatinger smiled thinly. 'Of course that's true. But I daresay the average citizen is hardly cowering in a basement somewhere, despite all these storms and your reactions to them. It isn't the end of the world.'

Stephens resisted still another impulse to shout a reply. What galled was that Tatinger, as usual, had a scintilla of truth on his side.

Despite everything that was happening, the vast majority of Americans still had no idea that this day was all that unusual. Even this fantastic number of tornadoes in a single day – more than eighty, now – meant little when spread over the breadth of America. For most, the news tonight would be surprising, and comfortably abstract: the storms would have hit somewhere else.

They would not be abstract for the 350 or so now known dead, the 800 or more injured seriously enough to require hospitalization. History was being written this day. It was the worst storm day in the recorded history of the United States.

It had quickly become axiomatic, after the storms of April 3, 1974, that the country had suffered the 'storms of the century.' The statistics had been staggering: at least 310 dead, 4,000 injured, property damage of more than $1 billion. That day's storms had left tracks of more than 2,100 miles, more than some earlier entire years. Even the famed tri-state tornado had included only seven known funnels, while the April 3, 1974 storms had counted more than 145.

Today's toll, however, would go higher: more deaths, more injured as slow reports kept filtering in, more property damage, more flooding, more of everything that was bad news.

Stephens hurried to call Dayton. He had some ideas about extra telephone calls, and if Cincinnati couldn't help, maybe Columbus could.

He wondered if there would be time for another quick personal call, too: to Mo. He knew all the odds were in her favour, but the worry nagged.

Monument Valley, Kentucky

A few big globs of rain banged into the dirt road as Milly Tyler, gasping for breath and dizzy, staggered along the fence line fronting the Lovett house.

Small, covered with pink asbestos sheeting, the house looked poor and frail against the rising wind. The small young shrubs planted along the foundation would not have been strong enough to stand firm against any wind, and the one whipping them now was becoming frenzied. Milly could see the slats of the pink-and-white aluminium awnings at the front windows bending and bowing, and they were humming like a musical instrument. The house was new, and the Lovetts had done much of the carpentry themselves; Milly did not like the idea of using it for a shelter. There was no choice. Set on a little rise, the structure was the only one in view, its gravel driveway leading up to a garage or carport that was still in the future, and the shed out back and down the slope was, she knew, infinitely flimsier.

The wind beating at her, Milly staggered up the driveway. She was sweat-soaked, but the wind felt muggy even against her wet skin. The sky overhead was low, bluish, clotted. The air seemed to have a kind of emulsion in it, as if it had somehow been filled with oil: the wind was more than wind because of this extreme density in the air.

Gasping for breath, Milly reached the side of the house. 'Jason?' The wind whipped her voice away and there was no reply.

'Boys?'

Again only the wind replied.

She hurried along the side of the house, feeling the momentary respite it provided from the harsh wind. Her vision was pink-tinged and there was pain throughout her chest and her legs. She wondered if her old heart could take this. She told herself, as she had several times during the run up the road, that she had lived a good life, she had only one vice – the pipe – and if it was time for her to go, then she was ready. If she could just warn Jason and the boys, she would accept whatever happened after that.

She stepped from behind the house and the wind almost caught her off balance and knocked her down, but she caught herself just in time.

From the back of the house she could look down the slope to the three pecan trees and the old shed with its bright plastic awning rigged up on the downwind side. The tykes and Jason evidently were inside because she could not see them. Beyond the shed and the pecans, she could look down farther to a fence row, and then out across the valley.

The funnel was halfway across the valley. Milly's sense of distance was warped by the size of the thing, but she knew it was only a few miles away. Cloud formed an inverted V that was blacker than night, and from the bottom extended the funnel. It curled and swung from side to side as it moved, clearly coming in this direction. Milly could see debris flying around the base as it chewed its way through a plowed field. The sound was not anything to seize attention yet. It sounded like any of the trains sounded at night, rumbling along.

Milly fled down the slope. She reached the shed and pulled the rickety door open. Inside, sheltered by extra pieces of plywood and the plastic tarp, Jason and the boys were on the ground in straw with the cow. The flare of a Coleman lantern showed that the cow had birthed, but was not back on her feet yet.

'Grammaw!' Kent yelped, turning excitedly. 'We saw it! She just had her baby!'

Jason looked up, startled. 'What are you doing here, Mrs Tyler?'

'Storm,' Milly panted, holding to the door frame for support. 'Run—. The house.'

Whether it was her words or the look of her, she would never know. But Jason seemed to understand instantly. He jumped up so fast he knocked over the lantern. Quickly setting it aright, he doused the gas flow and the twin mantles began to fade. He took one regretful glance at the cow and the folded-up calf, stepped over them, grabbed Kent under one arm and Adrian under the other like feed sacks, and practically knocked Milly out of the way as he barged outside.

He took one quick look over the top of the shed toward the southwest and then ran for the house with the boys under his arms. Milly stumbled after him. The wind was worse. Lightning split the dark. Thunder pealed.

Half-blinded by flying dirt, Milly stumbled across the little patio to the back door, a wooden door with many little panes of glass in the top. Jason had put the boys down and was struggling with the doorknob. He turned and yelled something at her, his face contorting.

'*What?*' Milly screamed, cupping her hand to her ear.

'*—is locked!*' Jason's voice tattered.

Just down the hill now, the blackness was total. Milly saw the fence go. She did not know whether Jason had lost his key, or didn't ever have one during daytime chores outside. There was no time to ask and it made absolutely no difference.

Making a fist, she smashed a pane of glass in the door. Bright blood sparkled on the shards of glass. She reached through and turned the knob from inside. The door blew open and she sprawled to her knees on the clean linoleum floor.

Jason pushed the two boys in behind her and bent to help her up. She got to her feet and pushed the door closed. It was a struggle. Wind through the broken glass stood the little curtain straight out. She could hardly see now, it was so dark. The roaring was becoming unbelievable.

Instinct pushed Milly across the kitchen and into the living room; it was on the far side of the house from what was coming. She looked for a basement door, but of course there was none and she had known this, only forgotten it in her panic. Then she looked for the hallway, but there was no hallway because the Lovetts had used all the space; this living room was a corridor itself leading to all the other rooms.

There was no place to hide.

The living room had beige carpet, cheap but adequate furniture, a limestone fireplace wall, dual front picture windows that formed a single unit. Through the window Milly could see dust flying along the road, pieces flying off the trees. The edge of a roll cloud had passed over them and it was like looking out from under a shelf.

'You're hurt!' Jason told her, grabbing at her hand.

Ignoring him, she ran to the windows. The side panels cranked out. As she frantically moved them open a few inches, the pressure inside the house rushed around her on its way out. Milly noticed with slight interest that blood streamed down her wrist and spangled the wall as she worked the cranks.

Something began hammering against the house everywhere at once. Chunks of ice as big as a man's fist began bouncing around in the front yard. The newly planted shrubs and trees were laid to the ground by the wind. Lightning showed this because there was no daylight left. The roar became more incredible. Milly could faintly see across the living room to where Jason and the two boys huddled against the fireplace wall.

It was natural to get against the stone wall. It seemed the most sturdy. Milly knew they were wrong. Masonry would fly apart.

'*This wall is better,*' she yelled over the racket, pointing to the interior frame wall. They didn't hear or understand. She ran to grab Kent by one hand and Adrian by the other and haul them to the other wall, where she tossed them down and tried frantically to pull an end table over so that it would form a kind of lean-to over them. Adrian was crying.

'You'll be fine,' Milly crooned. 'No old fool storm can hurt us. That's good boys.'

Jason crawled over against the wall with the boys and hugged them. His face had a ghastly pallor.

It was not merely his face, however. The light inside the house had suddenly changed in a remarkable way. It was brightening, with a bluish-white cast like fluorescent tubing. Turning, Milly stared at the windows and saw that everything outside was bathed in this eerie, pulsing light.

Continuous lightning.

The pounding was louder and Milly knew the house could not stand, that they were all goners. Rain flooded the windows now and they looked like toys she had seen once in a city store – light boxes.

'I wanna go home!' Adrian wailed.

Something, somewhere in the house, splintered and broke.

Wind rushed through the doorway from the kitchen, carrying sprigs of brush, curtains, towels, pieces of newspaper and cardboard. Everything flew across the living room and pasted itself against the opened windows. The wind shrilled around them, holding them still in a mad collage.

The floor buckled as if someone had driven a hydraulic piston beneath it.

Milly was staring at the front wall. She saw it start to *move*. The wall showed a long crack at the ceiling. The crack widened and there were tearing noises and a split appeared down a corner. The front wall of the house had bowed outward and was torn almost entirely off the house. The front wall was flapping back and forth. A crack bolted across the ceiling. Red insulation material poured into the room from the attic.

Something else happened. Milly experienced a sensation of force against her, and thought she heard a monstrous explosion, and then she was lifted up. Then she hurt and she was across the room, sprawling against the sofa, and the small boys and Jason were on top of her. Dazed, she scrambled to a seated position.

The front wall of the house was gone. Part of the roof was gone and hailstones were hurtling in.

Out in front, not far across the road, a perfectly vertical column of blackness spun wildly. Its hollow interior was lighted by the strange bluish-white light that bathed everything else. The column seemed to be composed of rings of spinning clouds, one on top of the other like a stack of pale tyres, and as Milly watched, she saw one ring near the bottom work its way upward, seeming to slip over others above it until it was out of view. Boards and small trees and other unrecognizable objects hurled around and around the rotating column. She saw a small tree fly out of the column and flop to the ground like a killed fish. The sound was either too great for Milly's ears, or they had been broken by the intense pain she felt in them.

Jason tugged at her arm, yelling words she could not hear. He was on his feet tugging at her. She dazedly obeyed and got to her feet and found nothing broken. Her dress was half torn off and she was cold, the rain was lashing at her. She got Kent's hand, and Adrian's, and stumbled across the room after Jason.

He opened a door in the far wall. It opened onto a shambles. The front wall of the house was gone, much of the top was gone, and the roof over the adjoining room, a bedroom, had been dropped intact so that its timbers formed an angled shelter, tall at the centre of the house and down to the ground where the supporting wall had vanished in the front. Milly could see bedroom furniture partially crushed under the accidental lean-to.

Jason yelled at her again and crawled in under the timbers. He gestured frantically from inside. She understood. She pushed the tykes in to Jason and then crawled in after them.

It was darker under the timbers. Adrian was crying. His face was smeared with blood. Kent was not crying but he was bloody, too. Milly hugged them to her breast. Rain was leaking through the slanted timbers just over her head as she hunkered on the floor.

'We're all safe,' she said. 'We're safe, boys.'

With that, her hearing was back. The sound exploded into her mind. The sound was like it had once been standing near the railroad tracks when a steam locomotive went by very, very close: hiss of steam, clatter of big iron wheels, grinding of turbines, groaning of springs, hissing-banging-whanging crescendo of weight and fury, all of it blending into a single continuous roar of naked power, the kind that vibrated deep into your very soul, shaking you.

Milly rocked on her haunches, trying to comfort the tykes in her arms. Jason lay beside her, his eyes black slots in his face as he stared out at the fields in front of the wrecked house.

It was becoming more bright, a more normal brightness, and they could not longer see the funnel. Rain teemed down, making the yard a lake. Where the tornado had moved, the grass was gone and the earth looked like it had been polished with brooms. It was impossible to tell where the road had been, or any of the trees. The weed field across the ditch glistened, everything in it beaten flat. Standing in the field, upright and evidently undamaged, was a piano.

Beyond the piano, the field was littered with planks, uprooted trees, smashed bits of house and furniture, a great junkyard as far as she could see. And the few standing trees now becoming visible as the light continued to improve, and the rain began to slack, were filled with the storm's flags: bedsheets, towels, pieces of sheet metal, books, newspapers, pieces of cardboard.

Milly closed her eyes. She was afraid that if she looked any more, she would see people impaled on the trees, too.

*

Over Missouri

Bill Fredrick, bundled up, was working his cameras through the open window of the Cessna. He had a tornado track that formed a horseshoe pattern in the rolling woods below, and was taking his pictures most carefully.

So intent was he that Barbara James, the pilot, had to waggle the wings violently to get his attention.

Fredrick turned. 'What is it?'

She shrugged her long dark hair away from her headphones. 'We have a relay from Louisville. There's an Air Force pilot approaching the squall line near there. He's in an RB-71 at sixty-four thousand feet and plans to fly over it on the way to Minneapolis. They want to know if we can think of any observations we'd like him to make.'

'I can think of a couple,' Fredrick grunted. 'How do we tell him?'

'They'll give us a frequency.'

'Take it.'

While the young woman relayed the message, listened, and tuned to the new frequency with her usual cool professionalism, Fredrick was busy thinking exactly how to deal with the Air Force pilot up ahead a hundred miles and some ten-to-twelve miles higher.

The Cessna was near the Kentucky line now, working quite close behind the third squall line, which formed an ugly black wall in the sky some twenty miles to the east. The entire system was somewhat weaker here, allowing him to take the chance, but he knew it was full-fledged to the east around Louisville. One cell, according to latest reports that Barbara James was monitoring for him, towered over fifty thousand feet.

'Air Force niner bravo,' Barbara James said now over her mike, 'this is Cessna four four six eight lima, do you read? Over.'

The ceiling loudspeaker crackled with static and the pilot's voice boomed back clearly: *'Six eight lima, this is Air Force niner bravo, read you loud and clear. You have observations you want? Say instructions, please. Over.'*

'Stand by, niner bravo,' Barbara James said, and handed the microphone across the centre pedestal to Fredrick.

He formed his thoughts and pressed the red mike button. 'Air Force niner bravo, this is six eight lima. Give us your present position, altitude and heading, please.'

'Six eight lima, this is niner bravo. I am at sixty-three thousand five hundred, about eighty miles south of Louisville, proceeding on a heading of two hundred eighty-five degrees. I have the storm line just ahead of me and well below.'

'Niner bravo, do you see any cloud in that line that appears much taller than the others around it?'

'Affirmative, six eight lima. There's one real dandy slightly off to starboard. It appears at least five thousand feet taller than anything else around.'

'Niner bravo, can you alter course enough to fly directly over that tallest cloud?'

'Uh ... affirmative, six eight lima. Changing course now ... and closing at about twenty miles. I'll fly right over it.'

'Okay, niner bravo. As you pass over the tallest cloud, please observe its appearance on top and report any unusual observations. Over.'

'Okay, six eight lima. Anything special you're looking for?'

'Negative. Just tell us what you see, if anything. Over.'

'Roger. Understand. Stand by one.'

Fredrick held the mike in his hand. At the jet's speed, it would fly over the cloud within moments.

He expected no great burst of knowledge to come from the pilot's observation, but he had not been entirely honest when he said there was no particular phenomenon that he hoped to verify. On at least two other occasions, pilots of high-flying aircraft had reported that the tops of extra-high clouds of this type were not flat on top, as might be expected, but somewhat inverted. One with a poetic streak had said the top of the cloud looked like a morning glory. There were possible clues to tornado formation in this phenomenon, although Fredrick had not worked out details. He needed to know if this tallest cloud might be forming such a pattern, and, if it was, he could later determine whether it had also put tornadoes to the ground. In the long range, a pattern might develop, advance knowledge.

He had not wanted to tell the pilot to look for the inverted 'morning glory' top. Observers tended to report back what they thought you wanted them to see.

'I imagine,' Barbara James said, 'he's over it by now.'

'At the speed of an RB-71—'

The ceiling loudspeaker cut in: 'Cessna six eight lima, this is Air Force niner bravo.' The voice sounded different, excited.

'Go ahead,' Fredrick said quickly.

Gone was the professional ennui from the pilot's voice. *'Listen, I flew over this dude and now I'm swinging around for another look. I've never seen anything like it. The whole top of this cloud is a big swirl. It looks like a gigantic funnel going down into the thing! Over.'*

'Thank you, niner bravo. Do you happen to have camera equipment on board?'

'Negative on cameras. But listen. What about this geyser coming out of this thing?'

Fredrick tingled with surprise. 'Geyser? Say again.'

'Geyser! Geyser! Out of the bottom of the cone of this thing it looks like a geyser or waterspout shooting out the top, it goes up a couple hundred feet!'

The loudspeaker fell silent. Fredrick stared in surprise at the radio panel, as if it could explain anything for him. Did the 'geyser' mean a rotation so intense that material was being spewed entirely out of the cloud?

'I'm coming around again. I'm going to penetrate that geyser.'

'Penetrate?' Fredrick said to Barbara James. 'Does he mean he—'

'Fly through it,' she said.

'Hell!' Fredrick thumbed the mike. 'Air Force niner bravo, we can't predict what kind of turbulence you might encounter. Over.'

Silence.

Fredrick said, 'He could kill himself!'

'The RB-71 is a tough bird.'

'Tougher than whatever that geyser thing is?'

'It's too late now.'

Fredrick gritted his teeth. He could only wait for a report. He imagined the jet bomber swooping down to slice through whatever formation was erupting from the volcanic centre of the huge cloud. Did the geyser mean a strong upward thrust *within* the kind of swirling downdraft that would explain the conical top of the cloud itself? This had to be. It would be vital to learn whether the storm was developing tornadoes on the ground. Did the geyser simulate the power of a tornado on the ground? If so, the RB-71 pilot was in trouble.

'Cessna six eight lima, this is Air Force niner bravo.'

'Go ahead,' Fredrick said thankfully.

'*We penetrated that thing. We got a jolt and some ice crystals on the windscreen, but that's about all. That's a very strange thing. We never saw anything like that before. The other clouds are all much lower, and this one stands by itself, gold from the sun, with this blue-black top, an inverted cone, and the geyser is still shooting out the top. It has some rotation to it.*' The pilot paused as if to try to reassert a professional calm. '*Say if you wish other observations. Over.*'

'Negative, niner bravo. Many thanks.'

'*Okay, niner bravo out.*'

Fredrick turned to Barbara. 'Get me ground control, please. I want to see if they monitored that.'

The moment Barbara James's fingers turned the receiver to the special storm-study frequency assigned to the Cessna, the voice of Van Davidson snapped through the overhead loudspeaker: '*Cessna four four six eight lima, this is Davidson at control. Over.*'

'Six eight lima,' Fredrick replied. 'Did you monitor that talk with the RB-71?'

'*We got it,*' Davidson's voice came back tinnily, but clearly enough to carry with it a background chaos of ringing telephones and other men's voices. '*We have radar reports on that cell, which is moving northeast at about thirty knots. It is not associated with any tornadic activity on the ground that is being reported at this time.*'

'Van,' Fredrick shot back, 'we ought to watch that cell real close from the ground, with every kind of instrument we can put on any activity it might spawn.'

'*We were thinking the same thing. Stand by. We've got something on the other line.*'

Fredrick fidgeted impatiently with the mike in his hand.

Barbara James said, 'What can you learn from studying that cloud?'

'We don't know,' Fredrick admitted. 'But what if a major cell like that one develops a cyclonic rotation all the way from the ground to the top, up past fifty thousand feet? That might start some new thinking about tornadic-storm thundercloud structure. You can't predict—'

'*Control to six eight lima,*' the radio squawked.

'Go ahead to six eight lima.'

'*We want you to get to Paducah as fast as you can. Bock will have the second Learjet there as fast as he can, probably ahead of you. He'll have to use a secondary field because Municipal is all torn up. Suggest you head that way, flat-out, and we'll radio which field for the rendezvous.*'

Fredrick looked sharply at Barbara James as she banked the Cessna sharply toward the northeast. Into the microphone he said, 'Where am I going? What's the plan?'

Davidson's voice came back: '*You'll get radar vectors through the worst of the rough stuff going east. We plan to get you on the ground somewhere in Ohio just as fast as we can. We'll pick the spot after further reports on where that big geyser-top cell and a couple of rotating systems are headed. We'll get you in close to their path with as much equipment as we can jam in the jet in ten minutes.*'

Fredrick glanced at his watch. He asked his pilot, 'How long to Paducah?'

'Practically there,' she said briskly, scanning gauges as she increased power.

Fredrick took a deep breath. Nothing like this, as far as he knew, had ever been tried in precisely this way before. He was excited.

'*Six eight lima, did you read?*'

Fredrick pressed the mike button. 'Affirmative. We're on the way.' He turned again to Barbara James. 'Looks like you get to quit work a little earlier today than you thought.'

She smiled at him. 'Like hell. I intend to fly to Ohio with you. This is just getting interesting.'

Wednesday, April 9
4:20 p.m.–4:55 p.m.

XXZ
NNNNγγA
ZCZC WBC 341
TBXX6 KMKC 092100
SSFSS MKX SATELLITE NARRATIVE

BASED ON SMS-1 I-R DATA THROUGH 2100.

MKC FLOATING SECTOR IS B-3

IMAGERY OVER CENTRAL AND EASTERN US DEPICTS THREE SQUALL
LINES FULLY DEVELOPED IN ADVANCE OF THE WEATHER SYSTEM
NOW EXTENDING SOUTHWARD OUT OF CANADA THROUGH WESTERN
INDIANA . . . KENTUCKY . . . TENNESSEE . . . AND ALABAMA. DENSE
COVERAGE OF EASTERNMOST SQUALL LINE OBSCURES OHIO INTO
WESTERN EDGES OF PENNSYLVANIA, WITH LINEAR DEVELOPMENT
SOUTHWARD INTO GEORGIA AND FLORIDA. HIGH THIN CIRRUS
INDICATES NORTHERN EDGE OF SUBTROPICAL JETSTREAM OVER
GEORGIA. SECOND SQUALL LINE SHOWS WEAKENING IN CENTRAL
PORTIONS . . . KENTUCKY AND ALABAMA. EASTWARD DRIFT OF THIRD
LINE SPEEDING UP, ABOUT 50 KNOTS DURING LAST TWO HOURS.

BAND OF CLEAR AIR BETWEEN SECOND AND THIRD LINES
INDICATES SOLAR HEATING POSSIBILITIES AND MID TROPOSPHERIC
DRY AIR ADVECTION PLUS VIGOROUS SUBSIDENCE CAUSING DRYING
AT MIDDLE LEVELS. THE EXISTENCE OF BANDS OF CUMULUS
CONGESTUS CLOUDS INDICATES INCREASING CONVECTIVE
INSTABILITY.

DEVELOPMENT OF ALL THREE LINES TO THE EAST APPEARS VERY
EXPLOSIVE. BULGE IN LINE 2 IN SOUTHERN INDIANA-OHIO MAY
INDICATE POSSIBLE INTENSE THUNDERSTORM ACTIVITY IN THAT
REGION.

IMAGERY INDICATES CLEARING IN WESTERN US. SOME
SOUTHEASTWARD MOVEMENT HAS BEEN NOTED IN THE CLOUD
MASS NOW IN CENTRAL MANITOBA WITH NO APPARENT GROWTH.

XXX

Thatcher, Ohio
The young woman walking down the hospital corridor toward

Mike Coyle was young and pretty in her candy-striper uniform. He noted automatically that she had pretty blond hair and sweet hips and lovely little legs. Then he realized she was his daughter.

Jill appeared as surprised as he was. 'Daddy, what are you doing here?'

'I'm not checking up on you,' he assured her.

'I didn't think you were, silly.'

He hesitated, assimilating information in the mild aftershock of momentarily seeing his own daughter as a stranger, a desirable young woman. *She was pretty. She was almost grown up. Before long they would lose her, as they were already losing Billy, and before long they would be old.*

Jill pointed to her candy cart nearby. 'And don't try to tell me you only came by for a Hershey bar.'

'I won't, chicken.'

'Good.'

'It was a Clark bar.'

'Daddy.'

He relented. 'One of our office employees is in the hospital. I came by to say hello.'

'Mrs Ketwhiler?'

'Right. Our accountant's assistant. You know her?'

'I get to meet most of the patients. That's part of my job, you know.'

'I imagine you cheer up a lot of people, honey.'

She strutted a step. 'Just a bundle of sunshine.'

'It's good experience for you, too,' he added soberly. 'You learn a lot that will help you when you get to be a doctor.'

Jill's sunny face froze and she started to turn away.

'Hey!' Coyle grunted. 'What did I say?'

She turned back, eyes blazing. 'I've told you, Daddy. I *might* be a nurse.'

'If you can be a nurse, why not go all the way and be a doctor? This is the age of—'

'That's what I mean, Daddy!' And she was really very angry. 'Let me be what I want to be! Don't *push* me! All right?'

He accepted the rebuke badly, feeling his face stiffen. 'All right. Sorry.'

She grimaced. 'Oh, I know you don't mean anything by it, but you're always *pushing*. Pushing me. Pushing Billy. Pushing Mom. Can't any of us just be who we are?'

'I just want you to be the best,' he replied, still struggling with his surprise and dismay. 'I don't mean to force you—'

'But you always do!'

He looked at her awhile. 'I'm sorry,' he said finally.

'Oh, and please don't get that baffled, hurt look all over your face! Honestly, Daddy!' She stamped her foot. 'If I want to be a doctor, I'll be a doctor. If I want to be a nurse, I'll be a nurse. You don't have to push. Just let me alone, all right? Don't you know you're driving me and Billy up the wall with all your pushing?'

'I just want you to do well – have good lives—'

'We will, if you don't drive us crazy!'

Coyle sighed. 'Okay. Sorry.'

'Don't *say* it that way!'

He rallied himself. He could try to make it make sense later. 'Is this your early week or your late week, while we're standing here, anyway?'

Jill looked relieved. 'It's my late week.'

'You get off at seven, then.'

'Yes. I talked to Mom. She said she can pick me up.'

'Good. It doesn't appear very busy around this old place today, though.'

'Wednesdays are quiet. A lot of the doctors take the afternoon off to play golf, you know.'

'In this weather?'

'Is it raining yet?'

'Not much, if at all.'

'Then they're all out there. They're fanatics at it. You know how that is.'

'I'm a working stiff myself, love.'

She wrinkled her nose. 'I meant, you know about being a fanatic.'

He wrinkled his nose back at her. 'You better believe it.'

That was better; it established the proper bantering tone. She laughed, took hold of the handles of her candy cart, and pushed it on down the hall. He waved and went on to the elevators.

Leaving the hospital, he vacillated between memories of earlier times, such as when he had left the hospital after Jill's birth, and attempts to deal with what she had said about his pushing her and Billy too hard. It might be true that he had always pushed everyone ... and himself ... too hard. It occurred to him now that he knew no other way to live. He had never been a sports freak, not after the high-school football disappointment, but the Vince Lombardi quote he had used on his son – the one about excellence – was not just rhetoric. It was what he had built his own life upon.

The world was full of people who said that a job was 'good enough.' No job as ever good enough unless it was not only as good as a man could do it, but worked at so hard that it was *better*. Extending yourself; pushing yourself beyond what you had imagined were the limits of your endurance; those were the only ways to live. Nothing meant anything except the drive to excel, whether it was building a city budget or playing golf . . . or raising a child.

Now, perhaps from the viewpoint of his already deep depression, he wondered if he had not been wrong. If he had not tried so hard – cared so intensely – he could be a Purvis Rawlingson now, and accept things. If the drive to excel did not still flame, he could turn his back on Congress as just too much trouble.

If he were not the man he was, the flight of his children would not make him feel so much like a failure with them.

Driving away from the hospital, he headed along the most direct route leading back downtown. A quick check back at the office, and he could go home for the day. He might be able to talk this over with Mo, get her insights.

He drove through tree-shaded side streets to Chestnut Avenue, then southward through a section of town typified by old three-storey houses built in the teens and twenties. Bulky, perched atop little terraces created when their basements were dug out, the doubles and four-families peered out through heavy evergreens at FOR RENT and VACANCY signs amid solid kerb-rows of parked cars. Small children along the way were about half white, half black. It was a troubled neighbourhood; neighbourhood desegregation had never gone well in Thatcher, if it ever went well anywhere. The neighbourhoods were racially mixed only in an interim time of white flight.

A few blocks farther south, on a cluttered intersection, he passed an ancient A&P store and a small frame building housing Thatcher's last genuine confectionery. Some spot zoning in the next block had mixed old homes with a funeral parlour and a dry-cleaner's shop. Gas stations guarded all four sides of the next corner, with vacant lots and derelict cars nearby. The following block was residential again, the houses smaller, shabbier.

He made the light at Neuville Street, crossing the islanded boulevard to pass Anderson Park, with its rolling grass and creek that meandered past softball fields and tennis courts. The homes facing the park were large, and of the same vintage as those he had passed a few blocks north. These, however, wore fresh paint, and their lawns were elegant. In crossing Neuville Street, he had also crossed the *de facto* segregation line.

He could not drive casually through his city without relating things to a history. The transitional neighbourhood meant multi-family rezoning problems, trouble with the sewer lines in the area, spot-zoning fights he had fought, and lost. The Neuville Street racial boundary meant all of Thatcher's racial problems, including the real estate men's conspiracy which the Council would not strike at with a new ordinance or meaningful human relations programme. Now, driving into the shadow of blight cast by the elevated crosstown expressway, he was reminded of the grand urban-renewal programmes on the drawing boards – and how long they had been held onto the drawing boards by bond-election failures and nuisance litigation.

He drove up the entry ramp of the crosstown with some sense of relief. It took only a few minutes to get downtown now. The higher speed with the windows down was pleasant because the heat and humidity were so intense, despite low cloud banks hanging over the entire afternoon sky.

Some cars had their headlights on because the clouds, many with a curiously waffled appearance underneath, had made the day very dark.

Everything in Thatcher, he thought as he sped along, was either a nagging reminder of an old problem or a pointer toward one yet to be confronted. The visit earlier in the day by Andrews, the glass-factory president, was symptomatic. Thatcher was divided, quietly but implacably, along every conceivable political fault line.

If he were smart, Coyle thought, he would leave it. Thatcher would never be united. He should give it up and look out for himself, press on in a new direction.

Press on? *Push* on?

And so he was back to Jill, and the brief confrontation at the hospital.

He was still not sure he knew exactly what she had meant. He knew his failure to understand might be near the heart of his feeling of growing alienation from both of his children. There were times, now, when he was not even sure he understood Mo any more. Change was sweeping them along, and he was not sure how he felt about change any more, either.

He stopped at a Sohio station just off the downtown exit ramp, filled up with gas and got the proprietor's promised Cleanest Windshield in the Big Ten, thought futilely about the energy crisis, and drove into the late-afternoon traffic jam. He cut through some side streets, passed the old Coca-Cola bottling works and then some old hotels and rooming houses. Stuck in a line of traffic at Main Street a few blocks from City Hall, he flicked on the radio to the Thatcher station.

'—and that was the latest big smash from Birdseye, friends,' the disc jockey said. 'That was Birdseye, and this is Johnny Schottenstein, your man on the move with the sounds you will groove, coming at you right here on radio fourteen in good old Thatcher, Ohio. The time is fo-ah thirty fo-ah, and looking at the up-to-the-minute news on your news and music station, the Thatcher area and all of the state of Oh-ho-ho remain under a severe-weather watch at this hour, the Weather Bureau telling us we've got us some dandy thunderstorms heading our direction. These storms have given some of our friends and neighbours some real hassle in Indiana this afternoon. And this just off our wire. The Thatcher area has been placed under a tornado watch – dig it, friends – a tornado watch from now until seven o'clock this evening, and that's in addition to the severe-weather watch, I guess. The weather folks say a line of severe thunderstorms, with the possibility of a tornado, is moving in from the west, and they say keep your eye on the sky and your hands off that there dial, 'cause we'll have all the latest scoop for you right here on good old radio fourteen. I sure do hope this stuff moves in through before eight o'clock tonight, because that's when yours truly will have the mobile unit out at the Redlands Shopping Centre for some platters and some patter and some jive that's alive. Stay tuned, kiddies. Now for our next tune, a real boffo hard-rock sound from—'

Coyle shut the radio off as the traffic moved. He made a right turn, cut through a one-way alley going the wrong way, used a parking lot for a street, and pulled in behind the police station.

Inside, he found Chief Merrill with two of his men in the squad room.

'Chief, the radio said something about bad weather. Is that new?'

'It's new, all right,' Merrill frowned. 'Message is in on my desk, and the Dayton Weather Bureau just called to make sure we got it.'

'What's happening?'

'Well, the whole squall line will be here within the hour, I guess. You can already see a little lightning out to the west. Also, they say the worst part of the thing looks like it's drifting this way. They wanted us to batten down the hatches, or whatever you do when you're going to get wet.'

Coyle thought about it. Something sinister tickled the back of his mind. 'I wish we had tested those sirens again earlier today when the weather wasn't so bad that people might misunderstand what was happening.'

'Well, they'll work if we need 'em,' Merrill said.

'What about the areas that don't have coverage?'

'We can put something on the radio if things start looking hairy, I guess.'

One of the patrolmen said, 'The Wyandottes wouldn't have had that old camping ground here in the bend of the river if there was ever any tornado-type weather.'

'You'd better call the radio station,' Coyle told Merrill. 'Make sure you have a line open just in case something more comes in over the wire and you have to make an announcement quick.'

Merrill looked dubious. 'Okay, but I hate to bother them over nothing.'

'Just on the off-chance something might develop,' Coyle insisted quietly, 'your office is the nerve centre. I'll feel better about heading home in a little while if I know you've taken that extra precaution.'

'Consider it done,' Merrill said.

Coyle nodded and left the station, cutting next door to City Hall. He had to use his master key to get through the side door, and into a darkened hallway; things shut down at four-thirty, and this was one area in which every city employee was prompt.

Finding his way to his second-floor office, Coyle looked over a few letters left for him to sign. None was urgent. He signed them and dropped them into the out basket. Then he leaned back and thought about the weather for a moment. He did not want to be an alarmist. He knew nothing ever happened.

On impulse, however, he picked up the telephone and punched the number for the sheriff's office.

'Sheriff's office.'

'Is Sheriff Bergdall in, please? This is Mayor Coyle.'

In a moment, Bergdall's bluff voice boomed over the line. 'What can we do for you, Mister Mayor?'

'We have some stormy weather heading our way later this evening, Sheriff. I just wanted to make sure you were aware of it.'

'Yes sir, I am. I surely, surely am! We've got our own weather wire down here at the courthouse now, you know. I saw that last message. Of course nothing ever comes of these durned things, but I gave old Barney a call on the radio. I think he was probably *dee*lighted. He's out south somewheres, sitting on a hilltop or something, right now.'

'Will you have any other cars out, Sheriff?'

'Well, nothing special. We're handing out some summonses for the judge this evening. Did you have something in mind?'

Coyle's embarrassment got the better of him. 'No, I guess not.' Then he remembered something. 'Sheriff, do you happen to know if that emergency power generator is still parked next to the hospital?'

'Yes sir, as far as I know, nobody's moved it. We don't have a use in the world for the blamed thing, you know.'

'It just occurs to me, Sheriff, that you might have a man drive by there and make sure the unit has plenty of fuel. You never know. If we were to have a lot of lightning or something, they might need to fire that relic up.'

'That's a sterling idea, Mayor! I've got a man heading out that way anyhow, and I'll just have him stop.'

'He might just make sure the hospital knows about the storm, too. I think they like to have a power-unit man on duty at times like this.'

By the muttering tone of the sheriff's voice, it was clear he was writing something down. 'I'll ... sure ... do ... her.'

Coyle hung up, thought about it another moment or so, and decided, what the hell, he was already under way. He called the power company and the other utilities. The engineer at the electric company seemed somewhat interested and said he would do some checking, just in case.

His calls completed, Coyle looked at his watch. It was almost five o'clock. He parted his draperies and looked outside. The sky was very dark, threatening rain at any time. There was lightning to the southwest.

He thought briefly about staying around awhile, then decided that was ridiculous. If he were not in such a pessimistic mood, he told himself, the idea of damaging stormy weather would never have entered his mind. All the things on TV about tornadoes had begun to make him a little punchy and overaware of them.

And he was already late, compared to the time he had promised Mo.

He turned off his office lights and went into the dark corridor.

'Friends, Romans, countrymen,' a voice boomed. 'Lend me your ears!'

Coyle turned. 'Hello, Purvis.'

Purvis Rawlingson, dragging his sports coat behind him, had just come from his own office. He fell in beside Coyle as they started downstairs.

'You think that's a pretty good line, Mike? Lend me your ears? You suppose I ought to write it down and send it to the Beltone people?'

Coyle grinned automatically. 'Great idea.'

'You know, by gollys, I was just in my office dictating a memo for you. I think this new Pride-in-Thatcher programme is finally really getting off the ground.'

'Oh?'

'Yes sir! You know, the Stranniger Store has done a real nice job fixing up that new store front. Really topnotch, I'd call it. And I talked today with Brack, over there at the jewellery store, and he says they're planning to put an entire new window unit in. A new sign, too, maybe, he said. I thought a nice letter from you, and from the manager of the Chamber, would encourage these folks that are taking a little pride in our fair city.'

'That sounds fine,' Coyle said, unlocking the front door so they could get out.

'A stitch in time, you know,' Rawlingson said.

'I know. Every little bit helps.' Now Rawlingson had *him* doing it!

'Every little bit does help!' Rawlingson said, as if it were profound. 'You darned betcha it does! If we get the good old booster spirit moving, no telling where it will end!'

Coyle locked the door after them and went down to the sidewalk. 'I'll look at your memo dictation in the morning, then.'

Rawlingson shoved his arms into his baggy jacket. 'By golly, I think I'm just going to circle the block and have another look at that new front on Stranniger's. It's really a dandy. Want to come?'

'I'd better get on home, Purvis.'

'Right! And wipe your feet, huh?'

'Right,' Coyle said, Rawlingson's hearty laughter following him around the corner of the building.

It would be nice to be like Rawlingson, he thought, getting into his car again. Then the smallest advances would be enough. He could become an entrepreneur in mediocrity too.

Then he rejected the thought because it was so patronizing. He did not really know Rawlingson that well, he told himself. He could not give in to bitterness.

But having rejected that mind-set, he found none to take its place. And he *needed* an attitude now, a stance from which he could deal with the things assailing him. What kind of man, ultimately, was he going to be? Where was his life heading? He had to make his decisions *soon*. Yet without a basic attitude toward experience, he was a blind man, groping.

His lungs ached as he started his car once more, and for no reason at all he was again near tears. He was so close to the ragged edge. He had to have rest.

At the west-side power substation where the telephone switching equipment had automatically moved Mike Coyle's call, engineer Harley Dean stood at the city line schematic chart, studying it. The mayor's call had certainly not alarmed Dean, but he had nothing better to do and he was curious.

Electric power throughout the city of Thatcher was essentially divided into four large grids. The oldest served the heavy industrial users south of the river, and flowed from the south-county transformer site. Downtown power and west-side power came from this station. The central and eastern parts of Thatcher derived their electricity from the old Number One station and transformer site on the bluffs, while a new site powered Country Club Heights and the other new additions to the north.

Ordinarily, power flowed through the system continuously, one segment borrowing from another as peak loads varied from place to place. The county system was the same, everything hooked together in power-borrowing arrangements, just as the entire region sometimes bought power from places as far away as Arkansas and Oklahoma.

Studying the chart now, Dean for the first time paid very close attention to the shunt stations and procedures that would be necessary to restore power in an area quickly if something happened to curtail electricity in a given area. There were simple enough ways to 'switch out' one section or one grid, and keep electricity flowing to other areas. There were ways to borrow power, too.

Although he was not at all alarmed, Dean reflected that the mayor had had his reasons for calling. It was a simple operation to call the other maintenance sites and just make sure that everyone was on the same operational wavelength – that they all knew what they would do just in case there was a little power outage or something.

And hell, Dean thought, if he did less, and then something happened, he would hear about it.

Protect the old job, boy.

Dean made the calls.

About five miles north of where Dean made the calls, a deputy sheriff stopped at the hospital, checked the diesel emergency-power unit, strolled inside, talked to the assistant administrator a few minutes, went to the coffee shop, made a pass at a nurse, struck out, and went on back to his car and about his business. The assistant administrator called the hospital custodian meanwhile, and the custodian left his basement TV long enough to rummage through his file cabinets and find a sheet of instructions about the power generator. The custodian grumpily read the instructions over again, tossed them back into the file, and went back to the old movie.

*

Downtown, Chief Merrill forgot that he was supposed to call the radio station.

At the radio station, newsman Leroy Prendergast did some rapid calculations and decided that he just had time to sneak out to the shopping centre, check those golf shoes they had on sale, and be back early enough to get the wire news together for the 6 p.m. report.

Leaving his desk in the cramped alcove they laughingly called a newsroom, he skirted the wire machine in the corridor to walk into the front business office. Everything was already dark, the girls having left early to beat the rain. The girls often left a few minutes early when the manager had gone to the country club, which was the case today.

Prendergast walked on deeper into the long, narrow, concrete-block building. The small ad office was black and deserted. The front studio was also empty. Bright light shone through thick glass from the back studio, where Johnny Schottenstein sat in the inner curve of a horseshoe of equipment, talking a mile a minute into an overhead mike. Schottenstein had the next record cued on the turntable to his right, and as Prendergast waited, the disc jockey finished his commercial, let the turntable start rotating, and fanned the volume control with his left hand. The red bulb over the studio door went out, indicating the radio signal now fed from the turntable stylus and the mike was shut off.

Prendergast opened the door.

'Hubba hubba!' Schottenstein yelled, doing a double take. 'I thought I was alone in this place!'

'You will be in two minutes. I'm ducking out for a little while.'

'Holy shit! You mean I got to answer the phone and everything? I'm getting overworked!'

Prendergast glanced at the five-button telephone on the desk. Not a light was on. 'It's rough, I can tell.'

'Where you going?'

'Down to the shopping centre. I'll be back in plenty of time for the news.'

'You better be, mother! *I'm* not reading that turd!'

'Just answer the phone and keep it clean on the air.'

'Cool.'

'UPI says we're still under a severe-weather watch, so glance at the wire every once in a while too, okay?'

'Sure,' Schottenstein said lazily.

'I'll lock you in when I leave.'

'Yeah, man! I wouldn't want any teenyboppers getting in here after my bod.'

Prendergast shook his head wearily and left the station.

Birmingham, Alabama

The rain had stopped and it was cold. Swirling breaks showed in the soggy clouds overhead. David Kristofsen stood with his wife Susan on the debris-littered steps of their wrecked house, two suitcases nearby. The suitcases were not large, but then they had not been able to salvage much, either.

Scattered across the big front lawn and driveway were all kinds of vehicles: two grey trucks from the telephone company, insanely the first to arrive, as if the rubble would accept telephone calls; two panel trucks and a huge orange cherrypicker unit from the electric company; a blue pickup from the city water department; a black Ford sedan from the gas company; another Ford belonging to some kind of minor city official, and a police car. The fire department had come and gone. So had the health department.

And the ambulance, taking Mrs Jackson's corpse.

Workers were near the street gate, at the sides and back of the house, and inside it, repairing wires, shutting things off, doing whatever they did. Kristofsen watched them humbly. Beside him, Susan shivered in a rain-stained corduroy housecoat.

'The cab ought to be here any minute,' Kristofsen said.

Susan didn't say anything.

He wondered where the hell he was going to tell the cab driver to take them when he came – if he ever did. Maybe it was as crazy to expect a taxi as it was to be repairing the telephone lines.

Out at the front gates, where the police had sawhorses across the driveway, there was some slight commotion. Then a policeman moved one of the barriers and an olive-drab Chevrolet sedan pulled slowly in, followed by a medium-sized, canvas-topped army truck.

'Who's that?' Susan asked listlessly.

'I don't know. National Guard?'

'What do they want?'

'I don't know.'

The sedan moved slowly up the driveway, going two wheels on

to the soggy grass to get around one fallen tree. Broken glass grated under the tyres as it pulled up in front of the house. The truck was close behind, its heavy engine thrumming.

A uniformed captain got out of the car. He looked up at the house for a minute, shock clearly on his face. Then, frowning, he checked a list affixed to a clipboard. He sloshed through standing water to the front steps.

'Mr and Mrs Kristofsen?'

'Yes.'

'I'm Captain Walter Michels. Alabama Guard. We have troops here who will be stationed around your home to prevent any, uh, difficulties.'

Kristofsen watched the first few soldiers climb out of the back of the truck, splash into the driveway, and begin forming up on the muddy lawn. There were about a dozen of them. Then he understood.

'You're here to prevent looting,' he said.

'Ah, yes sir, not that we expect any, but to be on the safe side. We're securing the entire neighbourhood, so you can rest easy on that score.'

Susan asked sharply, 'Do you think someone would find anything to steal?'

Michels jumped, startled. 'Ma'am?'

'What do you think might be left for someone to steal?' Susan demanded shrilly.

'Ma'am, I don't know, but our job is to protect—'

'You might as well go protect a dump! What makes you think—'

'Susan,' Kristofsen muttered, embarrassed.

'It's ridiculous!' Susan snapped, and her eyes were not normal. 'Why should we have any more functionaries pawing over our things? Tell me, Captain, do you see anything worth stealing here?'

'Susan, stop it,' Kristofsen said more sharply.

'No! I—'

'I said stop it!'

She stared at him.

'He's here to help us,' Kristofsen told her.

Michels said lamely, 'We'll protect everything just as it is. That's our job.'

'Thank you, Captain. We appreciate that.'

Michels started to turn away, then swung back around. 'Sir, after I give my orders to my men, I'll be heading toward downtown. I'd be glad to give the two of you a lift.'

'We asked the police to have a taxi come for us.'

'Yes, sir. The only thing is, uh, the storm took out a couple of cab companies, and the rest are all piled up, you know, with radio communications messed up, streets blocked, everything else. I'm not sure when a taxi might get here, if at all. So I'll be glad to take you somewhere.'

'Thank you,' Kristofsen said. 'We can use a lift.'

Michels splashed across the driveway to his men. He issued some orders and they filed to the truck to hand out rifles. Then they started moving around the house, taking up stations at regular intervals.

'It's mad,' Susan said softly. 'There's nothing to steal.'

'We don't know that. Whole rooms of things might be okay, just blocked off.'

'Who would come and steal at a time like this?'

'People.'

She looked at him. 'There isn't anything left.'

'Even if there isn't, we got through it alive. That's all that matters.'

Her eyes glistened. 'I want my sewing machine to be all right.'

It had been the first thing they bought after they were married, and an investment in the future. They had paid it out over a two-year period.

'We'll find it,' Kristofsen told her.

'And what about your manuscript?'

The smile was not genuine, and felt tight on his face. 'No problem.'

'You mean you think it's all right?'

'That part of the house is gone. So we don't have to worry about that manuscript any more.'

'Oh, poor David.'

'No. You know how long I've been stuck. It's no loss.'

'You can write it again.'

'You can never write the same thing over again, and I don't want to. The story was sick. I'm better off with it gone.'

'You're just saying that.'

'No. I might "just say" a lot of things. I *mean* this.

'Oh, poor David,' she repeated with genuine sympathy.

He took her in his arms. 'It doesn't matter. It doesn't matter a damn baby.'

And it was the truth. The loss shocked him, but it did not hurt. The feeling he had lived with for months was now becoming clear for the first time by its absence. There was *no more house to live up to:* no more rooms of furniture, flood of bills, maintenance programme, maid, cook, gardener, visitors, speaking schedule, parties, pages of manuscript vainly gone over and over again while the fine electric typewriter hummed in the silence of desperation and blockage. It had been wiped away, and his burden was lightened.

The feeling had been claustrophobia.

Despite all this, the need to reassure Susan moved him to speak. 'We can find another place . . . start again.'

'I don't want another place like this.'

'You loved this place.'

'We were happier in the trailer house.'

'With *ants*, like the old one?' he asked.

She laughed through the tears. 'Yes. The ants, too.'

The captain walked back up to them. 'Sir, Ma'am. We're ready if you're ready to go.'

Kristofsen and his wife waded to the car and got in the back seat. Michels got in the front with a driver, a corporal. They drove down the flooded driveway to the front gates. Along the way, Kristofsen saw that the muddy grass was covered with sheets of paper that looked like pages of manuscript. Kristofsen felt a gust of hysteria. At last he had a perfect title for the book. But Margaret Michell had already used it.

The car pulled out on to the street, which was all but unrecognizable. Great old trees lay across it in jumbles of power lines. Cars had been tumbled and lay like crushed toys in front yards. Houses were piles of lumber and bricks. Repair and emergency vehicles stood everywhere.

As the car made its way through a tree-strewn intersection, Kristofsen reached out and took Susan's hand. She allowed this, but her hand was lifeless. She kept her face averted. Kristofsen knew, then, that even an event like the storm could not erase the troubles between them. A storm smashed; it did not heal.

'We're going to be all right, Susan,' he said.

'*Are* we?' she asked.

'Yes,' he said, but he was not sure.

The highway east of Dayton, Ohio

Chris O'Conner leaned over the steering wheel of the Datsun to peer out at the clouds. 'Doesn't look too bad, kiddo.'

His wife Janet, a pretty blonde who looked especially fetching today in a new pink pantsuit, pointed ahead, to the east. 'Look how all the clouds are so much blacker up toward Thatcher, though! It's a lot worse where we're going.'

O'Conner, a red-haired man of thirty, made a face at her. 'Want to turn back?'

'No. You got off work early and everything else so we could be there for Mother's birthday.'

'It would be silly to turn back, right?'

'I guess so.'

'On we go, then.'

From the back seat, Annie piped up, 'Daddy, have we got storms?'

'Nothing bad, honey.'

'Then how come we brang our umbrella?'

'So we wouldn't get wet, cuckoo.'

'How come we brought raincoats, too?'

'So you'd ask questions, you question machine!'

Annie giggled at that. Janet smiled. O'Conner was pleased with himself. It might rain a little, but all the radio and TV alarms, and so forth, had really gotten Janet uptight. The chances of being hurt in a little thunderstorm were – what? – one in a million? The government had an awful lot of money to waste, using so much of it to scare people.

'Daddy!' Annie piped up a few minutes later.

'What now, question machine?'

'When are we gonna *get* there?'

'Fifteen or twenty minutes!' O'Conner promised, and pressed a shade harder on the accelerator to try to make his prediction hold. Lord, it was black up ahead!

Wednesday, April 9
4:59 p.m.–5:28 p.m.

NNNN
ZCZC
WWUS RWRB 092200
Z Z Z Z Z

SPECIAL MARINE WARNING BULLETIN
NATIONAL WEATHER SERVICE TAMPA FLORIDA
ISSUED 4:55 P.M. CDT APRIL 9, 1975

A SPECIAL MARINE WARNING IS IN EFFECT FOR THE COASTAL
WATERS OF CITRUS . . . HERNANDO . . . PASCO . . . PINELLAS . . .
MANATEE . . . AND SARASOTA COUNTIES OF FLORIDA UNTIL 6 A.M.
CDT THURSDAY MORNING . . .

RADAR INDICATES A LINE OF INTENSE SHOWERS AND
THUNDERSTORM ACTIVITY MOVING INTO THE ABOVE COUNTIES . . .
THIS ACTIVITY IS INTENSIFYING VERY RAPIDLY AND WILL LIKELY
CAUSE HAZARDOUS CONDITIONS FOR MARINE INTERESTS FOR THE
NEXT SEVERAL HOURS . . .

THIS LINE OF SHOWERS AND THUNDERSTORMS IS MOVING
EASTWARD AND SOUTHEASTWARD AT NEAR 30 MPH . . . ALL
MARINE INTERESTS FROM SARASOTA NORTHWARD SHOULD EXERCISE
THE GREATEST CAUTION . . . SMALL CRAFT ADVISORIES ARE IN
EFFECT ALONG THE FLORIDA WEST COAST . . .

FURTHER WARNINGS OR STATEMENTS WILL BE ISSUED AS
CONDITIONS WARRANT . . .

XXX

Freesburgh, Ohio
In an eerie, pearl-coloured light, the cloud put down a funnel. It
touched down a few hundred yards south of Freesburgh, a cross-
roads community of about three hundred fifty persons, most of
them elderly. There was no siren in the town, and no other
warning.

Old Mrs Simpson was on her back porch, arranging flowerpots
so they would catch the rain, and she saw the funnel coming
across a broad field, where it exploded a small storage building.
Mrs Simpson screamed, and in the sudden stillness just before the

strike, her neighbours heard. Mrs Ablavack, next door, opened her side window to see what the problem was, and saw her back fence blow down. Then the wind hit her house and threw her back inside.

The funnel moved directly across Freesburgh.

It smashed the Ablavack house and then the Simpson place and then the Smiths' and the Zink property. The schoolhouse exploded in flying bricks. An uncanny roar blanketed the area and a total darkness came. The flasher light at the highway intersection took off to the north. Down went the Gulf station, the drugstore, the grocery, the barbershop, the post office, the houses along the street fronting the tree-shaded Grant Library. When the Turner storage barn blew up, missiles – planks and timbers – filled the air. One of these, a four-by-four oak beam, went entirely through a parked school bus and embedded itself in a solid rock wall. A propane storage tank exploded into flames. A row of newer homes on the hill to the north flew apart like Tinkertoys before the hand of an angry child. Some hail slammed to the earth, and then a quick, hard rain, and then it was over.

Where Freesburgh had been was now a naked intersection of two country roads. There were debris and rubble and felled trees, and the insane sound of a stuck car horn, the flames of the propane explosion which had caught a fallen house afire, and the wailing of someone crying.

The twister, still on the ground, rumbled out over open land, moving northeast, on a line for Thatcher, a little over twenty miles away.

Monument Valley, Kentucky

'Land,' Milly Tyler shivered. 'We can't stay *here*.'

'Somebody will come along,' Jason said. 'We've waited this long.'

'We might wait forever. How do we know anybody can get over the road now? It's cold. We have to move.'

'Where will we go?'

'My house, silly.'

'What if your house isn't there any more, either?'

Milly set her jaw. 'At least we'll have the cellar.'

'It's a hard walk, and the road is awful muddy.'

'Did mud ever hurt anybody? Are we made of sugar?'

They were standing in front of the wreckage of the Lovett house, and overhead the sky was a little brighter, with even a few breaks that allowed brief glimpses of clear blue. The wind had slacked off, too, but it was cold and all of them were shivering, soaked to the skin. The two little boys were huddled under a piece of plastic in the house debris, out of earshot.

'We'll all catch our death staying here, Jason,' Milly added now. 'We just have to hoof it.'

'Can you make it, Mrs Tyler?'

'Foof! I made it here, didn't I?'

'You don't look too . . . good.'

Milly smiled at Jason, who was soaked, his clothing half torn off, and chalky with fallen powder from Sheetrock partitioning. 'Jason, you just don't look too good yourself. But if you can make it, I danged sure can.'

'Okay,' Jason said miserably.

Milly marched to the wreckage. 'Come on now, boys.'

Kent peered up at her from under the plastic. 'What are we gonna do?'

'We're going back to your granny's house.'

Adrian made a whimpering sound. 'I don't wanna!'

'Nonsense! Now come on, young man!'

'No! Another one might come and get me!'

'Are you going to be scared of a little wind? Be a big man, now!'

'I'm *not* a big man!' Adrian wailed. 'I'm just a little kid!'

Kent began crying, too.

Milly quickly knelt, throwing her arms around them, hugging them. 'My land, all *right*, now, you two! Listen to me. Will you listen to your granny? I was scared, too.' Their eyes raised, saucer-like. 'Of course I was! But that old cyclone didn't get us. We got away. That's the only cyclone that's ever been in this valley and there won't ever be another one. It was just a sort of mistake, got the wrong address. Now it's gone. See the sun trying to shine? The cyclone is *gone*. Now we have to walk back to my house, and we'll have some more pie. All right? All right, then. Come on. Be good boys for Granny.'

Adrian sniffled, rubbed his fist across his nose, and let her pull him to his feet. Kent, seeing this, and being the older brother, had no choice if he was to avoid disgrace.

'Here we go,' Milly said, taking them each by the hand.

They walked to the muddy stretch that had been a road. Jason hesitated, but Milly pushed by him and started out with long strides. Her feet slipped in the mud, but she kept going. She was chilled, shuddering. She was cold, but she recognized that the shuddering was a companion of shock. *Just keep yourself together, old girl,* she told herself. *It's up to you now.*

'I wonder who all it hit,' Jason muttered as they trudged along.

'It was big,' Milly said. 'A lot of people got hit.'

'Do you think it hit town?'

'Well, I don't know. I first saw it near Steptoe.'

'I hope Mr and Mrs Lovett are okay.'

'I'm sure they're okay, Jason, but they'll be mighty upset when they see what happened to their place.'

'I have to try to find a telephone – tell them.'

'Maybe the telephone will be working at my house again after a while.'

'If not, I can hike to the highway.'

'Someone will be along, Jason. Count on it.'

They walked for what seemed a long time in silence. Milly got no warmer. A pain crept across her chest. She tried to ignore it.

'What about the old cow?' Kent asked after a while.

'Yeah!' Adrian chimed in, troubled.

'She's all right,' Milly told them.

'Yeah, but when we went back down there, there wasn't no shed or no cow or no baby or *nothing.*'

'That old cow,' Milly lied, 'is probably just fine. She probably went into the woods somewhere to hide that baby. Cows are smarter than people. They know what to do. She probably has that baby in the woods, and tomorrow Jason can come back and find her and the baby both.'

'I think that cow blew up in the sky!' Adrian said thoughtfully.

When they reached the oak bridge over the creek, they found the water sluicing over the top, rushing an inch deep over the planks which had been washed clean of tar and gravel. Foam boiled over the sides, making the whole structure tremble. Milly knew they could either try it or stand around all night, so she pretended she was not afraid and led the way across quickly, and without incident.

Over the next little hillside, the storm's damage was not so apparent. Pieces of trees were down, and here and there a trunk was split, twisted open to raw pulp. This area had been on the edge of the worst damage, and that made Milly have more hope for her own house. Despite the nagging pain throughout her chest, she forced herself to walk a little faster.

As they walked on, she tried to keep up a string of chatter, pointing out felled trees and fallen limbs. The television set was her mentor, and she had followed closely when NBC showed a special on the effects of a big Alaskan earthquake. Many months later, children had still been traumatized, experiencing irrational fears and lapses into near-hysteria. She hoped to keep Kent and Adrian as calm as possible by pretending a normalcy of her own that was entirely feigned.

She had over-exerted herself, then had been scared half out of her wits, soaked, hurt, and over-exerted again. She was more wobbly than she wanted to admit.

And the chest pains had begun to frighten her, too. She had always exercised. She had never felt pains exactly like these.

After a while, Kent popped up again. 'What if there's *another* tornado?'

'Foof. Won't be.'

'But I see more clouds!'

'Clouds are normal, boy. Clouds are good. They're God's way of carrying rain around in the sky.'

Jason said huskily, 'The boy is right, though. There are more clouds building.'

Milly had been concentrating mainly on putting one foot before the other in the mud. Now she looked up wearily. They were in a small valley, and it was not far now to her house. She could not see the house yet, but the view was unblocked out toward Steptoe Mountain. Jason was right; the tykes were right: new blue-black clouds had begun to gather over the mountain's greeny bulk, and she saw distant lightning in them.

'Nothing to worry about,' she said. 'Lightning never strikes twice in the same place.'

'Yeah!' Adrian piped up. 'But how about *tornadoes?*'

'Now you just hush, young man, and no more nonsense!'

They crossed the hill and went through a ravine. Water was not quite as deep in this one, and the bridge was secure. They went up the next hillside. They reached the crest, and could see down into the area of Milly's house.

It was there.

Dear Lord, Milly thought.

They went down the hill and to the house. Twigs littered the lawn, and a few shingles had been blown off the roof, but everything else was intact. Spotnose ran out from under the porch and wrapped himself around Milly's muddy legs. He was paranoid from fright.

Milly scooped him up. 'Jason. You need to take the boys inside and get them out of those wet cothes and put them in the bathtub. Can you do that?'

'Yes, ma'am,' Jason said.

'We don't need no bath!' Kent cried.

'You're a walking mudhole, Kent. You and Adrian go with Jason.'

'Aw!'

'Go! And Jason, you can find some clothes that belonged to my husband in that back-bedroom closet. You can change, too.'

Jason nodded palely and led the boys inside the house.

Milly patted Spotnose for a moment. Despite the chill in the air, she sat down in the rocker on the porch to get her breath. Bright-yellow sparks dazzled her eyes and she almost fainted. Startled, she got up again, looked around and found her pipe where she had dropped it, refilled it, began to smoke.

If more storms were coming, she thought, it would just have to catch them at supper table. She intended to rest herself a minute or two, then fix supper. They all needed some warm food in them.

Warm food might even help the pain in her chest.

Kansas City

Buck Tatinger stood in a corner of the weather room, sipping coffee, aloof and mildly amused. It was as if his effort at sardonic distance increased in direct proportion to the seriousness of the situation, and it was an attitude that Ed Stephens could not fathom.

His heart sending stabs of pain through his chest, Stephens tried to screen Tatinger out of his mind as he talked to two of his aides, Bright and McAndrews. 'Extend the thunderstorm watch to all of Florida. The tornado watch ought to be extended as far south as West Palm Beach.'

Bright nodded. 'I'll call Tampa.'

'If they have any question, I'll talk.'

Bright hurried to a nearby telephone.

Stephens looked at more satellite pictures and charts handed him by McAndrews. The day's original Skywarn had covered all but the tip of Florida, but thus far the watch areas had been farther north. The easternmost squall line, however, was now intensifying and extending southward. New watch areas would increase the state of alert begun by the original Skywarn message.

Stephens looked at the day's activity report. Ruled legal-sized sheets on a clipboard, they were virtually blank some days, including only a little wind or a waterspout. Today, one man had done little besides try to keep the list current.

There were several pages of reports: tornadoes, heavy hail, damaging high winds, funnels aloft, lightning damage. As he scanned the list, Stephens could visualize the march of the great black clouds across America's heartland.

The list was past one hundred and fifty tornadoes. Some of these might not be verified on later check-out, but Stephens suspected that there were as many others that had not yet been reported over the glutted wires. As he watched, McAndrews handed a slip of teletype paper to the man on duty, and he inserted another entry at the bottom of the last page.

'Our casualty lists have just taken a big jump.' It was Harry Adams with another teletype message. He was pale and rumpled.

'What is it now?' Stephens asked.

'Dead: four hundred and seventy-five. Hurt: about four thousand.'

Stephens winced.

Adams explained, 'The wire services, AP and UPI, are really flooding in with pretty accurate reports now.'

'It shouldn't be that high.'

'We've never had this many storms in one day.'

Stephens angrily picked up a new chart. It showed the low-pressure centre itself in Kentucky, east of Paducah. The clouds associated with it flooded out into Indiana and Tennessee, and their closeness indicated how steep the pressure gradients remained.

'It's not losing any of its stuff,' Adams observed quietly.

'No,' Stephens said bitterly. 'And it won't. Not until long after dark. The whole system is going to sweep right on across.'

'Just what we predicted.'

'Yes. But what good does that do when some people won't listen?'

'If this many have died or been injured,' Adams said, 'think of how bad it might have been *without* the warnings.'

Before Stephens could reply, Bright came back from the telephone. 'Tampa is in full agreement and they want to know if we can send it before five-thirty.'

'I'll send it now,' Stephens said.

He walked over to the work counter behind the desks and sat down at the keyboard of a Sanders 720 cathode-ray-tube device. Blue and grey, it looked like a Selectric typewriter with a four-teen-inch TV tube set on top. The picture tube was dark, quiescent.

Stephens punched four keys. As he did so, small sans-serif letters appeared in bright green near the top of the screen.

JSCO

He pressed another button, sending this code to the computer in Suitland, Maryland. The symbols asked the computer what it had in a particular information 'bin.'

With no perceptible delay, the computer began answering. Faster than the eye could follow, bright-green letters began appearing sequentially across the screen, forming the model message:

JSCO
ZCZC
WWUS9 RWRC XXXXX
MKC AC XXXXX
RAWARC

BULLETIN
TORNADO WATCH NUMBER XXX

THE NATIONAL WEATHER SERVICE HAS ISSUED A TORNADO WATCH
FOR XXXXXXXXXXXXXXXXXXXXXXXXXXXXXXXXXXXXXXXXXXXXXXXXXX
XXXXXXXXXXXXXXXXXXXXXXXXXXXXXXXXXXXXXXXXXXXXXXXXXXXX
XXXXXXXXXXXXXXXXXXXXXXXXXXXXXXXXXXXXXXXXXXXXXXXXXXXX
XXXXXXXXXXXXXXXXXXXXXXXXXXXXXXXXXX

THE THREAT OF TORNADOES AND SEVERE THUNDERSTORMS WITH
LARGE HAIL AND DAMAGING WINDS WILL EXIST IN THESE AREAS
FROM XXXXXXXXX UNTIL XXXXXXXXX THIS XXXXXXXXXXXXXXX
XXXXXXXXXXXXXXXXX

THE GREATEST THREAT OF TORNADOES AND SEVERE THUNDERSTORMS
IS IN AN AREA ALONG AND XXX MILES . . . XXX NAUTICAL . . .
EITHER SIDE OF A LINE FROM XXXXXXXXXXXXXXXXXXXXXXXXXXXXXX
XXXXXXXXXXXXXXXXXXXXXXXXXXXXXXXXXXXXXXXXXXXXXXXXXXXXXXXXXXX
XXXXXXXXXXXXXXXXXXXXXXXXXXXXXXXXXXXXXXXXXXXXXXXXXXXXXXXXXXX
XXXXXXXXXXXXXXXXXXXXXXXXXXXXXXXXXXXXXXXXXXXXXXXXXXXXXXXXXXX

PERSONS IN OR CLOSE TO THE TORNADO WATCH AREA ARE ADVISED
TO BE ON THE WATCH FOR LOCAL WEATHER DEVELOPMENTS AND
FOR LATER STATEMENTS AND WARNINGS.
OTHER WATCH INFORMATION:
XXXXXXXXXXXXXXXXXXXXXXXXXXXXXXXXXXXXXXXXXXXXXXXXXXXXXXXXXXX
XXXXXXXXXXXXXXXXXXXXXXXXXXXXXXXXXXXXXXXXXXXXXXXXXXXXXXXXXXX
XXXXXXXXXXXXXXXXXXXXXXXXXXXXXXXXXXXXXXXXXXXXXXXXXXXXXXXXXXX
XXXXXXXXXXXXXXXXXXXXXXXXXXXXXXXXXXXXXXXXXXXXXXXXXXXXXXXXXXX
XXXXXXXXXXXXXXXXXXXXXXXXXXXXXXXXXXXXXXXXXXXXXXXXXXXXXXXXXXX

Double-checking his map references with Harry Adams, Stephens
worked quickly but carefully, typing in the new watch information for much of central and southern Florida. As he typed, the
symbols changed on the screen before him, the X's being replaced by specific data.

When the message read as he wanted it, he glanced over his
shoulder at Adams, who also scanned it.

'Okay,' Adams grunted.

Stephens pushed a typewriter button which sent the message
to the computer. The computer in Maryland would accept the
message, encode it for placement on the five regional RAWARC
circuits, and send it over the national teletype network.

'That ought to take care of that,' Adams said.

'Yep,' Stephens said, standing to light a cigarette.

Bells began ringing in the message centre. The tornado watch
for central and southern Florida was already being received
everywhere.

Thatcher, Ohio
At 5:18 p.m., lightning struck one of the high-power lines carrying much of Thatcher's electricity in from the Cincinnati area.
For a few moments, virtually all electrical power stopped at the
instant the bolt sizzled into the line, severing it. Lights in Thatcher's downtown browned out, then recovered. Safety switches
cut off the flow of power to everything south of the river, and

overload mechanisms shunted the flow so that a large, pie-shaped section of the city, from downtown northward in a widening area, remained with no electricity whatsoever.

At the electric company, the status board showed the area where the line break had occurred. The assistant engineer on duty downtown rang line maintenance, ordered a truck on the way immediately, sent a secretary scurrying to give the telephone operator a standard reply to the curious or irate calls sure to flood the switchboard, called his boss and explained the situation, and called the police department downtown to report there, too.

At the police station they didn't get the message. Incoming lines were all lighted already. Some people were calling to ask about their power outage; others were calling to ask about a bulletin that had just appeared on Dayton television, saying Thatcher was under tornado warning.

Chief F. D. Merrill didn't have time to talk to any of the callers. A situation that had seemed only mildly menacing five minutes earlier had blown up on him. He had a power outage. He had thunder and lightning overhead. He had a car reporting a funnel aloft – or something – just west of the city limits. He had an irate public wanting information, a blooming attack of heartburn, and a message in his hand just off the weather wire.

XXXCC
RB 84 XX
ZZZZZ
ZZZZZ
BULLETIN
TORNADO WARNING
EANS REQUESTED
NATIONAL WEATHER SERVICE DAYTON OHIO
ISSUED 5:15 P.M. CDT APRIL 9, 1975

A TORNADO WARNING IS IN EFFECT UNTIL 7 P.M. FOR PERSONS IN THE OHIO COUNTIES OF CLINTON, GREEN, FAYETTE, CLARK AND MURPHY.

A TORNADO HAS BEEN REPORTED ON THE GROUND NORTH OF FREESBURGH IN MURPHY COUNTY AT THIS TIME. THIS TORNADO APPARENTLY HIT FREESBURGH, DOING HEAVY DAMAGE, ABOUT 5 P.M. RADAR INDICATES THIS TORNADO IMMEDIATELY SOUTH OF

THATCHER. IT IS MOVING TO THE NORTHEAST AT ABOUT 40 MPH. THIS IS A LARGE TORNADO WITH HEAVY RAIN, LARGE HAIL AND VERY HIGH WINDS. PERSONS IN THE THATCHER AREA ARE ADVISED TO TAKE COVER IMMEDIATELY.

XXX

Merrill ran into the message room, where officers and clerical help were already swamped with incoming telephone calls and the constant crackle of messages coming in from patrol cars.

'Get me the radio station!' Merrill yelled.

'All the lines are tied up,' an officer called back frantically. 'This is the damndest mess I've—'

'Cut somebody off! I don't care who it is! Get that radio station right now! We've got a tornado coming right at us!' Merrill turned to the swamped radio operator behind the glass partition, sliding the glass back as he spoke. 'Get us thirty seconds of silence on the frequency. Get that siren box open. We're sounding them in twenty seconds.'

The radio operator jumped to key his mike. 'All Thatcher units. All Thatcher units. Begin radio silence for thirty seconds now. Maintain complete radio silence until notified in approximately thirty seconds. This is an emergency. Maintain complete radio silence.'

An officer named Slade asked the chief, 'Shouldn't we at least tell them what's going on?'

'After the silence,' Merrill snapped. 'After the sirens. Jesus Christ! If they don't know the emergency procedure—'

The fire chief ran into the room from the back hallway. 'When our TV came back on, Dayton had a bulletin—'

'I know, I know,' Merrill fumed. He was beside himself as provisions of the seldom-consulted emergency plan flooded piecemeal into his memory. He barked at the telephone desk, 'Get the hospital, too. Tell them we have a tornado warning, immediate. Start alerting all city department heads. Send people into City Hall to use their lines too. Somebody notify the mayor. He ought to be home by now.'

Slade said, 'I'll need the master key to City Hall to get people in there—'

'I don't have time to dig it out, Slade. Break the fucking door down if you have to! *Move!*'

Slade turned, yelling men's names as he passed the squad room.

'Get the sheriff,' Merrill ordered. 'I want to know what he's heard from Barney Reilly. Goddamn it, that crazy son of a bitch is supposed to *know* about these kinds of things! Where the hell is he?'

In the radio room, the operator keyed a small grey box. It broadcast a two-tone signal over the police transmitter, which would key the sirens.

'What do you do about the power?' the fire chief asked.

'What? What do you mean?'

'How much of the city is without electrical power?'

'Hell, I haven't had time to find out about that yet!'

The fire chief stared at him. 'Where the power is off, the sirens aren't going to blow – are they?'

'Oh, shit!' Merrill groaned.

Overhead, muffled by the bulk of the building, came the sound of the downtown siren blowing. How many others were working?

'Do you have the electric company yet?' Merrill bellowed. 'Do you have the radio station yet? Where's my call to the sheriff? Jesus *Christ!*'

Halfway across the city to the north, the Thatcher radio station had normal power. All the lights on the telephone in the studio were blinking frantically. One call was from the police.

Johnny Schottenstein, however, didn't know this. He was not aware of any of the calls. A Beatles album was playing on the big turntable, and Schottenstein was in the back room, humming along to the monitor speaker in the ceiling, as he blithely selected records that he planned to take in the mobile unit for his evening broadcast from the shopping centre. The back room was used for storage of records and tapes, and it had no telephone. It had no windows. It was insulated and quiet.

In his north-central residential section, Mike Coyle had reached home. The electricity had failed just about the time he walked in the door. He stood at the telephone in the hallway while Mo rummaged in the kitchen for candle-ends.

'Yes, Mrs Ralbovsky,' he patiently told his latest caller. 'My electricity is off, too. I don't know what's happened, but I'm sure the power company is working on it.'

'God,' he muttered, hanging up.

Instantly the telephone rang again.

'Is this the mayor?' a man's voice asked loudly.

'Yes,' Coyle said.

'Well, this is Rufus Jordan. I live at 2929 Steuben Way, and my electricity has been off for five minutes now. I want to complain about it!'

'Mr Jordan, the city doesn't supply electric power. The electric company is a public utility—'

'Listen, Mayor, I don't want any smart-ass talk, I just want some action. Last month I couldn't get my garbage picked up on schedule, and now I want to know what you're doing about this electric deal. We've got a freezer full of choice beef, brother, and if you think *we're* going to pay for it if it all spoils, I'll tell you—'

Mo came into the darkened hallway with a bit of candle lighted. The house had grown very dark, and outside the wind had begun to increase. She put the candle on the table beside the telephone, where Coyle had been jotting the names and addresses of callers, although there was no real reason for doing so.

Coyle put his hand over the mouthpiece. As the latest complaint spewed on, he told his wife, 'I'll get a long enough break here in a second to call downtown. I'm sure there's nothing to worry about.'

Six miles south of Thatcher, Barney Reilly sat in his Ford cruiser atop a slight rise in the rolling farmland. He had the window on his side rolled down, and leaned out of it, sampling the gusty, muggy, gritty wind. It was like night all around him. Gusts of wind rocked the car. Barney Reilly was so scared he couldn't quite see straight, but he had his radio microphone in hand and was talking a blue streak.

'I'm continuing to look east and south,' he said, yelling over the thunder, 'and this worst cloud I'm watching is very, very black and it's got a lot of lightning in it and when the lightning flashes I think I can see a funnel up in the cloud. The whole thing is whirling around. I've been watching this all this time and the funnel is still up in the air but it looks real bad. The way it looks like it's going, it's going to miss town on the east side. It's going northeast and it will miss town on the east side, but people over on that side better be ready. This is a real bad cloud, as bad as I've ever seen, but unless it changes direction, it'll miss Thatcher. I'm going to break here in a minute and turn the car around so I can watch it better because it's almost straight east of me right now, but I want to report that I can see more lightning farther east and it's very, very dark everywhere, but I've had this bad cloud watched all the way and it is not on the ground at this time. Unit six over to county.'

Slight static hissed in the loudspeaker under the dashboard for a few seconds, and then the sheriff's voice boomed back: *'Barney, we've got a report from the highway patrol of a tornado on the ground out there. Are you sure it's in the cloud? We're blowing the sirens here. I want to be sure we read you right.'*

Barney Reilly didn't speak for a moment. Holding the microphone at ready, he continued to focus every ounce of his attention on the funnel aloft off to the east. *There!* Lightning flashed and he saw it very clearly. There just could not be any mistake. He continued to stare single-mindedly out his window, watching for more lightning that would make him doubly sure.

He did not want to make a mistake. He had come out here many times to watch clouds, and he knew most of the guys figured he was a lunatic. They had never seen tornado damage, either. He was the expert. He knew what he was doing.

But he stared intently to the east, nagged by the slightest little doubt. The hypo didn't say they saw a tornado on the ground until they *saw* one. What—?

'This is county to unit six. Come in, Barney.'

Barney Reilly thumbed the mike. 'This is six, go ahead.'

'Did you hear my last? Is that funnel in the air or on the ground?'

Before Barney Reilly could reply, something flew past the windshield. It hit in the ditch beside him. It was a fence post.

The air was quite suddenly murky with powdery earth. Things were flying around and dropping all around the car. He saw a piece of a tree and a long board and a chunk of what looked like sod. The dirt and pieces of things began hammering the car. It was all insane, he couldn't make it out.

A length of stepladder crashed into the road less than twenty feet in front of his cruiser. Something splattered hard on the windshield and he recoiled, amazed that the impact hadn't shattered the glass.

More heavy, wet objects began hammering down.

Hammering down, Barney Reilly saw dazedly, *and hopping around in the road*.

Rain dashed against the windshield. Lightning dazzled nearby.

It was raining frogs.

And debris.

Barney Reilly could not breathe. The radio squawked something at him. Thunder obliterated meaning. He swivelled his head as another piece of something flew past, and for the first time in many minutes his scan moved entirely across the windshield, looking south, and then looking across the front seat of the car – past the doughnut sacks, old McDonald's wrappers and discarded coffee cups – to the right-hand window, which looked directly west.

Two or three miles away, an unbelievable ebony column swept across open field toward a farmhouse, silo and barn that appeared toylike by comparison. A dull glow inside the great vertical column lighted the scene in a grotesque amber light.

As Barney Reilly's eyes shrank from the impact of what they saw, the ebony column reached the farmhouse and barn. They seemed to explode in a vivid greenish light.

'Unit six, unit six!'

Barney Reilly thumbed the microphone. 'It's on the ground!' he cried. 'It's on the ground! It's past me and I'm okay, but it's on the ground! It's moving right straight at you! It's coming like hell! Oh my God! Oh my God! Oh my God!'

In the city, only eleven sirens worked properly. Some people were so puzzled by the siren sounds that they tried futilely to call the police or fire departments. Others went out into their yards or the streets and looked worriedly at the darkening sky and asked each other what they should do. Some went to basements. More, worried by the warning from Dayton television and now given a second warning by a siren, nevertheless peered from house windows, wondering what on earth they should do.

Many did nothing more because it was just too embarrassing to act scared.

In the areas where sirens failed to function, even those who heard a warning on television assumed that the sirens would blow if anything really severe was close at hand. Many others didn't think about it one way or the other.

In the part of Thatcher without any electrical power at all, there was neither TV warning nor siren warning. At McDaws Park, three Little League baseball games continued as umpires tried to finish an inning before the rain moved in.

At 5:28 p.m., technicians completed a jury-rigged power shunt at the electric company. Switches closed and electricity flowed back into those parts of Thatcher that had been without it for exactly ten minutes. In several thousand homes in the centre of the city, TV sets began to make bright-coloured blips on the screen as they warmed up again; lights glowed; appliances hummed; home-owners smiled at one another with relief.

It was now so dark that street lights came on.

And now, across Thatcher came the sound of a very great wind.

Columbus, Ohio

A huge shelf of ominous cloud extended over Columbus' far west side, and lightning flickered to the south. Pilot Roy Bock made a low, hot approach to the private-aviation airfield and set the Learjet down flawlessly despite gusting crosswinds.

'How's that for service?' he called back to Bill Fredrick, strapped into the first passenger seat behind the tiny galley.

'We're not here any too soon,' Fredrick replied, looking out at the gathering storm.

Bock, a youthful, curly-haired man who fancied himself the world's Number One hotshot pilot, jerked the jet off the active runway at the first intersection, screaming the tyres, then taxied too fast toward the terminal building. As he began to slow on the apron, Barbara James left the copilot's seat and came back to help Fredrick move the camera and recording cases out of the galley area and into the narrow aisle. The plane rocked sharply as Bock braked, almost knocking Fredrick off his feet.

Barbara James put out a hand to steady him. She was pale. 'That guy is a fine pilot, but I'll take my hotdogs at football games, thanks.'

'Well, he brought us straight through.'

'If you had been watching that weather radar display up front, your heart would have been in your mouth. I still don't know how we dodged some of those cells!'

The plane rocked again as Bock came to a full stop near the small, glass-fronted terminal. Like most private-aviation airports, it looked deserted on a day of weather like this; lobby lights glowed, but there was no sign of life inside the lobby, and the tower beacon rotated bleakly as it signalled alternating green and white in the gloom.

Bock got the door of the plane open and the ladder extended, then helped Fredrick carry down the heavier steel cases. Included in the equipment, in addition to camera and sound gear, was a small, portable wind-velocity instrument specially designed to withstand very high winds. There was also a severe-weather barometric-pressure device. Both instruments operated on batteries, and printed their data continuously on a shielded paper roll.

Fredrick carried the rest of the gear to the front door of the terminal. 'See if you can get through to Davidson on the lobby phone,' he told Barbara James. 'Tell him we're setting up and get any new information. Then, if the airport manager hasn't put in an appearance by then, maybe you could hunt him up while I'm setting up, here.'

Barbara James hurried inside. A stiffening wind made the door hard for her to handle.

'What do you want me to do?' Bock asked.

'Check and make sure this building has a basement,' Fredrick said.

'How come? You put this stuff under the ground?'

'Have you taken a look at that sky?'

Bock's face twisted into a grin of disbelief. 'You mean you want a hidey-hole?'

'If it gets bad,' Fredrick said, cutting some twine with his pocketknife, 'you're damned right.'

'I thought you chased these things, man!'

'In a specially instrumented van, yes. But I don't usually get out in front of them, and frankly I don't much like the feeling.'

'I sort of hope something does happen,' Bock told him. 'I've never seen a twister. That'd be a blast!'

Wednesday, April 9
5:29 p.m.—5:50 p.m.

NNNN
XVXXXVCZ
XX
229XC
X

SEVERE WEATHER STATEMENT
NATIONAL WEATHER SERVICE DAYTON OHIO
ISSUED 5:25 P.M. CDT APRIL 9, 1975

DURING THE PAST FIFTEEN MINUTES THUNDERSTORMS HAVE
INCREASED IN INTENSITY ALONG A LINE WHICH EXTENDS FROM
CINCINNATI TO XENIA TO SPRINGFIELD. THIS LINE OF
THUNDERSTORMS IS STILL BUILDING IN INTENSITY AT A RAPID
RATE. AT 5:15 THE POLICE IN SPRINGFIELD REPORTED HAIL MORE
THAN ONE INCH IN DIAMETER AND WINDS GUSTING 60 MPH.
THIS LINE OF THUNDERSTORMS IS MOVING EASTWARD AT 50 MPH.
PERSONS AHEAD OF THIS LINE SHOULD BE ALERT TO THE
POSSIBILITY XXXXXXXXXXXXXXXXXXXXXXXXXX

X
  X
    XX
Z Z Z Z Z

BULLETIN
TORNADO WARNING
EANS REQUESTED
NATIONAL WEATHER SERVICE DAYTON OHIO
ISSUED 5:28 P.M. CDT APRIL 9, 1975

A TORNADO WARNING IS IN EFFECT FOR THATCHER.

OFFICIALS IN THATCHER REPORT A TORNADO HITTING THATCHER
AT THE PRESENT TIME. RADAR SHOWS A HOOK ECHO DIRECTLY
OVER THATCHER. THIS TORNADO IS ON THE GROUND AND MOVING
THROUGH THE CITY. PERSONS NORTH AND EAST OF THATCHER ARE
ADVISED TO TAKE IMMEDIATE PRECAUTIONS.

XXX

Dayton, Ohio
People had nicknamed John McKinley, chief of the Dayton

National Weather Service office, 'Prez.' The joke had never bothered him very much. He was an easy-going man.

He did not feel easy-going now. Staring at the radarscope, he imagined some of the things that the intense echo directly over Thatcher was doing to that city.

'Prez,' Judy Baxter, his assistant meteorologist, said softly, 'I'm afraid they're really getting plastered.'

'They're getting plastered, all right,' McKinley grated.

In the adjacent office of the Dayton station, McKinley had extra personnel on duty. Three of them were now making emergency calls – to the Highway Patrol, the Ohio National Guard, the Red Cross, the Governor's office, area police and fire departments. A disaster plan, well-honed on the state level, was already being effected.

Thatcher would have disaster assistance soon.

They were going to need it, McKinley thought, his tired eyes fixed on the scope.

Thatcher, Ohio

The Thatcher tornado, one of three suspended under a single enormous thundercloud cell some nine miles in diameter and towering more than seventy thousand feet in altitude, was at its peak of life as it reached the southwestern edge of Southtown, on a northeasterly path that would take it through the heart of the city. It was one mile wide at its mouth, with winds of two hundred miles per hour crushing, smashing and destroying everything in its range, and could not be seen as a classic twister, but rather as a gigantic ebony obscuration from ground to sky, swirling, shrieking with a sound like none other in the world.

Trees tossed and dirt flew ahead of it. A few drops of cold rain spattered down or were hurled horizontally. Shrubs groaned, writhing in the force of twisting winds. And over the heavy thickness of the very air was the high keening wail of the wind.

At the southwest edge of Southtown, at a car-salvage lot, the edge of the blackness arrived. At this particular point, the tornado's rotational wind velocities were boosted because they were here parallel to the line of forward motion of the entire incredible funnel. Winds screaming two hundred miles per hour around the centre were also being hurled forward at more than fifty miles per hour. The effect on the salvage yard was winds exceeding two hundred fifty miles per hour.

The stockade fencing was smashed flat and then thrown into the air, disintegrating, vanishing. Wrecked or junked cars leaped up as if insanely alive, and flew. Dozens and then hundreds of old cars simply took off, sailing in all directions. The salvage-yard office building, made of concrete blocks, vibrated and shook. Its metal roof lifted up and sailed westward. The wind lifted desks and a torrent of papers and small parts out of the interior, and then the walls exploded.

The blackness tore down the power lines along Harkness Boulevard and exploded garages, storage buildings, service stations. A city bus pulled to the curb, its occupants spilled out into the street. Bricks showered down on them as the three-storey apartment building nearby began to disintegrate. The people dived for doorways. The bus was flipped on to its side and tumbled down the street end over end like a berserk giant's toy. A power line toppled sideways onto a steel-frame building already stripped of its aluminium siding and sparks flew and flames leaped upward. Somewhere, very faintly, there was the wail of a siren.

The blackness smashed through the industrial park. Whirling debris sang at bullet velocities. A great old smokestack became a fountain of brick crushing tumbled cars beneath it. Glass crashed. Metal twisted. Trees ripped out of the earth and simply flew away into space. There was a little rain, but it was horizontal.

The tornado brushed the downtown bridge, moving northeast. The placid river became an enormous whirlpool, waves twenty feet high throwing pleasure boats into the nearby park and playground area. Trees went down one after another with the unbelievable precision of a surgeon's scalpel. The downtown bridge twisted and bent, and inside its metal support structures overhead, cars became mangled wrecks. Then the insanity was across the north shore, exploding some old apartment units, knocking down power lines, flattening a shoe factory, going up onto higher ground very near the edge of downtown, and it hit the bluffs. Shanties and shacks and decrepit duplexes flew apart or into the air, timbers and bricks and rocks and furniture and a blizzard of paper and trash everywhere, and then the blackness was moving still to the northeast, and off beside the main, gigantic ebony obscuration, several hundred yards to its east, the cloud put down another tornado.

The second Thatcher tornado was small, and it danced, a silver snake in the sky. It touched down and blasted an apartment complex of forty units, shovelling in walls and destroying roofs. It lifted, and its tail wriggled, and then it touched down again, lifting a hornet's nest of brown debris from a row of houses and shops.

The two tornadoes, the one huge, great and black, limitless in its power and evil duration, and its smaller companion, dancing like a mad little child in jubilation with its parent's grotesque horror, swept deeper into Thatcher.

Wind rocked Chris O'Conner's small car violently as he turned off the highway and entered the hilltop trailer court. He had his headlights on. The sky was like night. He was scared now and trying to hide it.

'No problem,' he said. 'See? We made it.'

'Hurry,' his wife Janet urged nervously.

O'Conner's voice cracked under the tension. 'Are you crazy? I can't hurry. The wind is pushing us all over the road now!'

The narrow gravel roadway led through a little limestone gate and into the grove of trees covering the top of the hill. The roadway forked, then became several roads that were even narrower. O'Conner stayed on the central street, following its curve in under the trees and past the first mobile homes. It was a large court and the mobile homes were permanent, for all intents and purposes, seated on stone or concrete foundations, with metal skirts extending to the ground. Most of the long, low metal units had aluminium awnings affixed to their sides, extending out over block patios; there were trash-can units near the street, gravel sidewalks, clotheslines here and there, even some fences circumscribing units' tiny rented plots.

Everything looked deserted in the first block.

At the second intersection, where O'Conner turned on to a lane neatly marked with a street sign – HUMMINGBIRD LA. – he saw a man and two women struggling along the gravel sidewalk. They wore raincoats which were being whipped by the wind; they were obviously having trouble making their way. Before O'Conner could comment, he spotted others up ahead – a dozen stragglers or more, all moving in the same general direction, toward the centre of the park.

A piece of a tree limb dropped heavily into the street just ahead of the car. The car picked it up and started dragging it along loudly on the underside.

'Where's everybody going?' O'Conner wondered. 'Are they *crazy?*'

His wife did not reply. Annie hung over the back of the seat, watching solemnly and for once not saying a word, either.

Dirt flew through the air, peppering the car windows. Lightning flashed bright, and the thunder vibrated the car.

O'Conner crept the car along past more people walking hurriedly, bent against the strong wind. No one even looked up at him as he passed; their heads were down against the flying dirt.

The mobile home belonging to Janet's parents, Mr and Mrs McCoy, was just ahead. It sat at an angle across a lot formed by the forking of the lane. White, with pale-blue trim, it had an enclosed side porch. It was one of the biggest trailers of the hundreds in the park.

Thankfully O'Conner pulled up beside the McCoy Buick in the gravelled parking space. 'Let's get inside,' he muttered.

As he got out, the wind almost tearing the car door out of his grasp, he saw the front door of the trailer swing open. Mr McCoy came out, followed by his wife. They were bundled up like the others streaming by. McCoy struggled to latch the front door.

Janet, holding Annie tightly by the hand, met her mother in front of the cars. O'Conner joined them. The wind was very strong, and dirt particles stung his face. Over the lashing sounds of the wind in the trees, he heard another faint sound: a siren.

'Come with us!' Mrs McCoy said. 'This way! Hurry!'

'Where?' O'Conner demanded. This was crazy!

'The shelter!' McCoy yelled as he joined the group.

'What?'

'The shelter! The storm shelter! This way!'

There was no time to argue. The elderly couple were clearly frightened, and had already turned to hurry around the side of their trailer, falling in with others on the sidewalk. O'Conner scooped his daughter up in his arms and hurried after them.

'Where are we going, Daddy?' she asked, frightened.

'We're just going to get out of the rain that's coming,' he told her.

'Why don't we go in the trailer, Daddy?'

He didn't answer. It was all he could do to keep moving against the wind. He saw a woman fall heavily, obviously hurting herself; she got right up and moved along faster, limping. The trees had gone mad. A piece of metal skirt on one mobile home was ripped loose at one side and flapped loudly in the wind as they hurried past it.

Crossing the next lane, they walked between two trailers and came to the small, tree-encircled central plaza. In its centre was the limestone 'clubhouse,' which served as a community laundry facility as well as a game room for Ping-Pong and other table games. The flag on the small pole in front was cracking like a whip. People were pouring into the low, solid old structure that had once been some sort of army post headquarters.

In front of the building, Crump, the owner of the court, stood straddling a metal box with a crank on the side. The old man was cranking ferociously. The box was the hand-operated siren that O'Conner had been hearing.

O'Conner followed the others inside. No one stopped inside the main lounge, with its timbered ceilings and rock fireplace. They were going directly across the room and through a doorway. O'Conner followed his wife and her parents, falling in line.

The doorway led to a wooden staircase that went down. It smelled musty in the lower level. It was a long, low room, walls and ceiling studded with pipes and wires, lighted by a single bare bulb in a porcelain fixture. A row of large hot-water tanks stood along one side. There were a few pieces of dusty, discarded furniture and some storage cartons against the back wall. All the walls appeared to be poured concrete. The bare floor, also concrete, was black with dirt, moist with condensation. The entire room was not more than fifteen feet wide and sixty feet long. It was packed, and more people pressed down the steps against O'Conner as he reached the bottom. Voices racketed. It was very hot.

'There's a tornado,' Mrs McCoy called to him and Janet over the noise. 'Someone saw it and called. Mr Crump sounded his siren.'

'We don't have tornadoes around here,' O'Conner argued.

Mrs McCoy just stared at him.

A few more people came down the steps. Last came Crump, his

blue shirt darkened by sweat, his thick eyeglasses fogged up from the dense humidity created in the cellar by all the humanity. He struggled to swing a stout door closed flat against the floor opening above his head. People called excited questions at him, but he ignored the clamour until he had the door finally swung closed and latched.

'All right!' he called from the steps, the overhead light glinting off his spectacles. 'All right, everybody! Listen!'

The voices began to quiet. In the far corner, two or three people continued yelling at each other, oblivious. Others hissed for silence and finally got it.

Without the voices, the wind sound outside was very clear and loud.

Crump spoke over it, his reedy voice strained. 'We have a bad 'un coming, folks, just any minute. But we're all right here. We're cramped, but this basement is safe.'

'Is there a cyclone?' someone asked. 'How do you know?'

'I've got a battery radio,' Crump replied. 'When the electricity went off, I turned it on. I listened to the police.'

'Where is it?' someone called. 'Where's the tornado now?'

Crump shook his head solemnly. 'It's heading this way.'

Someone muttered an obscenity. A woman wailed and began to sob.

'We're safe here,' Crump cried. 'Most states don't have no law that says a mobile home operator has to have a storm shelter, but I built this one myself. It'll *hold*. You see these walls? Poured concrete. That's better than blocks, don't cost that much more. You see that ceiling, there? All right. Four-by-twelves, solid beams, set in the concrete. Then two-by-six subflooring, tongue-in-groove, and heavy plywood on top of *that*. That roof ain't going anywhere. It ain't falling in, neither.'

His words were having a calming effect.

The single overhead light went out.

Someone wailed.

'It's all right! It's all right!' Crump called. 'That just means my little generator unit ran out of gas. I didn't have hardly none in it to start with. It don't mean anything else. Chances are this thing will miss us anyway. We're just taking precautions, right? Just stay calm. Stay calm.'

Crump's lips kept moving as he continued, for a moment, to

try to be heard. But the sound outside the shelter made it impossible. Through the stout roof and the earth itself, the roar multiplied a thousandfold. It sounded like a dozen jet aircraft parked right on top of the doorway. The heavy ceiling vibrated, dirt sifted down into O'Conner's upturned face. He could not see much of anything. Someone had a cigarette lighter held overhead for its feeble illumination, and the tiny light flickered yellow on stricken, sweat-shiny faces – glazed eyes. O'Conner found his wife's hand and squeezed it, holding Annie close against his chest. *We're going to die*, he thought with absolute certainty.

The bolted door at the top of the steps cracked loudly and flew upward explosively. Grey light filled with rain smashed in. People shrank back from the lightning-vivid opening, crushing against one another. There was screaming. The roar became hellish. Against the roar, O'Conner could hear another sound, a *leit motif*, the groaning of wood against wood, the crash of rocks falling as the building over their heads came apart. He heard machine-gun pinging sounds, metallic, and chilled as he recognized them: *the nails were being pulled out of the timbers overhead.*

Crump was yelling shrilly for calm, but only an occasional word could be understood. The sound was worse than anything any of them had ever heard.

O'Conner clung to his wife and daughter, frozen in place, possessed by the elemental fear of annihilation.

Nightlike darkness stood at the windows of Mike Coyle's home. When lightning flashed brilliantly, it was to reveal savaged trees stopped in their wild throes as if by a strobe light. Rain smashed against the windows. The lights had failed again. Mo was re-lighting candles. Standing at the suddenly dead telephone, Coyle saw she was trembling.

'The phone's out again,' he told her. 'I've got to know what's going on downtown, and wires must be down. I should have stayed down there! '

'I don't care about downtown,' she told him. 'I wish Billy and Jill were here. I'm scared, Mike.'

He went to her and took her in his arms. 'Nothing to be scared of. This is the worst—'

Lightning and thunder lighted the room brilliantly and rattled everything in the house. The rain became maniacal. Outside somewhere came a sharp, loud, splitting noise.

'My God, that sounded like something in the roof!' Coyle started for the front door.

'Mike! No!'

'I'll be right back. I have to see what happened. I want to get a better look at the sky anyway.'

'Mike!' Mo called again, despairingly.

He opened the front door, conscious as he did so that air from the house whistled through the widening crack like pressure escaping from a vacuum can. He stepped on to the front porch and then went down into the yard. Trees and shrubs whipped restlessly, with increasing fury. He thought he heard a siren in the distance. He looked up at his house, standing in the middle of the yard, and could not see any sign of damage, source of the ominous cracking sound he had heard from within.

The sky over the rooftop swirled, grey clots of cloud darting past at incredible speed. Everything was very dark, and, turning, he saw that it was even darker toward the west. He heard sounds like thunder, but they were not thunder.

The wind suddenly increased sharply. He had already been braced against it. Now it hit with a force that almost knocked him down. It was a hot, humid wind, reeking of ozone.

As he turned back toward the house, the wind increased *again*, screaming. But now it was an icy blast that instantly brought tears to his eyes. His clothing whipped at his body with such ferocity that it stung. He took an uncertain few steps toward the front door. He was scared.

Someone, somewhere screamed. The noise increased by some factor beyond understanding. He turned toward the noise and could look southward, down his street.

Pieces were flying off houses. The sky was packed with debris of all sizes. He saw an entire billboard at least two hundred feet in the air, rotating swiftly like the blade of a helicopter, and pieces were sailing off it. He saw a chimney on a house a half block away fly to pieces, and then lightning flashed crimson, blindingly, and the thunderclap – or the wind – sent him sprawling.

He was on his face in the grass and the wind was all around him, trying to pick him up. Dirt choked his mouth and nostrils and he could not see. More lightning and thunder blasted. *It's going to pick me up. Jesus Christ!*

It was less than a dozen steps to the front porch, and the door flapping back and forth beyond. Fixing it with his eyes, Coyle started crawling. He clawed into the soft lawn soil with his finger-tips, fighting against the wind that felt like whips on his back and legs. Leaves, chunks of dirt and grass, particles that hit with the biting fury of fishhooks, smashed against him. He could hear the storm more clearly now, and it was almost upon him, the full brunt almost here, and there was a combination of hellish sounds: the scream of high, cold wind; the sizzling fury of a lightning stroke; explosive boom of thunder; and over all of this a terrible earthen roar, like the sound of a continuous atomic explosion.

The shrubbery around the front porch tore at him as he crawled up the steps and threw himself inside. Staggering to his feet, he fought to get the front door closed, and did not know if he succeeded. The house was quieter and yet like the inside of a huge drum. He reeled into the living-room doorway.

Mo ran toward him. 'What's *happening?*'

Lightning and thunder, seemingly simultaneous, blasted into the front yard. The sound and flash were like a great bomb.

Mo turned toward the window. 'Oh, no!'

In the lightning flashes, Coyle saw that their biggest tree had been split down the middle. It lay broken across the front yard, limbs and dense leaves piled onto the front porch and sidewalk where he had been moments ago. Shrubs whipped in a frenzy. The smell of dust and electricity and rain filled the air.

'Get back from the window,' Coyle said sharply.

He was completely helpless. That was the worst part. In almost every situation he had ever known, there was something he could do. There was nothing at all now. He had never seen savagery to compare with this. They were trapped.

Lightning flashed again. A great roar came. Pieces of trees flew past the windows. In the lightning flashes, Coyle saw the two old maples in front of the Shyer house next door.

He could not believe what he seemed to be watching in slow motion.

The twin maples rotated. Their branches went mad. The entire trees lifted straight up like rockets, dangling great black root balls that tore up earth, sod, pieces of sidewalk. They continued to rise straight up.

The house across the street was moving sideways, bricks flying.

Mo screamed.

The scream shocked Coyle into action. He pushed her back away from the window. She sprawled against the couch. The window exploded inward, shattering him with bright spots of pain. He saw blood on his hands and arms. Rain dashed in and the wind tore draperies down, hurtling over a floor lamp and everything on the desk. The sounds outside became a demoniacal roar, and an unbelievable hammering. The house cried out and began to break.

Coyle staggered to his wife's side, throwing himself over her. Something fell – a piece of the ceiling. He held on to Mo and tried to cover her with his body and hung on, burying his face in her hair.

Police Chief F. D. Merrill bawled across the chaos of the message room, 'Has anybody gotten through to the mayor yet?'

A secretary looked up frantically. 'The line is out of order. A lot of lines are out of order—'

Next door, the fire sirens sounded.

'Oh, God,' Merrill grunted, and ran for the front door.

He had to see it for himself. In the minutes since the great blackness had enveloped the downtown area, he had been locked into the onrushing emergency atmosphere of the front office with its clattering of radio messages and jangling telephones. Now for an instant he knew a feeling like claustrophobia, and he had to get out – see what the world looked like beyond the front doors.

He threw the front door of the office open and stepped out on to rain-wet pavement covered with tiny white pebbles – light hail. A cool wind gusted against his body. The sky was a boiling blue-black.

Street lights glowed. At one corner the traffic signal blinked red, then green. At the other corner nearby, the traffic signal was not in place any more; it lay in the middle of the intersection, smashed in a tangle of lines.

Neon signs flashed and pulsed, but there was no one on the street.

Cars lay on their sides and tops on sidewalks, across intersections. A Volkswagen had been thrown into a plate-glass window and was half inside the display of men's clothing, which was somehow, still normally lighted. Pieces of roofs were gone. Debris covered the street – bricks, boards, roofing, pieces of signs, wire and cable. The sound of distant sirens carried through the gusty, cool-wet air from all directions.Looking southeast, Merrill was stunned to see the courthouse truncated, the steeple and dome missing. He could not see the rest of the building over a department store, the roof of which was littered with the wreckage of a cooling-equipment tower.

From the side of the building came the clanging of warning bells. The doors were already open, and a fire truck wheeled out, lights flashing, siren blaring. A wrecked car was in the street. The fire truck hit it a glancing blow as it wheeled out, turned left beside Merrill, and started up the street. It began to brake almost at once and firemen jumped off, running, as it ground to a halt. They began playing out hose to a fire hydrant. Others ran toward the building on the far corner, the drugstore. Merrill saw flames shooting from the upstairs windows.

Another fire truck lumbered out of the side doors and headed in the other direction, down the side street. It turned north at the corner.

The buildings that Merrill could see had all been damaged. Roofs were gone in some instances, windows blown in, pieces of walls gone. They all stood. He knew the tornado had hit the downtown area a glancing blow, which explained why they still had power here. He did not know what had happened elsewhere; the reports were too many, too confused. It was as if everything in the normal fabric of the city had exploded in seconds. He did not know what was going on. He was frightened and helpless. He had units all over the place and all the news was bad. There were probably more fires, too ... had to be. How many were hurt or killed? He didn't know.

A woman who worked in City Hall ran down the sidewalk toward him. Middle-aged, with grey hair that still managed to be in place, she had a department-store package under her arm with her large brown purse.

'I have keys,' she told Merrill. 'I can open the city building.'

'Yes,' Merrill said. 'Do that, and—' He stopped.

She waited, eyes snapping, for instructions.

'Open it up,' Merrill told her, trying to firm up his voice and demeanour. 'We have some people in there using telephones. We'll need a lot more help.'

'What do you want me to do first?'

'I – don't know. There's so much—!'

'Contact department heads? Try to get all city crews on duty?'

'Yes,' Merrill said. 'Good.'

'What else?'

'I don't know,' Merrill said, losing his temper. 'How do *I* know? I'm not the mayor. I can't even find the mayor. I don't even have an assistant chief. I don't have enough help. I'm not qualified to handle something like this. Do what you think – do whatever you think is right.'

On the next corner, firemen were going up a ladder into the building. Hoses played water across the blazing roof. The flames had spread to the small department store next to the drugstore, and smoke billowed against the sky. To the north, the clouds exploded with lightning.

'It's not my fault,' Merrill said to himself, because the woman had turned to run toward the city building. 'I'm not in charge. I'm not qualified, it isn't my responsibility.'

He was face to face with the realization that this tragedy was too big for him. He could not hope to comprehend it or try to deal with it. He was a detail man. There was nothing wrong with being a detail man, he told himself. If anyone was at fault, it was the mayor. The mayor ought to be here.

An officer stuck his head out of the police station. 'Chief!'

Merrill turned.

'We've got all sorts of injury reports, Chief. The ambulance services are swamped. They don't know how to answer calls, where to take the people or anything. We can't get through to the hospital. Nobody knows what to do.'

'Coming,' Merrill grunted authoritatively.

He had no idea what to do, either. He was near panic.

The worst noise was past. It had begun to abate as swiftly as it had risen. Torrential rain pounded down in the lightning, but it was not as bad as before. Mike Coyle sat up, releasing Mo. She stared at him with the widened eyes of momentary shock. Part of the interior wall had come down beside them and they were powdered with chalky dust. Across the room, the carpet was soaked from the rain coming through the broken windows.

'My God!' Mo said huskily. 'You're all – *hurt!*'

Coyle looked down at his arms and hands, which were bright

with blood from small glass cuts. He flexed his hands experiment-ally. 'They're all little. I'm okay. Are you okay?'

'Yes . . . I think so.'

He got to his feet and helped her up beside him. Two sections of ceiling had come down, exposing beams. One section of Sheet-rock lay crumpled across the desk, and a second stood at a crazy angle against the foyer wall. Nothing else in the room seemed badly damaged, although the wall into the foyer did not seem quite straight.

Outside, the rain was diminishing very rapidly. Light grew at the window and the wind had vanished. In more distant light-ning, Coyle saw that the street was filled with big trees.

'I've got to get to the circuit-breaker box,' he told his wife. 'We've been damaged. If the power comes back on, we could have a fire.'

'I don't want to move,' Mo said. 'I'm afraid things might fall on us.'

'Stay right here. It's just in the kitchen closet.'

'Mike!'

Because it was the only thing he was sure he should do, he was obsessed with getting it done. He ignored his wife's cry and walked across the room. He went into the foyer. The front door had blown open and the way out was blocked by wet tree branches and leaves. The floor was covered with a fine grey dust. It made grating sounds under his feet as he made his way into the kitchen.

The kitchen seemed undisturbed. He found the circuit breakers and threw them all open. He checked the stove. There was no gas. He turned the valve back off. He walked to the back door and peered out.

The back yard was an alien landscape. No trees remained. The fence was gone, the shrubs were beaten flat. He saw the back of the Shyer house and did not recognize it for an instant. It was completely demolished. All that was left of the kitchen was a pile of rubble.

Picking up the kitchen extension phone, Coyle knew it was fu-tile to hope that somehow the lines remained. The instrument was dead. He felt a moment of something like vertigo as his brain tried to comprehend things. The house was damaged, perhaps wrecked. Billy and Jill were out somewhere. He had to find out if they were all right. He had to take care of Mo. He had to start doing things about the house. How widespread was the destruction across the city? He had to deal with that. He had to get to a telephone and talk to someone downtown.

If there was still a downtown.

He went to the basement and used a wrench to close the main gas valve. Then he went back to the kitchen and checked the sink. There was water. He ran cold water over his hands and arms, dried them on a towel as he headed back into the living room. The rain was stopping. He could hear a police or fire siren up on Glenbrooke Boulevard. Dust hung in the living-room air, starting to settle out. There was no one in the room.

'*Mo!*'

His voice echoed sharply.

'I'm here,' she called.

He rushed into the foyer to see her coming down the stairs. 'My God! You shouldn't be trying to go up there! You don't know—!'

'It's all right,' she told him shakily. 'I had to – see.'

He stared at her, unable to ask.

'Part of the roof must be gone,' she said. 'Rain is leaking in. The walls are all standing. I don't think it's – I think we can—' Her control broke and she sobbed, leaning against him.

'Mo,' he said, holding her. 'Listen. We have to get outside and see what's happened.'

'I want the children. Where are our children?'

'Jill's at the hospital, remember? She's all right. It's a strong old building.'

'Billy.' She recoiled, her eyes great with fear. 'He was going to go with the Tidwell boy.'

'They're probaby halfway across town,' Coyle told her, trying to convince himself as well. 'He's fine. I know he is. A thing like this won't cover an entire city—'

'We've got to find them.'

'I'll find them. Let's get outside and see what's happened.'

She made a visible effort to control herself. Raking her hand across her face, she looked for a second like nothing so much as a scared child. But then she got the control she sought and it was better.

'All right,' she said.

He went to the front door, his feet squishing in the wet carpet. The fallen tree limbs blocked the way, but he pushed into the cold, wet leaves, shoving them back and standing on them to let Mo follow him. There were not as many limbs as at first appeared, and after a moment of struggling he got them pressed aside and they were both able to climb through and over, and to the wet sidewalk. The yard was half covered with standing water, but the rain had stopped.

He looked first at the sky. Low clouds scudded past, fleeing north at high speed. They were much thinner now and the light was that of early evening. To the north, past the broken roofline of the house, the sky was inky blue, with intense lightning. He could not see anything but the darkness. There had been a tornado; he knew this; he could not see the funnel. The worst activity was already several miles to the north and east, an ebony wall across the horizon.

Slightly dazed, he looked across the front of his house, seeing the broken windows, wrecked roof, shattered porch pillars, the tree that had fallen across his car, crushing it.

The street was completely changed. The thought crossed Coyle's mind that their house had been blown to some other neighbourhood entirely. He knew this was insane, but nothing else made more sense.

The old trees were gone. Everything stood naked to the sky. There were jagged stumps, trees felled and lying in the street and in yards, huge root balls in driveways. Some of the houses across the street were unrecognizable, too: knocked sideways, parts missing, familiar walls peering out from behind great mounds of rubble. An electric line sparked viciously, smoking, in a puddle nearby.

Then Coyle became aware that other people were also coming out – across the street, down the block – people appearing, standing in shock to stare at what had happened to them and others.

As far as Coyle could see toward the west, it was the same. He could see much farther than he had ever been able to see before, because almost all the trees were gone. And some of the houses.

There was a sound behind him. He turned at the same time Mo did. The Shyers had come across the lake of their front yard and were now making their way around the tree debris in the driveway. Mrs Shyer appeared hurt, or shaken; in a robe, with her hair in curlers, she leaned on her husband's assisting arm. Shyer, in mud-splattered khaki pants and sweat shirt, did not appear in much better shape.

'Are you folks all right?' Shyer asked solicitously.

'We weren't hurt,' Coyle told them.

Mrs Shyer stared at the front of the house and then turned to Mo. 'Oh, my dear. It hit your house, too.'

'I was in the kitchen, potting geraniums,' Shyer said huskily, like a sleepwalker. 'The wind started and I went to the living room. I saw our trees. Did you see what it did to our trees?'

'Yes,' Coyle said.

Mo said, 'Both of us saw that.'

Shyer began crying without sound.

'Mo,' Coyle said, 'maybe you'd better take them in our place.'

'Is it safe?'

'Yes. I'm sure our house is safe. I think theirs is damaged worse. I don't know for certain, but I think we must have been on the edge of the thing. Look there. Even the houses on the other side of the street seem to be hurt worse than the ones on this side were. And it looks worse yet on to the west. I think it went through to the west of us and we were on the edge.'

Mo recoiled. 'If we were on *the edge*, what did it do to people nearer the centre?'

'I've got to find out.'

A new voice called nearby, 'Somebody help me? Please?'

They turned. A man waded the street, a small boy in his arms. The child was unconscious. Other people had begun to gather across the street. One woman was being supported by two men, and her face was bloody.

The man stepped up into the yard. 'He's hurt. The wall fell on him. Can anybody do anything?'

'We've got a first-aid kit,' Mo said.

Coyle decided. He called to the others across the street. 'We'll try to help injured people in my house. Some of you come help us move this tree out from in front of the door!'

Shyer said, 'I was a medic's aide in the Army. That was a long time ago, but—'

'You're the best we've got,' Coyle told him. 'Come on.'

Together they climbed through the fallen tree to get back inside the house. By the time they had found the bulky first-aid kit – bought a year ago to humour Jill, who had been to a first-aid seminar – the people out front had gotten the tree moved enough to allow easier entry through the door. The man brought his son in and placed him on the couch. Shyer knelt beside the boy, gently examining him.

'Where's the rest of your family?' Coyle asked the man.

'Down the street – up by the corner.'

'Are they hurt?'

'No . . . they're not—'

'Go down and tell them where you've brought your son. If they want to come up here, bring them. We're going to set this up as the first-aid station for the block.'

'I think there are some other people down there hurt. I heard people yelling—'

'Find out. Take a couple of these men out front with you. If you need more help, get more people to go with you.'

'I got no experience bossing people—'

'You give the orders, and they'll obey. Count on it.'

The man stumbled out of the house as others brought in the woman with a bloody face. Mo threw down some blankets and they placed the woman on the floor. More people were gathering in the yard as word spread. Amazingly, there seemed to be few serious injuries.

Coyle went to the telephone and tried it again. Mo came into the kitchen as he replaced the dead instrument.

She said tensely, 'I'm sure that little boy has a serious head injury. The woman isn't so bad. I'm going to have to tear up sheets for bandages. Everyone is cut from flying glass.'

'Mo,' Coyle said grimly, 'I'm going to have to get out of here.'

She turned, slack-faced. 'What?'

'I've got to get to a telephone. I've got to know what's happened to the city . . . try to get things organized.'

'If you want to organize something, go down the street where someone said some people are trapped in their basement!'

'I'm the mayor. There are probably places hit worse than we were. Nobody will know what to do—'

'You're going to *leave* us – like this?'

'You're all right. The house will stand. I have to start finding out what happened – give orders—'

'Let them follow that precious disaster plan that you sat up every night for months, working on!' Mo's eyes blazed. 'Mike,

I've never tried to tell you what to do, but your place is right here!'

'My place is trying to help the whole city!'

She watched him, saying nothing. Her lips opened and closed. He could see the intensity of her shock and anger. He thought she was actually going to spring at him.

'I've got to,' he said huskily. 'It's my job—'

She turned and rushed out of the room.

In the front of the house now was a growing babble of voices – more neighbours, more injured, more problems. Coyle almost gave in and decided to stay right here. Sooner or later the police would get through to him.

But if he could get to Glenbrooke Boulevard, there would surely be emergency traffic there. He could flag somebody, get to a radio or a telephone.

He had no choice. He knew the capabilities of the people who worked for him. Facts had to be gathered and decisions made. *His* decisions.

Looking toward the foyer door, he felt a great impulse to go back to the other part of the house at least long enough to try to explain it better to Mo. How often – how goddamned miserably often – had he made decisions like this that he hated, that he had to make because it was the job and the responsibility?

He again heard what sounded like a siren up toward Glenbrooke. There simply was no more time.

The back door was stuck. He had to wrench at it repeatedly to get it open. He cut across the mangled remains of his back yard and reached the alley and started north, walking fast, climbing over and around wreckage where it was necessary.

When the people emerged from the mobile home shelter, they assured themselves and each other that they were mentally braced for whatever they might see.

Chris O'Conner was one of these.

He was not prepared at all.

The storm was gone, a blue smudge to the northeast. Sunlight shafted through swollen clouds. The trees were gone. The rock building was rubble. Where trailers and cars had been was now only a broad area of knee-high debris, punctuated here and there by a shattered stump.

A fire truck was parked about a block away, on the edge of the colossal dump. Several firemen waded up to the dazed people emerging into the blinding evening sunlight.

'Are you people all right?' one of the firemen asked anxiously.

No one replied. No one knew what to say.

NNNN
ZCZC NNL 80
092300

Y
SEVERE WEATHER STATEMENT
NATIONAL WEATHER SERVICE KNOXVILLE TENNESSEE
ISSUED 5:50 P.M. CDT APRIL 9, 1975

THUNDERSTORM ACTIVITY IN EASTERN AND CENTRAL TENNESSEE
HAS DIMINISHED IN THE LAST HOUR BUT THIS AREA REMAINS
UNDER A SEVERE THUNDERSTORM WATCH VALID UNTIL 11 P.M.
CDT THIS WEDNESDAY NIGHT. THUNDERSTORM ACTIVITY, WITH
SCATTERED TORNADOES, REMAINS HEAVY IN SURROUNDING AREAS
AND THE THREAT HAS NOT PASSED IN THIS WATCH AREA.

FLASH FLOODING AND LOCALLY HEAVY THUNDERSHOWERS ARE
REPORTED OVER A BROAD AREA. PERSONS IN THE WATCH AREA
ARE ADVISED TO MAINTAIN THEIR ALERTNESS AND BE READY TO
MOVE TO A PLACE OF SAFETY IF CONDITIONS WARRANT.

FURTHER STATEMENTS WILL BE ISSUED BY THIS OFFICE AS
CONDITIONS WARRANT.

XXX

Thatcher, Ohio

'Mo,' a neighbour woman said anxiously, 'We've got to know what to do here. People keep coming in. Shouldn't we try to get organized better?'

Maureen Coyle brushed her hair from her eyes and stared at the big pans of water heating on the table-warmer candles arrayed on the stove in her kitchen. She was still partially dazed; she did not know how to answer.

'I'll be in in a minute,' she said.

The woman fled into the living room, where the clamour of voices was incessant.

Well, Mo, my dear, Maureen Coyle thought, *what are you going to do about it?*

She had always had a strong sense of privacy. Now the house had suddenly become a turmoil of people everywhere, many of them total strangers. She knew it was crazy to react to this after the damage to everything here she loved, but the turning of her home into a public hospital was somehow an added blow that loomed much larger than it reasonably should have.

The trouble was not with the people in the house, she told herself. It was the storm – the tearing up of everything, the uncertainty about Jill and Billy, not knowing even where they were, and not being able to guess how much of the storm's destruction here could ever be repaired.

She had not known how much the permanence of this house and these trees had meant to her. In a stroke she had been cut adrift.

She could not get over Mike's abrupt departure. She was hurt and angry. He had no right to leave now. His place was here. It could not be worse anywhere else, and she needed him desperately. She felt adrift, betrayed, abandoned.

She stood at the stove, imagining things she could have said to him.

Mrs Shyer came into the kitchen. 'Dear, if any of that water is hot yet—'

Mo glanced at the pans. 'It is.'

'I sent people out to get more towels and sheets.'

'Good.' Mo picked up a pan and carried it into the living room.

The room had been transformed into an emergency treatment area. Three people, two women and a man, lay on the floor. Makeshift bandages covered slashes on face or arms. There were two children on the couch now, one at either end, and the little boy was unconscious. An elderly man stood near the fireplace, awkwardly holding his left arm, which was broken. Two young girls sat on the floor, holding towels to their heads. Several others in the room, including two women trying to help, showed head cuts with a startling amount of bleeding. The floor was soaked and muddy and furniture had been pushed back against the walls.

Two men came through the foyer, supporting a third man whose leg dangled behind him. He was sobbing with the pain.

'Got a broken leg here,' one of the carriers said loudly. 'We'll put him right here.' As they stretched the man out on the floor in the worst possible place, right in the middle of the room, Mo recognized the speaker as Major Henderson, a retired army officer who lived more than a block away. Mo knew his name because Henderson had visited the house twice in the past year with complaints about city government.

'Hello, Mrs Coyle,' Henderson boomed, standing erect again. He was tall, sturdily built, with close-cropped blond hair and ruggedly handsome features. He did not look his age. 'We've got a few more casualties located.'

'We have just about all we can handle already, Major Henderson.'

Henderson glanced around, frowning. 'I can see that. You don't have things set up efficiently. I'll take over here. We need more medical-treatment area. The people who don't have bad injuries should be taken up to the corner. Ambulances ought to be getting through there pretty soon.' As he spoke, others in the room stopped to listen. Mo saw some of the concerned expressions. Henderson, however, didn't.

He pointed to the two girls sitting on the floor. 'You two. You're in charge of getting everybody else that can walk out of here and up to the corner. You,' he added, pointing to Mrs Shyer. 'You're to come with me and these fellows while we scout for more injuries. Mrs Coyle, my men can move that furniture out of the dining room—'

'No,' Mo snapped before thinking about it.

Henderson stopped, clearly startled. 'Eh?'

'We're not moving anything out of the dining room,' Mo told him. 'And these people are not trying to walk to the corner. Some are too badly hurt, and others are on the edge of shock.'

Henderson's broad face turned to a scowl. 'See here. In a time of obvious emergency, citizens have to cope. I'm trying to make the best of a serious situation.'

Mo's thoughts were racing as he spoke, and the thing uppermost in her mind was that she was not going to be bullied. She had already taken too much to be very diplomatic or anything else. And since she was already committed, she swallowed hard and went right ahead with it.

'Major Henderson, we have the medical treatment going as well as we can for this block. If you want to organize someone, go down in the next block and try there.'

'Is that any way to respond to an emergency situation?'

Mo surprised herself. His loud voice and scowl didn't faze her. 'I'm giving the orders here.'

'May I say, madam, that you're doing a very bad job of it!'

She turned to Shyer. 'Mr Shyer, go ahead with your work. You're doing wonderfully. And you two girls don't have to go anywhere. None of you do. Mrs Ernst, I do think you should be in charge of getting names and addresses of everyone. Someone has to think about fixing some food – some hot soup and some coffee – too.'

'I can do that,' another woman volunteered.

The mood in the room had changed, shifting quickly to a happier one that opposed Henderson, who still stood there, hands on hips, with his two friends.

Mo ignored him. 'We don't know how long we'll have to shift for ourselves, so I'd like to find some of the men to work along this block on both sides, making sure no one is trapped.'

'I'll help with that,' one of the men who had entered with Henderson said.

'Wait just a minute—' Henderson began.

'Wonderful,' Mo told the man with her best smile. 'You can work with Mrs Ernst on the names. I think we want to try to take a census of the block just as quickly as we can, to try to make sure everyone is accounted for.'

'I don't think—' Henderson boomed.

'Mrs Scarletti will be good on that, too,' Mrs Ernst chirped. 'She knows practically everyone.'

'Fine,' Mo replied. 'Is she here?'

'I think she's outside.'

Henderson, whose face had been getting only slightly less red than a good Bordeaux wine, turned and charged out of the room. His one friend hesitated, stricken, then hurried out after him.

The other man smiled. 'Sorry, ma'am. I don't know why old Mac has to act that way. Gives the whole service a bad reputation.'

'Forget it,' Mo told him. She turned and surveyed the anxious, trusting faces around her. 'All right, everyone. Let's get busy. Help the people who have been hurt here. Start collecting names and addresses, and checking houses. Pick a place to start fixing soup and coffee. If there are houses so badly damaged that no one should go in them, we ought to make sure no one does go in them.'

One of the teen-age boys in the foyer said, 'Do you suppose anybody ought to try to get some of that stuff out of the street? If an ambulance did try to come through here, or a fire truck, they'd never make it.'

'I've got a chainsaw,' another boy said.

'You can find some of your friends and try to clear away as much debris as you can,' Mo told them. 'Just remember there are power lines down. You have to be awfully careful about that.'

'I'll watch,' the first boy promised soberly. 'I worked for the power company last summer. I know about hot wires.'

'Good,' Mo said. 'Then let's all get busy.'

Everyone began moving with a renewed sense of purpose. Instantly the faces looked somewhat more cheerful and determined.

People were not aware of the things they were capable of, Mo thought.

And that obviously included her.

She had surprised herself by standing up to Henderson. The results pleased her out of all proportion to the achievement. Even a few months ago she would have knuckled under. Now she had not only stood up to him, but had done so without any sense of fear.

Henderson was significant because he marked the first time she felt, with complete certainty, that she could handle herself under pressure without fear of falling back into the old uncertain way of dealing with reality. The storm had come and changed things. She had already been changing. As the day wore on, she was discovering new aspects of herself.

It occurred to her now that she could meet her husband as an equal in a way that she had never done before. And that meant their sexual relationship would change, too.

There might be hope for everything . . . and an end to guilt.

Mike Coyle found the first dead in the first block north of his own.

By some fluke, the homes in the next block had been hit harder. Trees and power poles had all been felled and it was heartbreaking to see many of the stately old houses wrecked: walls down, entire structures pushed off foundations and then partially flattened, houses reduced to piles of brick and lumber. It was like a mad dream, and he was walking in a bombed-out German city after World War II. But he had known that experience only in films, and this was here and now. Shock crept through his bloodstream, a cold sludge.

Halfway up the block, a crowd of people were gathered in a yard where an old brick home had been smashed. Only one partial wall remained standing. Women clustered about, hugging their children, watching in mute horror, as a dozen men attacked the rubble with sticks and shovels, throwing pieces of the debris aside as they dug deeper.

Just as Coyle hurried past, one of the men yelled something. 'We've got him!' another man called. 'Here he is!'

One of the other men ran across the rubble heap and plunged into the spot with his bare hands. Tears streaked his face. He tore at the brick and broken cement despite blood that spattered from his hands.

A woman nearby, holding a small child in her arms, moved forward haltingly despite the attempts of several others to restrain her. Seeing the terror on her face, Coyle moved partway across the yard to find out what the men had uncovered . . . although he was afraid he knew.

The man on his hands and knees in the rubble continued to hurl pieces of things away. Other men tried awkwardly to help. There was an arm sticking out of the broken brick and concrete. The work quickly exposed a thin leg in Levi pants and a red tennis shoe. Then they got the rest of the figure uncovered.

It was a boy of about six. He lay on his back in a bent position. His body and his face and blond hair were dusted with a fine coating of masonry chips. His eyes were closed. He appeared to be sleeping.

'Jamey,' the man choked. He touched the boy's face, shook him by the shoulder. *'Jamey!'*

One of the other men looked up to the crowd and sombrely shook his head.

The mother wailed.

Coyle turned and hurried back across the yard, into the muddy alley again. He felt like he was fleeing. Fresh sweat had burst from every pore. He was sickened. He ran, jogging, his head down so that he saw nothing but the mud and his own shoes splashing in it with each step.

His first reaction was that somehow it was his fault. He knew this was an irrational reaction, but he had always been this way, and recognized it. The warning system had failed. People had not known what to do, where to go. The house where the little boy had died: it had had a basement; he could have lived.

It's your city, Coyle told himself, running. *You could have done more. You could have made it so they did get warned – so they did know better what to do.*

He kept running, dazedly punishing himself. He knew it was no time for self-flagellation; he had to find out what had happened, how broad the damage was, and he had to direct rescue efforts. The first step was to find an emergency vehicle and establish contact with downtown. Nothing else mattered. He could not think about the little boy any more than he could spend time worrying about Billy or Jill . . . or Mo.

He had to make himself be hard.

And it didn't matter how tired he had been just an hour ago.

Forced to a staggering walk by momentary exhaustion, he found himself nearing Glenbrooke Boulevard. The two-storey apartment complex that backed up to the alley had lost much of its upper portion. A utility pole hung from intact wires, its bottom half snapped off and gone. The insulators on the two nearest poles were smoking, and he could smell the burning insulation. He ran under the dangling wires, went past a low garage unit that seemed completely undamaged, and was on the sidewalk along Glenbrooke.

It had been a wide, tree-lined thoroughfare with an island between lanes. The trees were mostly down, houses in varying states of destruction. There were many people out on lawns and sidewalks, milling around.

At the intersection to Coyle's left, a block away, there was a bigger crowd, and flashing red lights. He saw an ambulance and a police car. He started in that direction, going into the street and running again.

Halfway up the block, a thick-shouldered man of about twenty ran into the street ahead of Coyle, grabbing at him. The man was naked to the waist, and barefooted. He had a small black book in one hand. His eyes looked strange.

'Stop and repent!' he yelled at Coyle. He caught Coyle's arm and spun him around, almost knocking him off his feet.

'Let go!' Coyle snapped.

'Stop and repent!' the man cried. 'Have you accepted the Lord Jesus Christ? It's never too late to be saved, until that final judgement!'

Coyle tried to pull free. 'Let go, goddamn it!'

The man hung on. His eyes danced without real focus. 'Accept the Lord Jesus into your heart and you shall know no fear!'

Coyle broke loose. The man staggered backward as his hold was broken. He fell on to the seat of his pants and sat there, blinking.

Coyle ran on to the corner. There had been some kind of multiple-car accident, one or more cars thrown into others, and the mound of crumpled metal in the centre of the intersection, much of it draped in power lines, was incredible. A man knelt in the wreckage, vividly lighted by the flare of his cutting torch. A woman who appeared covered with blood knelt on the wet pavement nearby, while ambulance attendants stowed another person on a stretcher in the back of their white vehicle.

Seeing the traffic officer nearby, Coyle went to him and introduced himself. 'Is your radio working? I've got to talk to them downtown.'

The policeman, a lanky youth, frowned toward his car with its flashing lights. 'The motor is on, sir. All you do is wait for a break and push the button on the—'

'I know how to operate it.'

'I'll be over there with you in a few minutes, sir. I'd better—'

'Right.' Coyle went to the police car.

As he half-fell into the front seat, the radio was blaring something about a fire call. He didn't get the details. Sobbing for breath, he pulled the grey Motorola microphone off its bracket and tried to figure out what to say. Before he could move into a tiny break in transmissions, another car was reporting the need for a wrecker on the bypass.

Coyle paused, his thumb on the mike button, and didn't hesitate after the terse downtown acknowledgement of the wrecker call.

'This is Mayor Coyle to headquarters,' he said. 'Mayor Coyle to police headquarters.' It crossed his mind that he was being hopelessly melodramatic. What else did you say? He raised his thumb and heard some other unit talking.

Losing his temper, he jammed the button again. 'This is the mayor. This is Mayor Coyle. I've got to talk to you people downtown!'

The loudspeaker under the dashboard went silent for perhaps two seconds.

'All units stand by. Go ahead, Mayor Coyle. This is headquarters.'

'I'm at sixty-eighth and Glenbrooke, with—' He glanced at the dashboard plaque – 'with unit sixteen. Is Chief Merrill in there?'

The response was instantaneous, a different voice, Merrill's: 'This is Chief Merrill. Go ahead.'

'I'm with unit sixteen. I'll get down there as quickly as I can. Where did the tornado hit? How bad is it?'

'It hit Southtown,' Merrill's flat voice came back. 'Then it crossed the river. We don't know exactly where. It went up through the middle of town. We don't know anything yet. Was your place hit?'

'I was hit,' Coyle said, 'but not too badly. Was downtown hit hard? Do you have full power downtown? What about the hospital? Is the radio station on the air?'

'It's a mess down here. We have power. About a third of the city is without power. The hospital lost power but they have the emergency generators working. They're starting to get a lot of injury cases. The radio station is on but we haven't gotten through to them. Lines are tied up everywhere.'

Coyle gritted his teeth. 'What parts of the city were worst hit?'

'It went right up the middle. We don't know much more yet.'

'Is Rawlingson there? Is Purvis Rawlingson there or next door?'

'Negative. He called. He's on the way, but he'll be coming on the bypass and he's probably blocked in the traffic.'

'What traffic on the bypass? Is a bridge down or what?'

'No, sir. People are flocking out, starting to drive around to see the damage. The west side was just barely nicked, and people to the north didn't get hit bad. Sightseers are all over the place already, messing everything up.'

Jesus Christ.

Before Coyle could respond, another voice chirped, 'Seven to headquarters.'

'Maintain radio silence, seven,' Merrill ordered. 'Go ahead, sixteen.'

The delay had given Coyle just enough time to react logically. 'Chief, I want you to get through to the radio station. Go on the air. They can patch you in over the telephone. Announce that we're declaring martial law. Tell everybody to go home, immediate curfew. Any people out in cars to see the sights, blocking emergency traffic, will be put in jail. Have you got that?'

'*I don't know if we have the legal authority to do that.*'

'I'm giving you a direct emergency order. Follow it. Do you understand me?'

'*Yes, sir.*' Merrill sounded sullen.

'Get some wrecker trucks on that bypass. Get an officer up there with a bullhorn. If people don't start moving out, use the wreckers to push them into the ditch. Do you understand that?'

'*Yes, sir.*'

'Call the hospital. Tell them to set up the west-side armory as an emergency treatment centre. That should take some of the load off the regular emergency room. Get Rawlingson in there and tell him I said to contact all the people on my emergency list. Tell him to divide the city into the smallest grids possible and assign a police- or fire- or street-crew unit to each one. I want a report on what's damaged, where, and I want it fast. Have you got all that?'

'*West-side armory ... Rawlingson ... emergency list ... divide it into grids. Yes, sir.*'

'I won't tie up your radio any more. I'm having this officer get me to a telephone. I'll call in as soon as I find a telephone that works somewhere. Keep your extra six-four-seven number open for my call. Understood?'

'*Understood, sir.*'

'Okay,' Coyle said more softly. 'Sixteen out.'

Two other patrol cars immediately tried to talk at the same time.

Coyle leaned back for a moment. He had pushed Merrill very, very hard. Everyone on the radio net had heard it. So Merrill would now be a permanent, and possibly extremely dangerous, political enemy. Well, to hell with it. Merrill would obey the orders whether he liked doing so or not. This was not a time to worry about some of the usual niceties.

The contact downtown, as fragmentary and frustrating as it had been, had left him feeling slightly better ... tighter and more alive. He did not really know how bad it might be yet. But he had taken the first step in trying to take hold.

They were taking another person out of the tangled car wreckage just in front of the police car. The man they were removing had to be dead.

At first, Jill Coyle had not realized how bad the storm really was. The hospital was old and sturdily built, and even the darkness at the windows, and the torrential rain and high winds, seemed unlikely to cause any damage. When the power failed, it took only two or three minutes for the emergency unit to begin operation, and things seemed almost normal again.

Jill was on the ground floor, near the emergency room, when the full fury came. She saw a doctor and several nurses standing well back from the emergency doors, watching the incredible rain and wind in the lightning-filled darkness beyond the glass. Then the emergency ramp began to fill with water, and custodial help hurried down with buckets and mops to keep it out of the tiled corridor. Then the telephones began to ring. A nurse snapped at Jill to help answer some of the calls, and she was confused but she did as she was told.

Everything was bad and more confusing. Many of the callers sounded hysterical. People were hurt everywhere, begging for help, for ambulance service. A lot of the city was without electricity. At least one tornado had been seen. It had done terrible damage. Every ambulance in the city was on call, with more calls backlogged. Streets were blocked by fallen trees and poles. Nothing made much sense. Jill logged the calls as fast as she could take them while another candy striper next to her used an unlisted line to call doctors, trying to find out where they were and whether they could get into the hospital at once.

In a little while the first ambulance came up to the entrance, hurling sprays of water. Rain-soaked attendants hauled in some stretchers, then began bringing in more people, helping them or carrying them like sacks of laundry. Jill had seen an emergency drill here once, but the confusion had been nothing like this. The emergency rooms filled immediately and another ambulance came, then two private cars, then another ambulance, and the hallway was filled with injured people, women sobbing, men groaning, babies crying, rain and blood mixing on the green-and-white tile, and there were four or five doctors and extra nurses working now, but it was still chaos, everyone running.

Rushing out of a supply room with a box of bandages, Jill was almost pulled off her feet when someone grabbed her arm and swung her around.

The tall, youthful man wore a white doctor's smock. He had a black bag in his other hand.

'You'll do, babe,' he told her. 'Come with me.'

'*Where?*' Jill demanded.

'Come on!' he called over his shoulder.

Jill rushed after him down the hall and to a side exit. There were two nurses, another candy striper, and another young man who might have been a doctor standing there waiting. They had some black medical bags and what looked like three laundry sacks stuffed full of boxes and equipment.

'She's all I could find,' said the thin young man who had grabbed Jill. 'Let's go!'

'Where?' Jill demanded. 'What's going on?'

There were propelling her toward the exit, and a car waiting outside in the driving rain.

One of the nurses told her, 'Honey, they're setting up an emergency treatment centre at the armory. We're going to help. Consider yourself volunteered.'

Jill gasped as they rushed outside and icy rain pelted her while they piled into the Chevrolet four-door. She found herself in the back seat with too many other people and several of the bulky laundry bags. Boxes inside the bags gouged heavily at her legs and almost blocked all her view. She could just manage to see the young doctor pile into the driver's side, slam the car into gear, and mop at the foggy inner surface of the windshield. 'Here we go, kids!' he said. He laid on the horn and pulled away from the exit much too fast.

'*I* can't help,' Jill told no one in particular. 'I'm just a candy striper!'

'You can help, babe,' the driver said, wheeling sharply around the corner of the building. 'Count on it.'

'But I haven't even had advanced first aid yet!'

He barked a nervous laugh. 'And I'm a third-year med student, kiddo. But we're all they've got. Hang on!'

Chief F. D. Merrill had done what the mayor had ordered. He didn't like it. He was so confused by the reports flooding in over the radio that he hadn't even had time yet to be very angry.

Standing in the doorway of the radio dispatcher's cubbyhole, he listened to the latest calls, trying to determine what was going on and how the mayor's high-handed orders were affecting traffic on the bypass.

'*We've got flooding here at the Baxter-Cline underpass, and two cars stalled, blocking everything. Need a wrecker fast.*'

'Have you got that?' the dispatch patrolman asked the woman from the City Hall force whom he had pressed into duty as a notetaker.

The woman nodded frantically over her notebook.

The patrolman keyed his mike. 'Ten-four, unit three. All wreckers in service. If you can find somebody with a chain, try to pull those vehicles out yourself. Otherwise, stand by.'

'*This is four. I've got a house fire at 2211 Castro.*'

'Message acknowledged, four. All fire units are out. They'll get to you when they can.'

'*The fire is spreading to another house.*' This message came in garbled by another.

The dispatcher sorted them out. 'Ten-four, unit four. Go ahead eleven.'

'*I'm blocked in the alley behind Treadway Department Store. Require assistance. Most of this block has been knocked down.*'

'Ten-four. Do the best you can. Don't expect assistance too soon. Other unit calling headquarters, go ahead.'

'*This is twenty and I can't cross the bridge to Southtown. All lanes are blocked by twisted metal. I can see at least four fires in the industrial area. The glass factory looks like it was hit bad.*'

'Ten-four, unit twenty. Proceed to the alley behind Treadway's and render assistance to unit eleven.' The dispatcher told the woman clerk, 'Get that fire info to the fire department.'

The woman fled the cubicle thankfully, her message slip in hand.

Merrill slid into her chair. He reached for the microphone. 'Let me have that just a minute.' He keyed the mike. 'Headquarters to unit eighteen.'

'*This is eighteen, go ahead.*'

'Ten-twenty?'

'*Interstate and Fourteenth.*'

'It that traffic jam opening up there yet? How is the wrecker doing?'

'*The people are getting off the bypass now and turning across the median to go back the other way. Northwest lanes are slow but moving and we're letting them make the turnabout. Wrecker unit has pushed two cars off the side. Owners of said vehicles very irate. But everybody else is now obeying the bullhorn orders to head back home immediately.*'

'Ten-four,' Merrill said, and then remembered something else. 'Have you seen Purvis Rawlingson's city car out there yet?'

'*Affirmative, Chief. He got through a couple of minutes ago. He should be arriving City Hall any minute.*'

'Ten-four.' Merrill slid the microphone back to his young dispatcher. The patrolman leaned forward to read a note that a girl on one of the telephones next door had just put on his message spike.

'All units, attention. Vigilance Ambulance Service unit proceeding from Prospect and Exchange Avenue, west on Exchange for west-side armory emergency medical-treatment centre, code three.' He paused, but kept the mike button depressed. 'Unit twenty?'

'*Go ahead to twenty.*'

'Are you at the Treadway location yet?'

'*Not yet.*'

'After rendering assistance to unit eleven, proceed direct to west-side armory for traffic control that location. Unit eleven, if your unit is driveable, proceed to the armory with unit twenty.'

Both cars acknowledged simultaneously in a squeal of garble.

Merrill left the cubicle as the woman clerk came back. He moved out of the frantically busy front office and into the corridor that led to his private room. He was sorely tempted to go in there and shut the door on all of it.

He had the feeling that everything that could be done was now being done. But it wasn't enough. Everything was piling up. The ocean was coming into their sandhole faster than they could shovel.

As far as Mayor Coyle's high-handed tactics were concerned, Merrill had to admit grudgingly that so far they had worked. They would get some lawsuits and a hell of a lot of bad press over the bypass incident. Still, it was clearing the highway. But Merrill was fuming about the way the orders had come across the radio for everyone to hear. Made him look like a damned idiot. Couldn't have that. The mayor understood nothing about police work and authority. Merrill was going to have to take some action . . .

The back alley door flew open and Purvis Rawlingson rushed in. He had no coat on, and his baggy pants and shirt were soaked.

'Greetings, friend,' he said solemnly. 'What's going on around here? Where's Mike Coyle?'

'He's on the way,' Merrill grunted.

'Listen! I saw a wrecker out there on the bypass, shoving cars off into the ditch!'

'I know,' Merrill said. 'That's the mayor's orders.'

'Is he crazy? That's bad PR for the city! We'll have lots of complaints!' Rawlingson squeezed his nose. 'I don't know how I would ever have gotten through if that wrecker hadn't done it, but you talk about bad PR!'

'The mayor wants you to call everyone on his emergency list,' Merrill said, glancing at his notepad.

'Yes indeedie,' Rawlingson grunted. 'Get right on that. First tell me what the situation is in a nutshell.'

'The mayor also wants you to go on the radio station and announce that we're declaring martial law. He wanted me to do it, but I haven't yet.'

'Why haven't you?' Rawlingson asked, astonished.

'I don't know if I have authority.'

'You can't worry about authority at a time like this, man! The mayor is right. Mike is within his rights under the emergency statute. I'll call the station right away and get on the air and announce that, and try to say a few words to steady people all I can.'

Scratch Rawlingson as a potential ally, thought Merrill. 'That's up to you, sir.'

'Now tell me what happened and where we're at.'

'Everything is confused. Barney Reilly saw the storm headed for our south side. A unit in Southtown reported a funnel going right up the west side of the glass-factory grounds and crossing the river near the bluffs. We've got bad damage to the Main Street bridge, traffic can't get across it. We've got fires all over the place and flash flooding. The damned thing went right up the middle of the city, nicking downtown.'

'The west side isn't hurt too bad,' Rawlingson offered.

'Yes, but the Harmony Trailer Court was wiped out, and so was Crump's. We've got a lot of people badly hurt – or killed – at Harmony. We've got several ambulances out there now.'

'What about Crump's? It's on a hill.'

'The firemen say it was levelled. But he had a basement or something. Nobody was hurt as far as they know yet.'

'Thank God for that,' Rawlingson breathed. 'Now what did somebody say about the City Lights Shopping Centre?'

'I think it was wiped out.'

'Oh, my God. That's a big shopping centre!'

'We've got ambulances and emergency units there, too,' Merrill said. 'We've got an awful lot of people hurt. We're beginning to get calls about people dead. We can't get it all sorted out yet. With so much of the city without power or telephone, and everybody so swamped—'

'Did Mike say anything about that? Have you talked to the power company?'

'He gave me some orders about setting up a grid system and assigning a unit to each square, to collect information. I sent a man over to your office and he was trying to start working that out with Mrs Benson.'

Rawlingson rolled his eyes to the ceiling. 'I'll get right on that, too. I'd better get right over there. I'll stay in touch on the intercom.' He turned and ran out the back way.

Merrill stood there a moment after Rawlingson had left. He wondered if Rawlingson was capable of getting things together in any meaningful way. What they needed desperately now was a really strong hand, someone who could take hold and *make* things work. Despite his anger at the mayor, Merrill found himself wishing that Mike Coyle were already down here with the rest of them. He was needed badly.

There were some hastily erected flasher barricades partway across Jackson Avenue at Barker, blocking travel farther west. Jerry Tidwell pulled his Ford to a halt and glanced across at Billy Coyle, on the passenger side.

'You can get around them,' Billy said. 'Go around them.'

'It's bound to be blocked on up there,' Tidwell replied. 'Look up there. You can see police-car lights or fire trucks up there a few blocks.'

'I don't care!' Billy said. 'We've got to get through!'

'I'll try it,' Tidwell said nervously, and inched the car around the barricade.

Billy had been at the Tidwell house when the heavy rain began. Some tree branches broke, and the Tidwell television antenna was bent. Nothing more happened. It was much blacker toward the east, toward Billy's own neighbourhood, and he and his friend stood in an upstairs window and worried aloud about how black the sky was in that direction.

A few minutes later, the radio had the first announcement.

'This is Johnny Schottenstein, friends, and I don't know how bad this is, we don't have any details at all yet, friends, but a tornado has apparently struck in a part of Thatcher. According to police reports and our weather-wire info, a tornado has hit Thatcher. That's right. We don't have any other details at this time. We do know electric power is out for part of the city. All we can tell you is to stay where you are and wait for more information. Radio Fourteen will have more emergency information as soon as we can get it. Do not call the station, friends. You'll only tie up emergency lines. Do not call the police or anybody else unless it's the worst kind of emergency. All we know at this time is that a tornado or something very bad, equally bad, has struck part of Thatcher. It has hit part of downtown and up through the central part of the city. Stand by for later information.'

'It's hit my folks!' Billy said.

'Maybe not,' Tidwell said solemnly. 'Let's try to call.'

The telephone gave a busy signal. Billy tried the Shyer house and also got a busy signal.

'I've got to get over there!' he told Tidwell.

'I don't know if we can get through. The guy on the radio said—'

'Jerry, it's *my folks!*'

Tidwell swallowed hard. 'Let's try, anyway.'

Now they had driven in from Thatcher's far west side, and the nearer they got to Billy's own neighbourhood, travelling straight east on Jackson, the worse the destruction became. Here trees were down, houses were unroofed, garages flattened, cars on their sides. Billy's sense of dread was at fever pitch. Ahead, the intersection near the City Lights Shopping Centre was clearly blocked by all kinds of emergency traffic.

The Ford's radio was on, and the music that had been playing was abruptly stopped.

'This is Leroy Prendergast, Radio Fourteen news,' the voice

said tautly. The sounds of telephone conversation echoed in the background. 'Thatcher has been hit by a tornado. The tornado moved through the heart of the city from Southtown to a point east of Country Club Estates in the time period of about five-thirty to five-forty-five. There has been widespread damage with many injuries and some deaths. The storm has now moved to the northeast and the immediate danger has passed.

'This reporter just returned to Radio Fourteen's studios, which were not damaged. Two support wires on our antenna were snapped, but the tower is standing. We understand from the police that emergency traffic is being blocked by people out in motorcars, trying to reach loved ones, or sightseeing, and the police say anyone doing this will be subject to arrest. Repeating, citizens are urged to stay home and off the streets, where emergency vehicles need the right-of-way. Citizens out on streets in their cars will be subject to arrest. That from the Thatcher police.'

'Oh-oh,' Tidwell grunted.

'We will be back in approximately two minutes with a complete and up-to-the-minute report on the storm as we have it,' the announcer said. 'We also expect to have a taped statement from a city official, Purvis Rawlingson, about official reaction to the storm and instructions for Thatcher's citizens. That will be in about five minutes. Stay tuned to Radio Fourteen.'

'They're completely screwed up,' Tidwell said. 'They don't know what's going on.'

'Why would Rawlingson be making a statement?' Billy demanded. 'Where's my dad?'

They had reached the block just before the one where all the flashing lights blocked the intersection. Here a half block of apartments had been unroofed, a row of billboards torn to shreds, a service station crumpled.

An ambulance passed them going the other way, lights and siren operating.

Tidwell pulled to the curb. 'Listen. See that cop standing right up there? I'm not driving any closer, not till we know what's happening. There's no sense having our ass arrested!'

'Maybe he'll know something,' Billy reluctantly agreed, and got out of the car to hurry along the sidewalk.

City Lights had been one of Thatcher's best and newest suburban shopping centres. It had not really been completed yet, although it already included three department stores, a grocery, and more than twenty smaller shops. Now, as Billy hurried along the sidewalk, passing bystanders on lawns and curbs, he could look over the jumble of firetrucks and police cars in the street and parking lot to see that the near end of City Lights simply did not exist any more. The long, low row of glass-fronted shops that had looked out onto a mall area had become rubble. The modernistic steel roof of one of the department stores lay astride wrecked cars in the lot like a great, crumpled aluminium bird.

At the far end of the shopping centre was the largest department store, and Billy had to squint to assure himself that what he thought he saw was actually there.

On the smashed-in roof of the store was a semitrailer truck, its boxy units bent but still attached to one another. The entire truck rig was upside down, its fat black wheels pointed at the sky.

'How the hell did that truck get up *there?*' Tidwell gasped.

'I saw it!' a shirtless old man replied beside them. He had no teeth and he smelled of whisky, and the hand he pointed with was shaking. 'The wind picked that truck up and turned it around and *flang* it on top of that store! It saw it with my own two eyes!'

A policeman walked up to Billy and Tidwell. 'You the two in that Ford that came up the street a minute ago?'

'Yes sir,' Tidwell said. 'We—'

'You're going to have to get it out of there. If we see you on the street again—'

'My name is Billy Coyle,' Billy cut in. 'I'm the mayor's son. I'm trying to get through to my neighbourhood to see if my folks are all right.'

The cop studied him. 'Where's the house?'

'About another mile east and a little south.'

'You're getting right into the worst path of destruction along here. There's no way you can get through.'

'I've got to!'

'Son, our emergency vehicles are going all the way down to the bypass to get around, if they have to get around. There's no *way.*'

'You wouldn't have any information, would you?' Billy asked.

The cop frowned. 'Wait a minute.'

Billy and Tidwell waited while the cop walked past his parked cruiser to another officer. The two of them conferred. The second officer looked across the top of the police car at Billy. Beyond them, firemen began hosing water into smoking rubble of what had been an auto-supply store. Another ambulance left the farthest shop area and came by much too fast, siren and lights blasting.

The cop walked back. 'Your family is okay. We heard your father on the police radio a while ago. He is proceeding downtown. Your mother is at home, as far as we know. But they're okay.'

Billy took a heavy breath and felt weak in the legs.

A fireman walked around the police car with a bullhorn. 'All right, everybody,' he blared. 'We're calling again for volunteers. If you want to follow orders and help move wreckage, we can use your help. Check with one of the officers at the barricade and then report to me over there by that red car. Able-bodied male volunteers.' He turned and walked away.

Billy and Tidwell exchanged looks.

'Why not?' Billy asked.

'You're sure you're okay?'

'My *family* is okay. That's what's important.'

Tidwell nodded. 'Let's do it, then.'

They walked to the inner barricade and confronted the same officer who had just helped them.

'You again?' the cop asked with a slight smile.

'We're volunteering,' Billy told him.

'Can we leave my old Ford parked down there, and help?' Tidwell added.

'It can be worked out, gentlemen. Report to the man at the red car over there.'

Billy and Tidwell hurried toward the group of other men and boys being given instructions by the fireman in a long red slicker.

Wednesday, April 9
6:10 p.m.–6:30 p.m.

NNNN XA

ZCZC

WWUS7 RWRB 092300

SEVERE WEATHER STATEMENT
NATIONAL WEATHER SERVICE PEORIA SERVICE ILLINOIS
ISSUED 6 P.M. CDT WEDNESDAY APRIL 9, 1975

NEW THUNDERSTORMS ARE DEVELOPING IN THE PEORIA AREA AT
6 P.M. CDT. THIS IS THE ONLY RECENT NEW DEVELOPMENT IN
CENTRAL ILLINOIS WHERE ISOLATED SEVERE THUNDERSTORMS AND
A FEW TORNADOES ARE POSSIBLE UNTIL 10 P.M. CDT. KEEP TUNED
TO YOUR RADIO OR TELEVISION STATION FOR LATER INFORMATION.

XXX

Kansas City

The tall wastebaskets in the communications centre were filled
to overflowing with duplicate messages and used paper rolls, and
there were pieces of torn perforated tape all over the floor. The
wall clipboards were stuffed, bulging with the day's flood of data
that continued to come in over the hammering machines. The
smells of dust, tobacco and machine oil hung blue in the air. A
standby machine was down, and a repairman had the top hinged
back and was working inside with a screwdriver.

Ed Stephens, rubbing his forehead in a vain attempt to relieve
a killing headache, stood at the vertical banks of aviation-
information machines, watching the bad news continue.

There was nothing new from Thatcher. It had been hit, and
hit severely. Stephens had no way of knowing more than that at
this point. His first frantic telephone calls on his own phone had
gotten recordings saying service was disrupted; angry later calls,
with him throwing his official weight around in desperation,
hadn't gotten him any closer to answers.

He knew the chances that Mo or her family might be hurt were
small, even if the city had had as little genuine warning as he suspected was the case. But he was getting another side of the storm
now, the side of a victim. His emotions lacerated him. He had to

know she was all right, that Mike and the kids were safe. And he couldn't know that, not yet.

Standing over the machines, he glowered at the messages. *I don't give a goddamn about some of these other towns. Not in the same way I care about Thatcher. Why can't I just try to find an airplane and go there?*

He knew, however, that it was an impulse he had to restrain. He would accomplish nothing. His place was here. Every storm, every town, every victim was his responsibility.

In the war, Stephens had learned a trick of will. In the worst danger he had been able to screen out the fear and concentrate on the job at hand. It had made him seem cold; it had also given him an efficiency that had saved his own and other lives.

He summoned up the trick now, gathering his emotional resources.

There was a job to do and he would do it.

Struggling with his feelings, he forced himself to think about the larger picture and what was taking place.

The southern portion of all three squall lines was losing a little steam. But the northern sections were blowing as strongly as ever. Surface winds well away from thunderstorm clouds were as high as sixty-five knots in parts of Ontario. Pennsylvania and West Virginia were beginning to experience low ceilings, extreme turbulence and gusty winds at the surface. Commercial air traffic had halted in Columbus, Cincinnati and Louisville. And as the clouds began clearing away behind the front itself, scenes of devastation were being revealed at dozens of towns and cities.

It was going to go on and on, Stephens thought wearily. At best, the system would continue to generate violence for another four or five hours; at worst, it would continue sporadically all through the night, and reintensify in the morning. By then, any final blows before the system moved into the Atlantic might strike at the major cities along the East Coast, with the kind of potential for mass tragedy that people usually imagined only in conjunction with atomic attack.

Harry Adams hurried into the room with some notes in hand. He spotted Stephens, walked over, and waited in silence as Stephens finished glancing at a few more sequence reports.

'Speak,' Stephens told him.

'New death and injury figures,' Adams grunted. 'These are

from AP, which seems to be collecting information faster than anyone else in this particular line.'

'What do they say?'

'Five hundred dead, four thousand injured.'

'Those are estimates,' Stephens snapped. 'Everybody is guessing, goddamn it, and it won't go that high.'

'I'm just telling you what their latest wire story says.'

'Did you go over the activity report?'

'Yes.'

'Leaving out some of the more questionable calls, what do you think our actual tornado count really is, to this time?'

'A hundred and ten to a hundred and twenty.'

'That much worse than April 3, 1974?'

'That's the way I read it,' Adams shrugged.

There had been more than one hundred forty-five tornadoes on April 3, 1974. The storms had left more than three hundred dead and four thousand injured in ten states. There was to this day some question about the final death count; a few persons had vanished, and whether they had been killed might never be known with any degree of finality.

Now, the mounting figures proved again how much more severe this outbreak had become. Nothing like this had ever hit the United States before, and might never come again. And yet the averages meant nothing in nature; a repetition of today's events should not, by any mathematical calculations, occur again *ever*, or at least not for centuries. But nature did not go by the book. Each day was a new start. No matter how great the odds, another savage system might begin developing tomorrow, or the day after that.

And, Stephens thought glumly, it really mattered very little, if you were caught in front of a tornado, or under a bolt of lightning, whether you were being maimed by the only cloud in the sky or one of hundreds. Statistics got even more abstract when viewed from the standpoint of the victims.

The number of victims today, although he knew that everything possible was being done, lacerated him.

He knew he needed some rest. He had never felt this tired and the feelings in his chest had never been this severe. He looked up quickly from the machines and saw little yellow stars in his vision for just an instant.

At the same time, however, Tatinger came in from the weather room. Ignoring the fact that a conversation might be in progress, he scowled and said, 'These casualty lists are frightening.'

'You mean, suddenly you see it's serious?' Stephens snapped, and then instantly regretted it.

'I told you at the outset, Stephens, that none of this is personal.'

'Sorry. I'm feeling the pressure.'

'I daresay. You look like death warmed over. Aren't you set up efficiently enough here to let someone else take over for an hour or two?'

'If I rested,' Stephens said bitterly, 'I would be a feather-bedding bureaucrat. If I don't rest, I'm inefficient.'

Tatinger's frown changed, and for the first time there was a hint of actual concern in his eyes. 'If that's the impression I've given, I regret it. I'm merely trying to ascertain the facts.'

'I know,' Stephens said wearily. 'And you come on the way you do because it puts people off guard, scares them, gets you better fact-finding results. I'm just a little tired.' He turned back to Adams. 'Where are the new satellite pictures?'

'In a few minutes,' Adams said.

'The new radiosonde information we asked for?'

'In a few minutes.' Adams paused a beat, then added, 'Ed?'

'Yes?'

'What about your sister?'

'I don't know anything yet. Telephone lines are down and everything else. My wife is trying to get through and she'll call if she learns anything. I've got Dayton trying to get more details, too.'

Tatinger said, 'Where is this sister of yours?'

'Thatcher, Ohio.'

'That city that was struck a while ago?'

'Yes.'

Tatinger's pale eyes showed amazement. 'And you just continue working here, when she might be hurt?'

'What should I do? Get hysterical?'

Tatinger did not reply. Stephens knew how sharply he had spoken, betraying the frayed edges of his nervous system. His chest . . . *Christ!*, it hurt now.

He took a deep breath and hid the fact.

*

Near Crossville, Tennessee

Hunched close under the big steering wheel of his truck, Les Korowiscz peered out through rain and slapping windshield wipers at the grey road ahead. The weather had been miserable for hours, he was tired, and it was still a long haul to Knoxville and home. His citizen's band radio had gone out and he couldn't get information on conditions ahead. But he was going to drive on through.

The highway ahead, twisting up a three-mile grade, was a brown slash across a slightly out-of-focus black-and-white TV picture. In his rearview mirror, Korowiscz watched a car's headlights approaching very fast, from far back. The headlights neared, flicked up once in warning, and a tan Chevrolet passed quickly, going eighty at least. Korowiscz maintained his own speed and watched the lone car vanish over the next hill. The guy was driving much too fast for safety.

Korowiscz clamped the dead cigar in his teeth and readjusted his rump in the seat. He had the speedometer on a steady fifty, not as fast as he liked to drive, but as fast as he felt he should go right now. Even the big rig's dual radials would aquaplane if pushed too hard on pavement this flooded with pounding rain. He had seen too many wrecks in his lifetime to want to join them.

The crosswind buffeted his truck despite his safe speed and its heavy load of fertilizer.

Far ahead, the worst of the storm was visible as a line of great blue clouds bulging internally from lightning. Korowiscz congratulated himself for having sat out the worst of this front's passage. The citizen's band radio under the dash had been alive for a while with reports of cars wrecked, trucks off the road or jackknifed. The commercial radio, before static had made it impossible to listen to, had made it clear that this was no ordinary little gullywasher that a man could negotiate without sweat.

Still, Korowiscz had to combat his impatience. He wanted to be home. He still hoped to get to the unloading warehouse in time to empty the truck tonight, balance the accounts, and have a couple of days of rest. He was tentatively due out again Saturday, a longer run next time, all the way to L.A. A moneymaker.

Topping the long rise, Korowiscz shifted through some gears, picking up a little speed lost in the final mile of climb, then began downshifting again as the grade downward increased and he needed the braking action of the engine. He tried the commercial band radio again and got only crashes of static.

A yellow Volkswagen came toward him from the opposite direction and passed cautiously, its headlights yellow in the grey murk. Then he was alone again, and starting up another long grade.

One way or another, Les Korowiscz had been climbing long hills all of his life. His earliest memories were of the smallest, dingiest apartment in a forty-unit complex in a neighbourhood that would have been called a slum almost anywhere but Pittsburgh. His three younger brothers had squalled for attention, and Korowiscz had been the one who usually responded, because his mother worked in a machine shop and his father was long gone.

As the oldest and therefore the responsible child, Korowiscz had quit school in the sixth grade. No big deal: school had always been a hassle anyway. He threw papers in the morning, sacked deliveries in a grocery in the afternoon, and then trailed around the earlier route of coal-delivery trucks every evening. They dumped your house coal in the street in those days, and a kid could get a lot of jobs hauling it to the house and dumping it through the coalbin window with a bushel basket. Forty cents a ton, good money.

Korowiscz and some of his buddies – Abramson, Jankowski, Riley, Stein and a few more – usually took Saturday afternoons off. They met at a vacant lot next to an abandoned warehouse, cleaned off the week's accumulation of whisky bottles and trash, and played football. 'Sandlot' football was precisely what the term implied in those days before World War II. But that didn't matter. Abramson had this radio that ran on batteries, a huge thing you could hardly carry, and they liked to turn it on to the Pitt game, or sometimes Ohio State, and play ferocious tackle, no equipment, while keeping one ear on the big leagues. Sometimes, when Pitt did something exciting on the radio, Korowiscz got his imagination all lathered up pretending *he* was a Panther, and then he would run wild in the sandlot game, bulling right over everybody but Jankowski. He had never been able to run over Jankowski, and had more fun when they were on the same side.

On one such Saturday, a stranger watched part of the game. After it was over he called Korowiscz aside. The man's name was Liebler, and he coached the local high-school team. He asked

Korowiscz to come out for the club. Korowiscz admitted that he didn't go to school, and figured that was that.

By Monday, somebody from the school had visited Mrs Korowiscz with a lot of talk about truancy, and Korowiscz himself had been given a full-time job in the janitorial department. His schedule was set up to allow him to attend class and take part in football. Within two weeks, Korowiscz had been given a blitz education by two teachers who liked football, he passed some courses for grades seven and eight, and was instated as a full-time ninth-grader, and varsity eligible.

He might have made good. He was on the second team within a month. Then he went out with Jankowski one night in Jankowski's old jalopy, and nobody would ever know who was at fault, but the jalopy ended up in a ditch, in the embrace of a Pontiac. When Korowiscz regained consciousness five weeks later, they said he would live and be able to lead a normal life, but no more football. It did not seem like such a blow. Jankowski got worse: he was dead.

School didn't last long after that, but a fan put Korowiscz on as a helper in his trucking company. Korowiscz started trying to build. First it was temporary local relief rides, then stand-in driver on county calls, then relief driver on longer runs. He drove trucks in the Army. He came back with some mustering-out pay and bought his first personally owned rig, a junker, incidentally, but enough to provide income that would qualify him for a bigger, better unit.

A long time ago. After that had come marriage, too many kids too fast, a house, more income, more work, more bills. But he was okay. He had a good rig now, the best. He might have virtually nothing in the bank, but he was a jump ahead of the bill collector, right?

He had come a long way.

Korowiscz drove on, watching the distant lightning, drumming his blunt fingers on the steering wheel. In a little while, he came around a broad curve in the highway and spotted the flashing tail lights of a car on the side of the road a mile or so ahead. He began slowing; he made it a policy to help motorists in trouble when he could.

Getting nearer the parked car, he saw that it was the Chevy that had passed him lickety-split several miles earlier. He had a mind to go right on by the smartass. But there the guy was, out beside the broken car, rain streaming off his leather jacket as he waved.

You needed help when you broke down on the road, not sermons. Korowiscz touched the air brakes and pulled the truck to a halt on the shoulder.

The driver, a slender, dark-haired man, slammed the hood of his crippled car and hot-footed it back to the truck. He opened the passenger-side door and climbed up. He had deeply inset black eyes and a jagged scar, not too old, on his left cheek.

'Could I get a lift?' he yelled.

Korowiscz gestured. 'Climb in, bo.'

The man clambered aboard, sneezing and mopping at his face with a soaked handkerchief.

'You lock that car?' Korowiscz asked.

'Yeah!'

'Okay.' Korowiscz made sure no one was coming, then got the truck moving again, slowly.

'The damned engine just quit on me!' the man said, still mopping. He had jerky, nervous movements.

'You probably flooded it with water, the speed you were going.'

'Maybe so.'

'Where you going?'

'Up ahead,' the man said, and then after a moment's hesitation, he added, 'Knoxville.'

'Well, there's a Shell station up here about three miles. I'll drop you there. They've got a wrecker.'

'I'll just ride on into Knoxville with you.'

'And leave your car?'

'To hell with the car.'

Korowiscz shook his head. 'Sorry, bo. Can't do it. See the sticker on the glass? No passengers except in emergency.'

The man put his hands in his jacket pockets, and seemed to shrink into himself with some strange tension. 'Knoxville. All the way.'

'Didn't you hear me? I just told you. No passengers. Nothing personal, bo, but—'

Which was when Korowiscz stopped.

Because the man had taken his right hand from his jacket pocket, and he had a black revolver in it.

'What's *that* for?' Korowiscz grunted, suddenly chilled.

The revolver pointed at his midsection. 'You're taking me to Knoxville.'

Korowiscz returned his attention to the road. 'Just what I need,' he said bitterly. 'Just what I *need*. A nut with a Saturday-night special.'

'I'm not a nut, friend,' the man said. 'And as long as you do what I tell you, you won't get hurt. Now speed it up a little, huh?'

'Oh, boy,' Korowiscz muttered. 'Oh boy, oh boy, oh boy.'

Huntington, West Virginia

'Call Dragoo,' George Abrams told his secretary, 'and tell him I'm cancelling our meeting here.'

'He's probably already on the way, sir,' the girl said, wide-eyed with surprise.

'Then stop him when he arrives,' Abrams bit off. He consulted his desk calendar. 'And call Jorsky and cancel that appointment, too. I'm not seeing anyone else today.'

'Are you sick, Mister Abrams?' the girl asked solicitously.

'No. I'm just busy. Get out of here and close the door behind you.'

The girl fled.

Be careful, Abrams told himself, *be careful! You have to hide however you feel. No one must be able to guess you're in trouble.*

But the trouble was most serious. Donna Fields would carry out her ultimatum. He had no doubt of that now. His investigator had missed something in her background . . . some hint that she was capable of blackmail.

But what had kicked off the impulse within her? Abrams thought about this, his memory flicking back over times he had been with her . . . things said, things done . . .

In a life that put him into contact with many women, he had very often indulged himself in brief encounters, but never more than once with the same partner. His wife, he knew, at least suspected that some of these affairs took place. She said nothing, perhaps believing that such a brief interlude meant little in comparison with the continuing relationship of a marriage.

He did not know this was her rationalization, because they had never discussed it. But at least an occasional quickie seemed to do no harm, and was accepted by her whether she hated it or not.

In political reality, this tendency to philander was so common that it was not the stuff of major scandal that could hurt him.

A continuing affair, however, including weekend trips and small gifts, such as he had enjoyed with Donna Fields, was another matter. This could be blown up by the media, could hurt him very badly. His wife might not be able to stand the shock of such a revelation, either, especially when details became known. With the occasional momentary partners, he could indulge in fairly routine sex. With a mistress, in a longer time frame, his more esoteric preferences became the centre of activity.

He did not consider himself notoriously depraved. But if Donna Fields had tapes, as she claimed, and if they documented the use of certain leather and rubber gadgets—!

Christ, it was impossible. It was a nightmare. There was no way to duck her demands. He had to meet them.

He knew a payment was only the beginning. She was a bitch and a whore, and she would bleed him. He would never be free of her.

But there was no choice. He had briefly considered the possibility of an accident that could befall her, but this was not an episode from *Columbo*; he could not under any circumstances arrange her death personally. And hiring someone was out of the question: that would only leave him with another blackmailer, and one with even more damaging information on which to make greater demands.

So he had to pay her. And ironically the demand had come at a time when expenses for the oil-company probe, paid mainly out of his own pocket for the publicity value, had stripped his personal accounts to the bone. The cash had to come from the campaign kitty. He could accomplish this, although it was unethical at best, probably a felony if he were caught. But he had to take this risk because to do otherwise was to court immediate disaster.

Abrams knew he had to hurry now, because there was another neighbourhood house rally tonight at 8:30. After that, he would work it out about getting the cash.

He left his office, filled with a very great rage and self-loathing. There was no way out ... there was no way out. The words pounded in his brain. Here he was, on the threshold of everything he had ever wanted, and a whore had turned it into a nightmare.

He would pay her. The act would make him her captive – he who had always prided himself on being smarter than anyone else, and invulnerable. But he could not think of this. He had to continue going through the details of his life. He had to have the will to maintain outward normalcy.

He could do this, he told himself as he walked out of his building toward his car. There had never been anything he could not do if he set his mind to it.

The feeling of entrapment, however, was like strangulation. It was like nothing he had ever felt before. It was hellish.

A brisk wind blew bits of trash around the parking lot, and he had to use his windshield wipers against the light, steady rain as he drove away. A more serious storm was coming, but stormy weather was the furthest thing from George Abram's mind. For him, the storm had already come.

Wednesday, April 9
6.35 p.m.–7:15 p.m.

NNNN
XXXA
ZCZC
WWUS7 RWRB 092330
ZZZZZ

BULLETIN
SEVERE WEATHER BULLETIN
IMMEDIATE BROADCAST REQUESTED
NATIONAL WEATHER SERVICE ATLANTA GEORGIA
ISSUED 6:30 P.M. CDT APRIL 9, 1975

THE TORNADO WARNING ISSUED AT 5:40 P.M. FOR THE ATLANTA AREA IS NO LONGER IN EFFECT. THE TORNADO THAT WAS REPORTED SOUTH OF CARROLLTON AT 5:30 P.M. HAS DISSIPATED AND IS NO LONGER A THREAT AT THIS TIME.

HOWEVER, THE TORNADO WATCH REMAINS IN EFFECT FOR ATLANTA AND MOST OF THE REMAINDER OF GEORGIA UNTIL 11 P.M. CDT THIS WEDNESDAY NIGHT.

XXX

Thatcher, Ohio

The name on the police officer's lapel tag was HOAD. He solemnly shook hands with Mike Coyle as he climbed into the car.

'Sorry you had to wait, sir. I know you're in a hurry, but ... well, I had to get those ambulances loaded.'

'I know that, Officer Hoad. Using the radio helped a lot.'

'Where do you want me to drive you, sir?'

'Can you help me find a telephone, preferably over on the east side near the airpark?'

'I can head that direction.'

'Good.'

Hoad backed the car around. Although it appeared in good shape on the outside, its interior was badly worn. As Hoad pulled away from the wreck site, heading east, the Plymouth groaned and hammered in every joint.

'You think this will get us there?' Coyle asked.

Hoad grinned. 'It runs, sir.'

'Your odometer says twenty-two thousand miles. I suppose that's really a hundred and twenty-two thousand.'

'The maintenance card is in the glove compartment, sir. I think you'll find it's three hundred and twenty-two thousand.'

'Christ.'

'This is one of the units we got as part of the Civil Defence programme,' Hoad said, driving swiftly and well past a line of houses without roofs. 'The way I hear it, we'd better keep them running because there won't be any new ones for a long while yet.'

'We're getting some new ones next fall,' Coyle said.

'Is that right?'

'Yes. I don't know how, but I intend to get them.'

Hoad believed him and immediately looked happier. 'Great!'

Someone else, Coyle thought, who would depend on him in a small way now. The city budget was not likely to have any air holes in it for new cars, but they were already on one of the lists in Coyle's desk downtown. He would get them someway . . . if he was still in Thatcher.

But there was no time to think of that side of his life now.

The cruiser, moving about fifty miles per hour, was approaching what looked like a traffic jam a few blocks ahead. There were fire trucks in the jam, and dense smoke billowed overhead. A few people ran along the sidewalk.

Hoad flicked a switch, activating his siren. The sound vibrated through the skin of the car. Hoad slowed and inched his way into the array of fire trucks and city vehicles. An old warehouse was afire, flames shooting from dozens of windows, and firemen were playing water on the old brick walls. In the intersection, several civilians were directing traffic.

'Who are those people?' Coyle asked.

'I imagine just people,' Hoad said. 'Helping.'

The cruiser bounced over some fire hoses and inched through. Hoad accelerated on the far side.

'It didn't look much like Thatcher back there,' Coyle said. 'We're usually not very long on volunteers to do anything.'

'Maybe people figure the town needs their help a little more than usual right now.'

'How bad is it over the city? How much have you seen?'

'It's bad,' Hoad replied grimly. 'We're beginning to get out of the worst of it, but if you've been listening to some of these calls, you get an idea.'

Coyle had been ignoring the squawk of the radio speaker. 'It went up through the middle of town?'

'Yes, sir.'

'What about the hospital?'

'I guess it's okay, but I think they're swamped. Lot of people hurt.'

Coyle thought feverishly as Hoad was forced to detour a few blocks around a small corner shopping area that had been smashed so badly that debris blocked the intersection. Some city sawhorses had been put up as a warning, but there was no sign yet of a city crew working to clear things off.

There was an enormous problem in clearing streets for emergency traffic, he thought. Someone had to co-ordinate all calls of blockage, and give orders to the street crews. The big city map in the planning department could be used to pinpoint reported closings and the work of the crews. In this way, ambulances and fire trucks could be kept up-to-date by radio of possible routes to calls.

'Does this car have one of those CD walkie-talkies in it?' Coyle asked.

'Yes, sir, in the trunk.'

'Is it working?'

'It was just the other day, sir.'

The walkie-talkie might be useful. Visualizing the scope and complexity of the problems faced at this moment, Coyle had an idea of how co-ordination could be speeded.

If Purvis Rawlingson was following the disaster plan and emergency list, calls would have been made by now to many state and regional agencies. Help was probably already on the way. Emergency shelter had to be found for the homeless. Special kitchens had to be set up to feed people. Trouble with electric power and gas had to be worked out with the companies, on a priority basis. More places had to be set aside for the injured . . . and for the dead.

The cruiser passed a small delicatessen in flames. There was no fire truck. Several ordinary citizens were trying to fight the blaze with garden hoses strung together from nearby houses, which did not appear badly damaged. Some of the bystanders waved at the police car, not asking for help but simply waving, as if they felt some kind of friendly bond. Coyle had never seen anything like this before, either.

'Another few blocks up here and we ought to get to an area where phones might be working,' Hoad said. Then he picked up the radio microphone, having picked up some message of meaning out of the constant chatter.

'Go ahead to sixteen,' he said.

'*Sixteen,*' the radio blatted back, '*what's your ten-twenty?*'

'Sixth and Francis, headed east.'

'*You have Mayor Coyle with you?*'

'Ten-four.'

'*How long till you reach a telephone?*'

'Estimate two or three minutes.'

'*Ten-four.*'

Hoad slammed the microphone back on the hook. 'They're anxious.'

'I am too,' Coyle admitted. 'It's been—'

His words were cut off as Hoad grunted something angrily and hit the brakes of the car. It skidded and he swung the wheel expertly, drifting it toward the curb. Up ahead in front of a small store were several men and boys.

The right front wheel of the car banged into the curb. Hoad popped his door open. The men and boys in front of the store broke in all directions. One man dropped a large object he had been carrying. The TV set broke open on the sidewalk.

'Sorry,' Hoad grunted, and piled out of the car.

The officer ran out in front of the car, his revolver coming out into his hand as he moved. The males had vanished into two nearby alleys. Hoad did not pursue, but stopped in front of the store and looked around angrily. The front glass was all gone from the store, and its window and display area were filled with TV sets and other appliances.

Hoad jogged back to the car, holstering his big .357 Magnum. He got in and reached for the microphone again. He was sweaty. 'Sixteen to headquarters.'

'*Go ahead, sixteen.*'

'Looting at a damaged store, Ninth and Francis. Request assistance so I can take the mayor on to a telephone.'

'*No units available, sixteen. Suggest you proceed.*'

'Shit,' Hoad grunted angrily. He pressed the button. 'Ten-four.' He put the mike back on the hook and started the car again.

'They'll come right back again,' Coyle said.

'I know.' Hoad pulled from the curb.

'Why didn't you shoot?'

'You don't shoot, sir, when a kid is running from a theft. An officer doesn't use his weapon except to protect life, or in some other emergency.'

'I've read of cases where an officer killed a fleeing burglar.'

Hoad was angry. 'Am I supposed to shoot a kid for a TV set?'

'No,' Coyle said. 'Of course not.'

They drove the next block in silence. At the far intersection, a number of people, black and white, were milling around a service station that had been flattened. Hoad pulled in, left the motor running, got out to talk to the men over the top of the car.

'Anyone hurt in there?'

'Don't look like it,' a massive black man relied slowly.

'You people know that appliance store up the block there?'

'Myers'? Sure.'

'The front glass is broken out. I just ran off some people looting the place. They'll be right back.'

People stared at Hoad, at the car, and at Coyle. No one spoke.

Hoad said, 'If a few of you folks drifted up that way, maybe they wouldn't steal any more stuff.'

A tall, skinny white boy in an Ohio State tee shirt sifted out of the crowd. 'We'll mosey down there, officer. There ain't going to be any stealing in this neighbourhood.'

'That's right, brother,' the black giant said, rubbing his fist into his palm.

'Thank you,' Hoad said cheerfully, re-entering the car.

'Are telephones working around here?' Coyle asked.

A woman pointed. 'That one in that booth over yonder is okay, I think. Several people have made calls on it the last little bit.'

Coyle waved his thanks as Hoad made a U-turn in the inter-section. Coyle went into the booth. He dropped a coin and got a dial tone. The call went through immediately.

Chief Merrill sounded rattled again. The noise in the background was considerable, and sounded like excited people yelling at one another. He said the grid system had been started, but no one could put the pieces together yet and really get an accurate picture of what had happened where. Under Coyle's quick questions, he revealed that street flooding had not been as serious as it first seemed, but everything else was looking worse as more details came in.

Coyle asked Merrill to get Purvis Rawlingson on the line.

In a moment, Rawlingson's voice came on over a quieter phone. Rawlingson sounded chipper. 'Howdy-doody, friend.'

'Where are you?' Coyle demanded, instantly angry at the man's calmness.

'I'm in your office right now, Mike. I've got some people in here with me and we're setting up your wall map with the grids. I've sent out a call for all city employees, and quite a number are already downstairs, taking calls, helping organize things. I've talked to the National Guard, incidentally, and they're sending units right away. I didn't know exactly what we have to deal with here, so I made sure they're sending not only labourers and soldier types, but food-preparation units and a medical support team. Oh, and by the way, were getting a lot of help on the way from Dayton, too. Medical personnel, some ambulance and fire units.'

Mollified, Coyle felt slightly ashamed of himself. Rawlingson had dug right in. 'Have you broadcast something to the people?'

'Right. I have indeed. I explained as much as I knew at that time, told people to stay in their homes, tried to be sort of positive, you know? Then I got Mrs Wilcox, you remember her, the county health department, and she read some things about emergency sanitation. Good stuff, Mike, really.'

'We have all that old fallout-shelter stuff in buildings all over downtown,' Coyle said. 'Get some people breaking it out. The rations might be useful, and if we have pollution in the city water-supply lines, the canned water might be used, too.'

'I've got people checking all our city lines, and making tests on the tap water right now.'

'Good. Listen, Purvis. Are emergency vehicles still having trouble with blocked streets? Are there still more calls than anybody can answer?'

'Oh my, yes. It's a mess, and no one can get a handle on precisely what some of the priorities should be—'

'I'm near the airpark. This police car has one of our CD walkie-talkies. The thing will reach you downtown if I'm up in the air and you go to a roof or someplace like that. I'm going to hire a helicopter if I can find anybody over there, and take a ride over town. Maybe I can pinpoint problem areas, give you some kind of real idea of what's happened and where help is worst needed.'

Rawlingson sounded enthusiastic. 'That's wonderful, Mike! A great idea! If you go to the airpark, drive right to the Allied office. Jack Jennings, the man who took all those pretty aerials for the Chamber last year, has a trailer house right next to his business out there. I'd lay money that you'll find him ready to go.'

'Break out one of your walkie-talkie units,' Coyle said, 'and tune it to the top channel. I'll be talking to you just as soon as I can find the guy and get in the air.'

'Mike?'

'Yes.'

'You're all right? Not hurt or anything?'

'No. I'm fine.'

'And Mo?'

'Mo is all right. She's at the house, or what's left of it.'

'The kiddos?'

Coyle swallowed. 'I don't know about the kiddos yet, Purvis. But I'm sure they're okay.'

'Get down here as soon as you can,' Rawlingson said, and then the brave front in his voice faltered and almost broke. 'There are people everywhere in here, Mike, and a lot of them are scared and upset, and it's hard to . . . to tell them all what to do all the time. I guess we sort of need you.'

'I won't be long, Purvis,' Coyle promised. 'Hang in there. And be ready with a city map and a tape recorder in case I have some notes to give you from the air.'

Rawlingson tried to rally. 'Live in fame, go down in flame?'

Coyle hung up and rushed to the police car.

Jill Coyle was totally unprepared for it.

One large meeting room in the southeast wing of the armory had been hurriedly cleaned up for use as a treatment area for the most seriously injured. Set at the end of a long, broad corridor that provided access to the yawning main arena in the old brick fortress, the room was about fifty feet square, with two walls of high, metal-framed windows. Old-fashioned white globes hung down on pipes from high ceilings studded with plumbing. The globes provided a yellowish illumination that was badly needed now because the windows, grimy and coated with sweat, looked out on the grey wetness of evening.

Metal tables had been set up around the room for use in examinations and treatment. Emergency medical equipment and supplies had been rushed in from everywhere and dumped, with the result that everything was chaotic. The room was full of people: doctors, nurses, medical aides and young, frightened helpers like Jill, and storm victims on tables, on stretchers, on the floor, ambulance attendants, other volunteers. There was a constant bustle of people being moved about, the roar of voices, groaning and crying, yelled orders. The long hallway outside was similarly packed, stiflingly hot, and dense with the odours of sweat, blood, faeces, urine, mud and rain.

Jill was at one of the tables in the back of the room, packed in as deeply as anyone. Bathed in sweat and faint, she tried to keep her wits together in the roaring confusion. An older doctor had come in and grabbed her up as his aide, and she was being a very bad one.

They had a middle-aged man on the table and others around them on the floor.

The victim on the table was bald, with a mountainous chest and stomach thrusting up under a dirty tee shirt. His upper arms and a shoulder showing through a hole in the shirt looked like they had been sandblasted. He was conscious, peering out of a face coated with what looked like asphalt. A gash on his arm had been bleeding badly, but the doctor had that stopped now and was sewing a place on his hand. Jill watched the needle go in and out, puncturing the man's flesh. She felt numb with horror.

'I'm okay, Doc, right?' the man asked huskily over the din.

The doctor, whose name was Livezey, glanced up through thick glasses. He had been at an early party or something because he had been wearing a formal black suit on his arrival at the armory. His coat was gone now and his white shirt and cummerbund were splattered with blood.

'You'll live,' Livezey told the man.

'I know it. You know how I know? I hurt too bad to be dying.'

'That's a myth, brother. But in your case the facts support your theory about not dying, anyway.'

The man's pained eyes swung to Jill. 'It was weird.'

Jill found her voice. 'What – happened to you?'

'I was in the garage. Just got home. Started in the house and the wind came and the roof of the garage flew off. I heard my wife scream, but the wind blew me out the door into the back yard, and the next thing I knew I was flying through the air. I lit in the alley, got thrown into a bunch of trash cans.'

'Is your wife here somewhere too?'

The man started crying silently, the silvery tears sliding down over the asphalt cheeks.

'He doesn't know about his wife yet,' Livezey grated. 'She hasn't been found yet. Christ, girl!'

'I didn't know!' Jill whispered.

'Well, *think!*'

'I'm – sorry.'

Livezey tied a quick knot. 'That takes care of that. The people out in the floor area can do the rest.' He turned to two college boys standing against the wall. 'Okay. Take this man out front.' He rummaged in a box and handed some packages to Jill. 'Tell them out there to dust this powder on his abrasions. Press-bandage the arm and shoulder. Clean him up as well as they can without taking more skin.'

Jill clutched the little cardboard boxes to her chest. 'How do I know who to tell out there?'

Livezey's eyes flared. 'How the hell do I know? Use your head! And hurry it up back in here as soon as you've told them! We've got a lot of work to do!'

The college boys lifted the heavy man. Despite himself, he cried out in pain. They stopped, stricken.

'Move it!' Livezey barked.

They obeyed. Jill followed them through the maze toward the far door. They skirted a table on which a child was screaming as a doctor and a nurse worked together on her bloody face, past a table where two sweating volunteers were tugging at a woman's leg while another doctor and an aide held her down flat.

'Harder, dammit!' the doctor grunted. 'You've got to get it back *somewhere* near the right place!'

Jill slipped going into the hallway. The floor, she saw, was slick with blood.

Stifling the gag reflex, she followed the boys with the heavy man. They weaved through the tormented turmoil of the hall. There were people everywhere, lying out flat, sitting, standing. Far at the other end, the doors were open and men were bringing in more stretchers.

After the workroom and the corridor, the main armory was vast, echoing, cavernously roomy. Arena floodlights shone down through high girders, picking up spinning motes of dust. Bleachers stood empty on the sides of a gleaming wooden basketball court. The glass backboards were in place. Here and there women had set up tables, and seemed to be working swiftly on some sort of records.

Crossing the wooden floor, Jill and the boys came to a concrete portion. A National Guard tank sat there, dully gleaming. Beyond the tank, the floor was littered with people lying on blankets or stretchers. They seemed to be lined up neatly, in groups, and Jill could see other volunteers working on someone here, kneeling to take another's identity information over there. But she could not see the exact pattern of any of it.

'Lacerations?' a woman called at her and the boys. 'Over here!'

Jill followed, giving the woman the packages and the doctor's instructions.

'We're not fools, dear,' the woman said sweetly. 'We know what to do.'

Jill fled back toward the room. She had to fight the impulse to turn in the opposite direction, run for the door, and then just run and run. She was afraid she would be sick at her stomach if she even thought about the way she felt.

She did not, however, run. She seemed to be watching herself as she made her way back through the corridor people and into the room. The heat and noise blasted her as she entered. She choked back nausea and kept going.

Livezey had three patients on the long worktable at the same time. He was at the near end while two volunteers were cutting clothing from the other two people. There was a lot of blood. Sweat was dripping off Livezey's pointed nose.

His patient was a boy not much younger than Jill. His eyes were squinched shut and he was trying to be brave as Livezey probed around at his left leg, which lay at a strange angle.

'Well, son,' Livezey grunted, pulling a hypodermic syringe out of a box, 'I'm afraid we can't handle a fracture like that over here.

You'll have to go to the hospital. We can help the pain a little, though.'

Livezey handed Jill the syringe. 'Give him this and get him carted out of here. First ambulance heading east, take him to the hospital.'

Jill cringed from the needle. 'I can't give that!'

'Why not? Do it!'

'I'm a – I'm just a – candy striper! I sell candy! I don't—'

'Goddamn it, girl! Can't you see I'm busy here? Just stick it in his arm and push the plunger!' Livezey made her take the syringe, and turned to the next patient down the line.

Shocked cold, Jill stared at the needle. She looked at the boy. He was watching her. He looked dazed.

'Please,' he whispered. 'You don't know how bad it *hurts*.'

Jill put her hand on his arm above the elbow, pressing it down. 'Hold still now,' she choked. *Am I really doing this?* She did not believe it. She poised the needle. She couldn't do it.

Yes, she could. She had to. She did. The needle went in. She pressed the plunger and watched the ampule empty. She withdrew the needle and saw a single bright droplet of blood follow it out. She pressed bare fingers hard against the droplet in a convulsive effort to hide it – stop it.

She felt a deep, primary chill that she could not identify.

'Girl!' Livezey yelled. 'Come here! Quick!'

Livezey was working over the next patient. The lean doctor had tools spread out on a white cloth and he seemed to have one hand *inside* the man's chest on the table. Blood was fountaining out.

'Here!' Livezey barked. '*Now!*'

Jill stumbled against him, seeing nothing but the incredible amount of blood. *Where does all the pressure come from?* Livezey threw down an instrument of some kind and grabbed her right hand and thrust it down into the hole in the man's midsection. The hole was hot and slick.

'There,' Livezey grunted frantically, manipulating her fingers. 'Feel that? Feel it? Grab it. That's it. Hard! Squeeze harder! Hold it!'

He moved swiftly, reaching for some other glittering tools. Jill could not see clearly. She could feel something hard and slippery between her fingers down in the hole. It felt like a worm. It was harder than a worm. It was an artery. She could feel the pulse behind her fingers. She was holding an artery closed to stop the bleeding.

'See funny things in a disaster,' Livezey muttered, getting both hands inside with hers.

Jill hung on and closed her eyes.

'Brought in for chest pain, possible heart,' Livezey said as he worked. 'No blood, so he goes on the second row. Then somebody opens his coat and he's got a five-inch length of wood stuck right in his gut. Damned thing was blocking off most external bleeding. When I pulled it out a minute ago, that was some gusher, eh? Hang on a minute more. We're doing fine now. That's the girl.' He kept on muttering as he worked, but a woman at the next table was crying hysterically, and other voices were raised, and Jill knew a moment of blackout as she clung to consciousness by sheer effort of will and necessity.

It would never end, she thought. It would just go on and on. How had Daddy ever thought she could be a doctor? She would never even be a nurse. Not after this. She had had enough. And here she was, and maybe Daddy and Mom *both* were in another place like this, being treated like butcher meat.

She was vividly aware of the contrast between this and the visions she had had: of her in crisp whites, smiling, serene, in command, standing by the patient's bedside and taking his pulse and knowing just *everything*, and the patient looked just like Burt Reynolds.

'Okay,' Livezey said. 'Take your hand out now.'

Jill withdrew her hand. It was a gory mess. She wiped it on the front of her uniform in a spasm of fear.

Blood had a rank odour. She had never known this before, but now the room reeked of it. Looking around, she saw Livezey still working on the man's wound. At the next table, a doctor was looking into a woman's eye with a flashlight. Nearby, a nurse was administering oxygen through a mask to another woman whose lips were blue. Volunteers hefted another victim off a table swathed in white bandages but grinning.

The young medical student who had driven her here was watching her from halfway across the room. She was startled at the recognition. He winked and went back to whatever he was doing to someone.

One of the other doctors rushed across the room to Livezey. 'Hank, they're bringing one in you'll have to handle.'

Livezey's head jerked up. 'What is it?'

'Woman of twenty-five, twenty-eight. No ID. Wind rolled her car and knocked hell out of her, threw her out, tumbled her down the road like a cabbage. She's in really bad shape.'

Livezey stared at his fellow doctor.

The doctor added, 'Seven months pregnant.'

'Oh, Jesus Christ,' Livezey winced. He took a deep breath, re-asserting total control. 'Okay. Can you finish this man for me? I've got him clamped, but you can see . . .'

As Livezey swiftly showed the other man how to finish work on the puncture victim, Jill lost his words because she was watching the ambulance attendants bring the new patient over. The body was slung in a heavy white sheet that showed massive bright-red stains. Grunting and pale, the men put her on the table with infinite care.

'Put this man over there for Doctor Harrington,' Livezey snapped, and, as they complied, lifted the sheet from the woman. 'Now let's see.'

Jill had said she would not make a sound. The sound, how-ever, came from her.

Even Livezey flinched. 'Shit fire.' He turned to the equipment boxes and slipped, almost falling. 'Will someone,' he bawled, 'get some goddamned sawdust on this goddamned bloody floor?'

Jill could not take her eyes from the figure in the sheets, no matter how badly she wanted to do so.

Livezey swung back around, a stethoscope in one hand and another syringe in the other. 'Give her this, girl. Either arm. Quick. I've got to see if the baby is still alive.'

'I *can't*!' Jill sobbed.

'Christ, you did it before! Here!'

'I can't,' Jill said, 'because I can't tell – I can't find—'

Livezey's face showed his comprehension. He reached into the bloody sheets and grabbed up something, and as he raised it, it became recognizable as one of the woman's arms. 'Here. Now Jesus Christ, *hurry!*'

Mo Coyle was so busy and so tired and confused that she did not recognize him for an instant as she turned and saw him standing there in the kitchen doorway. Only fragmentary impressions first registered: his height, his dark hair, his eyes, the dirt and mud all over his suit. Then it came together in a little chill of surprise.

'Martin,' she whispered.

He came to her and tried, anguished, to take her in his arms. 'My God, I was so worried—!'

She moved back sharply. 'No!'

He almost reached for her again. His face showed havoc and his lips moved silently for a moment before he seemed to understand. His hands dropped to his sides. 'You're all right.'

'Martin, how did you get here? You shouldn't be here!'

'I know,' he groaned. 'But I knew it came close to you and I drove as close as I could, and then I just started running. The closer I got, the worse it was. Then when I saw all the people, I thought it meant—' He heaved a great sigh.

'Is your wife safe?' she asked. 'The children?'

'Yes. I called. There was some minor damage, but we live far enough west. God, Mo! When I thought you might be hurt, or worse—!'

Mo was getting over the initial surprise now. She could even feel the subtle chemistry move within her body as he stood close to her, so intensely masculine and alive and caring. Her heart was crashing around.

'You need to get to them,' she told him. 'They need you now.'

He grimaced as if in pain.

'Are you hurt?' she asked quickly.

'No.' His grin was ironic. 'That was such a bad line you just gave me. My place being with them.'

'It's true.'

'I know. I don't want to go with them. My place is here with you. I can help. I know engineering. I can inspect houses, do whatever else you want—'

Mrs Ernst bustled in from the living room. 'Mo, dear, do you have any more pencils and paper?'

'Look in the bottom drawers of the desk, Mrs Ernst.'

The woman nodded, smiled tentatively – questioningly – at Martin, and hurried away again.

'Just let me stay around awhile,' he said intensely.

There had been other times when their changing relationship, with all its tensions, had threatened to blow up. Looking into his face, Mo knew that this was the worst possible time for any kind of real decision. And yet it was here – she had known for some time what it had to be – and it was now.

'Martin,' she said, 'go to them. I mean it.'

They knew each other very well. From the first they had often communicated without many words. The way Mo spoke was sufficient, and Martin searched her eyes and saw the rest. In the instant of silence between them, the voices from the other room becoming loud and individual through the kitchen's quiet, it was all said.

All of it.

In Mo's imagination – or was it memory? – she saw and heard all the words they might be saying, things that needed saying, perhaps, and could have been said truly if they had not been clichéd by time. They could have said it was over completely now, and no regrets (a lie), and no one was going to collapse because people went on, and they would never forget each other, and the experience had changed both of them, and wasn't it too bad that somehow they could not remain friends. But pretence of real love had been over for a long time already, which made even the clichés unbearable now.

'I'll go, then,' he said.

'Yes,' she said.

'You want me to go. I mean, even after today, you want it ended.'

'Yes.'

His face twisted. 'Mo, I'm sorry it didn't all—'

'Martin, don't.'

'Yeah.' He grinned falsely. 'Right.' He walked to the back door and looked at her again. 'So.'

'I want to . . . thank you,' she said.

'Oh, babe,' he said softly. 'Thank *you*.'

He left then, and she cried a little. But it was all right. She was here where she wanted to be. She felt unburdened, and cleaner. Her life, if she could maintain it that way, would be with Mike and the children, and that was what she wanted . . . in this house, if possible . . . if the storm had not taken that away, and if everything else worked out.

She got busy again.

Broken cloud lay over Thatcher's twilight. To the east were ranks of dark cloud, and to the west were new clouds filled with lightning. As the helicopter sped low over the heart of the city, heading south, Mike Coyle could see the spread of the destruction.

Up from the still murky industrial area south of the river, across the bluffs and through a mile-wide section slashing through the heart of the city, the path of damage showed like a sickle swath. Near the centre of the path, the ground showed yellow-brown, and row upon row of house foundations gleamed bare, strewn with timber and rubble. To the east of the main path was an irregular strip of devastation that seemed blotchy, without real pattern, as if a second and smaller tornado had skipped along, touching here and there. It was only well away from the centre of either swath that the rolling dark of trees re-established itself; even the downtown area looked different, the courthouse truncated, the old central park barren and denuded. Coyle could see that downtown lightning was partly extinguished, several blocks dark while neighbouring ones glowed brightly, the lights showing tumbled cars, fire trucks working against pluming smoke.

As the helicopter neared the river, he saw how the main bridge was twisted in the centre, its main section heaved upward and shifted to the side. Little brilliance points flashed at either end – flashers on sawhorses blocking the way.

'We're nearing the river west of the old bridge,' he said into the walkie-talkie. 'I see quite a bit of smoke in the industrial areas. How many units do we have down there?'

After a slight pause, Purvis Rawlingson's voice came back scratchily on the hand-held instrument's speaker: *'The regular fire station down there, Mike, plus two police cars and a sheriff's unit.'*

Coyle gestured to the pilot to swing somewhat southward, heading for the long, flat-topped buildings that composed the glass factory. 'It doesn't look like the glass plant was hit too badly. Their power line is down and I see rubble in the parking lots, but the roof is intact. The furniture factory was partly unroofed and I can see fire trucks, but no smoke or flame. But there's heavy smoke over toward the bolt works, Purvis, and, my God, it really hit hard farther down in Southtown, along Bixbie Boulevard. We've got to get some more fire trucks down here, more ambulances!'

'Some of the trucks from Dayton are getting close, according to their radio, but we don't know how to get them to Southtown with the bridge out.'

Coyle told the pilot, 'Head west along the river.' Into the radio he asked, 'What about Rockville Bridge? We're heading that way.'

'Rockville is okay, but the streets over there are all blocked and nobody could get through from there to Southtown proper.'

Coyle scanned the streets and roads below, on the south side of the river. He could see trees across many, but others seemed relatively clear. 'Purvis, I think I can give you some routing that would let those units get through without having to move too much debris.'

'I don't know, Mike. Are you sure you want to divert the Dayton people down there? We've got a load of trouble on this side, too—'

'Yes,' Coyle snapped back, losing his temper, 'and we've got all the emergency help north, too. We're not worrying about who pays the most taxes or anything else, Purvis. Have you got radio contact with the people driving in from Dayton?'

'The police have.'

'All right. You send instructions that they're to bear south on the old Rockville Bridge.' He raised the transmit button and told the pilot, 'Swing us back around the other way so I can get the best view of these streets.' He pushed the button again. 'Did you get those orders, Purvis?'

'I got 'em, Mike, but I don't know how wise this is.'

'Just do what I tell you, and turn that tape recorder on. I'm going to dictate to you the routes that look the most open. Okay. Are you ready? Do you have the recorder on?'

'It's on, Mike.' Rawlingson sounded hurt.

'South River Road is blocked on the east because the power lines are down,' Coyle broadcast, 'and lots of trees were felled. But you can go west on the River Road to Allen Road and go south on that. There might be a little trouble, but only a tree here and there. They can follow Allen Road to the blinker light at the old crosstown pike. They should turn east there. . .'

He signalled the chopper pilot to make another wide turn. As the pilot complied, he kept dictating instructions. He knew the emergency vehicles could make it, and he took satisfaction in knowing that Southtown would have its first real help in force because he was up here.

Within five minutes he had completed the routing.

'*The first units are five miles from the bridge now, Mike,*' Rawlingson told him.

'Okay. We're heading north to try to get you a better idea of where the worst areas are to the north.'

'*We know we've got a real problem around Stevenson Park. That's right at the centre of the path, as nearly as we can figure out. But everything is blocked for a quarter mile in every direction.*'

'Stevenson Park,' Coyle repeated to the pilot.

'I know where it is,' the pilot said, and touched the controls. The chopper canted slightly forward as it picked up speed.

The park, south of Mike's own neighbourhood in the central section of the city, was in the middle of Thatcher's historical preservation district. Streets in the area followed the oldest, original plot lines, and had no rhyme or reason to them. The wending ways were considered either charming or ridiculous, depending on the viewer. As the helicopter neared the area now, however, Coyle could quickly see that the nongeometric street patterns around the old park had added to the chaos wrought by the storm.

Trees were down everywhere. The great old Victorian houses were wrecked unbelievably. And the curving, cul-de-sac streets could not be picked out at all because the blockage from trees and debris was total.

Smoke wisped up from numerous small fires. As the chopper swung even lower, Coyle saw people out in bare spots, frantically waving for help. But there was no sign of help. The entire section, eight blocks square, had been sealed off. The nearest emergency vehicle was a lone police car a dozen blocks north.

Coyle ordered the pilot to fly over the patrol car. It was in an intersection, and the officer was out of the car, struggling with limbs of a felled tree. He probably could not see that if he got this tree out of the way, he would only open the way to a dozen more beyond.

Coyle picked up the walkie-talkie. 'Purvis, this is Coyle. Are you there?'

'*Here, Mike.*'

'The houses around the park have been hit very, very hard. When are you going to get some fire trucks in there? You need to get some street crews in there to clear a way, and those people need help fast.'

'*We know it's bad up that way, Mike, but we can't get through.*'

Coyle gritted his teeth. 'I just told you to get street crews to start chopping through. There are some signs of fire, and many of those houses have been flattened. There are bound to be injured people in there!'

'*Mike, I'm not arguing with you. But we don't have anybody to send. All the crews are swamped. We've got every available man at the City Lights Shopping Centre.*'

'How many people are trapped in there?'

'*Oh, we've got everybody out now. But the merchants need a lot of help salvaging inventory.*'

'These people around the park need help more than your merchants and their inventories! Get those street and fire trucks into the preservation district, now!'

'*Mike, we can't get through! How are we going to get through? We've only got a couple of chainsaws in the whole street department!*'

'They're at City Lights, you said. The farm and garden centre out there has a big display of saws and garden equipment. Take what we need.'

'*There's nothing in the budget for it! The owner will object!*'

'Purvis, I'm giving you a direct order under emergency powers. To hell with what the owner says. Charge those saws or just take them out of there, I don't care. Just *get* them and get those crews moving!'

'*I don't think this a wise move, Mike. I beg you to reconsider.*'

'Do it!'

'*Yes, sir.*'

Coyle slammed the walkie-talkie on the floor in front of him and gave the pilot new instructions. There was time to swing north toward the far end of the tornado path, and try to get more information about needs up there.

By the time he had completed the brief swing, he could see the fire trucks and other units streaming away from the City Lights Shopping Centre, heading toward the old park section. Three or four police cars were already on the site, and two officers were at work with chainsaws which puffed little wisps of white smoke as they bit into old trees blocking the street. Coyle felt an angry satisfaction. The people in the sealed-off neighbourhood would start having some help within a few minutes.

'Purvis, this is Coyle.'

'*Go ahead, Mike.*'

'I've done about all I can up here. We're heading back to the airpark.'

'*Mike, can you land your helicopter anywhere downtown?*'

Coyle glanced at the pilot.

'We can do it,' the man said dubiously. 'It's against regulations, but in an emergency I can put it down beside the old courthouse if you tell me to.'

'We can do it if we have to, Purvis. What's the problem?'

'*Mike, I don't want to ... put it out on the air. But just get on down here. Please. It's necessary.*'

Coyle thought about it for a few seconds before keying the unit. 'Okay, Purvis. We'll land on the old courthouse lawn and I'll get there on foot as fast as I can.'

As the chopper banked sharply to the south, he wondered what new crisis Rawlingson – or fate – had cooked up for them all.

ZCZC WBC 599
ACUS KMKC 092400
MKC AC 092400
MKC AC 092400

SPECIAL SEVERE WEATHER OUTLOOK NARRATIVE

VALID 092400 TO 100600

THE SYNOPTIC SYSTEM PRESENTLY CENTRED OVER KENTUCKY AND ILLINOIS CONTINUES TO GENERATE THREE DISTINCT SQUALL LINES. EACH SQUALL LINE IS ACTIVE AND IS EXPECTED TO REMAIN ACTIVE AT LEAST UNTIL 11 P.M. CDT THIS WEDNESDAY NIGHT. SEVERE THUNDERSTORM WATCHES VERY LIKELY WILL BE EXTENDED UNTIL 2 A.M. AND POSSIBLY LATER FOR ALL AREAS REMAINING EAST OF PASSAGE OF THE TROUGH LINE . . .

THE SECOND SQUALL LINE PRESENTLY EXTENDING FROM CENTRAL INDIANA SOUTHWARD INTO THE HUNTSVILLE ALA AREA HAS BEEN WEAKENING BUT INCLUDES SEVERE AND UNUSUAL ELECTRICAL STORMS WITH VERY INTENSE LIGHTNING AND LARGE HAIL ASSOCIATED WITH CYCLONIC CIRCULATION IN MANY CLOUD CELLS. THIS LINE WILL BE MOVING INTO OHIO WITHIN THE HOUR . . .

THE ENTIRE SYSTEM IS EXPECTED TO REACH THE EAST COAST OF THE US BY 6 A.M. CDT THURSDAY MORNING . . . RAPIDLY CLEARING CONDITIONS WILL FOLLOW FRONTAL PASSAGE . . .

THE STATES OF PENNSYLVANIA . . . WEST VIRGINIA . . . VIRGINIA . . . MARYLAND . . . DELAWARE . . . NORTH CAROLINA . . . SOUTH CAROLINA . . . GEORGIA . . . AND FLORIDA MAY EXPECT SEVERE WEATHER WATCH INFORMATION TO REMAIN VALID UNTIL 6 A.M. CDT THURSDAY APRIL 10 AT THE EARLIEST . . .

REVISED WATCH AREA BULLETINS AND FORECASTS FOLLOW . . .

XXX

Monument Valley, Kentucky

Rest: that was all she needed, Milly Tyler told herself.

But she remained seated in the living-room rocker when some-one knocked on the front door. She knew from her view from the window that the truck belonged to the sheriff's department. She let Jason go to reply while the two boys, pale but clean now in their nightclothes, stood up from watching the TV and waited to see who the caller might be.

'I just wanted to make sure you folks had power and telephone and all back in operation,' the voice said.

Recognizing Ed Higginbotham's tone, Milly called, 'Jason, let the man come in. He shouldn't be standing out there with the wind blowing rain all over him, poor soul!'

Jason swung the door wide and Higginbotham, streaming water off a long black slicker and cowboy hat, stepped diffidently inside. 'Evenin' Mizz Tyler. Everything all right around here now?' He was a tall, homely man with a cactus for a nose.

'We're fine and dandy, Ed,' Milly chirped. 'The TV shows might be better, is all.'

Higginbotham grinned, as usual not knowing exactly how to take her. 'You've got your lights, sure enough. I seen a telephone crew east of here. Is your telephone working?'

'We haven't had any calls going out or coming in, either. There the thing is. Maybe it's on and maybe not.'

'Would you mind me checking, Mizz Tyler? Just for my report?'

'Land sake, are you going to fill out a form on that, too? It's no wonder we have crime. Go ahead, go ahead, for land sake!'

Higginbotham tiptoed ponderously across the linoleum and lifted the telephone receiver. He listened. He replaced the receiver. 'You got your line working, Mizz Tyler.'

'I'm sure the widow Jenkins is mighty pleased,' Milly said acidly. 'She's the one always on the party line.'

Higginbotham bent from the waist and studied Milly acutely.

'What are you *staring* at?' Milly demanded.

'Pardon me, ma'am, but you look a little poorly.'

'So do you, Ed Higginbotham! Is there anything else nice you want to say?'

The deputy sighed. 'Well, ma'am, the Lovetts have about finished up anything they can do tonight up at their place. They said they'd favour it if Jason would just stay here tonight, do anything you might want did.'

'Jason is welcome,' Milly said, ignoring the continuing pain in her chest, 'and thank you.'

Higginbotham grinned at Kent and Adrian. 'You fellers over your scare?'

'We weren't scared!' Kent boasted.

'Heck no!' Adrian chimed in. 'Us? Scared? Aw!'

Higginbotham winked at Milly. 'Well, I guess I'll be going, then, and I'm pleased you're all feeling so chipper.'

Milly smiled and waved him off. He clomped back to the door and left, yelling back to Jason that it sure was raining, which any fool already knew. Milly remained in her rocker, breathing carefully and listening to the rain. She was terribly tired, and the bath had not refreshed her at all.

Closing the front door, Jason looked at her and noticed. 'If you're tired, ma'am, no reason why I can't set up a while longer with the boys, here, and you can go ahead to bed if you want.'

'Well, Jason, I might just do that,' Milly decided.

'I'll shut everything off and be sure the doors are locked.'

'Good. Will you tykes be all right if Grammaw goes on to bed?'

'Sure we will,' Adrian said solemnly. 'And we can watch the real late movie, too!'

'You can *not*,' Milly said. 'You can go to bed after the news.'

'Aw!' Kent groaned.

Milly wagged her finger at them as she climbed laboriously to her feet. 'Mind, now!'

They both subsided, and Jason nodded to her, signalling that he would carry out her orders.

Feet dragging in her open cloth slippers, Milly went down the short hallway to her bedroom in the back of the house. Rain drummed evenly on the windows and she could hear the sigh of a light breeze. The room smelled faintly of sachet and Sir Walter Raleigh.

Milly sat on the edge of the bed and considered a good-night smoke. She decided against it. All she wanted to do was stretch out and wait for the Anacins to take better effect, so she could forget the pain and sleep. In the morning, she told herself, she would be fine again.

With a weary sigh, she leaned over to remove her slippers. Dizziness struck.

She plunged forward toward the floor. It happened too quickly for her to cry out. Her head and shoulder hit the nightstand, toppling it.

The crash carried faintly into the living room. Jason started as he heard it. The boys seemed not to hear it at all, perhaps because so much was happening on TV.

Jason got up without saying anything to them and walked back into the dark rear hallway. 'Mizz Tyler?' he called softly.

Getting no reply, he went hesitantly to the bedroom door, peeped in.

He turned and ran into the living room. Grabbing the telephone, he heard someone's voice chatting.

'Get off the line!' he pleaded. 'Get off the line! This is an emergency!'

'Who *is* this?' a woman's voice demanded after a moment's shocked pause.

'I'm calling from Mizz Tyler's house! She's hurt – sick or something – maybe a heart attack! Get off the line, *please!* I've got to call to get an ambulance or something right away!'

There was a gasp, and the line opened instantly. It was a world's record for the widow Jenkins; as he frantically dialled the operator, Jason wondered if it would be fast enough to save Milly Tyler's life.

West of Knoxville, Tennessee

The rain had diminished to a steady, hard drizzle. Les Korowiscz still had to maintain total concentration on the highway ahead, however, as the side wind buffeted his rig. It was not very easy watching the road when the slender man beside him continued to hold the revolver aimed at his chest.

'Look,' Korowiscz said finally. 'Could you maybe just hold that thing, but not point it right *at* me?'

'You take care of driving. I'll take care of the tool.'

'Look, bo. Maybe we could talk about this. What am I supposed to call you, anyway? Have you got a name?'

The man's eyes snapped nervously. He looked crazy, twitching and moving the gun constantly in a tight circle that never left Korowiscz's body. 'Lee. That's my name. You just drive.'

This was progress, Korowiscz thought hopefully. 'Look here, Lee. Maybe if you and I—'

'I said *drive!* and shut up!'

'Okay! Okay!'

Lee's features twisted. 'You won't get hurt if you just do what I say.'

'Right, pal. I understand. Just take it easy.'

It was one hell of a mess. They had more than two hours left until Knoxville. Korowiscz did not have any idea what might happen then. It was up to this Lee character, not him. A .38 had a narrow vocabulary, but you listened carefully. Maybe the nut would just bail out someplace and go about his business. Korowiscz had to hope devoutly for that. He was not about to try anything heroic. The son of a bitch could have the whole rig if he wanted it. Korowiscz just wanted to get out of the deal in one piece.

They drove in silence for a while. The highway was bleak and deserted. Korowiscz wondered at the complete absence of traffic coming from the east.

'How much farther?' Lee finally asked.

'A hundred miles, about.'

'You're going too slow. I want you to go faster.'

'I can't! This wind is bad and the pavement is slick. I told you that.'

'Are you trying to pull something on me?'

'Hell no, I'm not trying to pull something on you! I want out of this deal just as much as you do – maybe more.'

'Not more,' Lee said blackly.

Korowiscz decided to risk the question. 'Is somebody after you?'

'Yeah.'

'The cops, I guess?'

Lee didn't reply.

Korowiscz turned on his headlights against the gathering gloom. They did not help much. 'Did your car really blow up on you back there?'

'You think I'd ride in a stinking truck by choice?'

'And you just happened to flag me down?'

'You were the first thing that came past, except for a farm truck that wouldn't stop.'

'I wish,' Korowiscz said fervently, '*I* hadn't stopped.'

Lee's face twisted in a crazy grin. 'You had the milk of human kindness.'

'I didn't really mind,' Korowiscz said carefully. 'I'll take you where you want to go and drop you. I mind my own business—'

'*Goddamn you!*' Lee screamed. 'Don't *beg* me!'

Shocked by the outburst, Korowiscz swerved the truck slightly. He regained full control.

'Don't beg me,' Lee said more quietly, going in a split-second from a scream to a whisper. 'I don't aim to hurt you. It makes me mad when people think I'm going to hurt them. Don't make me mad.'

'Right,' Korowiscz breathed. 'Right.'

They drove on in silence. Korowiscz did not try any more talk. He had heard enough stories about truckers beaten up, or worse. He had no intention of adding to that list if he could help it. He intended to do exactly as he was told.

No grabbing for the gun, no tricks, nothing. After all, maybe the guy would just hop out in Knoxville. If he was running from the law, he was in a hurry. Korowiscz would give him no trouble whatsoever.

In another few minutes the highway spiralled gently down out of the hills and began a long curving route through a valley area. As the truck came down around the bottom curve, Korowiscz could see several miles out ahead through the half-darkness.

'Oh-oh,' he muttered.

'What? What?'

Korowiscz raised one hand from the wheel to point ahead.

About two miles ahead, the highway was a dull-yellow blaze of car headlights and emergency blinkers. The tie-up was at a point where the highway crossed a narrow stream. Whatever had happened had happened on or very near to the bridge.

Korowiscz started going down through gears, slowing well in advance.

'Don't do that!' Lee shrilled.

'I have to! It's blocked!'

'Go on through! Go right on through!'

'I can't! Look for yourself!'

They were close enough now to see that the stream had leaped out of its normal boundaries, causing all the problem. Water sluiced brown over the bridge surface itself, a few inches deep and running hard. It was out of its normal banks on both sides of the bridge, too, water lapping close to the highway out of drainage ditches alongside the shoulders. There were three cars stopped on the bridge in the westbound lanes, and three more on Korowiscz's side, with two others parked off the bridge at either end. People were out of some of the cars and sloshing around on the bridge in the drizzling rain.

'What's going on?' Lee demanded. 'Why is everybody stopped?'

'You know as much about it as I do. It looks to me like we've got a car flooded out, or spun out, on both sides.'

'What are we going to do? We've got to get on through!'

'First I'm going to stop.'

The gunman did not protest further as Korowiscz brought the rig groaning up close to the bridge, pulling off on the shoulder as far as he dared, considering the flood waters lapping just a foot or so below the level of the gravel. He put the truck in neutral and set the hand brake.

It was easier to see what had happened now. A venerable Studebaker blocked both eastbound lanes. The hood was up and several people were clustered around it, flooded out by the rain. In the other lanes, a recent-model Pontiac had skidded into the bridge railing and was sideways.

'Somebody is going to have to shove somebody off there,' Korowiscz said, putting his left hand on his door handle.

'You're not going anywhere!'

'If I walk up there, I can show them how to push that old Studie out of the way.'

'Let them figure it out!'

'Sure. And we can sit here an hour or two while they do, right?'

Lee's eyes darted around; sweat gleamed on his shallow cheeks. 'What is it you want to do?'

'I want to walk up there and get those people organized, and get the bridge cleared. If that creek is still rising, the water on the bridge is going to get worse. It might *really* be blocked after a while.'

'All right,' Lee grimaced. 'We'll both go.'

'Fair enough.' Korowiscz reached for the handle again.

'Just remember I've got this tool in my coat pocket.'

'I'll remember, bo.'

The hard, flat drizzle stung Korowiscz's face and bald spot as he clambered out of the cab to the soaked pavement. Lee hurried around the front, ghastly pale in the headlights, to confront him. He had both hands jammed in his coat pockets and appeared on the verge of real panic.

'Nothing to it,' Korowiscz said softly, leading the way up toward the snarled cars.

It was clearer now what had happened. Evidently the old Studebaker had hit standing water on the bridge, and the driver had braked to a quick halt, stalling his engine in the process. The Pontiac on the other side of the divider had tried to stop abruptly in response, perhaps to offer assistance, and had skidded out of control. The Pontiac was badly crumpled and might require a wrecker.

Korowiscz led the way on to the bridge. Icy water was less than ankle-deep. People peered out at him from the steamy windows of a Buick and a Ford as he passed their cars. All the drivers were out in the middle of the bridge.

The Studebaker starter was whining as the old man behind the wheel tried vainly to get a spark. The battery sounded almost gone.

'Looks like we've got a problem,' Korowiscz told the men cheerfully as he reached them.

'It won't go,' a beefy-faced businessman grunted.

The driver of the Studebaker, an old man, peered out of his window. 'I don't know what's wrong. I just had it worked on.'

'What we ought to do, sir, is push you on across the bridge. Then we can let everybody else get by. Somebody can take you on up the road here a couple of miles; there's a gas station up there.'

'Well,' the old man said fretfully, glancing across the seat at his wife for corroboration, 'that's okay, I guess, if somebody will give us a push.'

Korowiscz turned to the heavy-set man again. 'Is that your Buick next in line, there?'

'Yeah,' the man said dubiously. 'But I don't want to scar up my bumper.'

'Looks like the option is waiting for a wrecker.'

The man grimaced as others watched him. 'Okay. I'll pull up slow and you can direct me. If the bumpers don't fit, I'm not going to do it.'

Korowiscz nodded. As the Buick driver walked back to his car, he asked if anyone was hurt in the facing lanes. No one was.

The Buick fired up. The driver inched it forward. The bumpers fit reasonably well, and any scars would be to the Studebaker, which wouldn't show them among all the others it already carried. Korowiscz went through the business of directing the pushing of the Studebaker off the far end and on to the shoulder a scant few feet from where flood water lapped at the gravel.

Lee, the gunman, stayed close, silent by Korowiscz through the operation. Everybody was revving engines to get going again. It would be possible for the drivers on the other side to back up and use the cleared lanes, as long as no one was coming from the other direction.

Korowiscz signalled the Studebaker driver to roll his window down again. Just as he did so, there was the start of distant flashers – red and approaching fast – in the far lanes a mile or so east.

'What's that? What's that?' Lee grunted.

'Looks like the hypo is arriving on the scene,' Korowiscz said.

'Get back to the truck! We're getting out of here!'

'Are you crazy! If we tear out of here without telling him what's going on, he'll *know* something is up.'

'Don't try to tell me what to do,' Lee hissed. 'No tricks – I won't fall for any tricks!'

'I'm trying to get myself out of this with my whole skin,' Korowiscz shot back honestly. 'If we stay here and get people moving, then we get in the truck and go on with no problems. You think *I* want to draw attention to us now?'

'And have me caught? Sure!'

'And have you waving that gun around, you mean!' The patrol car was getting close, throwing water as it braked, red lights pulsing. 'Just do it my way, goddamn it, Lee, and we won't either of us have any problems!'

The gunman darted fearful glances all around. He appeared almost out of control. He had no time to think. 'Okay. Okay.'

Korowiscz heaved a sigh and bent over the Studebaker to speak through the window. 'Sir, if you want to step out, I'm sure the highway patrolman over there will want to talk to you, and you'll be able to get a ride with him.'

The old man pulled the keys from his ignition. 'All right, all right. Madge, go ahead and get out. The policeman will help us now.'

The old man opened his door on Korowiscz's side.

The woman on the far side opened that door, inches from the flooded shoulder ditch.

'Lady, get out *this* side!' Korowiscz grunted.

Too late.

The woman stepped down onto the muddy gravel. Her feet

slipped. She cried out and fell. Half-turning, she went over the narrow embankment, hitting in the muddy water with a huge splash.

'*Madge!*' the old man screamed.

The Buick, just pulling by, rocked to a halt. The highway patrolman jumped from his car, running. Lee exploded an expletive and tried to grab Korowiscz's arm, missing. Korowiscz, acting reflexively, was already halfway around the back of the Studebaker.

The old woman was in the boiling water over her head, crying out and thrashing around in her ridiculous fur-collared black coat. The current had already tugged her a few feet from the shoulder, and into a gushing rivulet where drainage water moved swiftly toward the creek itself.

Korowiscz reached out to try to grab her hand, but she was too far out already. He hesitated an instant and she screamed again and went under for perhaps two seconds.

Korowiscz dived in after her.

It was colder than all living hell, driving his breath out of him as he hit and went all the way under. He came up sputtering, shocked by the cold and fighting to stay afloat in the heavy clothing. People were running around on the road and he could hear the gunman's shrill, hysterical voice. *So shoot me, you prick.*

The old woman was a few feet away, being swept toward the ditch that poured runoff water into the main body of the creek. *In* the thing, it didn't look like a creek; it looked like an ocean. Korowiscz stroked to try to get closer to the woman and got ducked again, choking on gritty water. This made him mad and he fought much harder, throwing up brown spray, and he managed to get almost beside her. He reached for her shoulder and missed, reached again and caught her left arm. The effort promptly ducked both of them.

She was sobbing and screaming, clutching wildly for his face. She almost took both of them under still another time. Korowiscz got one of her arms pinned, and the current swung them around so that their faces were only inches apart.

'*Hang on to my back!*' he bellowed.

'*Yes!*'

He turned partway, being carried ever farther from the road. Her fingers clawed at the back of his neck, and then caught in his shirt. The movement turned both of them around in the water, but Korowiscz could manoeuvre with her hanging on in this position. He shook water from his face and saw a tree hanging down into the water just at the mouth of the ditch gushing into the creek. The tide spun them around twice more and threw them into the cutting branches. He grabbed one and it broke. He grabbed again and the branch was big enough to act as a snare. The water boiled over him and the woman, but their movement had been halted.

Korowiscz got another blurred look at people running off the road and coming along the muddy little finger of earth that extended out to his snag. 'It's okay!' he yelled to the woman. 'Just hang on!'

Half-blinded, he began working his way hand-by-hand into the roots of the tree. The water had numbed him and he could not feel much, but there was enough bright pain in his hands to help him hold tightly to the wet branches.

His feet hit something – a rocky upslope. He caught a better grasp in the tree and heaved himself upward. The bank was there, blessedly muddy but solid. Clawing into the mud, he pulled himself partway out of the water, the woman a heavy weight on him as the water's buoyancy was removed.

Then the other people were around him, hands grabbing, excited voices, the old man crying, the woman crying, hands dragging her and Korowiscz all the way out of the water.

'Heroic!' the old man babbled. 'Such a heroic thing to do!'

Korowiscz, remembering the gunman, rolled his head in the mud to see where he was.

On the bridge, the highway patrolman had someone – Lee – spread-eagled on the side of the Buick. The patrolman had his gun out and was patting Lee's pockets.

'Your friend went sort of crazy!' someone panted as Korowiscz sat up. 'He tried to attack that officer. We all had to grab him. With you in the water at the same time, I tell you, that was a mighty exciting couple of minutes!'

Korowiscz gulped in some air and felt a great urge to laugh. They were all eager to help him get unsteadily to his feet.

'Is your friend in bad trouble now?' the old man asked solicitously.

Korowiscz removed a ruined cigar from his pocket, examined

it, and tossed it disgustedly into the raging water. 'I sincerely hope so,' he told the old man.

Columbus, Ohio
The sky to the south and west was a terrible greenish black, and wet wind blasted across the expanse of runways and grass, making it hard for Bill Fredrick to stand by the instruments. He was quite near the lobby door and only about forty paces from the inside stairwell that led to the basement, where he had already ordered everyone else to go.

Roy Bock, of course, had refused.

Standing braced against the rising gale, Bock grinned down at Fredrick as he knelt to try to wedge the legs of the camera tripod against the metal fence for greater stability. 'What do you figure to learn from this?' he demanded.

'If a tornado comes right through here,' Fredrick gritted, 'nothing. Because the cameras and everything else will end up in Lake Erie or somewhere.'

'Aren't you getting a little uptight, man? I thought you experts were cool.'

'I know enough to know when to be scared.'

'What chance is there to get hit anyway?' Bock pressed. 'I've heard the chances of one of these things actually hitting a place is like once every two or three hundred years, and that's in Texas where they have the most.'

'Statistics can fool you a little, Roy. Oklahoma City has been hit something like twenty-six times since 1892.'

'This isn't Oklahoma City, though. This is Ohio. That cloud out there don't look all that bad to me.'

Fredrick paused to look to the southwest. The sky was black from ground to infinity. Directly overhead, wisps of grey cloud extended down from darker masses, and could be seen whirling ominously. Fredrick had a prickling sensation on the back of his neck.

'Roy,' he said, 'get the hell into that basement.'

'Not me, boy. If something comes, I want to *see* it.'

Fredrick turned again to the southwest.

And froze.

Off beyond the southwest airport fence, a mile or two away, the air had suddenly taken on a pearl quality. From a blue-black shelf of cloud extended a long, grey hose. It curled slightly to the south near the ground, and he could see debris being sucked up into its maw.

'Come on,' he told Bock, grabbing his arm.

'Hey!' Bock cried, pointing to the tornado Fredrick had already seen. 'Will you look at that!'

'Roy, come on!'

'This might be the only chance I ever get to see one of these things!'

Fredrick left one of the movie cameras locked to the *run* position, grabbed Buck by both arms, and shoved him bodily into the lobby. It was deserted, and against the glare of the fluorescent lighting the windows looked black. The wind-speed indicator on the wall was spinning wildly, some gusts taking the pointer to the peg.

'We're getting to that basement,' Fredrick told Bock. 'Come on.'

Bock pulled free. 'I'm not going, man. You think I'm scared? I've never been scared of anything in my life!'

'If you've got any sense, you'll be scared of this! Come on!'

Roy Bock grinned at him and refused to budge.

Fredrick, growing desperate, grabbed at his arm again. Bock pulled free. Fredrick caught him once more. They struggled. Bock shoved him backward and Fredrick, although a big man, almost went sprawling.

'Roy, goddamn it—!'

'I ain't going!' Bock yelled, angry now. '*You* go, if you're scared!'

Fredrick hesitated. There was nothing in sight that he could use to brain the man.

But there was no time left. Beyond the darkened windows, which seemed to pulse now with the force of the wind, he could see that the grey hose to the south and west had grown enormously. It had reached the south fence a mile away, and he could see chunks of wood flying around. It appeared that the tornado was about four hundred yards in diameter.

'It's coming right at us,' Fredrick told Bock, struggling for calm in his voice. 'I'm getting belowdecks.'

'I'm staying here,' Bock grinned, and turned his back to face the window.

Fredrick grunted an obscenity, turned, and ran for the stair-well.

Bock felt a moment of elation. He had spent much of his life, as a boy and man, proving that there was nothing that could frighten him. He had just proved it again.

He watched the tornado through the front glass. It had come through the fence, and he was amazed now to see that the thing was tearing up chunks of asphalt, right off the runway, as it came over.

Planes parked on the transient ramp nearby fluttered and strained at tiedown chains. The wind howled. It was very difficult to see very far. The lightning helped.

Bock thought what a story this was going to make. He imagined it being told by Fredrick, too. *'They always said that S.O.B. was crazy, and now I believe it! I tell you, that tornado came right over the building, and Roy was just standing there at the front glass, watching it, sort of smiling. God, what courage!'*

The tornado crossed the grassy area between runways twenty-seven and twenty-one. Huge pieces of sod flew through the air, whirled around. The tetrahedron swung around insanely and then blew up. The length of the tornado changed colour, or seemed to, becoming broader and black. It roared into the row of hangars along the south ramp. Twelve-foot steel doors flew off the hangars. The first one in line seemed to lean, and then a wall fell outward and the three-storey roof lifted straight up. *That roof must weigh ten tons*, Bock thought.

The next hangar was slapped sideways, collapsing like an accordion. Hundreds of windows in the wall of the next exploded, the shards creating a kaleidoscopic effect. The planes parked along the pavement were all chained, but the entire line went crazy as the blackness passed near them. Cessnas, Pipers and others thrashed about. Chains broke. Some planes began hurtling along the ground. Others seemed to take off straight up. Some disintegrated.

Bock felt a pang of concern. He had not really known a tornado was this strong. He turned and looked across the lobby, but there was no one else in sight.

The blackness reached the front of the terminal building. A piece of broken concrete weighing three hundred pounds or more hurtled through the front glass like a howitzer shell, smashing everything in its path. The lights went out. The roar was deafening. Pieces of the ceiling began coming down. The blackness blew the front windows inward, and the evil wind hurled Roy Bock all the way across the lobby and against the closed door to the basement. The walls caved in and Bock was crushed to death.

By this time, Columbus knew the tornado was moving in.

The flight service station and Rudy Murphy's boss at the radio station agreed it was time for Rudy to get the traffic chopper safely home.

'I'm already just west of the river, downtown,' Murphy argued. 'Why don't I just sneak out that way and have a look? I'll keep my distance.'

'*Columbus radio, roger,*' the FAA man said tersely. After all, a traffic chopper was a special commercial vehicle, and the pilot was always the final authority.

'*Rudy,*' the air man from the station called, '*Jonesey says cool it.*'

Murphy grinned and hung up the microphone. He had never seen a tornado.

He banked the helicopter away from the downtown area, following Broad Street to the west. Under sullen, blackening clouds, he flew swiftly, following the ribbon of lights made by evening traffic out toward the Hilltop. Gusty wind buffeted his light craft, but he maintained control with practised ease.

'I'm out about the Wheatland–Oakley area now,' he told his man at the studio, 'and you're right. That's a mighty ugly-looking cloud out west of here. I'd say it's about at the Westland shopping centre right now. It's got some lightning in it, too. I'm going to swing south, down toward Sullivant Avenue, just so I don't get too close to the thing. It looks real narrow.'

'*Rudy,*' the voice came back excitedly. '*It's no joke out there. We've got phone calls and cop information. There's a tornado in that thing.*'

As the words came in, Murphy chilled, seeing it.

From the base of the cloud, which seemed about eight hundred feet above ground level, a broad pale funnel extended. It was on the ground and he could see landmarks.

'Put me on the air!' he yelled. 'I see it! Put me on the air now!'

'Okay, go in ten seconds, on the tone.'

Murphy fought the controls and his tiny chopper bucked and rolled in high gusts of wind. All his senses were riveted on the awful thing hanging down out of the cloud. A lark had become the most exciting thing that had ever happened to him.

The tone sounded in his earphone.

'This is Rudy Murphy in the Earlybird Whirlybird,' he yelled over the increasing wind noise, 'and I'm about at Sullivant Avenue and Terrace over the Hilltop. There's a tornado on the ground near Broad Street, near the GM plant, people, and this is no joke. I'm as close as I dare to get to this thing, a great black cloud, a silver funnel hanging down out of it, and oh, people, I can see things being torn up, I'm getting in just a little closer. Everyone on the west side, take cover. This is no joke. This is real. I'm in the chopper and this tornado is moving west of the GM plant now, it is crossing Broad Street and it is moving east and a little north. People north of Broad street on the Hilltop, get in your basement. Take cover. This thing is real.'

Murphy swung the gyrating helicopter around in a tight circle, fighting the wind as he got his bearings more precisely. He kept the mike open so no one would cut him off.

'The tornado is just crossing Broad Street and it's going to go right along north of Broad, moving toward Huron, Roys, those streets along there. I can't tell if it's going to hit the businesses along at Hague and Broad, but it's going to hit some on north Hague for sure.'

A panel light flashed, indicating the studio wanted in. Murphy released his button.

'*Rudy,*' the air man said, '*the police and Weather Bureau and everyone else say to just stay with it as long as you can. Keep talking and telling exactly where that tornado is.*'

Murphy did not even acknowledge. He was far too excited and awed. Keying the button again, he started telling the precise location as he could see it at the moment.

He did not know it, but Rudy Murphy was winning a national medal. The Columbus tornado was destined to kill only two persons, and injure fewer than twenty. Officials would estimate that dozens might have died, and scores would surely have been injured, if Murphy had not been in the air – and on the air.

Medals were the farthest thing from Murphy's mind at the moment. He was talking a blue streak, something he did very well, and flying the chopper, something he did equally well. He was so busy he did not even have time to realize how scared he was.

As the squall lines continued to move with inexorable power, there were quirks, pranks, miracles and disasters, all a part of the storm.

A large tornado, lighted from within a scummy green, moved into Harrisburg, Pennsylvania, at 7 : 41. People said the sound was that of a jet airliner at very close range. Sixteen blocks were damaged, and an industrial development park reduced to rubble. Hospitals filled, and hailstones as big as oranges pelted ambulances trying to deliver more casualties. The tornado moved east out of Harrisburg and struck the town of Middletown a little before eight o'clock.

In Middletown, a widower named Henry Lattigan was on his way to shelter in the basement of his home when the wind began screaming. He had a very old kerosene lantern, fully fuelled. He paused at his dining table to light the lantern because power had failed, but as he got the wick lighted, the storm intensified and he ran, leaving the lantern on the table.

After the storm had passed, Lattigan crawled out of his basement to find part of his house wrecked. To his astonishment, Lattigan peered out through the shattered front wall toward the street and saw a flicker of light in the darkness. It was his lantern, standing upright in the middle of the street and still burning normally.

In eastern Kentucky, Mile McClory was at the controls of a diesel locomotive hauling forty-one loaded freight cars westward. The rain was very bad and the lightning constant, but McClory was an old-time railroader and was not unduly worried.

When big pieces of trees began flying by the cab windows and the train began to rock on the tracks, McClory reached for the brake. He never got to it. He was thrown sideways and had an incredible sensation of being airborne. There were a few moments of terror and vertigo, then a grinding, crashing impact that left him on the floor of the cab. There were sounds of gravel and dirt sliding, and the engine was being torn apart underneath.

When McClory got back to his feet and looked out, he saw, in the flashing lightning, that the engine was on its wheels in the middle of a grainfield. The track was forty yards away. Some cars remained on the track, others were on their sides, others had been flung through space – forty-ton projectiles – along with his much heavier engine.

The lightning revealed a horizontal white cloud in the sky to the northeast. As McClory watched, it picked up a house and threw it aside like a petulant giant who wanted something nicer.

No one saw a tornado in Parkersburg, West Virginia, but a rock chimney exploded on a residential street and one of the sixty-pound blocks was carried half a mile to the east, where it crashed through the living-room window of another home and killed a sixty-year-old woman playing Parcheesi with her grandson. The boy was not injured.

Near Atlanta, in a cocktail lounge called Captain Kidd's, a barometer behind the bar pegged at twenty-eight inches of mercury as frightened patrons stood at windows, watching a twister pass almost directly overhead. It was probably the same tornado that touched the ground a few miles east, virtually destroying a rest home. The home's recreation room had a pool table in it, the balls racked and ready for play; after the storm, survivors found the pool table in a creek two hundred yards away. The balls were on the floor of the recreation room, under pieces of the roof. The balls were still racked.

In North Carolina a farmer named Atwood drowned. He was in a makeshift earthen cellar beside the dam of a farm pond. The dam broke, pouring his cellar full in a twinkling. The Atwood property suffered no other damage.

An airline pilot flying at twenty-one thousand feet over Tennessee reported great flocks of small birds flying in disorganized patterns in all directions. Another pilot not far away said he saw many birds – robins and starlings – apparently *falling past* his altitude of thirty thousand feet, from some much greater altitude.

Despite the havoc, most Americans east of the Mississippi spent reasonably normal evenings with their TV's, complaining about continued programme interruptions for weather bulletins. Most experienced only some heavy rain, a little wind and lightning. Even in the most epic outburst of severe weather the country had ever known, the individual's chances of escaping were very, very good.

Near Atlanta, a man named Henried was saved by his fondness for gadgets.

Henried had watched the NBC 'Today' show that morning, and knew about the Skywarn. At lunchtime he went by a discount electronics store to look for a stereo-loudspeaker switching box, and happened to notice the small weather radios on a display table. Prices ranged from less than twenty dollars to more than a hundred dollars.

He asked the clerk about them.

'Weather radios like these cheap ones are fixed-frequency,' the clerk explained. 'All weather stations broadcast on either 162.55 or 162.40 Hz. You buy the frequency for your local station and you're in business.'

'These fancier ones are also regular radios?'

'That's right.'

'One-sixty-two Hz is FM,' Henried said, to show the clerk he wasn't dealing with an idiot.

'Right,' the clerk said. 'So you get static-free reception even in a storm.'

'That makes reception line-of-sight, too, though, like television.'

'Half the population has coverage now. More stations are being added. We have a local station. They usually start at three hundred watts, and they'll be upgraded to a thousand watts as money becomes available.'

'I live a few miles out of town. I wonder if I could get anything.'

'Look. Try the radio. If you can't get reception, return it and we'll give you your money back.'

Henried compulsively walked over to one of the most expensive units on display.

'You don't need anything that grand,' the clerk smiled. 'That kind of unit is for a school or business. See? You turn it on standby. Then it will just sit there on the shelf, quiet. But if there's a warning, the station broadcasts a special tone that the radio hears. It then turns its own volume up so people will hear it.'

'Do the stations broadcast all the time?'

'Weather information, yes. They can go on live at any time.'

'My wife will kill me,' Henried said after a minute's thought. 'I'll take one of these little red ones.'

That evening, the little radio told Henried that a storm was near his neighbourhood. He took his wife to the basement. Wind unroofed his house. His wife, shaken, said that they would probably have survived without her husband's latest gadget, but she did not sound very emphatic about it.

Wednesday, April 9
8:05 p.m.–8:30 p.m.

ZCZC WBC 623
ACUS KMKC 100100
MKC AC 100100
MKC AC 100100

BULLETIN
SPECIAL WEATHER STATEMENT
ISSUED AT 8 P.M. CDT APRIL 9, 1975

TORNADO AND SEVERE THUNDERSTORM WATCHES HAVE EXPIRED
AND ARE NO LONGER IN EFFECT FOR

MISSOURI
ARKANSAS
ILLINOIS
WESTERN KENTUCKY
WESTERN TENNESSEE
WESTERN MISSISSIPPI

SEVERE WEATHER WATCHES IN THESE AREAS TERMINATED AT
8 P.M. CDT.

TORNADO WATCH INFORMATION FOR AREAS TO THE EAST OF THESE
STATES REMAINS IN EFFECT. RADAR PRESENTLY INDICATES SEVERE
WEATHER ACTIVITY EXTENDING FROM WESTERN OHIO SOUTH
THROUGH EASTERN KENTUCKY AND TENNESSEE INTO ALABAMA
AND GEORGIA. ANOTHER BAND OF ACTIVITY CONTINUES IN WEST
VIRGINIA, A PORTION OF PENNSYLVANIA, VIRGINIA, THE
CAROLINAS AND PORTIONS OF FLORIDA . . .

XXX

Thatcher, Ohio
The helicopter settled on the courthouse lawn, its blade breeze
driving back a small crowd of straggly onlookers. Mike Coyle
thanked the pilot, hopped out, and ran, bent over, from the
machine. The people standing along the brick-strewn edge of the
lawn were shirtsleeved, dirty and hollow-eyed. Coyle thought he
saw some familiar faces of shopkeepers and small merchants.

One of the men recognized him at once. 'Hello, Mayor!'

Coyle waved. He pointed at the unbelievably wrecked upper

portion of the courthouse tower. 'Our poor old courthouse.'

'Nobody was in it. Charley, here, got the janitors out just in time.'

Coyle saw that he was about to be drawn into a conversation, so he kept walking swiftly toward the street, 'I've got to get to City Hall.'

The skinny man pointed. 'Look at that power pole there.'

Coyle looked at it. It appeared *furry*. He walked closer, and to his amazement saw that it was covered with imbedded pieces of grass and what looked like straw. He touched his palm to the pole. It was straw, all right, along with millions of blades of grass. They had been driven into creosoted wood.

The skinny man grinned crookedly. 'Takes a wind to do that, eh?'

Coyle shook his head and cut across the street. He had two blocks to go to get to the city complex. He had to move into the street at the corner to get around fallen bricks, and then in the next block the sidewalk was littered with pieces of roofing material and broken glass. A police car blocked the intersection. Here and there a merchant was in front of his shop, trying to nail up plywood or provide some other makeshift fronting. The small buildings had been hit a light blow, compared to some of the things Coyle had already seen, but the blocks were like a city after war.

He was a block from City Hall when light rain began again. As he dodged past an overturned car, he heard someone calling his name from down the street he had just crossed.

He turned and saw a rotund, coatless figure waddling up to catch him. Cecil Upshaw owned Thatcher's biggest downtown department store, and was personally as much a tradition in town as was his old family-owned business. Ordinarily the dapper embodiment of a Victorian picture-album photo, Upshaw was ragged, spattered with mud or some other substance, and both his white shirt and dark trousers were torn.

He reached Coyle's side, breathless, his face glistening with sweat. 'Hello, Mike. Glad you're here. My God, isn't this terrible? Just awful, awful. Everyone has suffered terrible losses. Are you on the way to City Hall, I suppose?'

'Yes,' Coyle said. 'Your store was badly hit?'

'Not as bad as some others, but that's why I chased after you.

Mike, you've got to get more emergency help downtown, here. We have inventories to protect. We need emergency construction help – everything.'

'Cecil, you'd better call in as many of your own employees as you can persuade to come to work, and get them on it. I'm just heading down to the office to get more information, but what I already know is plenty; you won't be getting any emergency help out of us tonight, and maybe not for days.'

Upshaw's face twisted. 'What kind of attitude is that for the city to take? Who deserves more consideration than your leading businessmen? If what I heard about help being sent to South-town is correct, it seems to me that a lot of favouritism—'

'Listen, Cecil! The people who need help the most are going to get the help first!'

Upshaw's eyes bulged. 'Let go of me. No need to get excited—'

'If some of you bastards worried more about somebody else once in a while, maybe everybody would be better off.'

'Southtown is getting all this help—'

'Southtown was hit harder than downtown was. There are people hurt and probably dying in a lot of other areas, too. Don't talk to me about your goddamned inventory. Just take care of it yourself. We'll help when we can, *if* we can!'

Upshaw stared at him with watery eyes. 'Don't ask what your country can do for you? That kind of a line?'

'Christ,' Coyle said explosively, and turned to hurry away.

At the front door of the city building, a middle-aged, over-weight woman in a pale housedress was arguing with a policeman beside his car. Seeing Coyle, she ran toward him, catching him on the building steps. The rain misted into Coyle's face as he turned in answer to her cry.

'Mayor Coyle,' she cried, 'you've got to do something! You have to help me!'

'What is it?' Coyle asked.

'He's gone – missing – and I don't know where to turn! I can't get anyone to help me look!'

'Who's gone, Mrs—?'

'Barnes, Mrs Walter Barnes, and his name is William, and he—'

'How old is he?'

'Five. He's five years old. I live in the Greystone Apartments on Third Avenue, and windows were knocked and he's gone.'

Coyle signalled the policeman to come over. He told the woman, 'We'll do all we can, Mrs Barnes. You have to realize that there are many temporary separations. My own son and daughter weren't at home when this thing hit.'

'Oh, you poor man! You poor, poor man!'

'I'm sure they're all right, Mrs Barnes. William is all right too, I'm sure.' The policeman had reached the steps. 'Officer, you'd better taken the information from Mrs Barnes, here.'

The cop frowned. 'Sir, I'm not sure you want to—'

'Mrs Barnes, tell Officer Kincaid about your boy. Start with a description.'

'Well,' the woman sobbed, 'he's not special or anything. He's yellow, a tabby, and he has a nametag—'

Coyle must have jumped violently as the realization hit. The woman cried defensively, 'He's all I have in this world!'

Coyle turned and pushed into the building.

It was chaotic. All the offices were open, ablaze with light, and crowded with unusual activity. Some card tables had been set up, and two telephone men were stringing in extra telephones. Women from the city clerk's office were already making and taking calls on one set of lines. As Coyle entered, a National Guard sergeant brushed by him, hurrying out with a handful of city street maps. 'Sorry, sir.' Blackboards had been dragged into the foyer and already had many hurriedly chalked names and emergency messages on them. Colye saw other uniformed Guardsmen.

Purvis Rawlingson rushed out of the clerk's office, his face twisted by the strain. 'Mike!'

'You didn't want to say something on the radio,' Coyle snapped.

Rawlingson looked around, his shaggy mane hanging into shocked eyes, as if trying to assure himself no one would overhear. In all the noise and bustle no one was even looking their way.

'Purvis, what *is* it?'

'We have a new message from Dayton, Mike. There's more bad weather on the way.'

Coyle could not quite believe it. 'Coming here? Soon?'

'Thirty minutes or so, they said about thirty minutes.'

'What kind of bad weather? What did they say *exactly?*'

Rawlingson was so badly shaken he had to start the sentence twice. 'More of the – bad weather like before. I mean another squall line. We're under a new tornado alert kind of thing. They said this new line has bad lightning and wind and hail and maybe another tornado.'

Coyle closed his eyes. It simply was not possible, he thought. But his instincts tried to panic. He felt a great impulse to turn and run – try to get back home to Mo.

Rawlingson choked, 'I was just waiting for you to get here. We haven't made any public announcement yet. But I'm going to have them blow the sirens right now – all the sirens we can get to work – and all the police cars will blow their sirens, and all the workers will tell everybody to take shelter, we can be ready this time—'

'What about rescue operations that are going on?' Coyle asked.

'We'll stop for now. I hate it as bad as you do, Mike, but we don't have any choice, we'll blow everything and broadcast the warning and get everybody in hiding, as safe as they can be—'

'No,' Coyle snapped, cutting in on Rawlingson's near-hysterical burst of words.

Rawlingson stared, shocked.

'If we have thirty minutes, Purvis, we'll use them. And we won't blow sirens or anything like that ... not yet. Remember how it's supposed to work? The alarms go off when a tornado is sighted – verified – and nearby, a proven threat.'

'Oh, my God, Mike! We got caught with our pants down once! We can't risk having the same thing happen a *second* time!'

'How often has this city been hit by a tornado?' Coyle shot back.

'What?'

'How often—'

'Once! A little while ago! You know that! I don't understand—'

'We're not going to panic, Purvis. We get ready, yes. But we aren't going to panic and run off in all directions at once. No sirens, not yet, anyway. We'll make an announcement on the commercial radio and on the police band. I'll go on the building PA and tell everyone what's up. We'll get cars out – spotters.

But we won't go all to pieces just because we're under a watch.'

'If we had paid more attention earlier today—'

'All right! But that doesn't mean we *over*react this time!'

Rawlingson's eyes seemed to droop. 'Mike,' he said hoarsely, 'if we get hit another time, and we aren't ready—'

'Right,' Coyle shot back bitterly. 'It will be on *my* head, right? It's my responsibility, is that what you were going to say? Fine. I'm telling you what we're going to do, Purvis, and what we aren't going to do. And to hell with where the blame will fall if I'm wrong. It isn't like this was the first time I started hearing the I-told-you-so's even before we did something.'

'Mike, maybe we ought to call the Council in on this.'

'There isn't time. We wouldn't be able to locate half of them. They've got their own problems. Some of their houses or places of business were hit. And it's my responsibility. I'm telling you how it's going to be.'

Rawlingson did not seem capable of comprehending. 'Why did Dayton send us this message if they didn't want us to do something about it?'

'They do want us to do something about it, Purvis. We're going to. Get somebody into my office so I can dictate a statement for you to read on the city radio circuits, the police and fire emergency. Call the radio station and make arrangements for me to telephone a statement onto their tape machine in five minutes. Get the building PA turned on; I'll make an announcement in here right after I talk on the radio.'

Rawlingson blinked. 'You'll tell people here *after* you broadcast the news?'

'Right.'

'Mike, I don't know if that would be good PR—'

'*Damn* PR! Which message is going to get to the most people? If this is urgent, we go in the order of priority.'

Rawlingson sighed and pulled at his ear. 'You're a hard man. I guess it takes that, sometimes.'

'Purvis, just *do* it and analyse my character later.'

Rawlingson shuffled off glumly. Coyle hurried to his own office, and had a secretary there within two minutes. He dictated a brief, factual statement: a new storm was coming; it might be violent; it would be watched; four police cars would be sent south and west of the city; if the sheriff's department could send anyone, these units were to co-ordinate by radio with city police to provide the best continuous coverage; radio and siren warnings would be sent only if another tornado or very high winds were imminent; in the meantime, salvage and rescue work were to go on.

By the time the girl had run to type the message for Rawlingson to read, the radio station was waiting on the line. Being careful to keep his voice as flat and unemotional as possible, Coyle dictated a similar message into the silent tape recorder at the other end of the line.

When he was finished, he heard some switching on the line, and Leroy Prendergast came on. 'That it, Mike?'

'For now, yes. Listen, I think we ought to keep this line open.'

'Right.' Prendergast paused. 'Say, listen.'

'Yes?'

'What you're doing sounds right to me.'

'Leroy, thanks.'

Waiting for the microphone line from the PA amplifier to be strung into the downstairs lobby, however, Coyle had time to reconsider. He did not dare show his own uncertainty, but it was there, in spades. Down deep, he was frightened. What if he was wrong? What if lightning *was* going to strike twice? Would people be caught because he *thought* this was the right thing to do?

He thought about Mo, and about the kids. Where the hell *were* the kids? Something inside his chest ached.

Purvis Rawlingson, accompanied by a young janitor, hurried across the lobby trailing an audio card. 'It's all set, Mike.'

'It's working?'

'It should be.' Rawlingson flicked a switch on the small microphone. 'Testing, one, two, three.' His voice boomed through the building, coming from ceiling loudspeakers that usually carried only Muzak. People glanced up from hectic work, appeared in office doorways.

Rawlingson handed Coyle the microphone.

'This is Mike Coyle,' he said, hearing his own amplified words bounce back. 'Please let me have your attention for a minute, whatever you're doing. This is important. Please let me have your attention.'

Voices stilled through the building. More people came to doorways, and there was hurried whispering as word spread that Coyle was standing in the lobby. Within seconds, every doorway was filled, and other people were straining to see from inside rooms. Coyle knew the same attention was fixed on his voice in the fire department, the street-crew rooms, next door in the police department.

'We have a new message from the weather people in Dayton,' he said, and instantly saw the anxious expressions. 'This is an advisory kind of thing only. Please remember that. They say a second squall line is approaching Thatcher.'

There was a general hubbub, and someone called out, 'Oh, no!' Other voices joined in, and for an instant there was confusion.

'We don't know how severe this new storm may or may not be,' Coyle said, his voice booming, amplified. 'We are sending out spotter cars to keep watch on the situation. If they see something bad – *if* they see something bad – they'll radio back, and we'll sound the alarms and give everyone time to seek shelter.

'In the meantime, we all have vital work to be doing. Let's keep at it. I guarantee you that we have spotters out, and we're alert. There will be ample warning if we need it. Let's not panic. Let's do our jobs.'

He paused again, thinking he was finished. In the clerk's office, however, he saw two or three women crying. The silence was funereal, shocked.

So he had to say more. He felt suddenly very tired. Why did the job have to have this component? Why did the man in charge always seem to have to carry everyone else's morale on his back? This was one of the reasons he had started this day so tired, he thought: he had carried too many people too long; he could no longer support it.

But he had to support it.

'Let me say just a couple of more things,' he said, and faces turned back to him. He saw the fear and uncertainty . . . and the trust.

'We're all scared right now,' he said slowly, struggling to keep his voice under control. 'But we're doing the right thing, proceeding this way. I was in a helicopter a while ago, and I saw what's happened to Thatcher. We've been dealt an awful blow. People are hurt . . . dead. There are parts of the city that may never be the same again.

'But I'll tell you this. If we stick together now, we can whip this thing. We're getting the spotters out. We'll have warning if anything happens. We're ready ... as ready as we can be. Please stand with us tonight. You're doing great work. Don't let the *possibility* of something wreck all our efforts. I'll keep you informed. In the meantime, let's all ... keep on our jobs, here.'

He handed the microphone back to Rawlingson.

He had failed, he thought. It had been a moment that cried out for something fine, some rhetoric. He hadn't given them anything but what they had always gotten from Mike Coyle: talk about work, talk about hanging in there.

To his amazement, he realized that there was a new sound.

The workers were applauding him.

Some were weeping, but they were standing, applauding.

Then they began bustling back to their jobs.

'Mike,' Rawlingson said, patting him on the shoulder, 'I sure hope this works. I'm with you, my friend.'

Rawlingson's good-hearted gesture of support was the last straw. Coyle had to turn away quickly because somehow this sequence of events had touched something deep in him, something he had imagined was lost. He had to turn away so no one would see the tears in his eyes.

Birmingham, Alabama

Sitting in front of the motel-room television set, David Kristofsen sipped his lightly spiked coffee and felt afterwaves of shock and fatigue filter through his body. Across the room, Susan sat at the telephone, talking to another of their friends. The TV announcer was talking voice-over films of the wreckage around the city.

It was good to be in the motel room. It felt secure. Rain was pounding down outside, but it was only rain, the TV said: the worst of the storm system had passed the area. In his newly purchased and rather silly-looking karate-style bathrobe, Kristofsen had two Libriums in under the scotch, and he was savouring the fact that they were alive.

'Yes,' Susan told the person on the telephone. 'All right, Billie. We'll call you in a few days.'

Kristofsen watched her as she hung up and frowned over the telephone book. She had bathed, too, her hair was in rollers, and she was wearing a newly purchased pink robe and bunny-rabbit slippers. She looked quite beautiful to him.

'Finished?' he asked hopefully.

'Just the Lockridges,' she said. 'I have to call them.'

He nodded, vaguely disappointed, and returned his attention to the TV. He heard her dial and begin to talk, and then he allowed her voice to become only a pleasant background sound without content.

They had come to the motel from the house, and had been among those lucky enough to find a vacant room before storm victims took every unit in town and hundreds of others began taking potluck with Red Cross volunteer shelter. They had gone out again almost immediately, still manic in reaction to what they had been through, and walked to an undamaged shopping centre nearby. Their salvaged clothing included all the wrong things, so they bought sleepwear, toiletries, new slippers and shoes, a bottle of scotch, a probably illegal refill on the Librium prescription. Then they had come back here again, stripped, and went into the steaming shower together, giggling like kids. It had been a long time since they had bathed together, but somehow it had been more comradely than sexual, and they did not try to make love. They opened their new purchases, dressed – she in jeans and a sweat shirt, he in corduroys and a lumberjacket – and went to the motel dining room. The food had not been very good, but it was substantial. Finally they had come back to the room, changed into new nightclothes, turned on the TV.

Kristofsen had then called his parents and his agent. Susan called her parents, too, and then began talking about others they should contact if possible, to see if they were all right, to share experiences.

'Don't make any more calls, okay?' he had asked her a little while ago.

'I have to, David,' she told him.

'Later. Just sit here with me awhile.'

'In a little while.'

So he had nodded stiffly, a little hurt and withdrawn, and watched the television news, which continued on and on. Her responses to him proved, he thought, that the storm and their losses had not worked any magic between them. There was still the remoteness. Maybe that was natural. Maybe he was the crazy one to have this feeling of great need at a time like this.

Waiting for Susan to finish the last call, he tried to concentrate on the television summary. It was impossible. All the wreckage looked alike. It was impossible to tell what anything had looked like before. His own street had been shown a while ago, and he had not recognized it until the announcer named it for him.

Mentally he went over inventories. Things lost, things that might be salvaged. He thought again about the manuscript and felt sure it really did not matter. He thought about Mrs Jackson. *How will we ever find another maid as good as she was?* And then he was shocked by his own selfishness.

Susan hung up and left the telephone. She walked to the bed and sat beside Kristofsen, watching the pictures for a moment.

He sought her hand on the coverlet. 'Finished?'

'Yes. I had to let them know, David.'

'I know.' He tried rather badly to smile at her.

She got up and started to move away.

'Susan, let's talk.'

She looked down at him. 'About what?'

'About what happened. About what we do next. Anything!'

'I'm so tired, aren't you?'

'Look, I'm sorry I hit you. I'll never do anything like that again.'

'Oh, David, let's just go to bed, all right?'

Driven, he held her with his eyes. 'Right after the tornado, I thought somehow – I got the feeling – that the storm blew a lot of bad things away for us. I thought that now maybe we could start over . . . fresh . . . the way it used to be.'

'Maybe we can.'

'But not if we fight.'

'Maybe,' she said slowly, 'we have too much practice fighting, now, to do anything else.'

'No. That's not so. We've lost our house and a lot of other things. We've got each other. We don't have all that damned crap and all that house to try to live up to any more. We can't let something like this happen and not have any meaning.'

Susan studied his face, puzzled. 'Is that what it was like for you? Did you feel like you were trying to live up to that house?'

'I didn't think about it,' he admitted, 'but yes.'

'I thought you were so proud of the house.'

'I was, at first.'

'I was, too,' she admitted.

'But later you weren't?'

'Not really.'

'Then we can start over,' he told her excitedly. 'The storm gives us a fresh start.'

'Is it that simple?' she asked him.

He was startled. 'What?' She did not usually talk to him exactly this way, as if she knew something that he didn't.

'David, do things really turn out in real life the way you try to make them turn out in your books? Is there really a silver lining? Did you ever consider the possibility that loss is . . . just loss?'

'No. I reject that.'

'It doesn't matter whether you accept or reject the idea. What matters is whether it's *true.*'

'It isn't true for us, Susan.' He reached for her hand, took it. 'We lost our way. We can find it again. Death and resurrection. That's what life is all about. We can get back if we *try.*'

She smiled, but it was a faint, sad smile. 'Is it always like that, David? A living, full-colour rendition of a great literary theme?'

He was astounded, and frightened by the coolness of her eyes. 'Susan, we can get back together complete, just the way it once was. All we have to do is try.'

'If we *want* to try,' she told him.

'My God, *I* want to! Don't you?'

'I don't know.'

'Susan!'

'I've been an object,' she told him with terrifying calm. 'I'm tired of that. Oh, I tried to be a good ornament for your life, the happy hostess, the wonderful party-giver. But it wasn't working, was it, for either of us? Now should we start in again on the same charade?'

Kristofsen stared at her, thunderstruck. How long had they been chipping away at the foundation of their love? Even in the early years, when it had been so fine and they had both been so sure, had they been killing a part of themselves as he worked night and day, trying to succeed, and she played the faceless, loving supporter? Then, with success, how much more had they thrown away as they rushed into the new life with hands clawed, intent on getting all from it that anyone ever had? *We have it coming to us*, Kristofsen had told her once, justifying some particularly outrageous purchase or plan. Had they grabbed for so much that now they had absolutely nothing of one another any more?

He looked at his wife. He could see in her expression that at last he knew precisely what she felt. He wished desperately that he didn't.

There would be no miracle for them out of the storm . . . no *deus ex machina* sweeping down to make everything all right. They were what they had become, unknowingly. There was no way either of them could tell whether fate had given them this shock opportunity too late.

'I want to try,' Kristofsen told her.

She did not answer him.

Thatcher, Ohio

The meeting in Mike Coyle's office included a major named Ott who was the local National Guard commander, Purvis Rawlingson, and a man named Armour who had come in with Guard units, representing the governor. The meeting had been planned to be brief and had already run on too long. They all had one eye on the clock, which showed 8:20, almost a half hour since the message had come in from Dayton about the new severe weather approaching.

'When the mobile kitchens are set up in the park,' Coyle told them, 'we'll make an announcement. In the meantime, we need a report on this new weather.'

'You can see it in the distance from the windows now,' Rawlingson said.

Coyle rotated his chair and looked for a moment out of the windows, their draperies fully drawn back. Over rooftops was the darkness of Southtown in the distance, and, well beyond, a sky that pulsed with distant lightning. 'It looks well off yet.' He glanced at his inside telephone. 'It's past time for Merrill to call back.'

'I'm sure he'll call as soon as the spotters make their next report, Mike,' Rawlingson said.

Coyle nodded and swung his chair back around. *Who's panicky now?* 'Okay. Major Ott, these first units that you have arriving are going south of the river. When do you expect more help?'

Ott rubbed his index finger through a tiny moustache. 'Within thirty minutes. Perhaps sooner. I understand that the orders have already gone over our convoy radio, and they'll swing north and begin taking up positions around that big shopping centre and along the streets you pointed out on the map.'

'And any medical personnel to the west-side armory?'

'Yes, sir. Correct. The first field kitchen will be set up there, too, since the Red Cross is organizing downtown, here.'

Armour uncrossed his legs nervously. 'I'm sure the governor is waiting for my call, gentlemen. I want to report to him directly.'

'Have you seen enough, or are there questions?' Coyle asked.

Armour's expression was grim. 'I've seen plenty. You can be sure the state is going to have a lot more help in here by morning. You need it.'

'I believe—' Coyle began, but the telephone rang.

He snatched it up. 'Coyle.'

Chief Merrill's voice was raspy. 'We've been talking to our people out south. The line is moving slower, but it's coming our way. Dayton says it's building up to the west now, too, and we can see that from here. I'm sending a couple of cars out on the west side, just in case.'

'Okay,' Coyle said. 'Have you had any word from the hospital on my personal matter?'

'We found a nurse who saw your daughter leave with some people headed for the armory. I just talked to one of our officers out there. He went inside, found your daughter. She's helping in the temporary emergency room.'

Coyle breathed a deep sigh. 'She's all right?'

'Yes, sir, I'm glad to say.'

'Thank God for that.'

'Mayor, I've got a unit very close to your house. Emergency crews are working through that area now. If you'd like to relay a message to your wife about your daughter—'

'Yes, Chief. If you can do that it would be great.'

Merril hesitated. 'I'm sorry we don't have anything on your boy yet.'

'Yes.' There was a dryness in Coyle's throat.

As he hung up the telephone, Rawlingson said, 'News about your kiddos?'

'My daughter is at the armory.' Seeing the expressions, he quickly added, 'Not hurt. She's a candy striper. She's helping with the injured.'

'Wonderful!' Rawlingson beamed and clapped his hands in genuine pleasure. 'And your boy?'

'We don't have any news about him yet. But the Tidwell house wasn't badly hit. He and the Tidwell boy left there after the tornado, so they must be all right.'

'Maybe they're helping somewhere, too.'

Coyle smiled, but did not say what he thought. He knew what Billy and most of his friends thought about Thatcher and most of the people living in Thatcher. It was hard to imagine them volunteering to help in any situation.

But at least both kids probably were safe. And now Mo would soon know that, too. It was a lightening of his burden.

Major Ott stood. 'If we're concluded for the moment, sir, I'll get back outside to my temporary command post.'

Coyle nodded. 'I'm going to go out for a few minutes myself. I want to see what's happening up and down the street.'

He stopped briefly to talk to a number of workers and volunteers in the offices fronting the lobby. The people cheered up when he stopped. They were scared, but he maintained an easy composure that they were eager to grasp at, and hang on to. He was very good at this, he thought. He had taken pleasure in this skill with people for years, but until tonight the skill had never really been tested.

Distant lightning pulsed. Overhead, thick clouds had moved back over the city, and vein lightning flickered at great altitudes. The air was thick, hot, humid, as it had been before the tornado. He could smell smoke, tar, gasoline fumes.

Many of the street lights were not working due to some partial line break, and the National Guard had set trucks at each intersection with generator-fed spotlights. The criss-crossing beams of brilliance glinted off broken glass, overturned cars, broad puddles of black water. In the distance were the cries of sirens. Somewhere nearby people were hammering something. From the dark interior of a canvas tent draped over a manhole by the gas company came the brilliant arc of a welding torch.

Coyle walked south. Bonfils, the jeweller, was in front of his shop, standing on a chair, using a staple gun to affix flattened pieces of cardboard over the hole that had been his small display window.

'I have everything safe in the vault,' he panted cheerfully. 'The glass company said they will get to me as soon as they can. You think that will be tomorrow? Ha!'

'The police will have foot patrols working, Mister Bonfils.'

'I know. My loss is so much less than anyone else's, I feel almost ashamed. I am all right, my wife is unhurt, our apartment was not damaged. My son and his wife were in Columbus, so they are fine, too, and the tornado did not go near their neighbourhood. We are lucky!'

'I hope everybody else downtown did half as well.'

Bonfils waggled a finger. 'Downtown will come back.'

At the next corner, the storm had freakishly dealt a strong blow to the three-storey building housing medical offices upstairs and the Hoffman drugstore below. A handful of spectators stood in the street, staring. The last fire truck was reeling in hoses. The building's side wall had been smashed in and there had been fire.

Ira Hoffman stood on the sidewalk, wringing his hands. His store was a black, sooty cavity.

'Ira,' Coyle said, putting a hand on his back, 'if it's any consolation at all, I know insurance companies work extra fast in disasters like this. It won't be long until you're back on your feet again.'

Hoffman stared. 'It was everything I have.'

'You'll rebuild.'

The old man spoke as if in a trance. 'Thirty years I had insurance with the same company. A few months ago I had vandalism – you remember the broken window and paint poured on counters? The company didn't pay it all. So my policy came up for renewal last January and I wrote them a letter telling why I was dissatisfied . . . why I would not renew.'

Hoffman turned to meet Coyle's stare.

'Oh, Ira. Don't tell me.'

Hoffman made a flattening gesture with his hands in the air. 'Nothing. There was no insurance of any kind. I had not renewed with another company.'

Coyle could not believe it. It sickened him. 'Oh, Christ.'

Hoffman turned back to the wrecked store.

Coyle wanted to say something. He did not know what to say. Of course it was stupid to let insurance lapse. Had anybody ever lived a week of his life without doing something equally stupid?

Hoffman was a good man. Now what did he have left? What could Coyle say, pretending otherwise?

He started to move away.

'Mayor?' Hoffman called huskily.

'Yes?'

'In a time like this, do you think zoning regulations would be waived?'

'I don't understand.'

Hoffman gestured toward the ruined building. 'This will be torn down. Some others will, too. I have a little cash. If zoning allowed it for a while, as emergency, I could get a trailer house, move it on to the lot. I can get credit from suppliers ... I could start again, if zoning would allow it.'

'Ira, count on it!'

Hoffman nodded wearily, but with some inner nobility that would not give up. 'I can do that. I can get a trailer and start again.'

Coyle went on, talking to others. They asked about the new storm. When he explained, they were mutely trusting. They told stories of where they had been and what they had been doing when the tornado hit. Coyle began to sense a sameness in the stories, a mythic quality. For no one here would ever forget this night. It would be told in their families, perhaps, for generations.

And yet there was little of the utter despair that he had expected. They might be too numbed yet, or there might be another factor operative here that seldom showed in this place, in this day and age. Was it possible that a catastrophe of this magnitude could actually bring out the best in people ... if they had a best to stimulate?

He walked back to City Hall more hopefully. There, Chief Merrill said an officer was bringing Mo downtown because she said her work was done for the moment in the neighbourhood. He also said volunteers were working selflessly, despite the threat of a new storm, to clear streets in many neighbourhoods. He also said a fourteen-year-old girl had been raped in the Gimley Addition, and there was looting at several small shopping centres.

Lightning flickered overhead. The new violence was moving in.

When he reached his own office, Coyle found the telephone ringing. He snatched it up. 'What is it?'

'Mayor Coyle,' one of the volunteer telephone operators said breathlessly, 'I know you're taking nothing but emergency calls, but this man on line two says he's family.'

'Who is it?'

'A Mister Ed Stephens? In Kansas City?'

'Put him on.'

The telephone clicked a few times.

'Ed?' Coyle yelled.

Remarkably, it was a perfect connection. Ed Stephens sounded like he was in the next room. He also sounded upset. 'Mike? Is that you? What's the situation there? Is Mo all right? The kids?'

It was very, very good to hear the voice of a man who might have some answers. 'Mo is fine, Ed. We haven't collected the kids yet, but we think they're okay, too. You were right yesterday, in spades. We got the hell knocked out of us. One tornado, and maybe two, came right through the heart of town.'

'Christ,' Stephens groaned. 'Casualties?'

'I don't know how many. I wouldn't want to guess. We have some killed and a lot hurt . . . a *lot* hurt.'

'Where were you when it hit?'

'At home. And yes, it did hit the house.'

Stephens did not speak for a moment, and Coyle imagined he could hear teletypes banging in the background. Finally Stephens asked, 'How bad is your damage?'

'Not bad. Not compared with a lot of others, Ed. Listen. Now your people in Dayton say we have another squall line coming.'

'Yes. You do. This storm is just unbelievable, Mike.'

'Ed, is this line as bad as the other one?'

'It could be. It is in places. For God's sake be ready this time.'

'We'll have spotters out. We'll be as ready as we can. But what I want to ask you is this. Am I right in not blowing any sirens we may have left, or sounding any other full-scale alarm, unless or until we actually see a tornado?'

'Or until Dayton gives you a wire warning. Yes. Your weather wire is still functioning?'

'Yes. It seems to be one of the few things we're sure of.' Coyle hesitated, listening to some long-distance chatter enter the circuit. He did not like revealing his uncertainty. But he was far past the point of stupid pride. 'Ed, I don't want to sound any sirens or anything unless we have to. People are shocked. They'll panic.

But Jesus Christ, what if I wait and then we don't *see* the thing in time?'

Stephens waited, too, before replying. When he did so, his voice was low. 'Mike, I can't tell you what to do. The chances of your getting hit again by another tornado are awfully slim. But some towns have been hit three times in one day.'

'I'm afraid of panic, though.'

'I understand. For whatever it's worth, I think you're doing the right thing. Have your spotters out, watch the wire, watch the sky yourself, and play it by ear.'

'I was hoping you could give me a neat assurance that I'm doing the right thing.'

'I wish I could, Mike.'

Coyle took a deep breath. He could see the lightning from his window, and it was nearer.

Wednesday, April 9
8:35 p.m.–9:15 p.m.

```
NNNN
ZCZC
WRUS RWRB 100130
ZZZZZ
```

SPECIAL STORM STATEMENT
NATIONAL WEATHER SERVICE TAMPA FLORIDA
ISSUED 8:30 P.M. CDT WEDNESDAY APRIL 9, 1975

..... COASTAL FLOOD WARNING .....

THIS APPLIES TO PERSONS ALONG THE UPPER FLORIDA COAST
FROM TALLAHASSEE TO CEDAR KEY ...

VERY STRONG SOUTHEASTERLY WINDS OF GALE FORCE ARE IN THE
PROCESS OF PUSHING HIGH TIDES ALONG THE UPPER FLORIDA
COASTLINE WELL ABOVE NORMAL. THESE HIGH TIDES ARE
EXPECTED TO CONTINUE TO INCREASE THROUGH TONIGHT
REACHING HEIGHTS OF BETWEEN THREE AND FOUR FEET ABOVE
NORMAL DURING THE MORNING HOURS THURSDAY. PERSONS IN
LOW LYING COASTAL AREAS CAN EXPECT SOME FLOODING BY
DAWN THURSDAY. TIDES WILL BEGIN TO RECEDE LATER
THURSDAY ...

XXX

From the West Coast of the United States eastward to a line extending roughly from Minneapolis to New Orleans, clear, cool skies allowed starlight to peer down upon the great land. Lights twinkled in the darkness of the prairies and farmlands, mountain masses jutted ebony bulk into a sky so clear the stars seemed very close, and airliners approaching the glittering sprawl of major cities reported visibility more than fifteen miles, the common jargon for virtually unlimited.

In places like Fort Dodge, Iowa; Topeka, Kansas; Miami, Oklahoma; and Marshall, Texas, night saw continued frenzied work by emergency crews clearing streets and roads, transporting injured people, mending power lines, welding gas pipes and water mains, securing temporary fronts for houses and businesses, evacuating late flash-flood victims, counting the dead. But the clear skies had begun to bring a feeling of some kind of returning normalcy, and in a hundred places, perhaps, workers stood up for a moment from a job of work, wiped away sweat, and told one another, 'It's over. At least we got through it alive.'

From Illinois eastward into Pennsylvania, the Virginias, the Carolinas and Florida, enormous thicknesses of cloud remained. The frontal system was weakening in the heartlands, but retained power of a magnitude no man could wholly comprehend. The farther east one wished to look, up to the actual cutting edge of violence, the more intense the activity remained. From a Detroit—Atlanta line to the east, the night was far from over. For many, the worst was still to come.

Charlotte, North Carolina, was skirted by a huge tornado at 8:35 p.m. Straight winds topping one hundred and twenty miles per hour smashed windows and signs and knocked over a five-hundred foot television antenna in Augusta, Georgia, at virtually the same time. The weather service and news wires clogged, ran eight minutes behind. The warnings and strikes and near-misses hit places like Cambridge, Covington, Lexington, Asheville, Macon, Dothan, Maryville, Athens, Valdosta, London, Durham, Lake City, Greenwood, Hanover, Trent. The Associated Press reported damage to several historic landmarks at Gettysburg, and in Winston-Salem, winds tore out more than seven thousand large panes of glass from a building scheduled for completion in 1976.

Thirty million Americans were watching the Wednesday-night movie with Clint Eastwood.

The cloud line moving across Huntington, West Virginia, included two cells whose altitude exceeded fifty-five-thousand feet.

Huntington, West Virginia

'With this weather, it's a wonderful turnout!'

'It certainly is, Mrs Traxler, and I appreciate your efforts.'

'My goodness, *I* didn't do anything!'

'You're the hostess, Mrs Traxler.'

'Oh, yes, of course! But my goodness, *you're* the attraction!'

'But it takes work to get people out like this.'

'Oh, I find much more interest in politics this year, don't you?'

George Abrams smiled at the woman standing beside him and replied with an easy cliché. She wiggled with pleasure and returned him an aphorism, which he volleyed with a trite metaphor, deep to the backhand corner. She got to it and came right back with an old saw.

It was the kind of conversation on which politics thrived. George Abrams was very good at it, handled it with the thinnest top layer of his mind, and was thinking about other things as it continued.

He was standing with his hostess against the high ledgestone fireplace wall at the sunken end of a long, cathedral-ceiling living room. It was a comfortable house, sleeky contemporary, redolent of new money. Little ruby-glassed candles flickered here and there on heavy glass tables. The carpet was light blue, streaked with silver, and the furniture mostly white leather. Track lighting cast soft shadows across roughly textured white walls, and the voices of spa-trimmed, salon-sleek young matrons tinkled softly quiet, well-insulated from the gathering storm outside.

There were sixteen young matrons in the room, not counting the hostess.

George Abrams had counted.

'But don't you really *believe* that we *all* must get involved?'

'Oh, yes, Mrs Traxler. A government is only as good as its people.'

'That's a wonderful way to put it!'

In Abrams's hand was a sheaf of longhand notes. He really did not need them any more; he had made this same little speech fourteen times in the past eight days. But they were good for the image of the hard worker, and he especially needed the image tonight because his nerves were so bad as a result of the day's events.

The neighbourhood caucuses, however, were too important to cancel just because Donna Fields had chosen this day to drop the bad news on him. He had to hide the things he was feeling, and do his stint. He was very good at hiding his true feelings.

'—as a result of Watergate, don't you think?'

'That, Mrs Traxler, and the energy situation. We have to face the issue of strip mining, for example.'

'Oh, yes!'

Ordinarily, Abrams thought, he would have enjoyed this caucus. He had found that there was a direct relationship between the amount of money a woman's husband had and how long she kept her looks. The young matrons in this room were uniformly well-coiffed, nicely dressed, handsome. There were two women here whom he would ordinarily have made it a point to speak directly to in his speech, because they were the cream.

One was a rather tall brunette who sat in a pale leather chair just a few feet away. While others were chatting, she remained aloof, and her dark eyes were often on Abrams when he glanced her way. There was a slight knowing smile in those eyes. She was sleek and well-curved, with long, darkly stockinged legs, and her eyes said, *Do you really think you can leave tonight without seeing if you can have me?*

The ageless question. Since his rise to some power, Abrams had learned that many beautiful women liked to ask it. And many replied in the affirmative. He had been approached in many ways, from this kind of mildly challenging stare to the night when a very beautiful woman had stopped him with her hand lightly on his arm near the exit and had whispered a deliciously obscene suggestion in his ear while her husband stood less than ten feet away.

Did they seek out men like him, men of power, because they felt they could somehow draw a power of their own? Was their goal that moment in bed when he had spent himself, was for a few seconds hopelessly without manhood and vulnerable?

He didn't know. But this dark-haired woman would be inventive in bed, athletic, challenging, arch, witty, finally passionate and demanding. He knew her type, just as he recognized the type of the other woman who had caught his eyes, a plump little blonde somewhat closer to him in the room. She was all cuddly curves and darling silvery curls and cuteness, and her husband would not understand her, poor thing, and she would begin retreating coyly the instant he showed interest, but it would be much the same in the end, only she would cry a little and sigh, and ask him to tell her he loved her afterward. *Do you love me? Oh, say you love me! Tell me now! Oh!* Come, come, come.

Lightning flashed vividly at the tinted windows, thunder bellowed, and some of the women tittered and looked frightened for him. He smiled.

Then he realised that Mrs Traxler had her hand on his arm, and had said something.

'I'm sorry, Mrs Traxler. What did you say just then?'

'I said, shan't we get under way?'

'Yes. Good. Whenever you say.'

'Ladies? Ladies? May I have your attention, please?'

Abrams put his speech notes in his coat pocket.

Mrs Traxler began the usual witty little introduction. It took more than a little storm to slow the campaign of a man like George Abrams, as his appearance here tonight amply proved. And now, before letting them hear from the great man himself, she wanted to make sure she knew just a few things about him which he was surely too modest to tell about himself.

As she began reading from the printed card Abrams had supplied, the women in the room settled down, smiling, being Good Citizens. Abrams glanced at the brunette and their eyes touched. The explicit sexual message bolted silently out of her eyes.

Abrams felt his bitterness try to overwhelm him. He had been so clever. There were so many lovely women ... so many who would ask nothing but the essentially neurotic thrill of having been a receptacle for his semen. Of all of them, why had he fallen prey to a Donna Fields?

He still did not know how he was going to cope with her blackmail. His wife must never know. No one could know. He had to get the money himself, and deliver it personally. It would go on and on, and there was nothing he could do about it.

As the introduction neared its conclusion, he briefly enjoyed the legs of the blonde nearby. Every man had a weakness, he told himself. His was not such a terrible weakness. He could go on. He was a good public servant, on balance. Much harder working and more honest than most.

'—and so, with great pleasure and real personal pride, I give you our own George Abrams!'

Applause tinkled across the room. So many pretty eyes, so many lovely smiles and sleek legs and hidden dark recesses of pleasure. And how artificial this all was, talking politics now, when so many other messages of a more basic kind were being transmitted ... would settle his fate with them at the ballot box.

'I appreciate your effort to be here tonight,' he told them, using his big voice easily to be heard over the wind and thunder beyond the walls of the big house. 'I want to assure you that my speech is not of the fire-and-brimstone variety. We're being given quite enough fire and brimstone tonight by that big speechwriter in the sky.'

They laughed delightedly, and so, having shown them he was

just a regular guy with a sense of humour, Abrams launched into his standard speech. He said the situation locally and nationally was far too important for jokes. Many old-line politicians, he said, believed voters did not want to face the serious issues. But he knew better. And he intended to examine issues here and now.

The storm howled louder. Lightning flickered brilliantly at the windows. The rain thundered down.

Abrams went on, speaking with all the proper pauses, frowns and inflections, a part of his mind continuing to probe at the problem at hand. He could not give up this quest, this chance for power. As much as it galled him, he would have to leave here and go get the money.

Moving into his three-minute segment on penal reform, Abrams experienced a moment of insight and sadness. How many dreams died this way, he thought ... how many compromises were made. He stood here now already soiled, and they could not know it. Donna Fields had already won.

A particularly loud thunderclap rocked the house. The lights dimmed for a few seconds. The unbelievable rain intensified. Abrams raised his voice still more, but he saw that the women were only half-listening to him now as they began to worry about this storm. Another crash of thunder rattled glassware.

He paused to take a sip of water, letting the ladies calm down, showing them he was acting perfectly normally.

It didn't work.

Thunder exploded again and the lights went out. Women squealed. The room was now illuminated only by the few ruby candleholders. At the windows the lightning pulsed insanely.

'It will be all right,' Abrams told them. 'I'm sure there's nothing to worry about.'

Mrs Traxler was nervously on her feet. 'Since it's so bad right now, Mr Abrams, do you suppose we should break for coffee, and then you can resume after this has passed?'

'Fine,' he agreed. 'Good idea.'

Voices blended as everyone began chattering. Mrs Traxler went into the kitchen and found more candles. A battery-operated radio sounded. One or two women went into the kitchen with Mrs Traxler, others milled about. Abrams lit a cigarette. It tasted stale and bitter. The fiftieth cigarette today? The sixtieth? At what point, statistically, did it become 99 per cent sure of inducing cancer?

A voice at his elbow said huskily, 'Storms terrify me.'

Abrams turned, knowing it would be she. He was surprised to find that she was almost his own height. Close to him she was even lovelier. He recognized her scent but could not name it. It fit her: a dark, gently insistent jungle-flower fragrance.

'There's nothing to be worried about,' he told her.

'I know that,' she replied. 'But my feelings often overpower me.'

'You have an advantage over me, you know.'

Her smile taunted. 'Oh?'

'You know my name, but I don't know yours.'

'Melissa.'

'That's a pretty name. I've seen it, but I've never known anyone by that name before.'

'My mother wanted me to be unusual, I think.'

'And *are* you?'

'Oh, yes. You'll be pleased.'

'Will?'

'Should I have been subtle and used the conditional?'

Women started crying out excitedly in the kitchen. Mrs Traxler rushed in. 'There's been a tornado! It must have just missed us!'

There were little shrieks, more excited talk.

'What happened?' Abrams demanded. 'Where did it hit?'

'It went right down the highway! The man on the radio said it's lifted up now – it's gone – but it went right into that shopping centre down the road about four miles, and it hit those Halray Apartments. He said it did terrible damage to the apartments and lots of people are hurt or killed!'

'Halray?' Abrams repeated sharply as it clicked for him.

'Yes! It did terrible damage, he said!'

A woman said nervously, 'I think I ought to hurry right home. The children—'

Others babbled agreement.

Abrams turned to Melissa. 'I know someone in Halray.'

'A friend?' She touched his arm, and despite the situation, the electricity was there.

He lied. 'A campaign assistant.'

Women were milling around, getting coats. The blonde came over, glanced briefly at Melissa, then gave Abrams the full battery of her eyes. 'I'm *so* sorry this meeting is being cancelled, Mr

Abrams. There were a number of campaign issues I really did *very* much want to speak with you about.'

'Maybe,' Abrams said, 'we can talk about them sometime soon.'

She looked dubious. Melissa had not budged, and that was not helping matters. 'Yes. That's a nice idea. I could . . . let me think . . . I could give you my name and telephone number, and then you could call me when you have time.'

He smiled into her transparent eyes. 'That's a fine idea.'

She already had it written on a little pink card.

Melissa asked after the other woman had joined the crowd near the doorway, 'You'll go to Halray to see about your friend?'

'Yes,' Abrams said. He moved toward the hallway, and nodded dully as Mrs Traxler handed him his coat. He was not thinking clearly because the sudden hope was too enormous.

Donna Fields lived in Halray.

He could not face the hope directly, because it was too good to be true, and too hideous that he could hope for it.

Women were leaving the house now, running through driving rain to cars parked in the driveway, in the street. Headlights gleamed through the rain.

Abrams pulled his coat collar up, waved to Mrs Traxler, and stepped onto the roofed porch.

Melissa was right behind him. 'Where's your car?' she asked.

He pointed. 'Down there somewhere.'

'I'm right here in front. I'll drive you.'

He didn't hesitate. He was not even sure whether she was offering to drive him a half-block, or to Halray. It didn't really matter. 'That's very nice of you, and I accept.'

They ran to the car at the curb, a brown Lincoln, getting pelted by the icy rain. Both of them were gasping by the time they fell inside the shelter of the big sedan. Melissa's long legs gleamed in the light of the dashboard. 'I'll never be the same!' she laughed, tugging at her skirt to make sure he didn't miss anything.

'Are you taking me to my car, or all the way?'

'Whichever you want.'

'You don't mind?'

For reply, she stepped on the accelerator, passing his parked car and throwing up massive water sprays as she headed for the intersection.

Once at the corner, they found the rain-swept highway deserted. She turned west and drove well and hard, with admirable competence. The sky ahead was aflame with lightning. After the first mile or so, Abrams saw billboards that had been knocked down.

'Do you think we'll be able to get into the apartment areas?' Melissa asked.

'We can try to get close enough to let me check on my ... friend. I have a card that ought to get us past the police.'

They drove another mile and came to a police roadblock. Melissa stopped at the police unit, with its flashing red lights, and Abrams showed the officer the emergency traffic card signed by the governor. The policeman waved them through.

'Do you always get your way?' Melissa asked, driving fast again.

'Always,' Abrams snapped. He was in no mood for casual by-play right now. Ahead he could see the shopping centre, flames shooting into the rainy sky, lights of fire trucks and police cars everywhere, and beyond, the flames were even greater against a backdrop of huge smoky clouds.

'Turn down the service road and we can get in the back way,' he told her later.

They skirted the shopping centre's huge parking lot. It appeared that nothing remained standing. The batwing main structure was crumpled, and firemen were playing long streams of water into the wreckage. Abrams saw ambulances coming and going.

At the far end of the lot, where the road led into the side entrance to the apartment complex, another police car blocked the way. Abrams could see beyond it, and the skyline of the James-town-style apartments was all wrong. Whole stretches of building had been wiped out. There were more fire trucks, ambulances, police units, people bearing stretchers, moving around in the rain and smoke. A long line of ambulances was waiting not far inside the brick walls.

The policeman came over to the car and Abrams showed the card again.

The officer shook his head grimly. 'Sorry, sir. You can't drive in there. You'd be running over hoses and everything else.'

'Can I walk in? I've got an employee in there.'

'I guess you could go as far as the ambulances, sir. But that's your risk. I can't be responsible.'

'I'll be right back,' Abrams told Melissa, opening his door.

'You can back up and park along the wall here, lady,' the cop said.

Abrams got out into the rain, which was steady, but diminishing. The heat and smoke of the huge flames reached him before he had gotten halfway across the jungle-littered patchwork of hoses in the parking lot.

On the wet pavement beside the ambulances, perhaps as many as twenty bulky shapes lay under canvas blankets. There was no doubt that they were dead; the living were being bundled into some of the ambulances.

Abrams went over, his heart crashing in his throat. A policeman eyed him suspiciously, but Abrams went ahead as if he had every right to do what he intended to do.

He raised the first canvas and looked at the face of the victim beneath it.

Five minutes later, he was back at the car. He got in quickly, anxious to turn off the automatic dome light because of what it might reveal of his face.

'Did you find your friend?' Melissa asked.

'Yes.'

'He's all right?'

Abrams looked at her, the great shock filtering down through his body.

'Yes,' he lied. 'Everything is fine. But I saw victims.' He shook his head in revulsion that was not feigned. 'I think I need a drink.'

'I know a place. It isn't far.'

'No, I don't think so.' He would be more careful now. 'It's a silly thing, but you know how it is with politicians in the public eye.'

'Then I have another suggestion. I'll take you back to your car and you can follow me home.'

He looked at her and saw the smile, the eyes.

'It's all right,' she told him. 'My husband won't be there.'

Unbelievably, something in him stirred. He rationalized. He had to act normally. He had to put this behind him. His wife would understand: he had already told her he would be very late, because he had imagined he would have to go downtown to get the money for Donna.

Easier, then, to accept.

'I suppose it's the least I can do, to see that you get home safely,' he told her.

'Yes,' she purred. 'I know that I often give the impression that I'm the strong type, but I'm actually a very submissive kind of person. I'd be frightened going into that big house all alone, knowing my husband won't be home until sometime late tomorrow.'

'Take me,' Abrams suggested, 'to my car, then.'

Melissa drove away from the scene of devastation. 'It will be nice to get out of these wet clothes. We can have a fire in the fireplace and a nice drink and just relax.'

'I think we're going to get along together very well.'

'I do, too. I'm awfully glad, aren't you?'

Abrams smiled, but said nothing in reply. It was not necessary. He leaned back and luxuriated in the Lincoln's leather upholstery. The taste of his regained freedom was marvellous. He had won. He would always win.

Monument Valley, Kentucky

Milly Tyler lay in the darkened room. She knew it was a hospital room. She could vaguely remember the excitement, the voices, the rocking of the ambulance that had brought her here, some of the things they had done to her in that bright room with the people who talked too loudly and hurt her.

Now she lay in the dark. There was something in her arm. Other things were attached to her wrist and chest, she knew a dull pain, and she was very tired.

Although her eyes were closed, she knew it when the figure came to her bedside. She saw him very clearly and knew who he was.

Milly, it's time.

No.

Milly.

No, it's not time at all. I've got a lot of life left in me. You just don't understand. I've got a garden to put in and everything else, and those tykes to take care of. Now you just go on and get out of here!

You're in the hospital. You know today was too much for your heart. You're not a young woman. Now come along.

Well now, Milly told the figure, you just listen to me instead! I am not about to go anywhere. Don't think you can bully me around. A whole lot of people have tried to bully me around. I don't scare easy, you know.

But you are afraid.

Yes.

Come.

Milly felt a wave of doubt. Maybe it wasn't fair to stay around any longer. She *was* old, he was right about that . . . and goodness knows she had enough excuse to go, after today. Maybe, even if she stayed around, she wouldn't be strong any more. They might want to put her in one of those rest homes.

And take away her pipe.

It wasn't really fair. Life never treated you the way it should. If you died, you were cheated. If you lived, you became surplus property. Why hadn't anyone ever written down the way life really was, how it always came down to this sense of loneliness and how ridiculous things became?

Milly, take my hand now.

No!

I'll help you . . . soothe you. You won't hurt any more. Everything will be just fine. You'll see.

Ha! Do you think that claptrap is going to impress me any? You can't fool an old fool, shade. So stop trying. Anybody who ever tells me that everything is going to be just fine – well, sir, I know what kind of baloney that talk is! Get away from me!

I can see, madam, that you refuse to co-operate.

I ain't a madam. I'm a Ms, and don't you ever forget it! And if you reach that bony hand out for me again, I'll scream so loud even these lazy rich doctors in here will come a-running!

The figure loomed slightly closer, and was somehow associated with the pain in Milly's skinny chest. The pain was very bad, and she knew her fool heart was acting crazy again, bumping around and missing beats and everything else.

Heart, now you just straighten up! I'm having enough trouble here already, without your playing the fool.

Milly, talk to me, not your heart. It's time.

You might say it's time. What do you know? Go on, now! Get yourself out of here! I don't even know for positive whether I even believe in you or not!

Milly!

No! I won't be bullied! I'm still a tough old lady, and you better believe it! You just get on out! Get out, I say! I mean it!

The figure began to dim. *To everything there is a season.*

Yes, and this is going to be the season for me to slap the snot out of you, you dumbhead, if you don't get out of here and let a body have some rest!

Milly ...

Milly was scared. No doubt about that. She had *never* been so scared. But she was not about to show it. She glared right back, and saw that she might be winning. This astonished her. She wasn't whipped yet. Not by a long shot. She could throw a bluff with the best of them.

Milly. Come.

Foof! Don't bother me!

The room darkened. Milly was alone again. She slept. The crystal bottle over her head dripped fluid into her bloodstream. The cathode-ray-tube device on a shelf beside her was quiet, and the screen showed a regular pulse in the vivid-green lifeline it portrayed. Milly had a battle yet ahead of her, but she had won the crucial skirmish.

West of Knoxville, Tennessee

Sheeting black rain lashed the truck as Les Korowiscz, driving on familiar ground now, pushed hard for Knoxville. He was less than thirty minutes from the turnoff for home.

He was holding the speedometer on 60. He was in a hurry.

He couldn't wait to tell his wife and kids the whole story. They would be aghast, probably wouldn't believe a word of it. Like when the kids had been smaller and he came back from a transcon run and fed them whoppers about meeting dragons and everything else on the road. They would go nuts when they heard this one!

Korowiscz was wearing old clothes borrowed from the police back up the road, where they had taken the nutty gunman. His own soaked clothing was on the floorboards on the empty passenger side. He hadn't called his wife. She would be retroactively scared when he told her about it ... if she believed a word of it before the papers came out tomorrow, which he doubted.

The gunman's name, the police and highway patrol had discovered, was Burton. It took some searching around on the teletype, but they found out after a while that Burton had escaped late Monday from the state penitentiary in Oklahoma. The car he had burned up just before hailing Korowiscz had been his second or third stolen vehicle, no one was quite sure which just yet. He was a lifer, a killer, two murder counts.

Considering the complexity of the situation, mixing the highway accident and near-drowning in with Burton's capture, the authorities had let Korowiscz go in amazingly short time. He had given them a statement on a tape machine, and they said he would have to go back to testify; but once they had checked him out, they had let him get on the road again. They said he would probably get a medal for saving the old lady.

A *medal!* Pretty silly, and he had told them so.

The cops had wanted him to spend the night in their town, rest up, or even check into the hospital just to make sure he was okay. But he wanted to highball it home. So they had agreed, finally, and scrounged up these clothes he was wearing. Dried off, warm again, with some good coffee in him, he had gotten back onto the road.

Thinking about what fun it was going to be, the wife and family calling him a liar, he pushed the truck a little harder, allowing the speedometer to slip up to 65. He could feel the big rig swaying in the wind gusts, but he had everything under control very nicely.

He relighted his cigar and resettled his rump in the seat. He could imagine the way he would tell *this* whopper, making sure they didn't believe it until they got tomorrow's papers.

He was very tired, shaking a little in reaction to all the excitement, the icy water. But deep down he felt good.

'Oh, my darlin',' he bellowed, 'oh, my darlin', oh, my darlin', ClemenTINE!'

The truck topped a rise and started downhill. The wind-driven rain lashed the windshield, the wipers only scantly staying ahead. The road as far as Korowiscz could see ahead was deserted. The speedometer inched up to 70, and Korowiscz allowed this.

'Drove she ducklings,' he sang, 'to the water, every morning, just at NINE—!'

The speedometer touched 75. A particularly strong wind gust hit the rig broadside. Four or five big radials stopped throwing off excess water, all at the same time as a critical speed-mass ratio was exceeded, and as the truck ploughed into an invisible depression in the pavement, these tyres aquaplaned, becoming airborne on a wafer-thin cushion of water and air.

Lightning bolted blue-white just ahead. Korowiscz dropped the cigar from his mouth and got off the accelerator. The wind gusted again and the back end of the trailer began to slide, coming around. His heart suddenly in his throat, Korowiscz grabbed for the handle that activated the rear-unit air brakes.

Pressure hissed.

Too late.

The trailer continued to come around. The entire assembly began to jackknife. A tyre dug in and blew out. The truck hit the centre median and threw up oceanic waves of mud and torn sod. It turned over, bursting into great chunks of wreckage, and cargo went everywhere, and the cab was hurled upside down into a concrete underpass drainage culvert. Flaming gasoline streaked brilliantly along a hundred-yard strip of the rain-drenched median, reached the smashed cab, broke into a huge flower of yellow light, and killed Les Korowiscz.

Wednesday, April 9
9:20 p.m.–10 p.m.

NNNN
WWUS RWRB 100200
ZZZZZ

BULLETIN

ALL CLEAR

NATIONAL WEATHER SERVICE INDIANAPOLIS INDIANA
ISSUED AT 9 P.M. CDT WEDNESDAY APRIL 9, 1975

THE SEVERE WEATHER WATCH FOR THE WESTERN HALF OF
INDIANA IS CANCELLED.

THE SEVERE WEATHER WATCH FOR THE EASTERN HALF OF INDIANA
WILL REMAIN IN EFFECT UNTIL 11 P.M. CDT THIS WEDNESDAY
NIGHT.

THE ALL CLEAR AREA IN INDIANA INCLUDES ALL COUNTIES WEST
OF A LINE EXTENDING FROM SOUTH BEND THROUGH INDIANAPOLIS
TO LOUISVILLE KENTUCKY. LIGHT RAIN CONTINUES OVER MUCH
OF THIS AREA BUT THE THREAT OF SEVERE STORMS HAS ENDED.

IN THE AREA OF INDIANA EAST OF THE SOUTH BEND . . .
INDIANAPOLIS . . . LOUISVILLE LINE THUNDERSTORM ACTIVITY
REMAINS. PERSONS EAST OF THE LINE ARE ADVISED TO REMAIN
ALERT TO THE POSSIBLITY OF STRONG STRAIGHT WINDS, LARGE
HAIL AND AN ISOLATED TORNADO . . .

XXX

South of Thatcher, Ohio

Barney Reilly sat very still in his hail-dented sheriff's cruiser, the
microphone ready in his right hand. All around him, the lightning flashed and pulsed blindingly, and heavy rain pounded his
cracked windshield.

It was just a little unbelievable to the dazed deputy that he was
out here again, still on watch, after what he had already been
through.

The first tornado had missed him by less than a mile. After
radioing its track to headquarters in Thatcher, he had done the
only thing he knew, driving the cruiser into the nearest ditch.
There he hunkered down while fierce wind, driving rain, and

large hail pounded the car for what seemed a very long time.

When the fury began to subside, he had picked himself up off the floorboards of the car to find most of the glass broken out or cracked, and the painted surfaces looking like a mob had beaten them with hammers and clubs. The tornado's worst blackness was to his north, over Thatcher, at that time.

Nursing the car out of the ditch only because there was gravel riprap on the sides and he had cleated tyres on the back, Barney Reilly had proceeded shakily toward town, his radio temporarily blacked out by wild electrical disturbances. Then he had come upon the first devastated farmhouse, and helping injured victims had kept him busy.

That was, it seemed, a long time ago. The new storm was nearing now, and he had his orders – to stand watch again.

He watched.

It was frightening once more.

Clouds, afire with internal lightning, seemed to stretch from horizon to horizon. Barney had watched them scud swiftly in over his vantage point on Mile Hill, and he knew he was being approached by the most intense cells in the long, pulsating line. The clouds off to the east and west lighted themselves repeatedly with blinding flashes, and their thunder boomed in a constant symphony. He could see bolts hissing to the ground in all directions. None of this, however, was as frightening as what was taking place right around his car at the moment.

He could hear wind in the cloud overhead as it seemed to drape itself almost to the ground around him. The cloud was broad, fat, an ugly roll of grey, and its interior was aglow with an amber fire like the light of ten million light bulbs. The thunder was a continuous boom, without appreciable breaks from one crash to the next. Along the bottom of the cloud he could see wavy lines of fluid-like electricity, snapping from one area of intense illumination to the next. On the edges of the cloud, against the backdrop of other cells with their own lightning, he could see crimson pulsations, flecks of shooting green.

The air reeked of what Barney took to be ozone.

Barney Reilly knew as much about lightning as most people, perhaps more. Somewhere in the mess on his car's floorboards were several storm pamphlets from Washington. One of them was on lightning, and Barney had studied it.

People liked to say that lightning never struck twice in the same place. Folk wisdom characterized a very remote chance as about the same chance as being struck by lightning. Barney knew, however, that the chances were not quite as remote as people liked to think.

At any given moment there are 1,800 thunderstorms in progress around the globe. Lightning strikes the ground about 100 times each second. The average annual death toll from lightning in the United States is about 150 persons, with another 250 injured – sometimes blinded or rendered permanently deaf. The cost of lightning damage in this country exceeds $100 million per year.

When ordinary clouds grow into the towering giants known as cumulonimbus, complex interactions of electrical fields and charged particles occur. Large electrical charges build up within the cloud, and, through complex processes associated with the formation of raindrops, electrical imbalances build up. Negative charges build near the base of the cloud, with positive charges in the high upper reaches. As the cloud passes over the ground, the negative charge in its base induces a positive charge in the earth below, and for several miles around. As the cloud moves, the charged area beneath it moves, too. Current flows up poles, trees, or other tall objects as the opposite charges seek equalization. The air, however, is a good insulator, and the charges build.

Lightning occurs when the difference between charges becomes great enough to overcome the resistance of the air. The potential may be as much as 100 million volts before the sequence of events which we see as lightning actually takes place.

A typical cloud-to-ground stroke begins with what is known as a pilot leader, a current that passes out of the cloud to ground, too faint to be visible but creating the first breakdown in the air's insulation and opening the path for electrical energy flow. A second surge, called a step leader, quickly follows the first, rushing to the ground in pulses of 100 feet or more at a surge, pausing and stabbing deeper and deeper until a conductive path of ionized particles has reached very near the ground. At this point, discharge streamers extending from the ground upward intercept the step leader and a conductive channel is formed. A stroke leaps upward from ground to cloud at a speed approaching that of light itself. The force is so great and so instantaneous that atoms and molecules of the air are energized and sometimes changed into new configurations. This burst creates lightning's brilliant flash, and it all happens so swiftly that we think we see lightning striking down, when in actuality the final stroke is upward and what we see is the earlier step-leader movement in the opposite direction.

Once the initial stroke has been completed, others may follow. The outburst will not subside until all charges have been equalized, and in a very powerful cloud, with ongoing processes building new imbalances continuously, this may take a long time.

Current peaks may reach 200,000 amperes or more. Tremendous heat is generated. Strange configurations of electrical discharge, from cloud to cloud, in strange shapes, with terrifying whistles and thunder, may be encountered.

Barney Reilly knew most of this, but it still did not prepare him for what he was experiencing now. He was being engulfed in the ferocity of the electrical outburst. Lightning lit up the landscape as brightly as the sun. Clouds shaped like great balloons pulsed with multicoloured lights, as if they surrounded incredible Christmas trees. Some nearer ground strokes looked fiery red, others bluish green. The clouds pulsed, but never went dark. The thunder boomed and exploded unabated.

As quickly as the most intense activity surrounded him, however, it began to subside. He saw that the most brilliant light was now behind him – headed for Thatcher. Suddenly the clouds seemed higher overhead. The lightning veined the sky, but at greater altitudes, and he could hear his radio again.

'Barney, go ahead. Come in, Barney.'

He pressed his mike button. 'I'm here and okay. Worst of the line has just passed overhead. From the looks of it, you'll have it over town inside five minutes.'

'Do you see any tornadoes? Do you see any funnels?'

'No. Negative. Very, very bad lightning and thunder, but no twisters.' Then, because the sheriff actually did sound properly concerned *this* time, Barney tried to console him: 'It's bad electrical stuff, but shucks, you ought to see some of the stuff we used to experience down there in Bluejacket.'

'Are you coming back in now?'

'Right. Affirmative.'

'Ten-four.'

The sheriff was irritated with him.

Amused at the thought, Barney Reilly backed his cruiser across the narrow asphalt road and turned the wheels to start back. He had no intention of hurrying; the storm had bothered him and he wanted no more of it . . . no driving fast and *catching* the damned thing. But the boys at the office would never know he had had a queasy moment or two this trip. He was too proud of lording it over their new-found fear . . . and willingness, all at once, to listen to what he had to say about twisters and such.

As he pushed the car into gear, there was a low, screaming roar overhead. He ducked. For a mad instant he thought he was back in World War II – was getting shot at by a distant howitzer. But the scream was even uglier, if that were possible, and louder, and before he could react, a huge burst of greenish light exploded into the field less than a mile from his car. He saw smoke and an old oak tree slowly falling, and the thunder rattled the entire cruiser.

The rain magically ceased instead of intensifying, as he had always thought it was supposed to do after a lightning stroke nearby. He glanced once more into the field, now dark again under flickering high lightning, and then he started to ease out on the clutch to get moving.

As he peered ahead, he instantly stalled the engine.

Something large and red with fire was coming up the road right at him.

My God, I'm a dead man.

The object was a fireball. It was ten feet tall, threw off bits of flame like a pinwheel as it rolled up the slight hill toward the car, and had a wild, eerie humming sound somehow related to it. Barney knew they would ask what the sound was like. Harmonicas. A hundred harmonicas playing the same chord. Infinitely louder.

Barney's hair stood on end and his scalp prickled. He knew great forces of electricity were surging through and around him. His mouth was so dry he felt choked on his tongue.

The ball rolled nearer, about fifty yards away now, looming larger and more brilliant. As it rolled, it changed shape, became a huge doughnut of flame. It was twelve or fourteen feet tall now, six feet thick, pure crimson fire, hurling off sparks.

The musical humming changed pitch, becoming a growl. Barney's radio screamed static. His headlights dimmed. Little blue flames danced along the top lines of the front fenders.

The doughnut rolled on to the crest of the hill and sizzled past the car, not missing it by more than ten feet. Sparks, red and green, like pieces from a cutting torch, showered the car. Barney threw himself on the seat, face down. A murky heat washed through the open side window, and was gone.

Barney sat up.

Behind him, the doughnut rolled straight down the middle of the road, crossed the dirt-road intersection and the bottom, and vanished.

Lightning flashed overhead.

'Barney?' the radio said. 'Say your position, please.'

Barney Reilly shakily tried the car's ignition. The engine was still running. Everything seemed fine. In the lightning he could see that the sparks that had showered the car had made no visible impression on the paint, already dented by earlier hail.

'Come in, Barney.'

Barney put the car into gear and eased away. He was not about to answer the radio just yet. He needed a minute or two to make sure his voice was normal, would betray nothing.

Because he was not about to report what had just happened. He was not going to waste his time telling about something nobody would ever believe. He was prouder than that.

Thatcher, Ohio

Mike Coyle stood in the middle of the street in front of the city building. A few raindrops spattered down, then stopped. The air was hot, charged, filled with a murky viscousness like an emulsion. Overhead the clouds splintered themselves with blue-white brilliance, and just to the south the clouds were like greenish draperies from the earth to infinity above. Thunder muttered.

Purvis Rawlingson appeared in the doorway of City Hall. 'Mike?'

'Here!'

'Mike, do we sound the sirens?'

'No!'

'Mike, it's right on top of us! In another minute it'll be too late!'

'Do any of the spotters see a funnel?'

'No.'

'Does Dayton see a hook echo?'

'No, I have them on the line in there—'

'Then we're not sounding the sirens!'

Rawlingson made a moaning sound, and ducked back inside.

Coyle craned his neck to watch the clouds. He was frightened and angry simultaneously. *I'm wrong*, he thought. *People ought to be warned.*

But that was panic talking, he reassured himself. All the lines inside the city building were jammed, people calling in for information. The radio station was broadcasting his latest storm message on a continuous loop of tape. Every city soundtruck and police car equipped with a PA system was driving the streets, broadcasting the same message. *There is no tornado that we can see at this time. Stay under cover but do not panic.*

Coyle knew he was handling it the right way. If the earlier storm had not wrought such devastation, this electrical outburst would be looked upon as only an interesting phenomenon ... nothing of great consequence. But now they were all eager to overreact. His own fear proved that. Sirens now would create more panic, perhaps result in injuries as people fought one another for the best immediate cover.

The city's buildings suddenly changed only a few blocks away, and it took a minute for him to realize that their lights had failed. He turned and stared at the city-building complex. They remained lighted. Here the street lights continued as before. Lightning flickered.

Over the truncated courthouse, a portion of cloud seemed to burst into yellow fire. Perfectly round, it looked like a huge Japanese lantern at a garden party. Its centre was amber, but at the edges of its circumference it had tinges of blue and green. Pink streamers shot out of it, falling rapidly toward earth, going out as they fell.

A hot, moist wind gusted down the street, driving dirt and debris before it.

A police car rounded the corner and pulled up in front of the building. The back door popped open. Mo got out and ran to him.

He caught her in his arms.

'Are the children here?' she panted. 'Are they safe?'

'They're not here yet, honey, but Jill is on the way. She's in a police car. She's all right.'

Mo turned in quick response as thunder crashed and the cloud over the courthouse changed character, became totally blue for an instant, with threads of silver running in all directions. 'What's happening? Are we going to be—'

'It's okay, Mo! No tornado! No tornado!'

She stared at him with dazed eyes. He was startled. She had been like a rock through everything, but the new threat . . . unknown . . . had broken through her reserve.

There was no time for more talk. Clouds seemed to mushroom out over the sky, bursting into brilliant spasms of colour. One cloud, shaped like a huge urn, appeared to turn on to its side in the flashes of light even as they stared up at it. The lightning flashed red, blue, green, yellow. Then, as the thunder exploded around them, one entire pulpy section of sky flamed with a bright, rich red, as if it were filled with blood. A wind gusted and across the sky appeared a long, sinuous grey streamer, with what looked like luminous teardrops spilling out from either end.

The lightning was so continuous that to Coyle's dazed senses it did not seem that the flashes were of light . . . but that the sky was flashing *dark* now and then. The street lights had gone mad, turning off and on in response to the light sensors in their globes.

The clouds boiled and flashed crimson again, and then changed shape and were yellow. Out of tendrils from the cloud directly overhead spurted long, snakelike streamers, and as they extended downward they became bursting stars like Fourth of July skyrockets. The sky turned amber and then went black, and out of a growing pinpoint spot of brilliance came a new shower of falling red balls, ten or fifteen at once. One of them bounced off the roof of the city building and vanished just as Coyle ducked, hugging Mo against his chest for her protection. A green, egg-shaped cloud flashed, turned on from inside like a neon tube. Black wisps of cloud boiled around the light like smoke from a furnace.

Lightning suddenly unfurled itself behind the buildings just to the east – as if the sky was covered by stage curtains, and they hung gleaming pearl-white down to the ground, shimmering, waving in some unearthly electrical breeze. Another ball of yellow flame pulsed on and off, on and off, with the regularity of a strobe unit. Flickering blue lights arched overhead, faded into grey, and suddenly became orange stars.

Thunder rattled the buildings. A hard rain began teeming down, ice-cold. The sky turned greenish blue, a single continuous flame.

Gasping, Coyle dragged Mo to the entrance of the city building and pressed her against the wall under the shelter of the overhanging roof. The centre of the electrical storm had descended on them now, and he felt paralyzed. He held his wife and looked out, stupefied, as green streamers of light seemed to flow like melted lead from the clouds atop the buildings. There was a burst of purplish brilliance. There seemed to be no sound at all because it was *all* sound, an unending, sense-battering explosion of thunder, and the greenish light changed and was gone and a fantastic explosion of yellow lit up every window of nearby buildings, every brick in every wall, every thick, viscous raindrop in an instantaneous strobe-light effect.

Red balls of fire, like shots from a Roman candle, darted on to the street in a dense shower. A great yellow flash, and then a pink one, momentarily blinded him. Mo was trembling against his chest.

In the street below them, the door of the patrol car sprang open. The police officer who had driven Mo here jumped out. It was raining with brain-numbing ferocity, and the officer was hatless. He had blond hair, cropped close. He looked up at the sky with panic in his face and started up the steps toward shelter.

An orange streamer of pure electrical energy lanced downward. It seemed to strike the building across the street, and then it bounced. It hit the top of the scrambling officer's head.

He became illuminated.

For just an instant, Coyle felt every hair on his body stand straight on end, every pore tighten and quicken, as the electrical spasm went to ground. It was as if something in his body *leaped out* toward the annihilation.

It was an instant, so brief a time that it was incomprehensible. The policeman glowed like the filament of a bulb.

Then it was gone, black. Across Coyle's retinas the place the bolt had been was now a dazzled after-image of yellow and green. He blinked.

The officer collapsed and tumbled back down the three steps he had climbed.

Coyle shoved Mo nearer the door and dashed out into the pounding rain. He heard her cry out, but ignored her. Red and bluish fire slammed around him. He almost fell on the streaming concrete, took the last two steps down to the fallen man's side.

He grabbed the policeman's shoulder and rolled him over, ready to lift him and carry him to safety.

It was no longer a man, or even a human figure. The face was glistening char. The movement of being rolled over sent an acrid little puff of smoke into Coyle's nostrils – the sickening stench of burned flesh.

Coyle's stomach reacted and he staggered sideways, going to his knees in the gushing rainwater, and everything came up. A blast of thunder rocked the very pavement. Streamers of pink and blue filled the sky. There was another terrible clap and he saw bricks fly from the smoking corner of a building at the next corner.

He climbed to his feet, irrational.

'*Goddamn you!*' he screamed at the sky. '*Goddamn you, haven't you had enough?*'

The sky boiled, pulsing yellow.

He staggered back up the steps to the doorway, grabbed Mo at the door, and thrust her inside. He looked back and saw the police car, its door standing open, and the body on the pavement. He went into the building behind Mo.

The lobby was jammed with people. Many were on their knees.

Coyle's ears pained sharply and the building was filled with a fine brown dust as some pressure change sucked at its every pore. Beyond the front doors, the air seemed to be composed of solid falling water, and it was afire, and coloured green.

Kansas City, Missouri

Ed Stephens stood at the worktables in the weather room with a half dozen of his forecasters. New hourly charts were in, and the prognosis for most of the country by tomorrow looked excellent. The surface chart showed continuing very serious activity in the eastern third of the nation, but the latest satellite photos, just delivered, showed some small sign of hope even there.

The forecaster named King pointed to one of the large black-and-white photos. 'It's bunching up through Kentucky, as if the lines are caving in on one another.'

'Yes,' another man said. 'But if you'll notice . . .' He paused, glancing at Stephens, because satellite photography analysis was really not his job.

'Speak,' Stephens urged him.

The man pointed to the long, ragged line of cloud depicted across the Carolinas and Florida in the infra-red pictures. 'We just don't have any of the extreme cloud height in here that we saw earlier. And this area in northern Florida is quite thin. And up here,' he added, tracing his index finger into Pennsylvania, 'you don't have any signs of the kind of massive circulation we were seeing earlier in the day.'

The men paused, respectfully waiting for Stephens to agree or disagree. He studied the photos, correlating the visual data with some of the things given him on the charts.

He wanted to believe the storm was finally beginning to lose its punch. But there was tremendous potential remaining. Only five minutes ago, a tornado had struck near Columbia, South Carolina. The latest word was that the cloud had weakened, but tops everywhere remained sufficiently high to promise further bad news, and all the other elements remained as well. Nightfall, cooling, and subtle changes in the winds aloft were weakening the line of storms, but it was not over yet.

'Let's look at Raleigh,' Stephens suggested.

They crossed the room to the radar-information machines. King pulled the card for Raleigh, lifted the receiver, inserted the card, punched the 'start' button, got the warbling tone. In moments the machine started its swishing action, feeding out the current picture seen by the Raleigh radarscope.

It was on 250-mile scan. Great patches of precipitation echoes fanned out to the north and south, and elsewhere were smaller, evidently more intense blips. The Raleigh operator had grease-pencilled the cell which had hit Columbia. It was clearly weak now. To Stephens's practiced eye, nothing in the panorama of clouds showed the characteristic tarantula look of a killer storm.

'We're coming out of the woods a little,' he decided.

'Columbus, Ohio, reports intense electrical storms in progress,' someone noted.

'Oh, there's no question that we're far from finished. But there's some definite easing off of the activity generally.'

King smiled wearily. 'It's going to clear.'

'Yes.' Stephens rubbed his hand gently over his chest. The pain was not quite so bad now, but the fluttering continued. 'You guys will have a nicer day tomorrow, which is good, because I won't be in.'

'You're getting rid of Tatinger?' King looked surprised.

'He's waiting in my office. I guess he thinks the fun is over.'

'I'll be glad to get rid of the so-and-so. I'd say you've earned a day off, between him and this storm.'

'It's not just a day off. I'm going to the doctor's office.'

'Is something wrong?' King asked quickly.

'Oh, no,' Stephens lied glibly enough. 'Just a long-overdue check-up.'

He wondered if events would make this true. Had the storm revealed the true extent of a heart condition that might force him out of this job, or was it only tension ... only a kind of early-warning system that he could control with diet, fewer cigarettes? He was not sure he wanted to know the answer, but he had been scared a number of times today. He would not put off certain knowledge of his condition any longer.

Harry Adams appeared from the message centre. 'You still here?' he asked with mock severity.

'I've still got a lot to do. Tatinger is in my office, and I'm waiting for that call to go through to Thatcher and everything else.'

'Well, at least Dayton talked to your brother-in-law and you know they're all right.'

'Yeah,' Stephens grunted explosively, betraying the relief.

'You ought to get home as soon as you can. You look shot.'

'I'll get out of here in another hour or two, Tatinger willing.'

'At least call your wife. Women have a tendency to wonder, you know.'

Stephens nodded and felt a pang of guilt. He left the weather room and walked to the silent area where a light shone from his corner office. He found Buck Tatinger engrossed in Weather Service bulletins.

Tatinger closed the books and looked up expectantly.

'Excuse me while I make a call,' Stephens told him, and dialled his home number.

'Hello?' she answered.

Her voice sounded good. 'I thought I'd let you know I'm among the living.'

'Are you about to come home? It's late.'

'I have Congressman Tatinger with me. I'm waiting for a call to go through to Mo. Then I'll head that way.'

'Don't stay too late. You sound tired.'

'I am, honey,' he admitted. 'See you soon.' And hung up.

He faced Tatinger with folded hands on the desk. 'You said you had a few final questions, sir.'

Tatinger nodded, as brisk and fresh as ever. 'The storm is ending?'

'The worst is over.'

'Does that mean you go back to routine tomorrow, then?'

'Tomorrow,' Stephens explained wearily, 'an entirely new batch of work begins. Special survey teams will go out to all the hard-hit areas: Birmingham, Huntsville, Muncie, Indianapolis, Thatcher, Detroit, all the other places. We help co-ordinate some of that work. The people at Chicago and Texas Tech and NSSL are involved, too.'

Tatinger made a note. 'I heard some of your people talking about a press conference.' He smiled, and the eyebrow went up. 'A little politicking, perhaps?'

'Harry Adams will handle that.' Stephens was too tired to lose his temper. 'We need to use this storm, if possible, for education. Far too many people were killed today. With better public awareness, many would have been saved.'

'What are your latest figures?'

'More than six hundred dead. More than seven thousand injured.'

'Property damage?'

'Christ, I don't know. A billion, a billion and a half.'

'Your system is impressive, but it doesn't work very well.'

'No. A lot more would have died without us.'

The eyebrow cocked. 'You sound sure of that.'

Stephens glared back at him. 'If I weren't sure of that, I wouldn't have the job.'

Tatinger snapped his leather notebook closed. 'All right, sir. I believe I have all the data I require.'

Stephens was vaguely surprised at the abruptness. 'You're finished?'

'Here, yes. I'm going to Denver, and then to Norman. And then back to Washington to begin drafting my report.'

Stephens said nothing. He glanced at the telephone, wishing the call to Thatcher would go through. His heart flopped around.

'You're not going to pry about the report?' Tatinger prodded him.

'No,' Stephens said defiantly.

'The Weather Service has this big computerized data-processing system, AFOS, on the boards,' Tatinger volunteered. 'You ought to know that I intend to fight implementation on that.'

'Much of AFOS is already in the pipeline.'

Tatinger ignored the remark. 'I also plan to urge the Weather Service to investigate fully into some of your communications lags.'

Stephens said nothing. His heart fluttered, the pain radiated like fire.

Tatinger stood. 'Well, then.'

Goaded, Stephens told him. 'You won't stop AFOS. Data retrieval in a tenth of a second ... think of what that means on warnings.'

'You're still a bureaucrat, Stephens,' Tatinger said with a smile. 'But I almost like you anyway. Thanks for a good show.' He extended his hand.

Stephens took it. 'I'll walk with you to the elevator.'

'I can find it. Good night.'

The congressman walked briskly from the office, swinging his thin briefcase jauntily.

Stephens remained standing behind his paper-strewn desk. He wondered how much damage he might have done himself with his damned quick tongue. He decided he would never know. Under the circumstances, he had done the best he could. With the pain in his chest, it was so hard to think clearly.

Tatinger would not stop progress, he told himself. It was already under way.

Thinking about it, Stephens felt tireder. Whatever the doctor said tomorrow, he already sometimes had the feeling that he was living in the past. He would not see the end of this technological revolution. Retirement would come ... possibly much sooner than he had planned.

At least, he tried to console himself, he would not be the only one to go. Hell, the Weather Service was composed mainly of older farts like himself, men trained in the fledgling years of World War II. A disproportionate percentage of the nation's seven thousand professional meteorologists were in the 51–58 age bracket. In another ten years it would not only be a new ball game. The team would be composed almost entirely of new, younger faces.

Stephens sighed, which made two sighs for the day, one past

his usual quota. He had nothing to regret, he told himself.

And much to do, even if tomorrow a doctor might end his career.

He left his desk and went back out, heading toward the weather room once more.

Thatcher, Ohio

When it began to be quieter outside, and after the lightning had faded, someone finally went to the front door of the city building.

Dazed and bewildered, people moved outside, on to the steps and sidewalk.

A light drizzle fell. The lightning was far to the east and north.

'It's over,' someone said.

Some of the women began to cry.

Purvis Rawlingson walked over to Mike Coyle. 'By gosh, you were right, my friend. Don't fire till you see the whites of their eyes, right?'

'Right,' Coyle breathed. Then, mentally, he shook himself. 'Make sure we have a verified all-clear from Dayton. Get it on the radio. Tell all the crews to get back to work. That officer's family has been notified?'

Rawlingson nodded sombrely.

'I'm going to find a car,' Coyle added, 'and try to get around town and see some of the things we have to deal with here up-close.' He turned to Mo, who stood by his side. 'I know you're tired, but I kind of wish you'd go with me.'

'I intend to,' she told him.

He looked at her sharply for an instant, as if divining that there was a weight of meaning behind her words that he did not fully comprehend. Then, however, glad for it, he turned away to signal someone.

Mo breathed deeply, realizing that the horror had purified her.

There was no way she could predict now what would happen to him, or to her, or to anyone. But there were things she did know, with a new kind of serenity. She no longer had to worry about what was best for him, and what might be best for her, because she was no longer trapped in any way. It was her choice, freely given, to make this life with him. He was a good man. There were none better. She was lucky. She had gotten through this crucible, and was stronger for it, and so was not threatened by giving of herself.

She felt no real regrets. She thought now she knew where she was going. If change intervened, as it had this day, she could cope.

Together, she and her husband could cope. Because neither was a cripple now, and neither had to be afraid, and hide the fear under bluster.

Mo was very, very tired. But there was a gladness in her, too, like a great, glowing jewel.

I love you, she thought, watching Mike. *And I love myself, too. And that makes it perfect.*

NNNN
ZCZC WBC 112
ACUS KMKC 100600
MKC AC 100600
MKC AC 100600
Z Z Z Z Z

BULLETIN

TORNADO WATCH CANCELLATION
ISSUED 1 A.M. CDT THURSDAY APRIL 10, 1975
IMMEDIATE BROADCAST REQUESTED

THE NATIONAL WEATHER SERVICE HAS CANCELLED TORNADO
WATCH NUMBER 873 ISSUED AT NOON CDT YESTERDAY FOR THE
STATE OF OHIO.

PERSONS IN OR CLOSE TO THE PREVIOUSLY DESIGNATED AREA CAN
RESUME THEIR NORMAL ACTIVITIES.

. . . KING . . . NSSFC . . .

XXX

Thatcher, Ohio
Thatcher's Main Street was cluttered with trucks. A crew from
the water department was down inside a sewer, trying to find out
why there was still some flooding in side streets to the south, toward the courthouse. Telephone men swarmed poles, checking
circuits. Gas-company workers were safety-testing major lines.
Several National Guard trucks were strung along the curbing.
The sounds of jackhammers and chainsaws mingled with the
more distant sound of a bulldozer snorting through rubble.

Mike Coyle stood on the steps of the city building, waiting.

His first tour of Thatcher – the post-tornado Thatcher – had
been completed a few minutes earlier. He and Mo had been unable to drive into some areas because of continuing street blockage. What they had been able to see had been sufficient to shake
them profoundly.

Coyle had not said it to Mo, and he would not say it to anyone
if he could help it. But Thatcher would never be the same. He

alone of everyone here now knew best, from the air and from a driving inspection, just how bad it really was.

It was so bad that he could not completely believe it.

The historical preservation district was flattened. Most of the big Victorian homes were already smashed flat. There was little doubt that the others, with some walls remaining, would have to be knocked down because they were beyond repair.

It was the same along much of the Central Parkway, and within a half mile of his own home. All the houses on Brenda Street, smashed. Everything on Linden Boulevard, smashed. The City Lights Shopping Centre, smashed. Ravenwood Addition, smashed. Del Park, smashed. Commercial development from one end of Parker Boulevard to the other, smashed. Trees gone. Shops gone. Power lines and poles downed. Businesses wrecked. Where tree-shaded streets had been, and pleasant, middle-aged homes, now only rubbled muddy fields marked by stumps. Street after street of houses fallen off their foundations, unroofed, walls knocked out, porches broken, cars thrown through walls. The Midtown School, smashed. Hanover Shops, smashed.

In Southtown, where distance to the only remaining bridge had postponed a visit, the National Guard's preliminary report was no more encouraging. The glass factory had taken a tremendous blow, but the furniture factory had fared worse; it was flattened, literally, and could never be put back into operation short of ground-clearing and complete new construction.

All the other firms south of the river had suffered, too. Everything along Blanchard Road was wrecked. Bendix, unroofed and two walls damaged too severely to allow occupancy. Buckeye, unroofed and gutted by fire. Acme, much the same.

The hospital was filled to overflowing. Many would be treated in private clinics, or in the armory, which appeared destined to remain temporary shelter for many injured for days to come. Others, hurt or homeless, were being moved into the remaining schools, the churches, the old north-side gym and the downtown YMCA. Somehow, with the Guard units and Red Cross and Salvation Army and many other groups helping, people were being herded into temporary shelter, were getting clothing as needed, and food. But all of this was only the first, temporary help. Only Coyle fully comprehended the scope of the job, and it stunned him.

As he stood deep in thoughts of its problems, he saw the police car come around the corner. It pulled up in front of the building. The door opened and Jill got out. She was frazzled and dirty, her pretty little dress splotched with ugly dark stains. She saw Coyle and ran up the steps and directly into his arms.

'Oh, Daddy, it was just *awful!*'

Coyle held her close. 'I know, chicken, I know.'

She clung to his chest, sobbing. Still a child, he thought, but almost a woman now. At this instant he could be her daddy again, but perhaps it was the last time, ever.

'That's a girl, now,' he crooned, patting her hair. 'It's fine now, honey.'

She drew back from him a little. 'Is Mom here?'

'She and your brother are both up in my office.'

'Billy's here too?'

'Your Mom and I took a quick tour of damaged areas. When we got back, Billy was waiting for us. You know what? After the tornado, he went up and worked with a volunteer crew for a long time. He finally strained his shoulder a little, lifting something, and they made him quit. But he says he's going to be back at it in the morning.'

She searched his face with an intensity that reminded him of Mo. 'Is our house all right? I want to know.'

'Our house was hit. But it can be fixed. I'm afraid we aren't going to have any trees for a while.' He hesitated, and then said as much to reassure himself as her, 'We can grow new trees.'

'Can we go see Mom and Billy?'

He took his daughter in through the lobby, even more crowded and hectic now as additional personnel had been thrown into the work. The Guard had its central radio-control transmitter set up in the water department. The Highway Patrol's mobile disaster-relief unit had also moved in some communications gear. An information desk, designed to help people find one another, and ask about the fate of friends or relatives, had mushroomed into a clutter of twenty or more women working at a dozen card tables, everyone stumbling around over all the temporary telephone cables.

Upstairs, Mo murmured softly as Jill entered, and they embraced. Billy, muddy, his left arm in a sling, grinned like a maniac. For a few minutes they all jabbered at each other. Jill was the one who finally, cupping her hands around a steaming cup of coffee, broke the conversation.

'I've never been this tired in my life,' she whispered.

'You need to get right home to bed,' Mo told her.

'Is that possible? Is the house all right?'

'The roof, what's left of it, might leak,' Coyle grinned. 'But the sky is clear out there now. From what I was told a few minutes ago, they're restoring electrical power in that neighbourhood right now, checking house by house and switching in from poles that are intact. I turned our circuit breakers off, but you could turn them back on if the power company says to, couldn't you?'

'I don't even know where they are,' Jill admitted forlornly.

'Aren't you going home too?' Billy asked.

'Ah, God, I've got to stay with this another few hours, anyway.'

'Mom?'

'I might stay here with your father,' Mo said, 'a little while longer, anyway.'

Coyle met his wife's gaze. Without words being spoken, the tour of the city had drawn them still closer. There was a communion between them at this time that was stronger than anything they had ever known. He did not understand it. He did not question it, either. It was there and he was thankful.

Billy said, 'I could go with Sis. I know about the circuit breakers and all that bull.'

'You can take my car,' Coyle said. 'The police won't stop you when they see the city plates.'

'What will you do later?'

'If I'm half as tired as I am right now, I'll let a cop drive us home.'

Billy frowned, hesitant. 'You're sure it's okay for us to go on?'

'Sure.' Coyle handed him the car keys. 'Drive carefully.'

Billy looked at him. 'Dad.'

'Sorry,' Coyle grinned. 'I'll never learn, will I?'

The kids left, and Coyle was alone in the office with his wife. They smiled at each other.

'How wrong can one man be about one boy?' Coyle mused.

'I was proud of him tonight.'

'I was proud of all of you tonight.'

After another pause she asked, 'What's next?'

He took a deep breath. 'Engineering reports on downtown

buildings. They're on that right now. At seven in the morning, I meet with city homebuilders in the library's all-purpose room, to talk about emergency-shelter building and to get help co-ordinating damage assessments and repairs. There isn't going to be any cheating or price-gouging. And no bribes. We'll have some kind of priority system on repairs and demolition.' He paused, thinking about the tremendous problems that lay ahead, and then all at once he was thinking of something else.

'Will we ever get over that woman's look?' he asked.

'I don't know,' Mo replied softly.

It had been in one of the smaller-home neighbourhoods. The houses resembled a lumber-yard's dumping ground. As firemen sifted through wreckage, Coyle and Mo had driven up in the car and paused at the curb.

A woman had been standing there with two friends. She was perhaps fifty, no longer young and no longer slender, wearing a faded-blue dress which revealed bare upper arms thick with fat, the colour of pie dough. As Coyle stepped out of the car, the woman recognized him. Her face was tear-streaked, and she started to take a step toward him.

Then she stopped, turned back and looked at the crushed wreckage of her home, turned back to him, uttered a little moaning sound and tossed her arms up, like a referee tossing up a basketball for a jump, and she turned and walked away, her face in her hands.

Nothing had communicated the complete helplessness of the victims as she had done . . . without words, without an attempt, really, to do more than simply surrender to whatever pain, anguish, dismay was in her.

There was going to be so much of that. Tomorrow, with daylight and the subsiding of the first shock, it would be much worse for many people.

Coyle shook his head now in his own dismay. 'I'd better get downstairs and see if we have anything yet on new supplies from Columbus.'

'I'll wait here,' Mo said, 'and take any messages.'

He went into the hall and started for the stairs. As he started down toward the lower-level commotion, he met Purvis Rawlingson, a great shabby bear, hurrying up. Rawlingson looked surprised.

'Mike! I've been looking for you!'

'I've been in my office the last few minutes.'

'Listen, we have a problem.'

'No kidding!'

'No, no, I mean a new one. A political problem. Do you know who I've got in my office right now? Demanding to talk to us about city plans?'

Coyle felt his insides tightening. 'Who?'

'Cecil Upshaw and Bert Andrews. And Harrigan is with them.'

'Is Harrigan working miracles out of that Chamber of Commerce office of his tonight? The last time Upshaw's Department Store and Thatcher Glass were in the same room together was when they got into an argument about who had the better reasons for being against a bond issue.'

Rawlingson shook his shaggy head worriedly. 'This is serious, Mike. Upshaw is demanding to know how the Chamber and the city will work together to get downtown going again. Bert Andrews is livid; he says the first effort should go to the Southtown industrial section.'

'Why did Harrigan bring them here?'

'He didn't know what else to do.'

'It figures,' Coyle grunted, and headed for Rawlingson's office with Rawlingson hurrying, his loafers slapping on the tile floor, to keep up.

In Rawlingson's private office, a twelve-by-twelve room lined with old bookshelves that were crammed with memorabilia that would have fit in a set for a Sherlock Holmes movie, Cecil Upshaw and Bert Andrews stood glaring at each other across a tiny conference table. Harrigan sat at the table, between them in more ways than one. Upshaw was rumpled, dirty, wearing a rain-soaked white shirt and baggy trousers. Andrews had recently changed clothes, it seemed, because he looked razor-neat in a dark summer suit and tie. Harrigan's Levis and sweat shirt betrayed that he had been at home when the storm hit, and hadn't been back there since.

All three men looked up sharply at Coyle's entrance.

'Mike,' Harrigan breathed. 'I'm glad you're here.'

'See here, Mister Mayor,' Cecil Upshaw said abruptly. 'On behalf of the Thatcher Downtown Retail Merchants Association, I'm trying to get some preliminary facts on how we're going to cope with this downtown emergency.'

Coyle told himself to hold his temper, remain as calm as he

usually tried to be in ticklish situations. 'I'm glad you're concerned, Cecil. Of course this isn't just a downtown emergency.'

Bert Andrews's eyes snapped. 'Precisely my point, Mike. Good to hear someone talk some sense! Southtown has been dealt a terrible blow, here. Potentially catastrophic. The city and county have to band together on an immediate and broadspread relief and assistance programme.'

Upshaw bridled, 'The downtown merchants have been working for months on a comprehensive programme to restore shopping habits in the central city. Our whole quality of life is at stake here. Downtown is a symbol. It's the heart of our community. The two hundred downtown merchants expect prompt emergency action. We'll need help in obtaining emergency funding. Priorities have to be established. It's *very* important for us, as businessmen and citizens, to have assurance that every step will be taken to re-establish downtown as quickly as possible.'

'The glass plant is half wrecked,' Andrews snapped back, his cheeks splotched with ill-controlled anger. 'The furniture factory is so badly damaged that there's a serious question whether the parent firm will even choose to rebuild. The industrial base comes first and foremost—'

'Establishing a solid retail-credit business is at the heart of any recovery!' Upshaw said.

'How are people going to be buying anything downtown if there aren't any jobs in Southtown?'

'Gentlemen, gentlemen,' Harrigan said nervously.

'I came here for action,' Andrews said. 'Not insulting speeches.'

'I think you're right about that,' Coyle said. 'The speeches are already beginning to get on my nerves, and my nerves weren't too strong to begin with.'

'Mike,' Rawlingson said warningly.

'Shut up, Purvis.' Coyle's temper was going.

Rawlingson insisted gently, 'We can discuss things, work out compromise in various areas—'

'There's no compromising principle!' Upshaw snorted.

'And I agree with you on that,' Coyle shot back.

'Let's stay calm, Mike,' Rawlingson soothed.

Coyle, however, knew he was just a little too far gone now. He had listened to Upshaw and Andrews and others like them, patiently, with political expertise, for such a long time that it was almost a reflex. Tonight things were crumbling the walls of habit and wisdom. He plunged ahead.

'The city isn't going to set up any maniac priority schedules for downtown,' he told Upshaw.

'There!' Andrews crowed. 'I told you—'

'And we aren't going to go crazy pouring everything into Southtown, either,' Coyle added.

Both men's faces went slack.

'See here,' Andrews began.

'No, *you* see here. Both of you. You're two of the most powerful men in this community. You're not going to give up. But you're not going to be at each other's throats, either. Do you want to know what you're going to do? I'll tell you what you're going to do.

'Bert. You're going to get the Southtown business and industrial interests together. Tomorrow morning. Early. You're going to co-ordinate a damage survey. You're going to assign people to make contacts in Washington for emergency industrial aid. If your workers are going to be laid off, you're going to work with the unions to make sure payments go to those people either from your emergency relief funds, or the union's. You know a lot of people in the building industry. You're going to get your production people behind a project to locate building supplies in quantity, mobile homes, pockets of heavy unemployment in the trades that we're going to need, and need badly, on both sides of the river. You're going to work with Cecil, here, in setting up a cross-county task force to co-ordinate relief and reconstruction efforts, working with the city and the county.'

Upshaw began, 'I don't see—'

'Cecil,' Coyle went right on, 'you're organizing the downtown people in essentially the same way. And you're bringing the suburban merchants in. Don't look at me that way. If you don't all hang in there together now, you're going to turn slowly in the wind. You're going to get people working on help at the state level. You'll also police the insurance industry on claims. You'll work with the city engineering department on residential survey, with the homebuilders, and fair priority plans for repairs, renovation, removal.

'You'll both work with Harrigan and the Chamber. By the time you're finished work tomorrow, you'll probably have fifty committees going. I don't put a lot of stock in committees, but there's so much to be done I don't see any other way to handle a lot of these jobs. We're going to be working on assistance, placement, housing, demolition, building, health, surveying, employment, welfare, recruitment, transportation, food distribution, credit, insurance, and a lot of other things all at the same time. *You* two gentlemen are going to be the city's volunteer, unpaid workhorses in getting all the other elements of this town pulling together to pull *all* of us out.'

Upshaw and Andrews stood there staring. Harrigan puffed his cheeks out. From Rawlingson came a low, tuneless whistle.

'Well?' Coyle challenged.

'I don't know if we can possibly get things together in the way you suggest,' Upshaw said finally.

'It's fine and good,' Andrews added, 'to talk about community effort, but—'

'All right,' Coyle broke in. 'Maybe it's time for the I-told-you-so's. Do you remember the executive meetings about the bond elections?'

'That's not at issue here—' Upshaw began defensively.

'Bullshit! It *is* an issue! Do you remember the first plan? Two hundred and twenty-five thousand dollars for emergency and warning equipment? Do you remember voting that out because it was a frill? Do you remember the *second* bond plan? A hundred and seventy-eight thousand dollars for emergency and warning equipment? You voted *that* out because you said you knew it wouldn't pass. Do you remember the third bond plan? Ninety-two thousand dollars? Same category? Same tired excuses? Same "It-can't-happen-here"? This city was not just unprepared today. It had had plenty of warnings and plans for action and proposals, but the so-called "business leaders" of the community had been too busy fighting among themselves and standing for the cheap status quo. A lot of short-sighted assholes could have had this city ready, but they didn't even *try*.'

He paused for breath. Rawlingson looked like he might faint. The others stared, pale and obviously shaken.

Upshaw said slowly, 'We asked for it.'

'Yes,' Coyle agreed. 'But the point now isn't breast-beating. The point now is, Do we quit? or do we start trying to *help?*'

The room was very quiet. The men stared.

'Well?' Coyle challenged.

'It sounds,' Upshaw said dubiously, 'like we're going to be busy.'

Andrews suddenly grinned. 'And having some fun.'

'The first meeting is at 7 a.m. at the library,' Coyle said, hurrying to solidify his gains. 'I'll expect both of you to be there.'

Andrews nodded. 'Fine.'

'I guess,' Upshaw said guardedly, 'it's worth a try.'

'What's the option?' Coyle demanded. 'Quitting?'

Upshaw's shoulders squared. 'You're right. By godfrey! You're *right*.'

'Sit down,' Coyle said, 'and let me tell you some of the places I think we're going to have to start.'

Thatcher's two most powerful men obeyed.

Buckingham County, Virginia

At exactly 2:30 a.m., the low, swirling cloud put down a dark finger toward the earth. The finger extended itself tentatively, as if unsure, and then moved downward in the illumination of lightning. It became a tornado as it touched in the high meadow.

It was not a large tornado, and its winds were not much in excess of one hundred miles per hour. It was very narrow, and for a few seconds after it touched the earth, throwing up handfuls of grass and brush, it seemed undecided.

Then the tornado moved across the meadow. It reached a small apple tree, all alone in the middle of the expanse of waist-high grass, and broke the tree and tossed its pieces into a nearby fence with a contemptuous ease. The apple tree's trunk smashed one section of the barbed-wire fence.

Lightning flashed again, and thunder rolled. But it was not very frightening lightning or very impressive thunder, because the cloud and its companions were nothing like they had been a few hours earlier.

The tornado moved on another dozen yards, whirling, picking up little bits of grass and brush. Then, as if tired, it raised itself off the ground and shrank up into its parent cloud, and the cloud with its fellows trundled on east, toward the black vastness of the Atlantic, and oblivion.

This was the last tornado.

```
XXXXX
ZCZC WBC 104
ACUS KMKC 101200
ZZZZZ
```

BULLETIN
SEVERE WEATHER STATEMENT
NATIONAL SEVERE STORMS FORECAST CENTRE KANSAS CITY MO
ISSUED 6 A.M. CDT THURSDAY APRIL 10, 1975
IMMEDIATE BROADCAST REQUESTED

ALL SEVERE WEATHER WATCHES FOR THE CONTINENTAL UNITED
STATES HAVE EXPIRED.

THUNDERSTORM AND TORNADIC ACTIVITY ASSOCIATED WITH A FAST
MOVING PACIFIC STORM SYSTEM HAS NOW ABATED OVER THE
EASTERN COASTLINE OF THE US AND THE LOW PRESSURE TROUGH
ITSELF IS MOVING INTO THE ATLANTIC.

SOME LIGHT RAIN IS REPORTED AT THIS HOUR IN THE CAROLINAS
AND PORTIONS OF FLORIDA BUT NO SEVERE ACTIVITY IS REPORTED
OR ANTICIPATED.

FLASH FLOOD WATCHES REMAIN IN EFFECT FOR NINE STATES.

THE STORM ACTIVITY OF APRIL 9, 1975 GENERATED MORE THAN
150 AND PERHAPS AS MANY AS 185 TORNADOES. DURING THE
PERIOD FROM 1 A.M. CDT APRIL 9, TO 6 A.M. CDT APRIL 10, THE
NATIONAL WEATHER SERVICE ISSUED 44 SEVERE WEATHER WATCH
NOTICES OUT OF NSSFC AT KANSAS CITY AND IT IS ESTIMATED
THAT LOCAL NWS OFFICES ISSUED MORE THAN 1000 SEVERE
WEATHER STATEMENTS.

OFFICIAL CASUALTY ESTIMATES HAVE BEEN REVISED DOWNWARD
TO 620 DEAD AND 8000 INJURED . . .

NO TORNADIC OR OTHER DAMAGING WEATHER WAS REPORTED
OUTSIDE THE NWS SEVERE WEATHER WATCH AREAS. THE SHORTEST
LEAD TIME BETWEEN ISSUANCE OF A SEVERE WEATHER WATCH
AND THE START OF SEVERE WEATHER IN ANY AREA WAS 2 HOURS
15 MINUTES . . .

XXX

With the coming of dawn, from Kansas to the Cumberland Gap, men began the massive job of cleaning up and rebuilding.

In dozens of cities, repair crews had worked through the night, and continued with the help of National Guardsmen, state police, and citizens who chose to volunteer. Some were homeless, and were broken by the enormity of their losses. But even in places like Freesburgh, Ohio, which would never really exist again after this day, most survivors found, to their own quiet amazement, that life went on.

Small planes criss-crossed the continent, tracking, photographing, and analyzing tornado tracks. Teams moved into places like Huntington and Birmingham and Paducah to take more pictures, conduct interviews, make measurements.

Total tornado-track length already exceeded 2,500 miles. Property damage was about $1.5 billion.

National statistics showed that the average tornado killed two persons, but this figure was misleading because so many ordinary tornadoes occurred in open country, touching no habitation. One expert, noting the ferocity of the April 9 storms and the densely populated areas they had ravaged, expressed amazement that ten thousand persons had not died.

In Birmingham, David Kristofsen and his wife returned to their smashed house.

'It was a beautiful house,' Kristofsen said sadly.

Susan stared at the wreckage, saying nothing.

'We'll get a smaller house,' Kristofsen told her, knowing the risk he was taking, but facing it. 'Maybe in the country.'

She turned to him. 'Yes. I think I'd like that.'

In Columbus, Ohio, a jet from the Davidson team landed on the newly cleared runway at the west-side airport and picked up Bill Fredrick and Barbara James.

'Equipment?' the pilot asked Fredrick as he climbed on board.

'Gone,' Fredrick said grimly. 'Swept away.'

The plane became airborne shortly.

'It was my fault about Bock,' Fredrick told Barbara James, not for the first time. 'I should have just throttled him – dragged him down the stairs.'

'You did your best.'

'No, I didn't. Because as shook up as I was, *I didn't really believe that twister could kill anyone*. As much as I know about storms, there was that hidden pride. The kind of pride that people have when they think they're above tragedy. So I let Roy Bock stay up there. And he died. And I'll never forget it.'

'What are you going to do now?' Barbara James asked.

'Work,' Fredrick said, his mouth tightening.

In Monument Valley, Milly Tyler had visitors. They were not allowed to stay long. Milly's son Thomas was shockingly pale and upset. Milly told Nina that a little more loving might restore his colour. Nina blushed, and Kent and Adrian, who had sneaked in against orders (being Tylers too, after all), chortled with glee. They didn't know what their mother was blushing about, exactly, but any blush was funny.

In Kansas City, Ed Stephens mournfully dressed after the first portion of his long-delayed physical. When the doctor came back into the examining room, Stephens braced himself inwardly for the bad news.

'We're going to want you in the hospital overnight for some more tests,' the doctor told him, 'but there isn't much doubt about your problem.'

'How bad was the EKG?' Stephens asked bluntly.

'EKG? There was nothing wrong with the EKG.'

Stephens was floored. 'The flopping around in my chest! The pain! I even threw up!'

'Of course you threw up, stupid,' his sometime-handball opponent told him. 'You probably neglected to eat, and that's always deadly for an ulcer patient.'

Stephens put a hand to his chest. 'It's flopping around right now!'

'Of course it is! That's too much nicotine and too much caffeine. But the EKG shows you've got a heart like a rock. It's your weak gut that's making you sick.'

Stephens took a deep breath. Now that he thought about it, maybe the pain was a little low in his chest . . . sort of.

You didn't get thrown out of a job because of an ulcer.

'You're going to have a GI series,' the doctor told him pleasantly. 'You won't like it. Then you'll go on a diet and you'll cut out the smoking and coffee and several other items you'll swear you can't live without. You'll also try to control your tensions better.'

Stephens had a momentary impulse to tell his friend to go to hell. He was so relieved that he just grinned and felt foolish.

'I know your job is a strain,' the doctor said, opening a chart and picking up a pencil, 'but tell me just for the record: has there been anything – or anyone – new and especially irritating in your life just recently, a factor that might have kicked this off?'

'Except for a hundred and fifty tornadoes and Buck Tatinger,' Stephens said, 'I can't think of a thing.'

The doctor looked at him. 'What the *hell* are you grinning at?'

In Denver, Buck Tatinger rented a car and drove a considerable distance to a National Weather Service installation. He immediately insulted the section chief, and implied he was stupid, and made his speech about bureaucrats.

The chief became apologetic.

Tatinger smiled inwardly, knowing that here he was going to find some fat to peel off, unlike Kansas City, where he had scarcely found a damned thing to complain about.

In Thatcher, Ohio, the people worked to begin cleaning up. Daylight had shown the full extent of their devastation. They faced years of work, but everywhere the work was begun.

Mike Coyle rushed from one emergency meeting to another. After noon, he finally broke away long enough to go to his own neighbourhood. Cleaning up work was in progress everywhere. Billy had found some plywood to nail over broken windows and some sheet plastic to tack over holes in the roof. Jill was busily raking and cleaning up debris from the yard, and he found Mo inside, scrubbing at a carpet that would never be quite the same again.

Coyle held her.

'You know the Washington thing is out now,' he said. 'I can't leave now. There's too much that has to be done here.'

'Can it be rebuilt?' she asked him.

'Yes. We have everyone working, people are co-operating like—'

'Mike, I know what you're telling everyone else. But I saw some of the damage, too. Do you really think it will ever be the same?'

'No,' he told her. 'It's going to be better.'

She kissed him then.

'It's really okay?' he asked. 'You think I'm doing the right thing, for our future, to stay here in Thatcher?'

'Oh, my darling,' she said. 'If you only knew.'

And everywhere the work went on. For each thing there was indeed a season, and this time, after the destruction and fear and death, was the time for regeneration . . . rebirth.

More than twenty-two thousand miles overhead, the satellite diligently took its pictures and transmitted them back to Suitland, Maryland. But the pictures were very dull because it was a beautiful day.

J. D. Gilman and John Clive
KG 200 95p

They flew Flying Fortresses. They wore American uniforms . . . but they were Germans! KG 200 – the phantom arm of Hitler's Luftwaffe. From a secret base in occupied Norway these crack pilots plan their ultimate mission, the raid that would bring Allied defeat crashing down from the exploding skies. . .

Inspired by the best-kept secret of World War Two, this is one of the most enthralling novels of air warfare, espionage and manhunt ever written.

'Shattering' TELEGRAPH

Joe Esterhas
F.I.S.T. 80p

A sensational new film starring Sylvester 'Rocky' Stallone . . . F.I.S.T. is the Federation of InterState Truckers . . . F.I.S.T. is the story of Johnny Kovak, whose combination of punch and persuasion took him to the top of the truckers' union . . . of the wife he betrayed and the ambitions he tarnished . . . and of the dangerous allies who brought him down. A story peopled with characters as big and powerful as the trucks they drive.

Kit Thackeray
Crownbird 70p

Four men and one woman with a plan to change the face of Africa where the stranglehold of the Chinese is daily more threatening . . . Their mission – on orders from Whitehall – is an 'adjustment', violent if necessary, of the power politics of the Dark Continent.

Bernard Packer
Doctor Caro 80p

Who is DOCTOR CARO? He is a man with a past. A man who refused to die. His face and body were remade by wartime surgeons. He has changed his name and nationality again and again. As Henry Carr he comes ashore in the steamy South American port of Puerto Acero. Among the seamen and exiles, the whores and whoremasters, he stalks the man who condemned his family to the holocaust twenty years ago and half a world away . . .

'Superbly wrought' NEW YORK TIMES

Colin Forbes
Avalanche Express 80p

'When the luxury Atlantic Express pulls out of Milan Central Station it has aboard the highest-ranking defector ever to leave the Soviet Union. In the care of British and American agents, he is pursued across the Continent by the massed network of the Soviet's European agents. A blizzard is roaring across Europe and airlines are grounded. Tension mounts unbearably as *Avalanche Express* develops to its spine-chilling conclusion' LONDON EVENING NEWS

Robin Cook
Coma 80p

Why did the two patients who underwent routine minor surgery in Boston's greatest hospital never regain consciousness? Up against the scorn of the medics and the hostility of the establishment, one girl medical student starts to probe the coma cases steadily – and uncovers something unbelievably hideous . . .

You can buy these and other Pan Books from booksellers and newsagents; or direct from the following address:
Pan Books, Sales Office, Cavaye Place, London SW10 9PG
Send purchase price plus 20p for the first book and 10p for each additional book, to allow for postage and packing
Prices quoted are applicable in the UK

While every effort is made to keep prices low, it is sometimes necessary to increase prices at short notice. Pan Books reserve the right to show on covers and charge new retail prices which may differ from those advertised in the text or elsewhere.